"With brooding suspense and m[...]
Tide is unputdownable. A twisty, fast-paced, and utterly compelling read from master of the genre James R. Hannibal."

Tosca Lee, *New York Times* bestselling author

"In *Elysium Tide* readers will travel to Hawaii and a crime that seems to start small and then spirals into a many-headed Hydra that seems impossible to kill . . . or solve. Filled with twists, turns, and characters that kept the pages turning, the book felt like a vacation and a jolt of adrenaline at the same time. Be prepared to read this book in one sitting. *Elysium Tide* is perfect for readers who love a novel filled with mystery, twists, and the lightest hint of romance."

Cara Putman, bestselling, award-winning author
of *Lethal Intent* and *Flight Risk*

"James R. Hannibal's *Elysium Tide* is a compelling, pulse-pounding suspense and action-packed mystery that had me enthralled from beginning to end. Reading it was like watching a movie. Loved the Hawaiian setting, realistic/believable characters, and the multilayered plot. James is now on my favorite author list, and I can't wait for the next book."

Patricia H. Rushford, award-winning mystery writer
and author of the Angel Delaney Mysteries

"Maui's Road to Hana doesn't have anything on the white-knuckled suspense and hairpin twists and turns Hannibal delivers in *Elysium Tide*. Remember to breathe!"

Natalie Walters, author of Carol Finalist *Living Lies*
from the Harbored Secrets series, and *Lights Out*
from The SNAP Agency series

ELYSIUM TIDE

Books by James R. Hannibal

The Gryphon Heist
Chasing the White Lion
The Paris Betrayal
Elysium Tide

ELYSIUM TIDE

JAMES R. HANNIBAL

Revell

a division of Baker Publishing Group
Grand Rapids, Michigan

© 2022 by James R. Hannibal

Published by Revell
a division of Baker Publishing Group
PO Box 6287, Grand Rapids, MI 49516-6287
www.revellbooks.com

Printed in the United States of America

Library of Congress Cataloging-in-Publication Data
Names: Hannibal, James R., author.
Title: Elysium tide / James R. Hannibal.
Description: Grand Rapids, MI : Revell, a division of Baker Publishing Group, [2022]
Identifiers: LCCN 2021042938 | ISBN 9780800738518 (paperback) | ISBN 9780800741518 (casebound) | ISBN 9781493436279 (ebook)
Subjects: LCGFT: Novels.
Classification: LCC PS3608.A71576 E49 2022 | DDC 813/.6—dc23
LC record available at https://lccn.loc.gov/2021042938

Baker Publishing Group publications use paper produced from sustainable forestry practices and post-consumer waste whenever possible.

22   23   24   25   26   27   28   7   6   5   4   3   2   1

CHAPTER
ONE

Pediatric Surgery
The Royal London Hospital
London, UK

DR. PETER CHESTERFIELD WATCHED his chief resident cut a three-millimeter patch of flesh and muscle away from the boy's forehead above the eyebrow. "Easy, Anna. No sense in leaving a scar that might scare off the ladies."

"Michael's seven, Dr. Chesterfield." The resident passed control of her forceps to a waiting nurse, who held the patch in place, and then lifted a cranial drill from the instrument table. "He's not old enough to worry about girls."

"He will be someday, if we do our jobs right. Begin your burr hole."

"Drilling now."

Wisps of smoke rose toward the bright lights of the operating theater, carrying the smell of hot bone dust and cooked blood to Peter's mask—not the most likable scent in the world, but one he'd grown used to. When Anna finished, she stepped aside, and the lead surgical nurse handed Peter a multi-instrument scope. He immediately began his incision, cutting through the final layers of tissue that protected the boy's brain.

"Dr. Chesterfield." Once she had Peter's attention, the nurse, an older Black woman and a longtime friend, inclined her head toward the theater's microphone. A red light already burned next to the word RECORD.

Peter glanced at her and then at the line of students standing a respectful distance from the table. He sighed. "Right. Thank you, Carol. We can't forget our protocols, can we?" He raised his voice for the microphone. "This is Dr. Peter Chesterfield, senior attending neurosurgeon, Royal London Hospital. My accomplices today are doctors Anna Evans, chief resident, and Barbara Davies, a second-year neurosurgery fellow."

While he spoke, Peter maneuvered his scope through the folds and valleys of his patient's brain. "Today, we are conducting a four-hand, two-scope endoscopic procedure to remove a pesky adenoma growing from little Michael's pituitary gland. I will approach through the third ventricle while my accomplices take the nasopharyngeal route." He paused his work and lifted his gaze to the students. "Like Hamilton and Hickman fighting the Boers, we will attack this creature from both the north and south."

The students answered him with blank stares.

Cretans.

Shadows fidgeted in the tinted windows surrounding the upper level of the operating theater. More students, Peter supposed. They were everywhere, one of the hazards of attending at the Royal London and St. Barts, both teaching hospitals. To escape these hordes and practice in peace, Peter would have to commute outside the city to someplace like Surrey. But he had no stomach for long drives—or Surrey.

He punched through the wall of the third ventricle, steering his scope through a cavern of cerebral spinal fluid like Verne's *Nautilus* in the deep. "I'm almost there, Barbara. What's your status?" Peter knew her status. He could see the progress of her scope on his dual display, but if she wanted to be an attending neurosurgeon someday, she'd have to learn to work and talk at the same time.

"I'm at the cavernous sinus, Dr. Chesterfield. I should have a visual in—"

A flood of red wiped out Barbara's side of the display. An alarm blared from the monitor stack next to the table.

"Blood pressure rapidly dropping," Carol said, the barest tension tightening her voice. "Dr. Davies, you might have cut the internal carotid."

"Might?" Peter asked.

Barbara eased her controls up and down, staring at her screen. "I know. I know. I'm trying to get gauze on it. I can't see anything."

Peter would have taken over her scope, but in his current position, deep into the boy's ventricular system, he had to maintain control with at least one hand. If his line drifted too far to the left, the kid would fail every math test for the rest of his life. Too far to the right, and Michael might lose the ability to understand the concept of love, pain, or Saturday. "You have red out, Barbara. You need to clear your visual field. Get a larger suction tube in there."

"Already on it."

"Are you?"

While the surgical fellow fumbled with her scope tubes, Peter wrapped his gloved fingers around the boy's throat, signaling Carol with his eyes. "Pressure. Here. Like this. We have to slow the blood flow." He let her take over, then looked to the chief resident who'd made the first incision for him. "Anna, are you comfortable with the nasopharyngeal path?"

"Yes, Dr. Chesterfield."

"Good. Get another scope in there. Cut a one-millimeter square of tissue from the temporalis. We'll graft it into the artery as a patch."

Barbara worked her larger tube through the scope port and began clearing the cavity with suction and gauze. As the red curtain receded from her camera, the team got their first look at the damage.

Peter grimaced and shook his head. "Make that a two-millimeter square, Anna."

The tear might be two millimeters, but in the altered perspective of his tiny scope, the pressurized stream of blood pouring through it looked like a meter-wide gusher pouring from a breaking dam. The monitor in the observation room above repeated his display in seventy inches of high-definition glory. Peter imagined the students up there were getting quite the horror show. "Make your grip tighter, Carol. We've got to slow this bleeding."

"Doctor, the patient is exhibiting cyanosis." Carol's warning contravened his order, yet her hand tightened around Michael's small throat in complete obedience. "He can't take much more. Blood ox is tanking."

Peter's foot tapped the floor, loud enough for the rubber sole of his theater boot to be heard through the sterile overshoe. "I need that patch, Anna. In case you're not up on current events, Carol is choking the life out of this child to stem the tide while your partner in crime, The Barbara of Seville, sucks the remaining blood out of his brain. I'd say moving with purpose is the order of the day, wouldn't you?"

"I've got it. I've got it. Bringing the tissue up now." The third scope's display showed Anna following Barbara's red-soaked line up the channel. She reached the cavity, and together, they pushed the muscle tissue into the gap.

"Anna, hold it in place. Barbara, use your blunt electrode to solder the patch. Muscle side only. Make no contact with the artery."

Neither answered but followed his commands as if he were steering their fingers with his voice. The moment they'd soldered the full perimeter of the patch, Peter looked to Carol. "Release him. Slowly."

On the display, a trickle of blood spilled from a corner of the patch. Barbara gave the area another pass with the electrode, and the flow stopped. Peter checked the numbers on the monitor. Michael's blood oxygen and pressure slowed their plunge, leveled for a second, then rose.

Peter nodded. "Good." With his patient stabilized and in no immediate danger, he looked hard at the second-year. "Do you often try to kill your patients on the table or was that just today?"

Barbara sucked in a breath. "Excuse me?"

"You heard me. We brought this boy in with an eminently operable benign tumor that should have left him with nothing but a sore throat and a week of headaches. But you up and lacerate his carotid artery. Either you're a psychopath or neurosurgery isn't your bag." He pointed with his free hand. "Perhaps you should try the Royal Dentistry Academy next door."

The students shifted in their line. One of them coughed. Peter hit him with a glare. "You. Out. No one coughs in my operating theater." The young man lowered his gaze and headed for the door, and Peter returned his gaze to Barbara. "You, too. As soon as Anna has her scope clear, transfer control of yours and get out."

"You can't be serious. We're in the middle of a procedure."

"Which Anna can handle under my guidance. Out, Barbara. Now."

CHAPTER
TWO

PETER TOOK A LONG BREATHER in the attendings' changing room after the surgery. He had no desire to speak with the boy's parents. He'd never enjoyed that part of the job.

After removing Barbara from his operating theater, he and the more-than-capable Anna had finished the operation, assisted by Carol. Working from above and below in what had become known in neurosurgery as the Chesterfield pincer, they had removed more than 99 percent of the tumor. With minimal radiation therapy, Michael stood a good chance of never seeing it grow back.

Victory over death. He'd done it, as he had a hundred times before, some in far more pressing and far less pristine circumstances. Peter sank onto the bench between the lockers and dropped his head into his hands. Tomorrow, he'd step onto the battlefield again. And again the next day, and the next, over and over, until death—relentless—finally won. But such was man's plight.

The door slammed open.

Peter did not have to look up to know who'd entered. "This changing room is for attending surgeons only, Barbara."

"Which I will be in three months."

"Not if I have anything to say about it."

Barbara, for all the fury and drama of her arrival, stayed close to the door, arms crossed. "That kid had a prominent internal carotid. It could have happened to anyone." She thrust her chin toward Peter. "It could have happened to you."

He let out a wry chuckle. From the catch in her voice, he could tell even she didn't believe such a claim. "Stop making excuses and go. I was serious about the Dentistry Academy. I believe they're accepting applications for next semester until the end of the day. You can make it if you hurry."

"I'm reporting you to the executive board."

This was enough to make Peter lift his head. "You're reporting *me*? I'm not the one who almost killed that boy."

"You called me The Barbara of Seville."

"Oh. You caught that, did you?"

"If I had your lack of professionalism, I'd slap you."

Peter left the bench and raised himself to his full height of six foot three, not as a threat, but to remind her who she was talking to—the top attending neurosurgeon in the Barts Health Trust. He didn't have to say a word.

"You'll be sorry," she said, and walked out.

PETER FOUND MICHAEL'S PARENTS in the family room outside the children's ward, waiting for their son, and waiting for answers. He gave them the latter. The nurses would bring them the former soon after. He explained the complication of the injured ICA and assured them it had been properly repaired with no threat whatsoever of future damage, then gave them the good news of the successful Chesterfield pincer.

Both listened with grave expressions. The mother, a short redhead with eyes puffy from crying, nodded with real under-standing, almost like she'd been there for the whole thing.

When Peter finished, he paused and waited. He didn't do the job for the praise, but accepting it with the right amount of practiced grace was a necessary function of his position. He'd even come to tolerate the overzealous hugs often offered by the Welsh.

But these two, as Welsh as they came, offered no hugs and no praise. The father glowered at him. The mother reached up and slapped him across the face.

Carol appeared out of nowhere to rescue him and ushered the two away, promising they would see Michael soon. She cast Peter an apologetic glance. He answered with a shrug that said, *What was that for? I saved their child's life.*

"I guess Michael's mother is not as professional as Barbara." Nigel Avery, the group chief medical officer, pushed himself off the wall near the snack machines, where he'd been lurking.

"I saw you there," Peter said, turning to face him. "Those machines don't hide you, though they might if you used them less." Peter had recognized Nigel's reference to Barbara's rant. "Though I failed to see you in the changing room. Were you spying on me there, as well?"

"Not spying. Then or now. I never spy. I observe the goings-on in *my* medical group. And lately too many of those goings-on have involved you. I was not in the changing room, but Barbara came to me and lodged a formal complaint. She told me what she said to you, and what you said to her."

Things were coming together. Barbara had been busy. "I suppose she spoke to the parents after she spoke to you. That explains the slap."

Nigel shook his head. "Wrong. I ordered her to keep well clear of the parents."

"Then how did the boy's mother seem to know everything that happened in there?"

Nigel pulled Peter to the side, closer to his snack machines. Carol had returned with Michael and his parents. As they passed, the mother shot Peter a glare so violent, he could feel the heat on his cheek where she'd slapped him. Nigel followed the family with his gaze. "Don't you get it, Peter? I let them watch from the observation room. They saw the whole thing. More to the point, they heard every unfortunate civil-action-worthy word you spoke."

"You let them watch their own son's surgery?"

Nigel's thick chin bobbed up and down in a nod.

"Then you're a bigger idiot than I thought."

The chief medical officer turned to go, giving Peter a slow tilt of the head. "Follow me to my office, Dr. Chesterfield. It's high time we had a serious chat."

Nigel said nothing else of substance until they'd entered the sanctum of his office nine floors up. He closed the door and gestured to a chair. "I think we both know what I'm about to say."

Self-incrimination—the tool of administrators across England and beyond. Why level an accusation when you can make your underling admit to a whole host of sins in a game of Guess My Crime. Peter would not play, nor would he sit in Nigel's proverbial hot seat. He chose to stand. "I haven't the foggiest, Nigel. Please, enlighten me."

"You're a brilliant surgeon. Playing dense doesn't suit you."

"But it's fine for Barbara?"

"There," Nigel said, pointing at him. "That's the problem. Your mouth." He dropped into his chair. "Really, Peter. You don't have to say every odd thing that comes into your head. And you're always so dark. On your theater recordings, for instance, you often introduce your colleagues as accomplices."

Peter looked out the window toward Greenwich. Nigel had quite the view. He gave his boss the slightest shrug. "So?"

Nigel spread his hands. "It's a term for *murderers*."

"A bit of gallows humor. Nothing more."

"Then why do I never see you laugh?" Nigel sat back and sighed. "Your negativity is not healthy. I've let it go in the past, but today you became a liability."

For the first time in the conversation, Peter met his boss's gaze. "A liability? For kicking Barbara out of the theater after she nearly killed a child?"

"Barbara was not the only one to lodge a complaint—or rather, she nearly wasn't. The Firths spoke to me about you."

"Who on earth are the Firths?"

"Michael's *parents*, you numbskull." Nigel shook his head. "Perhaps you really aren't playing dense. Gwen Firth, Peter. She's the woman who slapped you across the face fifteen minutes ago. And an hour ago, you pushed a probe into her child's brain. The least you could do is learn her name." He stood and paced before his nine-foot-tall windows. "The father"—he glanced over his shoulder—"*Harry Firth*, told me he's grateful you saved their son, but he believes you are, quote, 'a menace to your patients and your colleagues.' He demanded the hospital put you under administrative review."

Peter finally sat in the chair. No patient or patient's family member had ever complained about him—not to his knowledge. Had Nigel prompted them? Was this some kind of vendetta? He had his suspicions. "Neither of the Firths work for the NIH, Nigel. Of that, I'm certain. So, how did Mr. Firth know about the administrative review process?"

"How should I know? The internet?"

Peter frowned. "And you said . . . ?"

"I reminded him once more that you were the one who identified the tumor in the first place and subsequently saved Michael's life." Nigel stopped his pacing at the center of the picture window—a polar bear in a suit, framed by gray sky and urban London. "And then I assured him I would deal with you."

Deal with you. That didn't sound promising. "What's it to be? The gallows at Tyburn? Drawn and quartered in the Old Palace Yard? Or worse yet, community service?"

Nigel's usual bear-with-a-honey-pot expression turned as grave as Peter had ever seen it.

"Hawaii, Peter. I'm sending you to Maui, and there's no way you're going to weasel out of it this time."

CHAPTER
THREE

The Elysium Grand Resort
Wailea, Maui

LISA KEALOHA CLIMBED the metal steps from the general admission bleachers to the VIP platform, reading faces as she went. While the spectators watched the blue-green water off the resort's beach, Lisa watched them. She hadn't seen any threats so far—just one kid having an allergy attack, which had been enough to clear a small space in the benches around him.

A horn sounded behind her, and she heard the splash of a competitor hitting the water. At the edges of her vision, the twin giant screens bracketing the crowd showed a freediver shooting through a series of wickets and hoops, propelled by a monofin. A tethered underwater camera drone chased her deeper and deeper as the course led her farther offshore.

Lisa reached the top of the steps and turned her attention to a tanned individual in a pink polo and white Bermudas. He was seated with the resort owner, Harry Alcott, and his wife at one of several white tables. Jack Carlisle. Maui's newest VIP. The chief had directed her captain to have someone check on him. As the senior detective on site, Lisa had drawn the short straw. "Good morning, Mr. Carlisle." She scanned the faces on the green lawn behind the platform as she spoke. "Enjoying the show?"

"Immensely," he said, sinking his Dallas drawl into the center of the word. "The Hawaiian Freediving Association has something fresh and new here, far more exciting than the last five decades of holding your breath and going up and down a rope. I'm happy to be a sponsor."

"And I'm sure they're grateful for your investment. The whole island is."

That earned her a chagrined smile. "Not the whole island. Otherwise, you wouldn't be here, now would you?"

An overstated point. Mr. Carlisle had received threatening social media messages and comments after purchasing more than thirty thousand acres of defunct sugarcane fields at the foot of the West Maui Volcano and stretching into the island's central valley. But Carlisle could take care of himself, as evidenced by the two bulky locals posted barely three paces from his table.

He offered her a chair opposite his guests. "Care to join us? Your chief told me his forces arrived on-site before sunup. By now, you must be starving. And ever since I bought my villa here at Mr. Alcott's new resort"—he gave a token nod to the white-haired man seated next to him—"the staff won't stop bringing me food."

"I appreciate the offer, but no. As you said, I need to focus on my reason for being here." *A different reason than babysitting you*, she didn't say. "Any new threats?"

"Read the comments on our Ono Beef Instagram feed and see for yourself."

Not worth her time. Mostly idle chatter and overstatement from the armchair warriors of Maui's environmental scene. "The evidence team is monitoring all your social media. They'll call me if necessary. What I meant was, have you received anything specific—phone calls, emails, direct confrontations at your hotel—anything to make me think a crazed detractor might take a shot at you?"

"Take a shot at me? Oh, dear. Now you *do* have me worried." The flatness of his expression told her just the opposite. This guy was in no danger. And bodyguards aside, he himself didn't seem to believe he was in danger.

Lisa made a note to have the captain thank the chief for wasting her time when she had bigger concerns. "Enjoy the show, Mr. Carlisle. And give the chief my regards." She walked to the back of the platform, making sure she was out of Carlisle's earshot, and raised a radio to her lips. "Patrol, you find my boy yet?"

"Been asking around. Nothing yet, Sis."

She gritted her teeth. "Call me *Detective* at work, Officer Kealoha." From the elevated platform, she saw her brother right where she expected to find him, at the Hula Dog truck picking some free snacks—*grindz* as the locals called them. "Don't make me tell you again." She switched to an accent she had left dormant for a long time. "Now put down da kine grindz and keep lookin'."

"Sure, sure, *Detective*. I give you a shout if I see Koa, ya? Patrol, out."

She held her position and searched the beach crowd crammed against a rope line thirty feet from the water—a collective living, pulsating organism, growing by the minute as more pushed in to see the local favorite Kelly Alana. Finding her target among all that movement was no easy task.

Show your face for me, Koa. I just want to talk. No arrests today, unless you do something dumb.

The post-calamity tourism boom had brought business and jobs back to Hawaii. It had also brought gangs from San Francisco and Los Angeles, causing an uptick in crime on the islands, with Maui experiencing a huge spike in auto theft. Those thefts had brought Lisa back.

It had been a strange homecoming, given her past. As a teen, she'd had a less-than-friendly relationship with the Maui PD. After six years away, five in the LAPD, she'd been invited by the Maui Investigative Services Bureau to head up their Criminal Investigative Division's GTF—their gang task force.

Kelly's slot is coming up, Koa. You're not going to miss your cousin's dive, are you?

There. She saw him at the north end of the rope line, hiding among the taller tourists. He had his eyes down, but the buzz cut and tattoos were just as she remembered.

"Patrol, I've got eyes on our boy. North end, at the rope. Get there, but don't show yourself."

Don't show yourself. What a thing to say to Pika. Trying to hide one of her oversize brothers in a crowd was like trying to hide a mako shark in a school of mackerel. And Pika was the smaller of the two.

After three weeks on the island, Lisa had to make some headway—to score a win for her captain so he could justify her presence to the chief. More than that, she wanted to show those who'd come up in the local department that she deserved this job, especially those who'd known her when she was a kid on the wrong side of the badge.

Lisa needed an in with the local criminal element. And she'd grown up with the perfect candidate—Koa Alana, the cousin that Kelly Alana saw more as a brother. She always had, even though he'd dragged both Kelly and Lisa into a lot of trouble over the years.

Lisa stayed close to the rope on her approach, minimizing Koa's view angle, but he'd always had sharp eyes. He saw her coming. "Hey, Sistah. I heard you back. Didn' believe it 'til now."

"Don't run, Koa."

"You see me runnin'? I don't care if you some big, scary LA cop now. I don't care where you been."

Funny, because he did look scared. Lisa had overtaken him in height after ninth grade, but Koa had always seemed bigger than her. Until now. She lifted the rope to let him through, and he came, glancing back at the tourists with a smile like he was some kind of celebrity.

"So you haven't been ducking me?" Lisa asked. "That's weird, because I've been asking around for three solid weeks."

"Then you must not be too good at your job, eh, Sistah? 'Cause I been around the whole time."

Her brother came up from behind, a head taller than the rest of the crowd.

If Koa saw him, he didn't show it. "Don't know nothin' 'bout you lookin' for me. You wanna talk, jus' call." He shrugged. "No big ting."

"Yeah. Right. What've you been up to since I left? Any new friends?"

Koa kicked the sand with a bare toe and gave her a laugh. "Wow. You serious? Jumpin' straight to 'Turn snitch for me, Koa.' Too bad for you. I ain't like that. I keep true to my *'ohana,* not like you an' that big dumb whale standin' behind me."

So, he had seen Pika. Good old Koa. Eyes in the back of his head. Years ago, those eyes had saved Lisa and others from spending their nights in Maui's youth detention center. But Lisa didn't remember that time of her life with fondness, not anymore. "Okay, Koa. My bad. How about a favor for a friend from your *hanabata* days? Events like this one have been pulling in a lot of activity—pickpockets, auto theft. It's making the tourists squeamish. Nobody wants that, not even you. Point me to something going down today. You can puff up all you want, but I know you've got rivals on the island now, maybe one or two big ones. I can take them down. Help me help you."

"Can't help you. Especially not today. I ain't here for dat, an' you know it."

"You're here for your cousin. Yeah, I know. Ever wish you'd taken a different path? Applied yourself? Ever wish you'd been more like her?"

Koa let out a huff and shifted his eyes to the water. "Yeah, right. A different path. You don't know nothin'." A slow smile spread across his lips—pride. "An', Sistah, ain't nobody like Kelly."

A booming announcement nearly drowned out the last of Koa's words. "Ladies and gentlemen, turn your eyes to the launch and greet Maui's own Kelly Alana!"

The crowd erupted in cheers as a slender Hawaiian native waved to them, seated on the rear deck of a cruiser. She lowered herself into the water and took a long breath through pursed lips. At the end of the breath, she raised her shoulders, then vanished under the surface.

All eyes moved to the big screens as the underwater camera drone took over. It seemed barely able to keep pace with the powerful mermaid strokes of her monofin. Kelly—this girl Lisa had babysat, carried in her arms not too many years before— dove almost straight down fifteen meters to pass through a green PVC wicket fixed to the seabed, then level through a hoop and into a slow descent through a curving hallway of suspended diamonds. The last of these included two upright bars, forcing her to turn sideways and cease her kicks to escape.

The curving hallway brought Kelly to Wailea's 150-meter dropoff, where she turned straight down again to follow a traditional freediving line.

"How long?" Koa asked, unwilling or unable to take his eyes from the screen.

Lisa shielded her eyes to check the running clock mounted on the launch. "Two minutes, twenty-four seconds. With all that exertion, her lungs must be bursting by now."

"Kelly don't even notice. She got the spirit of the *honu*, like our ancestors."

"You sure they weren't dolphins? Sea turtles never looked that fast."

Kelly ripped a plastic tag from the weight at the bottom of

the line and headed straight for the surface. Her score would be a combination of her time and the depth achieved in the final portion.

"Three minutes, nine seconds," Lisa said, anticipating Koa's question.

He didn't answer her, speaking instead to his cousin as she and her camera drone raced toward a rippling sky. "You got this, Sistah. Fly."

A few heartbeats later, Kelly burst through the surface and waved her tag at the judges. She showed them an okay sign to prove she hadn't gone hypoxic. The clock stopped. The announcer shouted into his microphone. "Three minutes and sixteen seconds. A new HFA women's record! Ladies and gentlemen, your hometown girl, Kelly—"

A series of sharp pops drew Lisa's attention to her left. One end of the bleachers collapsed. The spectators screamed.

CHAPTER
FOUR

The Elysium Grand

LIFEGUARDS, BROUGHT IN TO WATCH over the athletes, now turned and raced toward the injured spectators. The crowd at the rope bumped and jostled each other to get away from the unknown danger, taking even big Pika with them.

Lisa grabbed Koa's arm. "What did you do?"

"Nothin'. I told you, I'm only here for Kelly."

Above the noise of the frightened crowd, Lisa heard windows smashing. Car alarms blared. In a lot between the Grand and the neighboring resort, a trio of thugs hopped into high-end vehicles.

"Really, Koa? You'd risk killing these people for a diversion?" She let him go and ran. "Pika, cuff him!"

Koa called after her. "Lisa, that ain't my crew, I swear!"

Lisa had about fourteen seconds to close the distance—the average time it took to clone a key fob from a luxury car's diagnostic port. She pounded out twenty yards on the sand, hemmed in by the crowd, eating up most of that window.

The thieves were already on the move by the time she reached solid ground. She wished one of them had chosen to steal her

Toyota 4Runner, parked in the same lot. That would've made her life so much easier. But most auto thieves knew how to spot an unmarked cop unit. Lisa had known how, back in the day. With only a few paces to go, she punched her remote start. Seconds later, she tore out of the lot, grill lights flashing. "Don't forget to breathe, Lisa. Don't forget to breathe."

The LAPD had taught her to use that mantra to remind a partner to keep calm during a high-speed chase. But Maui didn't have LA's budget. The island's detectives didn't have partners. She rode solo, so she had to recite the mantra to herself. "Breathe," she said again after the pause that followed the technique's four-count inhale, and then she used a long exhale to slow her heartbeat.

The moment Lisa's radio connected to the net, she heard chatter. "—white with a red stripe. And a black Benz. I didn't get a good look at the other one."

"Charlie 1-6-5 is on Pi'ilani, en route to intercept."

"1-7-6 is on Kupulau, en route as well."

"Multiple injuries at the Grand. Send another ambulance. Rumors of shots fired."

Lisa cut in. "Break, break. This is Union 2-6, I'm directly behind the 10-80, heading north on Wailea Alanui. I have visual on a silver Corvette and the black Benz. I can't tell the make of the white one—maybe a Porsche—but you can't miss the red stripe down the center. Get air support moving, and we can wrap this up."

She knew the mistake she'd made the moment she released the mic switch, but dispatch gave her no opportunity to recover.

"No air support here, 2-6. You ain't in LA no more."

No kidding. Lisa didn't bother responding. "Charlie 165, can you get to Okolani and stop traffic?"

"On it, 2-6."

Stealing a car on an island in broad daylight. Not the best plan. The thieves had only one viable route out of Wailea—

Pi'ilani Highway. The other option was the beach road next to the resorts, but that would almost certainly get them trapped behind a fleet of golf carts or a busload of tourists, and they would know that.

As predicted, the stolen vehicles turned north on Okolani, giving Lisa a better look at the white car. A Porsche, as she thought. Flashing red-and-blue lights visible through the monkeypod trees ahead told her 165 had reached the intersection, maybe 176 too. She slowed. No need to risk her teammates' lives by forcing these jokers into a crash. Where could they go?

The Porsche had an answer for her. Leading the pack, its driver broke left, caught the curb at an angle, and smashed through a chain-link gate into a long green park. The Benz and the Corvette followed, fishtailing on the grass. Unbelievable.

Lisa hesitated only a moment before pressing her gas pedal to the floor and cranking the wheel. If the Corvette could handle it, her police-issue 4Runner should have no problem. She bounced over the curb.

Handle it? Yes. Comfortable? Oh, no. The jump to the grass nearly smashed her head into the Toyota's ceiling.

Mud spat out behind the sports cars' slipping tires, and Lisa gained. She could pull a PIT maneuver and spin the trailing vehicle on the grass, but a roll might kill the driver—not the most appropriate punishment for auto theft. She needed patrol to pull their weight and stop one of these fools with the road-blocks. One reprobate was all she needed. She'd get him to flip on his friends.

The park ended before she could close the gap. The Porsche punched through a hedge onto a residential road that intersected the Pi'ilani Highway. Lisa keyed her mic. "1-6-5, they bypassed your roadblock. They're turning north on Pi'ilani now. 2-6 is still in pursuit."

"We see you, 2-6. We're half a block behind. Got a plan?"

"Let 'em run. North of Kihei, they've only got two choices—310 or 311. One is empty fields, and the other is surrounded by water. No one to hurt. Take 'em there. Dispatch, send more units to block both routes."

"Copy, 2-6. Will do."

Lisa listened as the dispatcher coordinated the roadblocks. Maui PD might not have had any helicopters, but they had plenty of uniforms in Chevy Impalas, more than a lot of cities with far larger populations. Four cars raced down Route 310 from Maalaea and Waikapu, and five took 311 from Kahului. Lisa gave her three jokers space, once again hoping they'd ease off on their speed. They did, but not much, and when they reached the intersection, they split.

The Porsche took a hard left on 310, while the Benz and his buddy the Corvette blew through the T intersection to press north on 311.

"1-6-5, stay with the northbound pair," Lisa said. She wanted the leader. "The Porsche is mine."

Hawaii Route 310 ran between a thin strip of rocky, wooded coast and a three-mile-long salt marsh called Keālia Pond. With only two lanes and no off ramps or side streets, it made the perfect choke point. Cars sailed by in the southeast-bound lane. Lisa hoped they were the last. The roadblock should be stopping the rest.

When the road straightened, she saw the Maui PD units pulling into position. They'd brought in the island's only Bearcat—an armored Special Response Team vehicle with the look of a military MRAP. It must've been in the area. "Slow down, Brah." Her eyes drilled into the Porsche's tinted rear windscreen, willing the driver to hear her and obey. "You're not getting through."

The Porsche didn't listen. The gap between them widened, even though she had her foot on the floor. Lisa let up. If any civilians had made it onto the road behind her, she'd have to keep them back, and she had no intention of putting any more pressure on this guy.

The thief seemed oblivious to her efforts to give him room. He rocketed toward the barricade. The uniforms positioned behind the Impalas raised their weapons.

Shooting him wouldn't stop his momentum. She'd seen the chopper video of a vehicle running the barricade in LA. Every cop in her old department had. Not pretty. Lisa keyed her mic. "This is 2-6. He's not slowing. Move! Move! Get out of there!"

The uniforms backed away, then ran. Rapid gunfire erupted from the trees on the beach side—SRT protecting their Bearcat, their baby. The thief swerved away to the right. His tires caught the gravel, and an instant later his fender caught the guardrail. The Porsche cartwheeled into the marsh.

"No!" Lisa accelerated again, racing up to the accident scene with her dash lights flashing. She skidded to a stop twenty feet from the roadblock, hand already on her seat belt's release.

Last to arrive. First in the water. Lisa waded calf-deep through the salt marsh toward the wreckage. No smoke. No apparent fire. Glock drawn, she approached the driver's side. Between the thief's initial break-in and SRT's barrage of gunfire, nothing remained of the windows. A figure hung upside down in the shoulder restraint. "Let me see your hands! Show me your hands!" A pointless command, she knew. But she had to use it. This was an officer-involved shooting now. She had to check every box.

Others shouted variations of the same from behind her, just as pointless. Blood covered the deflating airbag and spread through the brown water, an oil slick without the rainbow sheen. The thief wore a bulky hoodie, probably to conceal the tools of his craft and maybe a weapon. Fat lot of good any of it did him. His head remained below the surface, and he showed no sign of struggling to find air.

"He's unresponsive! Watch him! I'm getting him out!" She holstered her Glock and drew a Smith & Wesson tactical knife with a hook blade on the spine—not a thing here on Maui, but a standard carry item in her previous city. It made quick work of the restraint, and she pulled the thief through the window. He felt light, even with the wet hoodie. Once she rolled his shoulders to get his nose and mouth above water, she knew why. Not a him. A her.

That face. Local. Young. It could easily have been Lisa's six or seven years ago. She felt for a pulse, then shook her head at the officers around her. "Stand down. She's gone."

CHAPTER
FIVE

The Elysium Grand

LISA RETURNED TO THE GRAND, hoping to get her eyes on the scene before any of her new colleagues ruined the evidence. Too late. Jenny Fan paced before the collapsed bleachers, issuing orders to the department's CSI techs. That girl moved fast. She hadn't even been assigned to the event, nor had Lisa heard anything about a second investigator being sent to the Grand. But she should have seen this coming.

On several occasions over the last two weeks, Jenny had made it clear that she should have been named lead detective for the new gang task force, not Lisa. She wasn't alone in that opinion. Jenny's fans among the rank and file outnumbered Lisa's three to one, and she knew it.

"Breathe," Lisa said to herself—for the same reason she'd said it at the start of the pursuit. She needed to keep her heart rate even. What would Clay have told her? *Defuse the situation, Lisa. Show them you're not a threat.* She missed him. But he'd chosen the FBI. And she'd chosen to come home.

"I got this," Jenny said before Lisa got within ten yards of the site. "You can read my report tomorrow. No need to supervise."

Breathe. Defuse. Lisa raised her hands. "I'm not trying to over-the-shoulder you. I'm just another set of eyes, that's all. Any fatalities?"

"None on our end. A few broken bones. Two concussions. One old lady thought she was having a heart attack, but the paramedic said she was fine. You? I heard you drove your thief into Keālia Pond."

Low blow. "Not me. SRT. And the other two vanished between Kihei and the roadblock. They left Franks and Mahoe in the dust after they split from the Porsche. Must have taken Kamaaina or one of the old dirt roads through the cane fields."

Jenny crouched beneath the mangled bleachers to direct an evidence specialist's camera. "Too bad for Franks and Mahoe."

"Wouldn't have happened if we had air support. And the girl would still be alive. We could have let them run home to their shop or boss—caught the big fish."

"No air support," Jenny said without looking up at her. "This isn't Los Angeles."

"So I've heard."

"You know what else we don't have?" A blond man in a white polo and a blue Maui PD cap poked his head out from the other side of the bleachers—Mike Nichols, the CSI liaison for Lisa's task force. "Boats. We're an island PD, responsible for the smaller satellite islands of Lanai and Molokai, each separated from us by nine miles of water, but we have no boats. What's up with that?" He tiptoed and pivoted his way out of the wreckage and walked over. "Detectives."

They both looked at him for a long moment. "Mike," Lisa said.

"That hurts. I have a title."

"It's too long for short conversations." She glanced down at a plastic baggie in his left hand. "What'd you find?"

"Bolts." He held the baggie up so she and Jenny could see the contents better. "These are the source of your mysterious gunshots and the reason the bleachers failed."

Jenny took the bag—a little fast, as if she needed to get a hand on it before Lisa—and held it close to her eyes, lifting her sunglasses. "Cut by explosive charges?"

He laughed. "Hardly. They weren't cut. Corroded is a better word."

"Corroded," Lisa said. "Like rust?"

"More like acid." Mike retrieved the baggie from Jenny. "I can't say for sure until I get these back to the lab, but from the smell and the orange residue, I'd say someone used hydriodic acid. Powerful stuff."

Lisa looked at the mangled end of the bleachers and tried to imagine someone standing beneath them, patiently pouring acid over the bolts, unnoticed by the spectators. "How fast does it work?"

"Fast. But the acid didn't have to do the whole job." Mike turned one of the bolts through the plastic so she and Jenny could see the cross section. Only a small part of that cross section was rough—corroded, like he said. The larger portion had sheared, leaving a smooth, clean surface. "With all those people in the bleachers, these bolts were under tremendous pressure. The acid weakened them, and once the first failed, the rest gave way. It would have sounded like a ripple of pops."

Jenny glanced at Lisa. "Our mystery gunshots."

Mike touched his nose with a gloved hand. "You got it."

Lisa remained quiet. She trusted Mike's analysis, but the whole combination of chemistry and car thieves felt off. "You ever hear of car thieves using this . . . this . . ."

Mike filled in the gap for her. "Hydriodic acid."

"That. You ever hear of boosters using it before?"

"Not car thieves per se, but gangs, sure. All the time. Hydriodic acid is a key chemical used in the production of meth."

"Meth. Great." Traditionally, the methamphetamine market was an Oahu thing, not a Maui thing. But it fit the profile of the gangs rumored to have come in from California. Lisa needed more information. Triggered by the thought, she looked up, scanning the beach and the resort lawn. "Where's my brother? What happened to Koa?"

CHAPTER
SIX

26 Knightsbridge Court
London, UK

"SOCKS." PETER HELD OUT an open palm, and Carol filled it with the same firmness she used when passing him a scalpel in the theater. He glanced down at a pair of light-blue low-cuts with the store's plastic hook still attached. "Carol, these are most definitely not my socks."

She had invited herself over, offering to help him pack with the proviso that all swim trunks and underwear be in the suitcase and buried under a layer of T-shirts before she arrived. "They are now, Peter. I picked 'em up on my way over, along with a few other things. Leonard and I will give you the bill when you get back." She handed him two more pairs—orange and pink. "Do you know how hard it is to find beachwear in London?"

"I don't. I really don't. I never go to the beach."

"You never go outside, honey. Not anymore. Way different from your past life, but I guess that was more duty than choice. Here." Carol slapped six plastic-wrapped shirts in a rainbow of colors down on the long ironwood coffee table he'd chosen to

34

use as a luggage stand. "These are called rash guards. I got you the long-sleeve version. Wear 'em whether you're getting in the water or not. Otherwise, your skin'll light up like Rudolph on Christmas Eve. I also put some sandals in there. The Hawaiians call 'em slippahs, so don't get confused."

Peter regarded the socks for a long moment, then placed the orange and blue pairs in his suitcase and tossed the pink ones onto the couch.

Carol frowned at him.

He frowned back. "I won't need any of it. Not ankle socks, nor . . . slippahs. I have no desire to go to the beach, or deep-sea fishing, or parasailing—or for anyone on earth to see what my toes look like, for that matter. I have no inclination to get caught up in any of the activities other doctors do on these certification shams the resorts put on. Other than the presentations I'm required to attend, I don't plan on leaving my hotel room."

"Actually, none of the presentations are required." She picked up the shirts, which he hadn't touched, and placed them in the suitcase. "Once you sign in at the resort's reception desk, you're good. Leonard took me to the one on Communication Strategies for Otolaryngologists last year in Waikiki. He bailed after the first class—which was Twitter Etiquette for Medical Professionals—and we spent the rest of the week on the beach."

Peter pointed at her. "See? That's my point. The whole thing is a waste of my time and the hospital's money. Nigel knows this. Frankly, I don't fully comprehend why he's doing this to me. Why am I being punished for Barbara's error?"

"This is not a punishment. It's an intervention. How long have I known you, Peter?"

He lowered his hand in resignation, knowing from her tone that a rebuke was on the way. "Long enough that you call me Peter instead of Dr. Chesterfield—since the third year of my residency, if I remember correctly. That's when you transferred to London from Brooklyn, six months after I transferred in from the unit at Buckinghamshire."

"When you were far younger than Barbara Davies is now. So don't think I haven't seen you on your bad days."

"I was young because I finished my schooling, my undergrad, and medical school early. And don't compare any mistakes I've made to Barbara's. I never sliced a child's internal carotid."

"I'll grant you, that's a doozie. Dr. Davies'll pay for it with lost opportunities for a long time, probably the rest of her career. She knows it too." Carol dug around in her cloth shopping bag and came up with six tubes of zinc-heavy sunblock. She bypassed Peter and tossed them straight into the suitcase. "For your face. Industrial strength. Don't let those surf-hippies give you any guff. If they ask whether it's reef friendly just . . . be you. They won't understand a word you say."

He moved the sunblock into a relatively ordered formation beside the rash guards. "Perhaps you should have bought me a straw hat too."

"Buy your own when you get there, and don't change the subject. We were talking about Dr. Davies."

"*You* were talking about her."

"Whatever. A sledgehammer slammed down on her in the middle of a surgery. Red out. The worst-case scenario for a neuroendoscopy. And what did you do?"

"I saw what was wrong, and I fixed it."

"You picked up that sledgehammer and hit her again, putting all of your"—Carol looked him up and down—"two hundred pounds behind it."

"One eighty. Thirteen stone, thank you very much."

"In that case, you'll need a belt for these." She handed him three pairs of flat-front shorts. They hung to the knees of the models on the tags. After the first wash, Peter imagined they'd come to his mid-thigh at best, like every other ill-conceived short pants purchase he'd made.

"The point," Carol said, "is that you messed up. Big time. You can't treat a colleague like that during a procedure. Besides, that's not who you are—at least it's not the young resident I met seven years ago."

"So, what? Maui is supposed to fix me?"

"This isn't so much a punishment as it is an intervention. Nigel cares about you. Both he and I can see what you don't. You need a break. And if you don't get one soon, you'll self-destruct."

To Peter's horror, Carol upended her shopping bag, dumping the remainder of her purchases into his suitcase to form a gaudy pile of pastels. She dropped the bag in as well and headed for the door of his flat. "Gotta go. I promised Leonard I'd have a combo plate from Burger and Lobster waiting for him when he finished his shift. Try to relax, Peter. Take a step back and get some perspective." She opened the door and shrugged. "At least enjoy first class on the way there."

Peter sifted through the pile in search of anything he could see himself wearing. "I'm not flying first class."

"What? Why?"

"Principle. Nigel booked me in coach, and I refuse to give him the satisfaction of paying for my own upgrade."

Carol stepped out into the hall, shaking her head. "Maybe I was wrong. Maybe you are being punished. And so are those poor flight attendants." She let the door fall closed behind her.

CHAPTER
SEVEN

Happy Valley, Maui

LISA GLARED AT PIKA across a platter of Kalua pork and cooked cabbage, several hours after the incident at the Grand. "I can't believe you let him get away."

"Koa's fast, Sis." He pushed out a hand to stop her from countering his excuse. "And don't say, 'Call me Detective.' We ain't at work. You coulda held him still for two more seconds 'til I closed in. But no, you had to go chase your car thieves. I mighta caught him if you hadn't given him a head start."

Lisa looked down at her plate, mumbling as she lifted her fork. "Or maybe you should spend more time at the gym."

Pika came half out of his chair. "Hey. The boy got legs. Always did. This ain't my fault."

Lisa's mother, seated at the head of their small dining room table, frowned at them both. "Enough. It's nobody's fault. From what the other ladies at the Oceana tell me, the beach at the Grand was total chaos." She slapped her son's thick arm with the back of her hand and lowered her voice. "Stop saying 'ain't,' Pika. If you want to make detective like your sister, you'll need to speak proper English."

"I got no interest in being a detective, Ma." Pika returned to his pork. "And I talk this way because that's how you raised us. You didn't start acting all *haole* until—" He went suddenly quiet, not under the hard look he was getting from Lisa but under the more powerful stare from their older brother Ikaia, who had just come from the kitchen with a pan of hot rolls in coconut sauce. At two inches taller and another two broader at the shoulder than Pika, Ikaia towered over them both.

He placed the pan at the center of the table and set to work removing his apron, never taking his eyes off Pika. "No more arguing. Ma only wants the best for you. Lisa's only doing her job. Eat, Brah. Let's have a nice meal."

Food. Ikaia's solution for everything. No fighting—not since middle school. From high school onward, he'd settled arguments among family and peers alike by looking big and mean and offering both sides the best grindz on the island. A peacemaker with a food truck. Lisa hadn't realized how much she missed that about him.

Ikaia might have shut Pika down, but their mother had the last word, as always. "I cleaned up my manners to get promoted at the resort and keep us in this house. If you hope to advance in the department, Pika, you'll do the same. End of story."

And it was. No one spoke again until half the *pani popo*—the coconut rolls—were gone. As often had been the case in Lisa's childhood, her mother, having established the silence, was also the one to break it. "How is Clay?"

Lisa would have preferred the silence. "I don't know, Ma. I haven't heard from him since I left LA."

"You could try calling him."

Why was that her responsibility? If Clay wanted to talk, he could call.

Pika piled on, grinning and glancing at the phone beside her plate. "Yeah, Sis. You could call him right now. What time is it on the mainland?"

She gave him a look that said *Shut up or I'll make you pay,* then turned to her mother. "I'm sure he's busy settling into his new post in Philadelphia. I don't want to bother him."

"'I don't want to bother him,'" her mother said, echoing her in a singsong voice. "With a daughter who thinks like that, I should get used to the idea of dying with no grandchildren."

"Ma, you have two sons, and both are older than me."

"I gave up on their prospects long ago." Her mother picked up a roll and broke it in half. "You know," she said, drawing out the word and eyeing Lisa's phone, "Pika's not wrong. What time is it in Pennsylvania, half past midnight? Single man like Clay. Big city. He's probably still up."

Lisa pushed back from the table. "I have to go."

"But you and Pika just got home," Ikaia said, standing with her. "I have *kulolo* in the oven."

"Save me a plate. I need to find out the story behind my dead car thief. Mia should have the autopsy finished." Lisa snatched up her phone. "Oops. There she is now." She dialed Mia and showed her mother the screen, knowing she couldn't tell the difference between the looks of an incoming or outgoing call. "See?"

She walked out the front door and down the porch steps. Mia had already picked up, and Lisa could hear her confused hellos before she got the phone to her ear. "Hey. Sorry about that. Tell me you have something."

Mia answered her with a giggle. "Your mom driving you nuts again?"

"You know it. I need a rescue. Fast."

"No problem. Come on down. I want you to see this girl's tox screen. Totally weird."

After the conversation she'd had with Mike, Lisa could guess where this was going. "Meth?"

"No. Your car thief was squeaky clean."

CHAPTER
EIGHT

Maui County Forensic Facility

LISA RUBBED HER BARE ARMS and frowned down at the diminutive Dr. Mia Chen. "I always forget to bring a jacket. It's so cold down here."

"Cheer up." The deputy medical examiner cast a glance at the covered body on her table. "I guarantee you're warmer than she is." She peeled back the shroud, enough to reveal the face. "Meet Angelica Puelani of Molokai. She had no ID on her. Mike's people pulled her basic info from her phone."

Angelica. The name fit the girl's features. Peaceful. Beautiful, despite the gray pallor of death and the gash on the left side of her forehead. If they had her phone, they'd be able to break down her life soon, assuming the evidence specialist team could work through the red tape. "Social media?"

"Nothing much there yet, but we did manage to find her mother using one of the accounts. She's coming over tomorrow on the first ferry to identify her. No tears when I told her. Just complained that she'd be missing a half day of work."

"Maybe she was in shock."

"Or on drugs. Probably a mix of both. I got the sense she was high when I called. That's why Angelica's tox screen surprised me. At least, that's one of the reasons." Mia peeled the shroud back farther, something she likely wouldn't do during the positive identification process the following morning, no matter what state of mind the mother was in.

No mother could take the sight of her daughter shot up and cut open like this. Lisa grimaced. "That's a lot of bullet wounds."

"Talk to your SRT friends." A touch of anger colored Mia's voice. "Tell them to save a few rounds for later next time."

"In their defense, she wasn't stopping. Your girl, here, charged the barricade at over a hundred miles per hour. If she'd hit the roadblock square at that speed, there's no telling where all that aluminum, glass, and steel would have gone. Gas and oil too. Like a bomb going off."

"I know." Mia replaced the shroud. "Doesn't make it any easier to dig slugs out of a healthy young woman. But you've hit on the other reason the tox screen surprised me."

"She didn't stop."

"Stop?" Mia let out a dry laugh. "She didn't even slow down, according to your own post-incident report. Something has to account for that kind of irrational behavior."

Lisa had been thinking along the same lines. She had a textbook answer ready, one that hadn't satisfied her. "Unreasoned, death-wish behavior indicates either suicidal intent or a lack of awareness consistent with synthetic stimulants. When I pulled her out of the car, I thought for sure I'd see signs of meth addiction."

"But you didn't."

Lisa shook her head.

"Me either." Mia headed for a standing computer desk. "Her mom may be a user, but Angelica was clean—consistently clean." She pulled up multiple pages of her report on the computer's dual monitors. "No meth mouth, no blood vessel damage, no burns. And before you ask, nothing in her phone or autopsy implies any other form of cognitive impairment."

"Suicidal, then?"

"Possibly. I can't speak to depression without a historical MRI or cutting into her brain."

"It's the only option." Lisa glanced back at the shrouded body. "If she had no drugs clouding her mind, Angelica had to know she'd die hitting that barricade. But she showed no fear."

Mia raised a small finger. "Ah. You're wrong on both your primary points, Detective. Depression isn't the only option, because it isn't the only cause of suicide. Fear is another major contributor. And your girl, here, showed fear. Maybe not with her actions, but postmortem, she's showing me plenty."

Lisa scrunched her nose. "How can a dead woman show fear?"

Mia flipped to the next two pages of her report, one of which included a picture of Angelica's heart. "Her bloodwork revealed highly elevated levels of cortisol, adrenaline, and norepinephrine, sometimes known as the fear or stress cocktail."

"Okay. Charging the barricade caused a fight-or-flight response. I can see that."

"Yes," Mia said, highlighting a section of text under the heart picture. "But in Angelica's case, the fear cocktail wasn't momentary or isolated. Look here. Her heart also shows significant calcification, way more than normal for her age."

"I don't get it. You're saying long-term fear hyper-aged her heart?"

"In a way, yes. The fight-or-flight cocktail increases calcium cycling to regulate the heart. In a normal, healthy young woman, one or two high-stress events wouldn't cause a difference large enough for me to measure."

Lisa studied the highlighted text, trying to reimagine the medical terminology in plain language. "But in Angelica . . ."

"In Angelica, the levels of heart muscle calcium are off the chart, as if she'd been constantly experiencing acute stress. This girl had turned fear into a lifestyle." Mia stepped back from the desk and looked Lisa in the eye. "I can't fully explain my conclusion. But to Angelica, death was a better option than being caught by the police. She didn't charge the barricade because she lacked fear of death. She charged it because she was terrified of living another day."

CHAPTER
NINE

Happy Valley

LISA WOKE TO THE SOUND of Ikaia bumping around downstairs, preparing breakfast burritos for his food truck. Her east-facing window was still dark. No sign of the sun. She checked her phone's screen. 5:11 a.m. "I have to get my own place."

Her mom had cleaned up her old room since she left—new bed, new paint. No more posters. No more Justin Timberlake. She didn't miss that one, but she made a mental note to find out if her mom had stored her panoramic shot of the Charger racing the Mustang in the 2005 NHRA nationals.

Lisa blinked. Had she just decided to ask her mom to dig up one of her old teen-dream posters? Sort of. She pushed aside the covers and sat up. "I *really* have to get my own place."

Her phone dropped to the floor, dislodged from where she'd set it after checking the time. Lisa stared down at the device, hearing her brother's voice in her head. *Yeah, Sis. You could call him right now. What time is it on the mainland?*

Too late then. But what was the time there now? She did some quick math. A little after 11 a.m.? Getting close to lunch-time for an FBI agent with cushy hours.

Surprisingly, the phone didn't leap into her hand. It stayed there on the floor, unmoving, uncaring, unwilling to make the decision for her. Lisa watched it long after the screen went dark, then picked it up and hit Clay's name, still in her favorites.

The line clicked open almost immediately. "Hey."

"Clay, I'm glad you picked up. I was—"

The voice on the other end talked over her. "This is Clay Parker. I'm not available, but if you leave your name and number, I'll get back to you as soon as I can."

Voicemail. Basically, a digital ambush. In Lisa's mind every voicemail message had the same meaning. *I know you called with important things to say that require a two-way interaction. Instead of that, I'm giving you until the sound of the beep to compose a concise but meaningful message that makes you sound neither dumb nor desperate. Good luck.*

She hung up.

When she walked down the stairs an hour later, Ikaia was stacking the last of his foil-wrapped burritos in coolers lined with silver thermal fabric. "You still here?" he asked.

"Not for long. Getting my own place. Checking out listings on my lunch hour."

"Sure you are."

"Wait and see." Lisa stole a burrito from the cooler marked *Egg Whites and Bacon* on her way past.

"Thief. That's Ikaia's Anywhere food truck stock. You gotta pay for that."

"Sister tax," Lisa said as the screen door fell closed behind her. "Don't like it? Call a cop."

LA HAD BEACHES, but not like Maui's. Even Malibu failed to compare.

Lisa picked up an Americano at Aimee's on Market Street, then drove to the lot at Waihee Beach to relax before work. In

LA, you could never watch the sun come up over the water. They only had one coast, and it faced the wrong way. But here she was, sitting on the hood of an old Jeep Wrangler, sipping coffee and enjoying her brother's cooking, with the full glory of the horizon before her.

Like old times.

Not really.

Lisa had woken up barely an hour ago. Her day was just getting started. Back then, watching the sun come up with Koa and the crew, she'd be teetering on the edge of a crash with a full night of stupidity behind her. How close had she come to being Angelica?

She took a bite of scrambled egg white and bacon and cocked her head. Maybe not that close. Koa had frightened her at times, but she hadn't lived in fear of him. She hadn't experienced the type of continuous terror that had calcified Angelica's heart. And Koa couldn't have changed that much. When he said the thieves weren't part of his crew, he wasn't lying. Lisa was sure of it. A crew or a kingpin who inspired that kind of fear was something new for Maui.

Lisa ate a little faster, chasing every other bite with the Americano. She needed to get to work.

There were protesters marching outside the division when she arrived at work. That came as no surprise. A woman of color had died with more than a dozen police-issue slugs in her chest. But the marchers didn't give her much trouble—far less than she'd have received in LA. One of them offered her a bottled water as she passed. This was still Maui, after all.

In the GTF section, she found Mike hanging out by her desk. A printed email in his hand showed crinkling from being held too long in nervous fingers. "Morning," he said with a smile too bright. "Did you get some breakfast? Coffee? Did you sleep okay?"

Lisa tossed back the last of her Americano and dropped the

cup in the recycle bin. She made the evidence specialist wait while she sat at the desk and unlocked her computer before finally looking up. "That was my coffee. I drank enough to make me personable, so don't look so scared. What's the story? Something happen with the auto theft case?"

"No." The paper disappeared behind his back. "That is to say, Mia told me you talked to her last night, so there've been no new developments since then."

"What about the other two vehicles? Did the graveyard shift spot anything?"

The question seemed to focus him. "Nothing. But I'm glad you asked. Detective Fan is on top of that." He shifted from one foot to the other. "I mean, way on top of it. She'll be high above it in—"

"Mike."

"Yes, Detective?"

Lisa rolled her chair to the side of him so she could see the email still gathering sweat from his fingers. "What is that?"

"It's from Detective Fan. She says it was practically your idea. You're the one who kept saying we should use the chopper."

The chopper?

Lisa felt the fight-or-flight cocktail she and Mia had discussed the night before flooding her bloodstream—much more fight than flight. "What chopper?"

He handed over the email.

Jenny had left the message in Mike's inbox for him to find when he came in that morning. Not Lisa's inbox. Not the inbox of the task force chief. No. She'd sent it to their evidence specialist, telling him to inform Lisa—like this was fifth grade or something. Lisa scanned the short paragraph. Jenny had coordinated a flight in the fire department's helicopter to search the island for the stolen Mercedes and Corvette. "The fire department has a helicopter?"

"We borrow the helicopter and their pilots from time to time for a flight." He raised both hands, to keep her calm or maybe to keep her from attacking him. "Super rare. The paperwork has to be in well before close of business on the day prior. When you mentioned it yesterday, I didn't think you'd be able to get a ride fast enough to matter. So, I didn't bother bringing it up." Mike paused, letting the confession settle in, but his face told Lisa he had more to say.

She sighed. "Keep going."

"Detective Fan is at the airfield now. The flight takes off in fifteen minutes. You'd never catch them, even if you used lights and siren."

"Jenny coordinated the flight yesterday without telling me, and then sent you the message? She didn't want me checking my email from home and showing up this morning to horn in on her chance to catch a break in the case. Is that it?"

Mike shrugged.

Lisa nodded, confirming her own assessment. "I'm finding it hard to like her." She opened her case notes and started to type, but then stopped and looked up at Mike again. "The fire department has a helicopter, but we don't?"

"Or boats. Neither of us have boats. Just sayin', I think that's worse."

She returned to her typing, logging the date and time on a new page. She could deal with Jenny later. By now the vehicles were in a shop somewhere. The chopper was probably a waste of time. "Where are we on pulling her contacts from the phone?"

"Mia is coaxing the mother into signing a permission-to-access form as we speak."

"What about those bolts you picked up? Learn anything?"

Mike brightened, a real smile this time. "Oh yeah. Hydriodic acid, as I suspected. It's a unique case—might get me published in the *Journal of Forensic Sciences*. I sent the report to your inbox."

Lisa clicked on the email and scanned the summary. Mike

used a lot of words—a whole lot. She glanced up at him to try to pull out the short notes. "This stuff ate through steel. It can't be easy to transport."

"Easier than you'd expect. A standard clear polyethylene squeeze bottle will do the job. Pretty common. Our saboteur could've squirted the acid on the bolts without much worry of getting hurt. No gloves. No goggles. The biggest danger would've been the fumes."

Fumes. "Could fumes from hydriodic acid cause sneezing and coughing?"

Mike snorted. "Oh yeah."

"The kid with the allergy attack. He must have been close to our perp when he deployed the acid." She closed her eyes, trying to visualize the bleachers. Had she seen the saboteur and walked on by?

No. Lisa would have noticed movement under the stands, especially when looking in the direction of the coughing, sneezing teenager. And she would have considered anyone under the bleachers worth checking out. But if the kid was still coughing when she walked past, she must've just missed the saboteur. Maybe that kid saw something. "We need to identify a teenage boy, probably between fourteen and seventeen, with slight build and brown hair. He was wearing a dark blue rash guard and black shorts, sneezing and wheezing for several minutes."

Mike grabbed a pen and pad and scribbled furiously, trying to keep up. "And who do you want on this?"

Instinct—and not the good kind—told Lisa to have Mike hand the job to Jenny Fan when she landed from her helicopter ride. Canvasing more than a hundred ticketed attendees from the freediving event to find an unnamed kid might take two or three mind-numbing days. But revenge assignments weren't Lisa's style, and Jenny's talents were better spent elsewhere. "Put Rivera on it. He's a detective-in-training. Grunt work will do him good."

Lisa felt a presence with them and glanced over her shoulder to see Captain Tony Griffith, head of the Criminal Investigative Division. She rose from her chair, shooting Mike a look that said *How long has he been standing there?* "Captain, I can be in your office in five minutes to give you an update."

"No need. I heard." Captain Griffith wasn't as big as Pika, but he wasn't small either, with a square jaw and hard features softened only by the rectangular reading glasses that seemed perpetually balanced on the bridge of his nose. Those hard features didn't look happy. "Fan is flying around the island with the smoke jockeys and you're about to send Rivera out to hunt down a sneezy kid. It's not much, Kealoha. What's your next move? Will you hunt down Koa Alana again?"

"No sir. I'll ask around, but I'm guessing he's made himself even scarcer than before." She shook her head. "This island's got plenty of places for a guy like Koa to hide—too many couches he can sleep on. But he's not the only one who might know something about what went down yesterday. I can think of a few other contacts."

Like Koa, those contacts had once been part of Lisa's circle, but she knew better than to say that part out loud. "This case is still fresh. Give me a day, Captain. I'll have something better than a sneezy kid for you."

CHAPTER
TEN

Hana Highway
Hana, Maui

LISA'S FIRST PARTNER in LA had once told her that all his old friends had started ducking him when he became a cop. He'd come to this conclusion after several had failed to answer his connection requests on social media.

That guy had no clue what it meant to be ducked.

She'd been down her list. Twice. Even the old acquaintances Lisa had been able to find when she first started asking around about Koa were nowhere to be seen. The few who could hold down a regular job had called in sick or taken days off. Most of them had no job—or at least no jobs with definite hours or locations.

The old hangouts were empty, except for a few kids who scattered when she arrived. She wasn't surprised. When Lisa had been their age, she could smell a cop too. Next time she would bring her Wrangler and bill the department for the gas.

Having run out of options, she found herself on Hana Highway, making the long drive to the east end of the island. The world called it the Road to Hana—two narrow lanes and more than six hundred hairpin turns through a volcanic jungle, beset by roving rain clouds and gobs of slow-moving lookie-loo tourists who'd made a day out of the drive. The tourists had no place to be and didn't care that Lisa did. She'd be lucky to get back to the division by dark.

All this because Koa's cousin, Kelly Alana's older brother, had decided to cut ties with his old life. Not that Lisa couldn't relate.

At two in the afternoon, she knocked on the door of a single-story duplex near Hana's tiny airfield. No one answered. She knocked again. "Jason Alana! You in there?"

Still nothing. Waste of a trip.

Lisa had started down the porch steps, dreading the return drive, when the door opened. "Lisa? Lisa Kealoha?"

She turned, and the man standing in the frame was so different from the kid she used to babysit that she almost apologized, thinking maybe she'd written down the wrong address. He'd added a foot in height since she'd last seen him, and traded stick arms for the muscles exposed by his tank top. The set of his stubbled jaw was hard, no longer the baby face she remembered. But the voice was the same. And the eyes—maybe a little darker, but the same in the way that a gaze never aged. "Hey, Jason. I tried to call. Your line was disconnected." Not her best opener.

"Old number," he said, crossing his arms. "Old plan. Pay as you go is cheaper." In the awkward quiet that followed, his eyes drifted down to the badge clipped to her belt. "I heard you were a cop now, but I thought it was LA."

"I'm back, working for Maui PD Investigative Services Bureau. I'm looking into the incident that ended your sister's competition yesterday. Several injured. One dead. Might be gang related." She looked past him into the small home. "Can we talk?"

"Sure, I guess." Instead of asking her in, he closed the screen door and wiped the dust off a couple of plastic chairs on his porch. "Have a seat."

Lisa glanced inside on her way back up the steps. Jason wasn't hiding a drug lab or bodies in there, but the place wasn't exactly tidy either. Black boxes littered the kitchen table, wires spilling out—computer parts or something. A frozen dinner box threatened to slide from the mountain growing out of the trash can. She sat beside him. "Didn't see you at the competition. Couldn't get the day off?"

"Work at the airfield's been busy. Plus, Hana Highway is the same nightmare it always was."

"So, why'd you move out here?"

"You know why."

The Road to Hana made a better shield than most castle walls. If it prevented Jason from reaching Wailea to see his sister dive, it also prevented Koa and his crew from making unwanted visits and bringing trouble by.

Lisa had used an ocean to do the same job, although she'd brought a year of trouble with her to the mainland. Between Maui and LA, it was a miracle that she'd managed to dodge any convictions that would have stopped her from getting her badge when she finally cleaned up. If she'd dragged that much trouble across the water, she had to wonder how much Jason had brought with him in the comparatively short jaunt down the Road to Hana.

When she said nothing, he made a little shrug and looked out at the monkeypods. "How'd she do?"

"You don't know?"

"We're not as close as we used to be. She still hangs with the old crew on occasion—one foot in and one foot out. I made a clean break."

Lisa hadn't heard that about Kelly. She had fans and articles in the sports magazines. She had a website, posing with her fins and her trophies—and the mayor. She looked like the ultimate clean-cut Hawaiian girl. But from what Lisa remembered about Kelly's proclivity for trouble, a trait she shared with her favorite older cousin, it made sense. "Koa?"

"He's the older brother she wanted. The protector. I was always just the tagalong."

"Until you got arrested." Lisa had found the record. Drug possession. Four years ago, Jason had been caught driving a small boatload of marijuana across from Maui to Oahu. A Coast Guard collar. Federal charges.

Jason laughed. "I was wondering when that would come up. You think because I did time, that makes me a suspect in your auto theft case?"

"I didn't say that."

"You didn't have to. You wasted your day, Lisa. I'm clean."

"Okay. I read the record, Jason. You never told the investigators where that weed was headed, or where it came from. It's not too late. Start sharing and maybe I can put a positive addendum in the file."

"An addendum?" He stood and faced her, looking mean enough for Lisa's hand to inch toward the Glock holstered at her waistband. "Is your addendum gonna get me a job?" Jason sighed and walked to the porch rail. "Did your file tell you I got a degree inside—an associates in information technology. But nobody wants to hire a tech with a felony record. Keep your addendum. It won't do me any good."

Lisa felt his anger. And she knew Koa had sent him out on that boat with the drugs as sure as she knew the moon set the tides. Koa had manipulated him with a promise of money or some other false treasure. He'd been manipulating Jason since they were kids. But this time Jason had been caught, and Koa had let him rot in a cell on Oahu for two years. So why protect him?

She still hangs with the old crew on occasion.

He wasn't protecting Koa. He was protecting Kelly. Jason wouldn't give Koa up if it meant giving up his sister. Lisa would never get anything out of him this way. She softened her voice. "Kelly was great at the competition. She was brilliant. A star."

He lowered his head and nodded. "Glad to hear it. At least one of us stands a chance without the mill. That place was the whole reason I got my degree. Bill Kline said he had a job waiting for me, for Dad's sake, because I was family. The Alanas are part of the land, he said."

"But the mill closed while you were inside."

"Yeah."

Lisa sat quiet for a time, and Jason seemed happy to let her. He was her last contact, and if he gave her nothing, she'd be left making the long drive back to Wailuku in the desperate and sad hope that Jenny Fan had spotted a stolen car on her helicopter ride.

She needed a different approach. "Listen, Jason. I'm not out here to give you a hard time. I'm here because I need your help. A girl is dead. You think she'll be the last?"

He turned, resting his hips on the rail. She'd chipped away at a bit of the barrier.

Lisa kept pushing. "Dangerous folks are moving to the islands these days, way more dangerous than Koa. If Kelly still has one foot in, like you say, she might be getting in with a crowd she can't handle."

This broke the tightness of his arms and brought his eyes up to meet hers.

Lisa nodded. "That's right. Maybe you two aren't speaking much these days, but you still care. I can see that. If you know anything about what's happening on this island, you've got to let me know."

His eyes fell again. "I can't help you there."

"What about old friends. You meet anybody on the inside that might have connections out here? Maybe in cars or meth?"

He shook his head.

"Come on, Jason. Give me something. Like I said, I'm not here to roust you. And if you're as clean as you say, you'll want to help."

He stayed quiet for a long time.

"Jason?"

"You ever hear of a Barrio 18?"

"Sure. The 18th Street Gang. Heavy hitters in Southern California. Big presence south of the border."

"Yeah, well, maybe now they're expanding west. That's all I'm gonna say." He left the porch and went inside.

So that was it, then. The Road to Hana was a bust except for one little snippet. Lisa already knew SoCal gangs were moving to Hawaii. Having one gang's name wouldn't do much. Now she had to root for Jenny Fan.

CHAPTER
ELEVEN

Hana Highway
Ke'anae, Maui

LISA LAID A HAND on the 4Runner's horn but received nary a glance from the sightseers moseying along in front of her. She considered spinning up the lights and siren, then decided against it. If a carload of tourists rolled over a cliff trying to get out of her way, she'd never hear the end of it from Captain Griffith.

So focused was her glare, attempting to push the sightseers up to at least the speed limit, that she nearly jumped out of her skin when her phone rang. The screen made no mystery of the caller's identity. She shoved a Bluetooth hands-free set in her ear, a requirement for officers behind the wheel, and pressed the device's single button. "Clay?"

"Don't sound so surprised. You called me, didn't you?"

"Well . . . sure." Her hand moved unconsciously to the horn, but she caught herself before she hit it. Perhaps sensing her frustration, the driver pulled into an overlook, and she sped past. "That was hours ago. I didn't expect to hear from you."

"You didn't expect me to call, because you didn't leave a message."

"Yeah. That. I know I should have said something, but—"

Clay stopped her before she could come up with an excuse. "I get it. In the four years we've known each other, you've never left me one voicemail. I don't think I've left any for you either. We like real interaction—preferably the face-to-face kind. Isn't that one reason we decided the long-distance thing wouldn't work?"

Lisa made it all of a quarter mile before a meandering Corolla halted her progress. She let out a frustrated breath and fell back against her seat. "I know. And I wasn't trying to . . . I mean, I just thought we could catch up."

"I'm all for that. What's up?"

That morning she'd had half a plan. Now? Lisa couldn't think of a thing to say. "Not much, I guess. Working an auto theft case. One related death."

"So, same as LA, but with better beaches."

He knew her so well. "Yeah. Except in LA, I'd already have the jokers in custody, and a girl who rushed a roadblock yesterday might still be alive. What about you?"

Clay fell silent for several seconds. "Can't talk about it. You know the drill."

She did. He'd been at the LA Bureau for three years before they both left town. Dinner conversation was always one-sided. She rarely got more than *It's an embezzlement case. That's all I can say.*

"We're looking into a fraud ring. That's—"

"That's all you can say, right?"

"Yeah."

Lisa sighed, and she could swear she heard Clay sigh on the other end. "Aren't we a pair."

"We were, right? We *were* a pair. But we both knew the Bureau would move me around for the first half of my career. I couldn't ask you to jump departments every three years."

"And when Maui called, I couldn't ask you to get a job at a surf shop."

"Exactly. And the distance isn't the only thing. I think . . ." His voice faded, almost as if she'd lost the signal.

"Clay? You think what?"

"Never mind. Doesn't matter what I think. And none of this means I can't occasionally dream about living it up with you on Maui."

So, he thought about it—dreamed about it. Lisa didn't mind hearing that. "Maybe your next assignment could be Oahu."

Clay gave her a rueful laugh. "Not happening. Every agent on Oahu is the son or daughter of a politician or the kid brother of someone in the director's office. I don't have that kind of star power."

Lisa almost smashed into the back of the Corolla. She slammed on her brakes and got a blaring horn from none other than the sightseers she'd been trailing before.

"You okay?" Clay asked.

"Yeah. Fine. Just bad Hana traffic. That and something you said. Star power. I was out here on the quiet side of the island to talk to an ex-con I used to know in my old life, fishing for info on new gang activity. But he's not going anywhere near trouble, not with the threat of a return to prison hanging over him." *One foot in and one foot out.* "I realize now I shouldn't have wasted the trip to talk to him. I should've been talking to his sister."

"She has the star power?"

"Local freediver making a name for herself." Lisa shook her head and chuckled. "I've known her since we were kids—used to carry her around in my arms when our families got together. Babysat her a few nights. But she isn't a little girl anymore. The same daring streak that used to get both of us in trouble when she trampled her mom's azaleas or climbed a bookshelf allows her to be a great freediver today. From what her brother said, though, it might also get her locked up for grand theft auto."

She heard Clay typing on the other end and immediately knew what he was doing. He'd done it a hundred times before.

"Clay. Don't dig into my case. We're not in the same city anymore."

"I'm not constrained by city boundaries. The F in FBI stands for federal, remember? And we have the largest auto theft database in the world. Let me see if I can turn up anything on Maui. Existing crews, known perps moving in—that sort of thing."

He was working harder than usual to make his argument. Lisa rolled her eyes. "That fraud case you can't talk about is boring you, isn't it."

"Boring me to death. Yeah. So can I help with yours or what?"

The Corolla inched forward, and Lisa followed. She had leaned on Clay a lot over the years. A *lot*, for more than just investigative work. If they were really going their separate ways, should she keep leaning on him like this? On the other hand, law enforcement professionals were supposed to do favors for one another. That's how the game was played, how criminals were caught.

"Fine," Lisa said, wincing as she spoke. "Dig in. Maybe take a look at 18th Street Gang members migrating to Maui. But whatever you find comes to me first, got it?"

"You're the boss."

CHAPTER
TWELVE

The Elysium Grand

"WHY AREN'T THERE ANY BOATS running between your islands?"

The man behind the counter at the Elysium Grand gave Peter a long blank look. "Mr. Chesterf—"

"*Doctor* Chesterfield."

"Dr. Chesterfield. Yes. Thank you. There are lots of boats. If you want, I can have the concierge set you up with a late dinner cruise. You can go out tonight."

Peter closed his eyes, trying not to let his frustration show. "That's not what I meant."

He'd been awake and in transit for thirty-six hours. Hannibal, crossing the Alps, had fared better both in the sleep and the legroom departments.

Carol claimed Nigel cared about him. Perhaps. Or perhaps Nigel had come up with the perfect plan to murder him. A transatlantic Air Lingus flight from Heathrow had brought Peter to New York. Nigel had chosen the Irish line with its shorter flight, ignoring the fact that British Airways flew perfectly good direct flights to the California coast every day. For the New York–to–

California leg, Nigel had placed Peter on a miniature subsidiary airline with seats that fell short of suitability for a full-grown human being. And after all that frustration, upon reaching Los Angeles, he'd still had two flights to go. *Two.*

The departure displays in LA showed multiple direct flights to Maui, but Nigel had booked Peter on a cheaper route through Honolulu. At that point, Peter had been tempted to throw his principles aside and buy himself a first-class seat straight to his destination, but he'd already stuck it out in coach and noisy airports for seventeen hours. What was another six?

Six too many.

By the time Peter had arrived in Honolulu, he could not have cared less about his principles, or anyone else's. He could not bear the thought of getting on another plane for the flight to Maui, no matter how short, nor could he bear another minute in an airport. He had come up with a simple solution. He would Uber to whatever docks these people had and take the ferry.

That plan had proved impossible, leaving him standing there on Maui at the Elysium Grand's reception desk after yet another flight, bleary-eyed and boiling inside. Peter rephrased his complaint in a way he hoped the receptionist could understand. "Why are there no ferries between islands?"

"Oh, we have ferries, Dr. Chesterfield. We have several departures a day from Lahaina to Moloka'i and Lanai. If you want, I can have the concierge book one for you tonight, or in the morning." The receptionist picked up the phone next to his computer and pressed a button. "Hey, Susie. This is Nikoloa. Could you—"

Peter motioned for him to put the receiver down. "I don't need a ferry now because I'm already here. That's not the question I was asking, and I think you know it."

He had decided early in his failed ferry-to-Maui endeavor that the Hawaiians set up the whole thing on purpose—a way of torturing the tourists. He would never get a straight answer.

Peter took his room key and laid down a twenty-pound note for a tip. "Forget it. Please have your porter take my bags to my room."

The receptionist lifted the note as if he wasn't quite sure what to do with it. "Sure, Dr. Chesterfield. No problem. Enjoy your stay."

Peter had traveled much more in his early career, although deployed might be a more accurate term. He knew better than to fall asleep immediately upon arrival in a new time zone. If he retired to his room, the allure of the bed was certain to overcome him. He resolved to stay awake by exploring the hotel instead.

The Elysium Grand. The name fit. Elysium—or the Elysian Fields—a Greek concept of a hero's paradise. Three-story columns and an additional seven stories of glistening balconies bounded a giant atrium with the largest shallow pool Peter had ever seen. He couldn't call it an indoor pool, per se, since the lines between indoor and outdoor blurred throughout the hotel. White statues of Greek heroes and their foes haunted this rectangular sea, locked forever in battle over black and gold canoes filled with tropical blooms. And at the center, a broad canopy of black jade covered the resort's largest restaurant, Okeanos, accessed by four arcing bridges of the same black jade.

The whole property had been quite recently remodeled under new management, according to a bronze plaque Peter found at one corner of the pool. The owner, one Harry Alcott, had blended the art deco style of the early 1900s with traditional Hawaiian elements. He'd drawn his color scheme and the resort's new name from a secondary meaning of the word *Elysium*. Swiss physicists had run a computer model to search the globe for new forms of natural carbon. The model had pinpointed Maui's volcanic underpinnings as the best possible location to find an ultra-dense, ultra-hard black carbon. The scientists described this theoretical stone as a form of black super-diamond and dubbed it Elysium, and Mr. Alcott had fallen in love with the idea it might be found on Maui.

A broad, white marble lane led Peter along the edge of the great pool to the rear of the atrium, where he rested his elbows against a railing overlooking the property. Waterfalls spilled from the atrium and fell two full stories to birth a sprawling network of fountains, rivers, grottos, and many more pools, separated from the beach and ocean by a green lawn. Before his departure, Peter had received an email from the Grand acknowledging that this lawn and their beach had been rendered off-limits for a short time, making a vague reference to some criminal incident. But the message had assured him that all would be well by the time he arrived.

And so, it seemed, it was. He saw no yellow tape or police barricades. The lawn and the white sands looked pristine. If any crime had taken place on those Elysian Fields, Mr. Alcott and his resort minions had wiped all trace of it away.

"Beautiful, ya?" An older Hawaiian gentleman in a flowered shirt and flip-flops sidled up next to Peter. "Never gets old. Like a new painting every evening."

Peter imagined he was talking about the sunset. The colors were, he had to admit, remarkable—like nothing he could ever see from his office near the Royal London. Gold and auburn played on blue-green water as smooth as fresh-blown glass. He shrugged. "It's not bad, I suppose."

The old chap leaned against the rail, a half-cocked smile on his lips. "Wow. Tough crowd. My grandpa always told me, when someone makes something pretty for you, you should say, 'Thanks.'"

After so many hours awake and uncomfortable, did Peter really look so approachable as to have invited this conversation? "No one made this view. The Earth's rotation brought that ball of flaming hydrogen over there to an angle such that its light produces more vibrant coloring. That's all."

The man stared at him for a time. "You must be one of the doctors here for the conference, ya?"

"Ya." Peter repeated the word without stooping to the offense of mimicking the old chap's accent. "A neurosurgeon."

"Impressive. We're honored."

"You work at the hotel?"

"Yup. So, tell me, Dr. Neurosurgeon, since you don't believe a benevolent Creator can paint a pretty picture with flaming hydrogen and light rays"—the deepness of the man's accent shallowed, vanishing along with his colloquialisms—"do you look with similar coldness upon the complex networks of nerve tissues, spinal fluid, and synapses you encounter on your operating table?"

Peter finally met the man's gaze and squinted. "Who are you?"

"Nobody important. Sunsets are one thing. But don't you ever wonder, when you're trying to rewire someone's brain, if maybe you get a little help?" He pointed skyward.

Peter had tolerated the conversation too long. "If you mean God, just say God. Because, for all I know, you could be talking about any one of the myriad sky deities from across the world and its cultures. But whichever of these you mean, the answer is no. If I were to depend on such supernatural help, I'd be risking the lives of my patients." He started to walk away but paused and turned. "And let me tell you this, friend. A lot of my patients pray to one deity or another before they lie down on my table, but when they rise again, I'm the one they thank." He gave the man a quick nod and walked on. "Enjoy the sunset and whatever delusions you've attached to it."

CHAPTER
THIRTEEN

**Maui PD Criminal Investigative Division
Wailuku**

A BLACK BENTLEY was double-parked in the lot outside the CID. As Lisa pulled in, she saw Jenny Fan making angry gestures by the driver's window. Lisa parked close by, in time to see Jack Carlisle behind the wheel, but the two had finished their argument by the time she shut off her engine.

She climbed out of the Jeep and shut the door, watching the Bentley drive away. "What did Carlisle want?"

"The usual. Hassling me about social media threats against Ono Beef. I told him that if he was worried, he should keep his bodyguards closer and quit driving around by himself."

Jenny seemed more testy than usual. Lisa lifted her chin. "No luck on your helicopter ride?"

"Total bust."

"Ouch. I'm sorry to hear that."

She was. Truly. Lisa didn't take any joy in Jenny's failure. They both wanted to catch the jokers who'd stolen the cars and sabotaged the bleachers—those who'd put Angelica in the position that ended her life. It didn't matter to Lisa who got the credit for breaking the case.

Okay. It mattered a little. And maybe she didn't mind seeing Jenny's frustrated expression as the two walked up the steps to the division doors together. But Lisa did her best not to show it. "We'll get them with groundwork," she said, trying to play the encouraging boss. "You'll see."

Mike was waiting by Lisa's desk in the gang task force section. He started to speak, but she cut him off. "Not a word unless it's to tell me your forensic team pulled a gem out of all that evidence they collected. I want something I can use."

He stammered—not a good sign.

Lisa dropped into her chair. "Fine. Just say what you were gonna say."

"Okay, first—good morning. As to the other thing, it's not great. Mia didn't get much from Angelica Puelani's mom. She and Angelica hadn't spoken in weeks. She signed the release allowing us to hack her phone and accounts, but we'll need to run the paperwork through the legal wickets at the network providers before we can begin."

"How long?"

"Two weeks. Ten days at best. Since Angelica's death doesn't qualify as murder, we don't have the grounds to expedite."

Two weeks to get a look at evidence already in her possession. Insane. The world either had too many lawyers or not enough. Lisa shook her head and took a sip of her coffee. "What else?"

"I mean . . . we're working all kinds of angles. We're processing the wreckage of the Porsche, we're analyzing Angelica's clothes to see where she'd been, we're using an algorithm to locate her anonymous social media posts, we're—"

Lisa snapped her fingers. "Stop. Rewind."

Like Maui, the LAPD had its evidence specialists. And like Mike, the specialists there were great at the science and cyber part of their jobs, but rarely great at sifting the good evidence out of the reams of data they created. A good detective had to become adept at helping the lab nerds break out the important clues. Lisa pulled an empty chair over and sat Mike down beside her desk. "This social media algorithm thing. Tell me about that."

"Sure. Melissa made it. She's the one on our cyber team with the red hair—I mean, it's more like copper when it catches the light. Melissa has three IT degrees, and—"

Lisa's coffee hovered at her lips. "Wrong details, Mike."

"Right. Sorry. Copper hair." He bobbled his head. "Who says stuff like that? Anyhoo, Melissa created a search algorithm as part of her master's work. Without *technically* violating any privacy laws, it traces a number of elements to identify an individual's anonymous internet posts."

"You're telling me Melissa found Angelica's anonymous accounts without waiting for the phone hack approval from her providers?"

"One. So far she's found one anonymous account." Mike left the chair and retrieved a printout from his desk. "Angelica posted regularly on a MetaHive group devoted to hypothetical burglary techniques." He made air quotes for *hypothetical* as he returned with the paper. "There were eight accounts, also anonymous, that interacted with Angelica's posts on a regular basis. Melissa cracked them all, and four belong to Maui locals." Mike sat down and handed her the printout. "This is a summary of the posts. The four names are at the bottom."

Lisa scanned the printout. Two of the four names stood out.

KOA ALANA
KELLY ALANA

"For future reference, Mike, *this* is a gem." She downed the remainder of her morning coffee and stood. "Print one of these for Detective Fan so she can look into the names we haven't seen before. And have your copper-haired IT girl and her friends look for ties to Barrio 18."

Jenny glanced at her across the office. "Barrio 18? The LA gang? Where did that come from?"

"Jason Alana."

"You could have shared that info."

"I am sharing it. Right now. Do some digging while I go talk to Jason's sister."

Mike tapped on his keyboard. "That's Kelly Alana, right? You've already got her scheduled to come in and talk to us this afternoon."

"I know." Lisa headed for the door. "But now I feel like surprising her."

CHAPTER
FOURTEEN

The Elysium Grand

LISA FOUND KELLY AND HER COACH at the Elysium Grand. An article about her rise to stardom claimed the two often rented two or three hours there at the hotel's Deep Dive Adventure pool. The hotel had designed the attraction to give scuba-averse customers a deep-water experience in the safety of a pressurized acrylic capsule. But at seventy-five feet long and fifty deep with utterly calm water, the pool had become a sought-after training location for scuba enthusiasts and freedivers alike.

The coral looked real enough, but Lisa had to wonder if the tangs and Moorish idols—or the rays and octopi—were fooled. Did they know their range had been limited? Or were they happy to live there, protected from the predators in the real ocean?

Looking deeper, she spied Kelly powering along the bottom, at one with the creatures. At the far end of the half moon, Kelly's coach crouched to hold a set of cards under the water with the number 3 displayed.

"Heather Johnson?" Lisa asked, displaying her badge.

The woman answered in a New Zealand accent, eyes staying

on her athlete. "We had an appointment to talk to you at the station this afternoon, Detective. You're interrupting a training session—an expensive training session."

"I thought I'd save you a drive. I know how bad 310 gets in the afternoon." Lisa hooked the badge to her belt, watching to see if the irony of the statement hit the coach. Angelica Puelani had died on that same road. But she got no reaction. "Forgive me, but aren't you *the* Heather Johnson? New Zealand's 2010 champion? If I'm not mistaken, you still hold a national record for the deepest dive."

The coach's expression changed. She glanced up. "You're a fan of the sport?"

"I'm a fan of the water, and freediving is one of the purest forms of water sport."

Lisa's statement was true, and an honest opinion, but she'd never followed freediving with any real interest—just Kelly and her career, because it was easier than calling and asking how she and her brother were doing. The same article that had led her back to the Grand to find Kelly had detailed the coach's history. And in LA, Lisa found that a little research and ego-stroking could loosen lips.

It worked.

"Okay," the coach said. "I guess I can watch my athlete and talk at the same time, especially if it saves us a drive later. And Kelly has a rest period coming up. How can we help the Maui PD? You know I spoke to your officers at the scene, right?"

"Yes. We have your statement on record. To be honest, as the lead detective on the case, I'm more interested in Kelly's perspective."

The coach eyed her for a moment, then flipped her card to the number 4 and made a thumbs-up sign in the water. Kelly shot straight toward them.

When Kelly broke the surface, Lisa noticed she was wearing a buoyancy compensation vest—the kind scuba divers wear.

Kelly took a few deep breaths, then blew in a tube to inflate the vest. She let herself bob there, blinking the salt water from her eyes. "Lisa? Is that you?"

"Hey, Kelly. We need to talk."

She waited, making small talk and getting details she already knew from the coach, while Kelly pulled herself out of the water and dropped the buoyancy vest in a barrel of fresh water to soak. Once she had Kelly's full attention, though, she opened with a statement she knew would put her off balance. "I saw Jason yesterday."

Kelly sat on a bench molded into a faux stone wall next to the pool and looked up, squinting against the sunlight. "Where?"

A strange question. Didn't she know where her brother lived?

"Hana. At the house he's renting."

"What'd he say?"

Lisa tried not to smile. Kelly was hiding something and doing a terrible job of it. Lisa would let her fear that Jason had given her up simmer for a while before bringing up the MetaHive connection with Angelica. "He said a lot of things. But right now, I want to know about the day of the competition. What do you remember?"

"Not much. I was focused on my dive. I finished, heard the announcer, then heard the screams. I was still in the water, so I couldn't see the crowd well."

"Anything before you went out to the launch—maybe someone you recognized on the beach?"

Kelly shook her head, looking away.

"Jason?" A prod—a reminder that she had spoken to him.

"Not Jason."

"So, someone else then?"

"No one."

Lisa cocked her head. "No one? The way you said, 'Not Jason,' makes me think you saw someone else. Somebody from the 18th Street Gang maybe? Barrio 18? That ring any bells?" Suddenly, she was fifteen again, watching seven-year-old Kelly squirm while she asked how her mother's vase had been broken. But back then, once she had the truth, she'd helped Kelly hide the broken pieces.

Not this time.

"Kelly? Who did you see?"

The shift from conversation toward interrogation got the coach's guard up. "A gang, Detective? Where are you going with this?"

"Just getting the facts straight. And Kelly has nothing to fear from me. She and I know each other from way back. Right, Kelly?"

"Yeah right. Until you left."

"We both left. Escaped, maybe, in our own ways. I went to LA and got my life straight. You turned a hobby into name recognition in a world-class sport. A different life." Lisa drew Mike's printout from her pocket. She kept it folded, a way of making Kelly wonder what was on it, turning up the heat. "Or are you still hanging on to part of the old life, Kelly. Is that it?"

Kelly met her gaze. "I didn't see Koa, if that's what you're after. He knows better than to distract me before I dive."

Not Koa. She hadn't lied just then. But if not Koa, who? Angelica? Had Kelly known they would steal the cars that day? Had she been a part of it?

Lisa sat on the edge of the bench beside her old friend, doing her best to avoid the little puddles of water. She held the paper in her left hand, close to Kelly, to let her feel the heat it carried. "Kelly, did you know Angelica Puelani, the girl who died trying to steal the Porsche?"

Kelly's gaze drifted between Lisa and the printout for a few seconds, then she shook her head.

"Are you sure? We're not too fancy over at the Maui PD, but we have some great evidence specialists—you know, the CSI types." Lisa opened the paper. "They tell me you and Angelica were besties in a MetaHive group devoted to the art of stealing cars."

"What?" the coach asked, standing up and glaring at them both.

Lisa raised a hand to keep her calm but left her focus on Kelly. "We both know you have more than hypothetical experience in that world. You were a kid back then, along for the ride. But this is different. This is serious. Angelica's dead, Kelly. Are you going to sit there and dishonor her by telling me you weren't friends?"

Seven-year-old Kelly had broken into tears over the shattered vase—spilled her guts with sobs and sniffles. She'd grown harder since then. But not too hard. Her bottom lip quivered.

"You have something to tell me?"

Silence.

"Maybe we should go to the morgue. I can show you Angelica's body. Give you a chance to say a proper goodbye before her addict mother has her cremated to the winds off Kiowea Beach."

"I did nothing wrong." Kelly stood and walked away. "I didn't steal those cars, and you know it."

The tears were free now, Lisa could tell, even though Kelly had put her at her back. To hide them, Kelly busied herself lifting the buoyancy vest from the rinsing barrel. She carried it to a rack of scuba equipment. "I knew you'd become a cop, Lisa. And I thought maybe you'd be the one cop any of us could trust." She hung the vest on a hook beneath the shelves of steel air tanks. "But now I—"

The whole rack tilted with a loud *crack*. Hundreds of pounds of steel tanks slid from their housings.

CHAPTER
FIFTEEN

LISA DARTED FROM THE BENCH and grabbed Kelly's shoulders to yank her away from the falling tanks. The two toppled into the pool. Lisa hit the water first with a back-stinging slap. They went under for less than a second before she got her body oriented and kicked for the surface.

"Kelly?" Lisa held her up, dragging her toward the edge. She wasn't moving. A trickle of blood rolled down her forehead. "Kelly, talk to me!"

Kelly stirred and sputtered. "I'm . . . I'm okay." She wriggled free from Lisa's grasp and grabbed her coach's hand. "Just stunned. That's all."

After helping Kelly out of the water, making a point of leaving Lisa to fend for herself, the coach sat her down on the bench and gingerly pushed the wet strands of hair away from her forehead. "More than stunned. You're bleeding. You might have been killed."

"I doubt it," Kelly said. "But if one of those had hit my knee or crushed my foot, my season would be over." She looked to Lisa and opened her mouth to speak, maybe to offer thanks for pulling her out of the way, but the coach cut her off.

"This interview is over. Kelly needs to get checked out." Her eyes darkened. "You want to talk to my athlete again, call my lawyer."

White-clad resort attendants came rushing in. One called on a handheld radio for a wheelchair. Another gave Lisa a hand climbing out of the pool. The rest formed an impenetrable wall of fussing and worry around the freediving star and her coach.

Lisa didn't bother trying to get through. Kelly wouldn't be hard to find after she got her head checked out. Instead, she removed her soaked oxfords and socks and walked barefoot to the broken equipment rack. The unit—a blend of shelves, round tank cubbies, and hooks formed from a high-strength composite—hung away from the faux stone wall at an angle, a few inches into a never-completed fall. It had tilted enough for the scuba tanks to slide free, but no more. The long bolts holding it in place must have partially given way.

Lisa tried to look behind the unit to verify her theory, but her eyes couldn't penetrate the shadows. She pulled out her phone, intending to use its flashlight, and realized that, like everything else on her person, it had been dunked in saltwater. Great. The phone was now a paperweight. She checked her key fob. Questionable. Her Glock? Salvageable, but she'd need to clean it soon.

She peered behind the unit, making one more attempt to see the failed bolts. They were present, not sheered or eaten through like the bleacher bolts. But it was too dark back there to see anything else. She'd have to send Mike over later to check it out.

Lisa abandoned the equipment rack and moved an attendant out of the way so she could dip her Glock in the rinsing barrel, washing off the salt water while the pieces of this case swished around in her mind.

Collapsed bleachers and now this. Lisa's instincts scoffed at the idea that one was sabotage and the other an accident. So, what were the common denominators?

The Grand. Kelly Alana.

One or the other was the catalyst for both incidents.

Lisa picked up a towel, dried her face, and then dried her gun, barely hearing the attendant who had gone into full panic mode at the sight of it—the same guy she'd pushed aside to get at the rinsing barrel. She ignored him and left the pool with the towel around her neck, dripping shoes hanging from one hand, Glock hanging from the other.

CHAPTER
SIXTEEN

The Elysium Grand

PETER HAD TO ADMIT the hotel chef knew how to poach an egg.

Breakfast had arrived without any request from Peter as he stepped out of the shower, and the waiter had insisted on setting it up for him outside on the lanai. When he tried to pay, the young man had refused to allow it and handed him a card in that fake cursive script that hotels and flower delivery companies loved.

> Peter,
> Relax and try to enjoy yourself.
> Consider this your first step.
> Best Regards,
> Nigel

Usually Peter drank a healthy mix of kale, fruit, and protein on the ride to his outpatient office, a stone's throw from the hospital. How long had it been since he'd paused his life for a real morning meal? A year? Two?

The beach. The water. The fresh-squeezed orange juice. He found all of it to be the opposite of relaxing. Yes, the food was good and the view beautiful, but Peter should have been at the office, studying the latest issue of Oxford's *Neurosurgery* or preparing for his next procedure, not sitting idle on a Pacific island like some Colonial-era governor. The whole situation stressed him out.

After finishing the egg, he picked up what he thought was a comment card, intending to leave his compliments and one or two helpful pointers for the chef. But it wasn't a comment card. Turning it over, he found another note from Nigel.

Physician, diagnose thyself.
Nigel
P.S. This was all Carol's idea.

Physician, diagnose thyself.
Peter needed no other clues to discern what Nigel—or Carol—intended by the jibe. They had tricked him into sitting down for what should have been a relaxing meal. It had caused him irrational stress instead. By implication, they wanted him to recognize the signs of a self-induced malady. Fine. He would play along.

He checked his pulse. Elevated. Sweating? A little at the hairline and on the upper lip, but Maui was far warmer than London. Headache? Growing.

Intellectually, Peter knew each of these, combined with his acknowledged stress during the meal, might indicate a workaholic in withdrawal. They might also indicate extreme frustration with meddling colleagues.

He tossed the card into the remains of his eggs and continued dressing for what promised to be an arduous day of accomplishing nothing useful at all.

With such low expectations for the day, Peter could never have anticipated the sight that greeted him in the atrium when he stepped off the elevator an hour later.

A woman coming from the pool area stalked past him in a drenched black-blouse-gray-slacks business combination, barefoot and towing an obvious storm cloud above her head. Most surprising of all, she made no effort to hide the gun in her hand.

Peter stopped an attendant who seemed to be following the woman at a safe distance. "Do many of your guests go to the pool armed?"

The attendant offered him a reassuring smile. "Don't worry. She's a police officer."

As if that explained everything. Were there criminals about? Why had she felt it necessary to draw the gun and go for a swim?

Peter watched the woman tuck her wet shoes under an arm and point a key fob at an SUV parked in the circle drive by the entrance. She clicked the button twice with an air of indifference, then chucked the fob into a fountain. "Yes, um," he said, keeping the attendant at his side. "I'm afraid I'm going to need more information."

"I did ask her to put the gun away, sir. But she said the saltwater that soaked into her holster hurt the polymer." He hurried off, waving at the woman. "Detective! Let me call you a cab. Please!"

The pool area had not finished spouting odd people or collections thereof. A small swarm of attendants came through next, surrounding a young woman in a wheelchair. She wore a wetsuit and held a towel to her head. When she pulled it away for a moment, Peter saw blood. Stranger still, the old chap who had wanted him to praise a sky deity for the sunset the evening before was the one pushing the chair. The group veered out of the atrium down an adjoining passage before they reached Peter, so he didn't hear what they were saying.

Guns. Blood. Old mystics pushing wheelchairs. And it was not yet half past nine. Were all American resort hotels this lively?

"I heard there was some excitement at the pool." A man in a bright blue flowered shirt and white pants walked up beside Peter, coming from the direction of the front desk. Dark hair.

Dark eyes. Peter would have pegged him as Mediterranean if not for the southern US accent. The man held a keen gaze on the passage where they'd taken the girl. "What happened?"

"I've no idea," Peter said, and continued toward the convention rooms.

Naturally, finding the first lecture on his retreat schedule forced him to navigate a small maze of boutiques selling the world's most expensive and unnecessary items. He escaped this gauntlet with relative ease and came upon an open-air quad. Twelve miniature lecture theaters surrounded a tranquil garden. They all seemed purpose-built for medical retreats, with demonstration tables, stadium seating, and lecterns, reminiscent of the rooms in which Peter had spent so many hours at Radcliffe. They were also empty, except for 1A, the room on his schedule.

Peter knocked on one of the open double doors. He was early and didn't want to be rude.

A balding man plugging his laptop into the demonstration table waved him in but said nothing.

Carol had mentioned that no attendance was taken, but surely at least some of the other doctors would arrive soon, perhaps coming in together from some morning beach activity. He picked a reasonable seat near the center of the hall, though neither dead center nor too close to the front, and waited.

9:23 a.m. Seven minutes to go.

Seven minutes passed with only one other individual coming in. He gave Peter a friendly nod and chose a seat in the darkest corner of the uppermost row.

The balding man with the laptop twiddled his thumbs for another forty-five seconds, glanced with uncommitted expectation at the door, then shrugged and dimmed the lights. Backlit by blue slides on a two-story screen, he introduced the conference title as *What's New for You in Doctor-Patient Relationships* and laid out a summary of available classes.

The slides did not differentiate between those that were required for the conference certification and those that weren't. Peter raised his hand.

The balding man acknowledged him with a curt smile. "Hold all questions to the end, please." Then he started a video dramatization of a doctor and patient and sat down in the front row.

The poor acting alone was enough to set Peter's mind adrift. He found himself attempting to link the soaked, gun-toting detective with the young woman in the wheelchair. An angry cop. A victim. No one under arrest. Something was out of place.

Peter always saw what was out of place, or in this case, missing. The criminal. Where was the bad guy? Why hadn't there been any other police present with vehicles to cart away an offender? The stranded detective—who clearly knew her key fob was going to fail—could have used the ride. But the attendant had been forced to call her a cab. And what was the man pushing the wheelchair's place in this? Peter had an inkling.

As if purely to answer his last question, the old chap came walking through the door.

He sat beside Peter and nudged him with a shoulder, keeping his voice low. "Hello there, Dr. Neurosurgeon. How's the conference?"

"You're the hotel doctor."

"Resort doctor, ya? But yes, guilty as charged. I like to pop in on these courses to keep current on the latest trends in medicine."

Peter almost laughed. "This is not medicine." He glanced at the screen. "Judging by the way that young man is holding his stethoscope, he's never been within ten miles of a medical college."

The balding man turned in his seat. "Shhh."

The old doctor pressed his lips together. "Relax, Alan. This is the most attendance you've seen at a lecture in months." He returned his attention to Peter and offered a fist to bump. "Dr. Tua Iona. Folks around here call me Tuna for short. And you are?"

Peter bumped the fist, though he'd never taken to the practice. Exchanging handshakes for fist bumps had never been a replacement for solid hygiene. "Dr. Peter Chesterfield, attending neurosurgeon at the Royal London."

"And you've been sent here under protest, maybe as a punishment?"

"Yes." Peter eyed him. "How did you know? Did Nigel call you?"

"No. Nothing like that. But trust me. You're not the only doctor to show up here with no interest in beaches or sham conferences." Tuna watched the video for several seconds, long enough that Peter thought the conversation had ended. But then he leaned close again. "I do find that doctors in your predicament, not drawn to beaches or adventure activities, sometimes enjoy accompanying me in my daily routine."

Peter took a moment to process what he was hearing. "You mean you want me to be your sidekick for a week?"

"Don't commit to the full week all at once. Try it out, ya? For instance, I have a young woman in my infirmary who took a knock to the head from a scuba tank. I could use a neurosurgeon's opinion."

"I doubt the hotel could afford my consultation fees."

"Not everything you do needs to be billed, my friend. Do it pro bono. Off the books." Tuna gave him a wink. "Think of my kind of lowbrow hotel physician work as your version of a vacation. You'd barely be using that big noggin of yours."

Peter had no interest in consulting on a concussion. He didn't get out of his proverbial bed for anything less than removing a tumor or a bullet. But he did want to know the rest of the two-part story that had greeted him when he stepped off the elevator.

"Tempting," Peter said, lingering on the word, then decided against it. "Sorry, mate. Perhaps on my next trip." The girl who'd lost the battle with the scuba tank had no need of his expertise, and in previous travels, he'd learned it was best never to get mixed up in local matters involving the police.

CHAPTER
SEVENTEEN

Maui PD Criminal Investigative Division

"BAD NEWS," MIKE SAID as Lisa stepped through the door to the CID.

She blew past him, continuing down the hall. "Let me guess. You couldn't find the spare keys to my unit?" She'd left the 4Runner at the Grand and taken a cab home to change. On the way, she'd hijacked the poor cabby's phone and sent Mike over to process the scene. By the looks of it, he'd already been there and come back.

"Nope. The unit's in the garage, and the damaged property report for the fob I recovered from the hotel is on your desk, waiting for your signature. Not really an evidence specialist's job, but I don't mind. You're welcome. I wrote in the remarks section that you showed particular dedication in attempting to wash off the saltwater by soaking it for a long period in the hotel fountain." He opened the door to the gang unit's offices for her.

Soaking the fob in the hotel fountain. Cute. She hit him with a long stare before walking through. "Thanks. Let's hope the captain appreciates your sense of humor. So what news is so bad that you had to wait for me at the front door?"

"Your faulty scuba rack. It was exactly that—faulty. No sign of foul play."

No way.

"That rack looked brand new, Mike."

"Correct. New rack. Fresh installation. But they used the wrong hardware. I got pictures if you wanna see."

Lisa needed a pattern. She needed him to tell her a saboteur had used acid to weaken the bolts, just like the bleachers. But that hope faded with every word out of his mouth.

She followed him to his desk, grabbing her chair along the way. Mike had the images open and waiting when he unlocked his computer screen, not shots of the scuba rack, but a wide shot of a maintenance room full of pipes and a closeup of crumbled brown rock.

"This"—Mike pointed with his pen to the wide shot—"is the pump room that runs the filters and circulation system in the deep saltwater pool. It sits behind the fake stone wall the scuba rack was bolted to." He moved his pen to the closeup. "And this is what happens when you use a long run-of-the-mill hex bolt and a nut to support that kind of weight. There are three such holes. The soft fake rock around the bolts cracked and failed—too much pressure on the nuts. There are several ways to support a heavy load with softer material. In this case, the installer should have used fender washers."

Lisa didn't mind getting her hands dirty, especially with American-made cars, but outside of the garage, she wasn't much of a DIYer. "Fender washers?"

"Big flat washer. Little hole, just large enough for the bolt to pass through. The surface area of the washer distributes the load. Otherwise, just tightening the nut can crack the rock. Chances are, the wall started to fail the day this was installed. It's a miracle this thing didn't come down sooner."

"So, poor workmanship?"

Mike touched his nose. "And the hotel is liable. Looks to me like they'll be paying Kelly Alana's hospital bills."

Fortunately for the Grand, the medical bills wouldn't be too high. Lisa had checked with the resort doc, an old friend who had nursed both her and Kelly's cuts and bruises in childhood, and learned he'd arranged for Kelly to stay in a villa at the hotel instead of sending her to a hospital. No great sacrifice for the hotel in exchange for dodging a lawsuit. If Mike had shared his findings with the manager, Lisa imagined Kelly was getting all the free room service she wanted.

Good for Kelly. And Lisa should be happy an unknown saboteur hadn't tried to kill her. But without a second crime to shine some light on her puzzle pieces, she was back to feeling around in the dark.

"What about cameras?"

"I checked, just in case. The Grand's head of security told me they don't have any cameras on the entrance to the pump room. Why would they? It's just pipes and stuff. There's a camera on the diving pool, but we looked through the footage together. Nothing suspicious. Sorry."

The office door opened. Jenny Fan grinned at Lisa. "I heard you went for a swim. You should probably do that on your off time. The rest of us are trying to solve an auto theft case."

"Funny." Lisa gave Mike a nod of thanks for his work and rolled her chair back to her desk. "The interview wasn't a total loss. Kelly Alana is hiding something. I could see it in her eyes."

"Her eyes, huh?" Jenny walked to the unit's coffee machine and began filling a mug that said *I'm Better Than You. Deal With It.* "Do your Hollywood judges accept eye-reading as evidence from the LAPD? Maybe tea leaves and tarot card predictions too?"

After the dunking she'd taken, Lisa had no patience for Jenny's abuse. She needed to reestablish the pecking order, or she'd never get the task force under control. "If I want your opinion of my methods, Jenny, I'll ask you for it. All I want from you now is a report of where you've been and what progress you've made in connecting the names Mike gave you to gang activity."

"Oh? Is that all you want?" Jenny took a sip of her coffee, set the mug on her desk, and pulled a large, off-brand phone from a hip holster. She used a stylus to scroll through her notes. "Let's see. Adrian Clark. That was an easy one, though not too fruitful. Our brothers and sisters on Oahu picked him up for armed robbery more than a month ago. No connections to Barrio 18, and while you were chasing poor Angelica to her death, Adrian was standing trial in Waikiki."

While you were chasing poor Angelica to her death. Jenny never missed an opportunity, did she? "Doesn't mean he can't point us to someone involved."

"Like I don't know that. I did a phone interview with him. Low pressure. He managed to get a lawyer on the line who said, 'That bleeding-heart haole judge gave him a sweet deal as a first-time offender.'" Jenny looked up from her notes and huffed. "First-time. Yeah right. Anyway, he told me he 'weren't gonna mess up a good thing by talking to no cops.'"

Jenny seemed to be flipping back and forth between her notes and her text messages. She was waiting for something. Stalling. Lisa narrowed her eyes. "We can revisit Mr. Clark later, once he's had more time to experience prison life. What about the other name?"

"Julian Ruiz. Twenty-three. Has an address here in Wailuku, but that was a bust."

"Because . . ."

"Because it's his dad's apartment. And let me tell you, that man is no prize either. Slammed the door in my face twice. Even if he knows where his kid's run off to, he won't give him up." Jenny lifted her mug with her stylus hand and made Lisa wait while she took a long drink. "But," she said, raising a finger once she'd finished, "I did find a garage in Kahului the younger Mr. Ruiz had rented. Judge Manu issued a warrant this morning, and the manager clipped the lock for me less than an hour ago." She went back to checking her texts.

Lisa knew Jenny wanted her to ask what she'd found. The woman had a master's degree in applied behavioral science and she clearly wasn't shy about using her knowledge to manipulate others, even her coworkers. Lisa wouldn't play her game. She kept quiet.

But Mike fell for it. "Oh, come on. What'd you find?"

"I'm glad you asked, Mike. Your friend Jerry over at the forensic facility has been helping me with the evidence." Jenny stalled them with another sip of her coffee, dialing a number on a video calling app as she drank. The line clicked. "Hey, Jerry. Why don't you show Detective Kealoha what we found?"

She turned the phone to offer Lisa and Mike a better view. The video showed the vaguely familiar face of one of Mike's colleagues over at the forensic facility. But after a disorienting jostle, it panned across a stripped-down, wheel-less vehicle on the back of a flatbed truck.

"Is that—" Lisa asked.

"Why, yes. Yes, it is. That's what's left of your stolen Mercedes Benz. And if we go ahead and discount the look you saw in Kelly Alana's eyes, I'd say it's our first big break in this case."

CHAPTER
EIGHTEEN

The Elysium Grand

PETER HAD FALLEN ASLEEP reading a digital copy of *Neurosurgery*. He preferred print materials for reading, but a pdf version of his favorite professional journal was the least of the indignities Nigel had foisted upon him.

He'd suffered through four more classes without Dr. Tua Iona—Tuna, as he'd learned to call him—to act as a distraction. The resort doctor must have been busy the rest of the day with his concussion patient, treating a boo-boo, as Carol might have said.

Three of the four classes had been rehashes of the same information despite varied titles like *Pronouns: Ask First, Don't Assume* and *Helping Patients Own Their Victimhood*. The fourth class had been more unique and the least objectionable. That one, *Don't PM Me: Horror Stories from #DoctorsOfInstagram*, had almost held Peter's attention.

Upon returning to his two-room suite, Peter had lain back on his bed with his pdf and succumbed to the combination of the rhythmic sound of the ocean waves drifting in through his open lanai doors and his lingering jet lag. He'd awoken hours later with the nightstand clock nearing midnight.

Fortunately, the Grand offered room service at any hour. He ordered a steak salad and asked the waiter to set it up on the lanai. Sitting down, he could not avoid the image of Nigel's note in his head.

Physician, diagnose thyself.

"Get out of my head, Nigel."

But Peter couldn't deny it. Faced with a moonlit ocean, an empty white beach, and palms swaying in a cool breeze, he felt his stress indicators rising—a workaholic in withdrawal. He'd felt more at ease walking into a cerebral artery bypass.

He chewed his steak and carried the diagnosis to its conclusion, assuming no treatment, as he'd done a hundred times with his real patients. Growing insomnia and habitually high cortisol levels would contribute to fatigue, leading to a general health decline. This, of course, had a high chance of causing neurological deterioration and a number of potential mental disorders, from mild phasic irritability to full-on depression. But long-term depression was not the worst news, since the increased statistical risk of diabetes, heart disease, and cancer would all likely kill him long before his time.

"My stars." Peter set his fork down and stared out at the waves. "Do I really have one foot in the grave?"

He wasn't ready to join a twelve-step group or anything, but Nigel and Carol might not have been too far off in their hinting. He frowned at his plate. A simple discussion might have served, rather than sending him halfway around the globe.

Peter had never been one to put off a treatment. If he needed to relearn how to relax, he'd better get started. Something easy, and preferably out of sight, with no one to watch him struggling to do what came naturally to most people.

The beach could not have looked emptier.

Ten minutes later, he strolled past the last of the pools and fountains and crossed the green carpet lawn to the resort's oceanside pathway. Thanks to the Grand's American devil-may-care attitude toward safety regulations, no gates or restrictions barred him from the sand or water. His only warning came from a small sign declaring NO LIFEGUARD ON DUTY.

Peter removed his wingtips and tied them to the temporary signpost. He doubted if anyone here had an interest in stealing a pair of size 12½ dress shoes or the equally large and sweaty socks stuffed inside. With his slacks rolled to the calf, he stepped off the path.

It had been years since Peter trudged through sand, and the atmosphere here was quite different, aided by the fact that he carried no heavy gear or weapons this time. Hours after the sun had set, the beach still held its warmth, ready to pass it on to a night wanderer through the soles of his feet and the soft flesh between his toes.

That sensation and a battle between the wonder and the science of it occupied Peter's thoughts for seventy meters or so, taking him beyond the recreation area and onto the beach below the property's villas. If he was to wholly commit to a cure for his work addiction, perhaps he should invest in one. He wondered what they cost and turned toward the ocean to appraise the view, imagining how it might appear from an elevated villa lanai with its own outdoor kitchen.

The surf interrupted his musings. It didn't look right.

Something floated out there, passing in and out of view on the white foam. Driftwood? Garbage? Peter waded out until the water touched the rolls of his slacks and peered harder, willing his eyes to adjust.

Not driftwood. A body.

CHAPTER
NINETEEN

The Elysium Grand

"HELP!" PETER RAN splashing into the tide, shouting over his shoulder. "Help! Call an ambulance!"

Who would hear him over the waves this far from the main resort?

The silt dropped away from the beach faster than he expected, and soon he was stroking and kicking in a full swim. The moonlight struck the victim's long dark hair with a different sheen than the water, aiding his effort to keep her in sight despite the surf stinging his eyes. "Hello! Can—" He coughed against the waves forcing themselves down his throat. "Can you hear me?"

No response.

Two more strokes and he caught the woman's arm. She wore a one-piece bathing suit and a pair of denim shorts—perhaps a midnight walk like his that had turned into a swim gone wrong. He rolled her over and pulled her shoulders to his chest, trying to remember less than a week of training from a decade before, and set off again toward the bobbing lights of the resort with a one-armed sidestroke. "Miss, can you hear me? I'm pulling you to shore."

Her head and arms stayed limp. Her skin felt cold. Peter was keenly aware he might be talking to a corpse, but until he knew for sure, decency and his oath drove him to act as if she could be saved. "Miss, stay with me. We're going to get you help."

Silt struck Peter's heel in mid-kick. The blessed sand had come up to find him again. Even so, he kept kicking, letting the tide carry him, until he felt the sand at his hip. He came to his knees and laid her down, cradling her head to keep her torso level.

She had a pulse. Faint. He pressed his cheek close to her mouth and nose.

No breathing.

One, two rescue breaths. Peter watched her chest rise and fall with each one, but when he stopped, her lungs didn't take over.

"Come on, miss. You can do it."

Two more.

The woman coughed, sending up a fountain of spray.

"Yes! Good. Get it out!"

She coughed again and moaned, and her eyes found focus on his. In that instant, he recognized her. The girl in the wheelchair. Tuna's patient. Her lids fell closed again. Her body went limp.

"No. No. Stay with me!"

Her breaths came soft and ragged. Peter had to get her to a hospital. With light but firm fingers, he checked her neck and back. Nothing out of place. "Miss, I don't feel any spine trauma. I'm going to pick you up now."

The girl was so light—almost nothing. Peter slogged through the wet sand toward the lights. "Help!"

A familiar voice greeted him. "Here! I'm here." Tuna, the resort doctor. He pointed to Peter's right. "Go that way. A path there leads straight to the hotel entrance. An ambulance is on the way."

Where had he come from? "You called them already?"

"I heard you from my villa, ya? Saw you dive into the water. Good man, Dr. Neurosurgeon."

"Peter." He was running, leaving the resort doctor behind

with his long strides, doing his utmost not to jostle her too much. "It's Peter. And you're Tuna, correct?"

"Correct," Tuna said from behind him. "What's her status?"

Glancing down at his patient, Peter saw no sign of life. Was she still breathing? Blood covered his arm. "She's bleeding. Back of the head." Two head traumas in the same day? An unlikely scenario. Peter didn't like it. "I can't tell if she's breathing. Come alongside me."

"Doing my best. We can't all be young and tall, ya?"

The path took them into a fantasy rain forest of broad leaves and exotic flowers that separated the ocean villas from the main hotel. Peter slowed on a bridge over a trickling stream, just enough for Tuna to reach him. They had to keep moving forward, but if she'd stopped breathing, that took priority.

The resort doctor laid a hand on her upper chest, then wet the back of it on Peter's shirt and held it over her nose and mouth. "Walk, please. Keep her level."

Peter obeyed.

Tuna nodded. "She's still with us. Barely." He glanced ahead, furrowing his brow. "I hear the ambulance coming up the drive. Run!"

Two paramedics were rolling a gurney from the van as Peter and Tuna broke out of the man-made jungle more than half a city block away.

"Help!" Peter shouted to keep them from rushing into the lobby. "This way!"

Seconds later, Peter laid her on the gurney, still moving. "Head trauma. Near drowning. Likely pulmonary edema. The patient experienced apnea caused by aspiration of ocean water—duration unknown, but clearly prolonged."

The paramedics eased the gurney to a stop at the back of the ambulance. The one closest to Peter shot him a glance. "You a doctor?" She gave her partner a nod, and the two hoisted the gurney up into the cabin.

"We both are," Tuna said. "Doctors Tua Iona and Peter—"

"Chesterfield." Without an invitation, Peter climbed in after the paramedics. He gave Tuna a hand up. "Dr. Peter Chesterfield. Neurosurgery."

The paramedic who'd posed the question reached past Tuna to pull the door closed while her partner jumped into the driver's seat. "I'm Wendy. Is this your patient?"

Peter stripped the plastic off an oxygenated bag-valve-mask device and placed it over the girl's mouth. "She is now." He started the oxygen flow and looked to Tuna. "Name?"

"Kelly Alana. She's the one who—"

"I know. The scuba tank victim." While the paramedic hooked Kelly up to the van's cardiac monitor, Peter watched his patient for signs of consciousness, gently squeezing the bag to help her breathe. "And now she has a brand-new head injury to compound her troubles. Take over the BVM while I check it out. Wendy, get an IV going with colloid solution. Do American paramedics carry diuretics?"

"We have furosemide."

"Give her forty milliliters. Also, this BVM has an inline adapter for a nebulizer. I take that to mean you have a stock of albuterol on board."

"Heaps."

"Hook it up. Two point five milligrams to start." He moved to Kelly's head and let Tuna take control of the BVM, then yanked a pair of nitrile gloves from a dispenser. "If Dr. Iona even thinks she's not breathing, you get a tube in, got it?"

"Like you said. She's your patient."

With his gloves in place, Peter probed the back of Kelly's head, looking for the wound. It wasn't hard to find. "Skull fracture. Lower right side of the occipital bone. It's deep."

"Strange," Tuna said. "I see the occasional bump or gash on a swimmer from rocks or coral, but never on the back of the head."

Peter didn't answer. Any words spoken in an operating theater that didn't apply directly to healing the patient went straight to his mental spam folder. Working in the back of an ambulance was no different.

He dug gauze out of the van's supplies with a glove covered in blood and pressed the wad against the wound. "She'll have a subdural hematoma. No question. She needs surgery ASAP to have any chance of survival." Keeping his hands in place to stem the bleeding, he turned toward the cab. "You, driver, tell the hospital to prepare for a craniectomy and subdural evacuation with an immediate cranioplasty to follow. Understand? Tell them the surgeon is coming in with the patient."

Tuna lifted his gaze from Kelly to give him a cautioning look. "We have surgeons on Maui. Good ones. You can't simply—"

"Watch me," Peter said, cutting him off.

Before the argument could continue, Kelly's eyes snapped open. Wild. Searching. Her pupils locked onto Peter. She grabbed Tuna's wrist and pushed the bag away. "Ho . . . hon . . ." Her words refused to form.

Tuna tried to return the bag to her mouth, but a voice in Peter's mind—one he'd never heard before—told him he needed to hear the girl. "Let her try to speak."

"Hon . . ." Kelly's eyes bored deep into his, as if the whole world hinged upon the two of them reaching an understanding. "Hon—" She gritted her teeth against an obvious surge of pain, then raised her voice. "Honu!"

Her mouth stayed open. Her body convulsed. The steady beeps of the cardiac monitor exploded into a rapid, chaotic string of tones and a piercing alarm.

CHAPTER
TWENTY

"V-FIB." WENDY THE PARAMEDIC slapped a green button on the monitor, killing the alarm and activating the integrated defibrillator. An automated female voice said, *Charging one twenty. Charging one twenty.* "Pads are in place. Make the call, Doc."

Charge complete.

Peter lifted his hands, signaling Tuna to do the same. "Now."

Kelly's chest arced, and the jagged line on the monitor resolved into a single peak. But it didn't hold. The automated voice persisted. *No sinus rhythm. Charging one fifty. Charging one fifty.*

Peter moved to her side and began compressions. "Tuna, intubate. Wendy, get 300 milligrams of amiodarone and one of epinephrine ready."

Charge complete.

"Clear!" Peter reached across his patient and pressed the button himself.

Kelly's chest arced. The monitor beeped, then dropped into a single flat tone.

"Kelly, come back!" Peter pumped her chest, feeling the crack of her ribs beneath his weight. "Come on!"

The steady tone remained until the paramedic silenced it. "Flatline, Doc. The system won't charge again unless it senses electrical activity."

"Override it. And push the drugs. We're getting her back."

The driver hit the brakes, and all three of them rocked back and forth with their patient. A nurse opened the doors, looking not the least surprised to see such a crowd in the van. "Status?"

Peter saved his breath for the labor of pumping Kelly's heart and let Wendy answer.

"Asystole." Wendy plunged a syringe into the IV line, while Tuna and the nurse jerked the monitor lines free. They rolled the gurney out. "I just pushed in 300 amiodarone and a milligram of epinephrine." She looked back at Kelly's face and shook her head. "No response."

At the outskirts of his mind, Peter heard a cacophony of voices. One demanded to know who he was. Tuna answered for him. He rode the cart with Kelly, focused entirely on his compressions. Around them, heat and humidity gave way to a rush of cold and the blue-white flood of fluorescents. They stopped in a trauma room. A nurse pulled him down long enough for a blur of green and blue scrubs to switch Kelly to a bed—the space of two pushes of the intubation bag—and he was back at it, continuous compressions now. The nurse who'd taken over for Tuna could manage the airway.

Peter pumped the compressions out at almost two per second, shoulders and back on fire, calling out new orders for amiodarone. Phrases he didn't want to hear floated past him.

"Still PEA."

"No activity."

"Doctor Chesterfield, it's time."

He kept pumping. The nurse at Kelly's head stopped squeezing the bag and sharpened her tone. "Doctor Chesterfield, are you hearing me?"

Not a nurse. The white coat registered with Peter for the

first time. Lazy American. "What are you doing, Doctor? Keep working."

A hand touched his shoulder. "Peter." Tuna's voice, soft but commanding his attention. "It's been forty-two minutes, Brah."

"I don't care. You saw her in the ambulance. She's a fighter."

The doctor who'd abandoned the bag glanced past Peter, eyes upward.

Peter knew she was looking at the clock. "Don't you dare," he said. "She's my patient."

The woman kept her eyes where they were. "And this is my ER. Either you call it, or I will."

He said nothing and kept up the compressions, but when Tuna pulled at his shoulders, he allowed it, falling away from Kelly's lifeless form. The ER doctor called the time, a barely audible echo behind the rush of blood in Peter's ears.

"I'm sorry, Brah," Tuna said. "You did everything you could. And I've known Kelly her whole life. But we have to face it. She's gone."

CHAPTER
TWENTY-ONE

Happy Valley

THE TINY CLOCK DISPLAYED on Lisa's department loaner phone said 2:07 when the call woke her. Mike had registered the device to her number and downloaded her contacts. The title on the screen said Medical Examiner. Mia.

"Um . . . Hey. What's up?"

"We've got a fresh body."

Mia needed to give her time to wake up before dropping bombshells like that. Lisa swung her legs out from under the covers and rubbed her eyes. "Okay. I'm up. Where's the crime scene?"

"No crime scene. Not even sure there's a crime. The girl died at the hospital—possible drowning following blunt force trauma to the head. Could be accidental."

Lisa held the phone away from her face and checked the time once more. Yep. 2:08. Weird. "In cases that are likely accidental, doesn't the ER put the body on ice and call us in the morning?"

"Usually. But there's some barefoot Brit here claiming it's murder. And your old friend Dr. Tua Iona is with him—goes by Tuna, right? He insisted I call you. He says you know the girl."

"I know her?" Lisa's brain snapped fully awake. "Give me a name."

"The freediver. Kelly Alana."

LISA STOPPED BY THE CID to pick up her official vehicle and dispatch a couple of units to the Grand to start asking questions. No way was this an accident.

When she arrived at the hospital, she saw Mia's barefoot Brit had lost a lot more than his shoes. By the looks of the gift shop T-shirt and the far-too-short sweatpants, he might have come in buck naked. Most of all, the detective in her took note of his feet—bandaged, with spots of blood showing through the wraps and no more protection than a pair of mismatched slippahs, flip-flops to a mainlander. She had no idea what a Brit might call them. What was this guy's story?

Lisa gave Tuna a nod. "When I saw Kelly last, she was in your care." The *How could you let this happen?* was implied. A little harsh. But she was still waking up.

The old doctor seemed to take it in stride. "I had the Grand put her up in a suite, ya? Checked on her every other hour till sundown. She was fine. Never left the room, to my knowledge. My plan was to release her in the morning."

"Fair enough. And you? What's your story?"

The Brit seemed willing enough to talk, almost eager. But as he opened his mouth to speak, she stopped him. "Hang on. Let's find someplace more private." She'd learned the tactic from Clay. When a subject wanted to talk, making them wait would hold the flood of words behind a mental dam. With that kind of pressure building up, when you finally let them speak, the dam would break and they'd often spill everything, including the parts they'd intended to hold back.

Lisa stalled for a few minutes, then commandeered one of the small meeting rooms where the Kahului ER docs preferred to give families bad news. She opened the door and closed the blinds. "In here, Dr. Chesterfield. Have a seat."

Tuna joined him, claiming the other seat across from her at the room's small table. She'd tried to send him back to the Grand, but he wouldn't hear of it.

The tall Brit set a pair of blue hospital trash bags on the table between them.

"Your clothes?" Lisa asked.

"Evidence. I carried Kelly from the water to the ambulance. Her wound bled into my shirt. Who knows what important fibers or fragments were transferred from her person to mine? Every detail matters, Detective. Are you aware that prior to World War I, if Archduke Ferdinand had not—"

"What about your shoes?" Lisa interrupted him, hefting a bag and letting it drop beside her on the floor.

"Those are still on the beach. I wasn't wearing them when I found her."

"You were walking on the beach, then?"

"Yes."

"Alone, in the middle of the night?"

"Lisa," Tuna said. "I think I can vouch for Peter."

She held up a finger to quiet him.

The Brit seemed happy to talk. "That's correct, Detective. I was alone. And so was she, from what I saw."

"What you're telling me, Dr. Chesterfield, is that you and the victim were both on the beach when she hit her head. She couldn't have been alone if you were there. Are you saying you went out there together?"

"No." Dr. Chesterfield scrunched his brow. "That's not it. Don't put false words in my mouth."

Tuna coughed, growing more insistent. "Lisa, I know what you're—"

She stopped him with another finger and flipped a page in the notebook she'd brought with her. "We'll come back to that."

She tapped the page with her pen. "Dr. Chesterfield, it says here in my notes that you're a neurosurgeon."

"Yes. Attached to the Royal London Hospital."

"Sounds fancy." She lifted her eyes. "I'm guessing a man in your position prefers fancy. And the Grand has a lot of fancy to offer. You probably have an oceanview suite or a villa. Am I right?"

He nodded—slowly. "A suite. Yes."

Lisa could see his guard coming up. She'd have to press harder before he shut down and called a lawyer. "Let me share the picture I'm getting. Rich doctor, unattached and feeling the freedom that comes from being far away from his home country, looks out from his lanai and sees a beautiful island girl out for a midnight walk. And a guy like you, loaded and"—she gave him a noncommittal shrug—"not half bad looking, you just knew she'd want to meet you. So, you headed out there to chat her up. Isn't that what you Brits call it? Chatting a girl up?"

He tried to answer, turning a dark shade of crimson.

Lisa gave him no space, feeling her own skin flushing with heat. Why had Kelly needed to die? Why now? "You went down to the beach, maybe watched her for a while to build up your nerve, then gave it your best shot. But Kelly wasn't having any of it, was she? You struggled. She fell and hit her head. You had to dunk her to make sure she stayed quiet, right? You had no choice. How'm I doing so far?"

His eyes burned. "I tried to save her life. We already told you, I'm the one who brought Kelly to the ambulance."

"Which only tells me you were the last person alone with her. No offense, Doc, but that makes you my prime suspect. And I find it strange that you keep calling her Kelly. First names are personal, Dr. Chesterfield, especially when referring to someone you claim you'd never met until you dragged her unconscious from the ocean. Did you know her? Because I did. And if I decide you're the one who killed her, I swear you'll curse the day you left your posh little country."

"I didn't take you for someone so dim, Detective. But you're rapidly proving me wrong."

"Excuse me?"

"You heard me. In all likelihood, the most verifiably brilliant mind on this island is sitting across the table from you, having been the first to find the victim and bringing a bag of physical evidence as a bonus. Statistically speaking, I'd say you've struck investigative gold, and you're throwing it away." He straightened, bringing his head well above hers. "Wake up, Detective. Instead of casting wild accusations about, you should be begging for my help. I'm willing to consult for you at no charge."

Lisa held him with a glare for a long moment, then closed her notebook with a *slap*. "I'm gonna have to say, 'No.'"

"Lisa, please," Tuna said, ignoring her warning finger this time. "Peter's not your killer—assuming Kelly was even murdered. And let's be honest. With the missteps of your youth and your shared history with the mill accident, you're more of a suspect than he is."

The missteps of your youth?

Lisa gave him a look intended to rip the tongue straight from his mouth. Tuna had often reminded her that he'd been working two floors away, in this same hospital, on the night she was born. Between Lisa and her brothers, he'd treated four broken bones and probably a hundred assorted maladies and injuries, some of which had occurred during less-than-legal adventures. But none of that gave Tuna the right to undermine her during an investigative interview. "Get out. Right now. Get out of this room."

To Lisa's surprise, Dr. Chesterfield also gave Tuna a dark look. "I'm perfectly capable of mounting my own defense. You should probably do as she says."

She waited, listening to the awkward squeak of Tuna's chair as he finally complied. When the door closed behind him, Lisa leaned across the table to glare at the Brit, reading his features. He didn't flinch, or even blink.

Maybe a different approach was needed here.

Lisa slapped the table with both hands and stood. "You know what? You're right. You're a material witness. I need you to show me exactly where you found Kelly. Let's get some coffee, Doc. Because the night's not over yet. You and I—and Tuna if he can behave—we're all going to the beach."

CHAPTER
TWENTY-TWO

Wailea, Maui

"THE MOST VERIFIABLY BRILLIANT MIND on the island?"

In Lisa's rearview mirror, she watched Tuna whack her British surgeon's arm with the back of his hand and give him a *What was up with that?* shrug.

"That's a bit presumptuous, especially with a fellow doctor sitting right there."

The Brit stared out his window, as he'd been doing for most of the half-hour drive. "I said that mind was sitting across the table from her. I could have been talking about you."

"You weren't talking about me."

"No. No I wasn't."

They were the first words he'd spoken since the hospital. Lisa's problem child. Smart. Maybe too smart. The wheels of his mind were clearly turning—calculating. But calculating what?

She parked the 4Runner short of the Grand's big awning, behind three squad cars and an equipment truck that had beaten them to the scene. "Why don't you go up to your room and change before we go out to the water, Dr. Chesterfield. I'm sure you're tired of moping around in borrowed sweats and slippahs."

"Sandals," he said. "Not slippahs. Cheap thong sandals."

"Here, we call them slippahs."

"So I've heard." The Brit popped open his door and winced as he set one injured foot on the asphalt. "I call them rubbish."

Tuna stood between them on the elevator on the way up to the surgeon's room, arms crossed and shifting his weight, like a chaperone on a date gone bad. "This is kind of you, Lisa, ya? Letting him change and all. I know how time sensitive this kind of thing can be."

Before she could answer, the Brit snorted. "She doesn't care if I change or if I'm comfortable. She wants to escort me into my room so she can assess the view from my balcony to see if her theory about me spotting Kelly from up there holds any water." He glanced at her over Tuna's head. "Isn't that right?"

Lisa gave him a thin smile. "I also don't want you hiding any evidence that might be lying around, so once you unlock the door, let me go in first."

"I'm familiar with American laws. I could demand a warrant."

"But you won't."

The elevator doors opened, and he stepped out. "No. I won't."

Walking out onto the lanai while the Brit changed, Lisa didn't have high expectations, but she had to account for all possibilities. The fact that she couldn't see the section of the beach in front of the villas—the place where Tuna said he had found his new buddy and Kelly—came as a relief, not as a disappointment. The sooner Lisa could officially rule Dr. Chesterfield out as a suspect, the sooner she could focus on her real theory.

Angelica and Kelly had both died because of the new gang activity on the island.

No matter what Mike said about the incident with the falling scuba tanks being caused by poor workmanship, Kelly's death on the same day removed all doubt in Lisa's mind. The two were related. And they were also tied to the collapsed bleachers, Angelica Puelani, and the stolen cars.

At the interview by the diving pool, Lisa had sensed con-fliction in Kelly. She'd had information she wanted to share, something she'd wanted to get off her shoulders long before Lisa showed up that morning. Maybe it had something to do with her online—and probably offline—friendship with An-gelica, but maybe not.

The falling tanks weren't deadly, but they could have taken her out of freediving for a while. Lisa decided they were a warn-ing. Someone in Kelly, Koa, and Angelica's world had sabotaged the equipment shelf as a reminder to Kelly to keep quiet. If that person found out she'd been talking to a Maui PD detective, there would have been consequences.

In the old island gang world—in Lisa's old life when Kelly and her brother Jason were too young to know it was more than a game—talking to the cops could earn you a beatdown. In LA, though, talking to the cops could earn you a bullet, and now LA gang culture had crossed the water. Kelly's death might be a sign of the future.

She walked back into the suite and rapped on the bathroom door with her knuckles. "Anytime, Doctor."

"You'll have to excuse me. I'm not accustomed to changing in a cramped bathroom while the local plod rifles through my things."

Cramped? Lisa glanced around. She could fit half her moth-er's house in his suite's two rooms, and she could fit the average Kahului apartment in that bathroom. "Don't make me drag you out of there. And I don't speak Brit. What'd you mean by 'plod'?"

The door swung back, and he breezed past her. "Google it."

On the way down to the beach, Lisa grilled him about why he'd been up so late, eating room service on the balcony. He gave her a jargony answer about circadian rhythms, bodily entrain-ment, and the hypothalamus. She didn't sense a lie, but it sure wasn't the whole story.

Flashlights darted about on the sand, carried by uniforms walking a search line from south to north. They had cordoned off the primary entrances with yellow barricade tape and posted guards at intervals to keep any predawn joggers clear. One of them lifted the tape to let Lisa and the others through, but Peter made them wait.

He freed a pair of wingtips from a NO LIFEGUARD ON DUTY sign and waved them at her. "See, right where I told you I'd left them."

"Yes. Thank you, Doctor. Because the location of a pair of shoes is solid proof of your innocence."

He pursed his lips and swung the wingtips over his shoulder, laces tied together, then ducked under the police line and trudged ahead toward the villa section of the beach.

Tuna walked beside her and touched her elbow to hold her back a pace. He lowered his voice. "Maybe cut him a little slack, ya? That man spent every ounce of his body and spirit trying to save the girl. I was there. How do you think he destroyed his feet? He ran barefoot over rocks, pavers, and asphalt, carrying her."

"My father used to call that being a tenderfoot. That might have been the most physical labor a rich surgeon like him has ever done."

Tuna gave her a flat look. "I'll let that little assumption slide, because you weren't there when he packed up his clothes. He gave you everything on his person except his wallet, his phone—which is just as dead as yours was after a dunking in salt water—and a coin."

His tone assigned a particular value to the coin. Lisa shrugged. "He kept a quarter, or a pound, or whatever? So what."

"Not that kind of coin. It was a military challenge coin, the kind members of the same unit carry with them. His service has clearly ended. Usually, that's when the challenge coins go into a display to be hung on the wall. But your rich surgeon keeps that one on him."

She'd seen challenge coins before. A lot of cops had them. A few precincts issued them in a similar tradition. "What unit?"

"It was a campaign coin, not a unit coin. Afghanistan. Royal Marines. Long before your surgeon was a rich London doctor, I suspect he was digging bullets out of his friends. So, I'll say it again, maybe cut him a little slack, ya?"

Lisa returned her attention to the tall, lanky man trudging through the sand ahead of her on bloodied feet. Maybe she'd missed the soldier in him on her first assessment. That didn't change anything. "Fine. A little slack. Emphasis on little. But don't think this means I'll let him bully his way into my case." She raised her voice to make sure the Brit heard the next part. "He still hasn't offered me any information of real use yet."

This bought her an almost instant response. "Honu," the surgeon said without looking back.

"What was that?"

"The last thing she said to us"—he coughed—"to . . . uh . . . to me, so it seemed. Honu. Tuna told me it's the Hawaiian word for the green sea turtle. But she spoke it as if the whole world depended upon her sharing that information before she died." He fell silent for a few steps, then slowed his long gait enough for Lisa and Tuna to catch up. "If I didn't know better, I'd say she forced herself back to consciousness at the end just to give me that message."

CHAPTER
TWENTY-THREE

The Elysium Grand

HONU. LISA GLANCED AT TUNA. Spoken by Kelly, the word had deeper meaning to them than to this doctor from the other side of the globe. But she kept that to herself. And judging by the solemn look Tuna gave her, he'd done the same.

On the villa side of the beach, Mike directed a team setting up work lights. Their high-lumen LED panels lit up the white sand until it almost glowed. He acknowledged her with a nod. Lisa nodded back, then looked to her problem Brit. "Okay, Doctor Genius. Show me what you've got. I need you to tell me exactly where you saw Kelly."

"Out there," he said, pointing at the water. "I mean, she was floating, which is, by definition, not a precise position."

"And that's exactly why I need you to be as precise as you can." Lisa lifted her chin toward a team of four men and women in wetsuits checking a crate of scuba gear. "Those four are part of our forensic dive team, and even with all their training, the water will make their search almost impossible. A good starting point can make a world of difference."

The Brit watched her for a few moments. She could see that

mind he was so proud of calculating again. He walked a few paces away.

He seemed lost, walking back and forth, looking from the villas to the ocean and back.

"You all right, Brah?" Tuna asked.

Dr. Chesterfield waved him off with a swatting motion but froze with his hand still in the air and stretched out the other arm. He closed his eyes.

Lisa and Tuna took a step closer. "I think he's got something," Tuna whispered.

Dr. Chesterfield's arms flopped to his sides with a loud slap. "This is wrong. Wrong, wrong, wrong. All wrong." Without so much as a glance at Lisa for permission, he started shouting at Mike. "You! With the lights. Have your people shut them off. Hurry up! And all of you keep quiet!"

The lights went out with an electric *clack*. The rumble of voices faded to a murmur, then silence.

Lisa didn't know whether she should be more annoyed with him for taking charge of her crime scene, or with Mike and the uniforms for obeying him faster and more completely than they would have if she'd given the same commands.

Her Brit, muddling around in confusion before, now seemed perfectly centered—a lost wanderer who'd rediscovered the path. He walked four paces farther up the beach, turned to face the water, and pointed about ten degrees to his right. "There. Give me a spotlight on the water, thirty meters out."

Mike did as he requested, focusing a light mounted on a tripod.

"Five meters to your left and six farther out. Yes. There. Right there." The surgeon turned to Lisa. "You wanted precise, Detective. There it is."

The divers needed no other prompting to enter the water.

He walked back to Lisa. "I can do more than point. Let me in."

"Why? Why do you care about my investigation, Dr. Chesterfield?"

"Please. Call me Peter. And I care because I took an oath."

"Liar." Lisa looked past him toward the dive team. She could see their lights panning back and forth under the surf. "This isn't about your oath. From what Tuna tells me, you fulfilled it when you fought to save Kelly. Try again. Why is a London doctor on vacation so keen to take part in an island murder investigation?"

He held her gaze for a time, then let out a quiet laugh and walked past her, moving in a slow half circle around Lisa and Tuna before stopping to watch the uniforms comb the beach. "How about I tell you another thing you don't know about this murder—perhaps prove my worth?"

"If you have something to say, I won't stop you."

He turned, eyes cold, though the look seemed forced. "I put my fingers into that big dent on the back of Kelly's skull—felt its depth, felt the bone fragments move at my touch, exposed and wet with blood. That kind of wound speaks to a man like me. It tells a tale. That wound is how I know for certain this was no accident."

She didn't know what she'd expected when she left the opening for him to speak, but it wasn't such gruesome detail. Maybe she should rethink her desire to rule him out. Lisa swallowed. "Go on."

"I'm sure Tuna will be happy to confirm this for me. Every good doctor knows that the skull brittles with age. A seventy-year-old in the ocean, with just the right dynamic of waves, might—*might*—receive a wound like that. But not a young aquatic athlete like Kelly. For a healthy woman of her age, the occipital bone, this one"—he touched the back of his head—"is too strong."

The surgeon lowered his eyes, then raised them and gave her a sad smile. "Not to be cavalier, but in physical terms, young people like Kelly really are thick-headed. At her height, even a fall on land could never have caused such a wound. At best, she was pushed or thrown down, adding force to gravity's pull. At worst, she was struck with a blunt instrument by an upward blow. Either way, Detective, I can tell you with utter certainty that Kelly Alana was murdered—bludgeoned in some fashion on dry land, then cast into the water to die."

An upward blow. If Lisa's theory about the gang world held true, a world in which Kelly's own brother said she was dabbling, then a skull-bashing blow made sense. And she'd seen more than her share of skull bashings in California. But not one of those had been delivered with an upward swing. Her killer was shorter than Kelly. There might be more, but at present, Lisa only knew one gang leader on the island who fit that description. Kelly's cousin. Koa Alana.

"Not bad," Lisa said. "Peter." She tried out his first name, risking the informal. It felt right. But she didn't want to give him the idea that he'd won her over. "You'll make a good medical witness, but don't think this means I'll let you—"

"Hey!" A diver came wading onto shore carrying his fins. With the other hand, he held an object high—round and smooth, about the size of a golf ball. It caught the lights with a black gleam. "We found something!"

CHAPTER
TWENTY-FOUR

The Elysium Grand

"IT DOESN'T STRIKE ME AS OBSIDIAN." Mike held the object close to one of the work lights, with Lisa and the two doctors gathered around him. Lisa's first assessment of it having a golf-ball-like shape had been slightly off. The thing looked more like a miniature soccer ball. "And I doubt it came upon this shape naturally."

"You're telling us someone dropped it?" Peter said. "Kelly's killer, perhaps?"

The evidence specialist shook his head. "I'll leave conclusions like that to Detective Kealoha. I *am* saying this isn't some volcanic rock we commonly find lying in the silt on our resort beaches. It's a cut stone, possibly synthetic." He dropped it into a bag. "We'll grind some dust off in the lab and get you more info tomorrow."

Lisa yawned. "You mean today." The shadow of Haleakala, Maui's eastern volcano, shielded Wailea's beaches from the rising sun, creating the illusion that the morning was still far off. It wasn't. "We've done all we can here. Bring the rest of your divers in, and pack it up. I'll see you at the CID. Come in an hour late."

"Oo," Mike said. "An extra hour of sleep. So generous."

"Don't push it. We could grab some coffee and head to the office now."

"An hour's good. Thanks, boss." Mike waved at the uniforms, whose beachcombing operation had decayed into random wanderings and chatting. "Yo! Pack it up. We're leaving!"

Peter followed Lisa as she left the beach. "Exactly what time is an hour late?"

It took her a moment to realize he was inviting himself over as part of the investigative team. "Half past never for you. Get some sleep. If I need your input, I'll call you."

"SHE DIDN'T EVEN ASK for my number."

After Detective Kealoha left, Tuna and Peter had decided that neither of them would get any sleep. Instead, they'd committed to getting cleaned up and meeting for the early-risers breakfast at Aunty Noelani's, the Grand's seventh-floor café overlooking the atrium.

"That's 'cause she's not gonna call you, Brah." Tuna used a sandaled foot to push a chair out for Peter. "Take a load off. Listen to the birds chirp. Enjoy your morning."

"The birds. Yes." Peter lifted a narrow menu from a rack and used it to shoo a house sparrow from the table. "There are plenty of those to go around. How does the local Ministry of Health feel about Aunty Noelani's and the big restaurant below doubling as aviaries?"

"Hawaiian birds are magic, Brah. No disease. Just go with it, and you'll be okay. And FYI, most folks call this place Aunty's. A favorite among the locals. Best coffee on the islands. The Grand trucks it in from a small-time grower over in Kaanapali—swapped his land over from cane to coffee long before the sugar crash. Now everybody thinks he's a prophet."

"Magic birds." Peter brushed another one away and took his seat. "Do you believe this coffee grower is a prophet?"

"Depends on your definition. Maybe the guy got lucky. Maybe he read the markets right. The signs were there. Maui was the last of the islands to abandon sugarcane. I'll tell you one thing for sure." Tuna took a sip from a porcelain cup and smacked his lips. "Growing coffee in soil that used to produce cane makes it sweeter. You won't find java like this anyplace but Maui."

"Coffee, huh? That's an interesting theory." A man with a familiar southern US accent, wearing a pink flowered shirt, turned around at the next table over. "I'll have to consider that thought as I expand my investments here."

The smile Tuna gave him in response seemed forced. "Peter, this is Jack Carlisle, a businessman new to the island. We're neighbors."

"Of a sort." Carlisle reached over to shake Peter's hand. "The resort keeps their good doctor in the last of the property's original villas, near the luau field. Dr. Iona's villa predates Mr. Alcott's revival of the Grand under his Elysium flag. I myself purchased one of the new models. All the bells and whistles." He grabbed his glass of orange juice and a plate of eggs and slid his chair over to join them. "But I'm being rude. Back to the introductions. I take it you're also in the medical field, Dr. . . ."

"Chesterfield. Peter Chesterfield. We've met."

"Have we?"

"Yesterday, in the atrium. You asked about the excitement at the pool."

"Oh, yes." Carlisle gave him an easy smile. "We didn't speak enough for me to peg your accent at the time. London, is it?"

Not even close. In Peter's experience, most Americans thought every British accent was a London accent. He didn't bother arguing the point. "I do work in London. Very good. But I'm afraid I'm not familiar enough with American southern to gauge your accent, sir."

"Texas hill country. East of Dallas. Born and raised." Carlisle shoved a forkful of eggs in his mouth. "My granddaddy owned a few hundred head of prime beef stock. Dad and I turned that herd into a multimillion-dollar corporation. And now that he's gone, a new breed of cattle is what brings me to Maui. The same sugarcane soil that makes Tuna's coffee a little sweeter will make my cows that much tastier to the American palate."

The rancher-turned-CEO prattled on about the variances between Angus and Wagyu and his own trademarked Ono Beef to be raised on the thirty thousand acres of former cane fields he'd purchased. Peter perused the menu and gave him an occasional nod, as if he was still listening.

After the food came and the waitress had passed out of earshot, Carlisle's demeanor shifted. He leaned closer. "Getting back to the excitement at the pool yesterday, I must confess, I came over here for another reason. I saw the commotion on the beach in the wee hours this morning. I'm sure I wasn't the only one. And when I looked out from my lanai, I couldn't help but notice you two gentlemen were there. I'm hearing that all of it—yesterday morning, last night—it's all related."

He let the statement hang over the table, waiting.

Tuna coughed. "We were there. Yes. But we can't comment, ya? Open investigation. You understand."

"Ah, come on. I know the resort staff sees everything that happens here—gets all the good watercooler scuttlebutt—and this time you saw more than your fair share. Let it out, boys. Give me something." When both Peter and Tuna kept mum, he frowned and lifted his chin. "My maid told me there was a drowning. A young woman. She said you and another man— Peter, here, I'm guessing—put the girl in an ambulance at two in the morning. Is that right?"

Peter didn't like being the subject of rumors floating around the resort, especially rumors driven by anyone wearing white pants and white canvas loafers. "As Dr. Iona said. We can't comment. Sorry to disappoint you."

The cattleman gave them a good-natured frown. "I can respect that. Good men. Both of you. But I won't be the only one asking questions." He nodded at the atrium below.

A small police army filtered into the hotel, some carrying cameras and other equipment. Guards had been posted on the beach after they left, and Peter assumed a new shift from the evidence team would now do a daylight search.

The guests looked restless, staring, murmuring to one another. More than a few snapped pictures or videoed the invasion with their mobiles. Watching them, Peter decided he couldn't blame Carlisle for his curiosity. He'd have to settle for disliking the man for his demeanor instead.

Despite his declaration that he'd let the matter lie, Carlisle remained at the table. The three passed the next half hour with small talk, most of which centered on Carlisle's view concerning English beef and musings about using some of his acres to push Tuna's favored coffee grower out of business while he waited for his herd to grow.

"What a creeper," Tuna said, shuddering as he walked with Peter to the elevators afterward. "For a moment there, I thought he was going to follow you to your room."

Peter pressed the up button and stood back. "Just as you appear to be doing?"

"This is different, ya? You and me, we got stuff to talk about—stuff we couldn't say in front of him."

The doors opened, and Peter waved a young couple on without them. He pulled Tuna to the side, to a balcony overlooking the pools. "What stuff?"

Tuna looked around, as if he worried that someone might overhear. "Honu."

Honu. The impact of the word caused Peter physical pain. The image of Kelly shouting it flashed in his mind, her body arcing as her heart gave out. Peter winced and shook it away. "You told me already. It's a sea turtle."

"No, Brah. Honu was much more than that to Kelly. To her, honu meant 'ohana. To her, honu meant family."

CHAPTER
TWENTY-FIVE

The Elysium Grand

"THE HAWAIIAN WORD is *'aumakua*."

Having taken the elevators down instead of up, Peter walked with Tuna along a black-and-gold garden path between the Grand's towering southern guest wings. Even with the coffee from breakfast, the adrenaline crash had begun to hit him, and Tuna said the fragrance of the garden's flowers would revive him. It wasn't working. "So, they're like family spirit animals?"

"Not exactly, Brah. According to tradition, 'aumakua can take many forms, not just animals. It's more about the form a visiting, deified ancestor chooses to take."

"Spirit animals. Deified ancestors. Either way, don't such things conflict with your views on God? I thought he was the jealous type."

"Oh, for sure. For sure. A lot of folks don't want to see it this way, but in my view, a lot of the old worship traditions like hula and 'aumakua don't mesh with Christianity—not if you take the Ten Commandments seriously." He rolled up a short sleeve to show Peter a blob-shaped scar. "We all made mistakes in our youth. This was one of mine. Used to be an octopus."

"Your family's mascot."

Tuna laughed, dropping the sleeve. "Yeah. You could phrase it like that. The Iona 'aumakua is *ka he'e*, the octopus. That scar used to be an artsy tattoo of one. I called him Uncle Apela, but he had to move out when I found Christ."

Peter caught a touch of sadness in his tone. "Sounds like you were sad to see him go."

"Oh, no. Not Uncle Apela." The old doctor shrugged. "He was just a figment of the imagination, ya? But here's the thing. A lot of people here take 'aumakua serious." He glanced up at Peter. "Real serious. More than a few of my family members stopped speaking to me when I suggested they kick their own octupuses to the curb. Wait. Octopieces?"

Peter shook his head. "Octopi."

"Doesn't sound right. Good thing I'm a doctor and not a veterinarian."

"And Kelly's honu?"

"Kelly was an Alana. Big family. Very traditional in many ways. Honu is a big deal to them. Big deal."

"Perhaps she was calling out to an ancestor."

"Nah." Tuna directed him down a sloped, winding path leading to a koi pond below them. "The family is traditional, and Kelly loved the honu symbol, but she never bought into the ancestor thing like her dad and her grandparents. I think she knew death had a grip on her, and I think she was trying to tell us a family member had pushed her into its path."

A family member. That seemed an important detail, but Peter didn't remember Tuna mentioning it to the detective. "Were you planning on keeping this bombshell to yourself?"

"You mean, should I tell Lisa? Brah, she already knows. She knew the moment you told her Kelly's last word. Lisa and the Alanas go way back. Kelly was *keiki* then, a child, but Lisa and her brothers ran with her older cousins. Got into all sorts of trouble."

Tuna told Peter about a freediving competition the Grand had hosted shortly before he arrived, and how there'd been trouble there as well. Collapsing bleachers. Stolen cars. "Right before the collapse, I saw Lisa talking to Kelly's cousin Koa. The kinda guy we call a moke. Big tough stuff among the local island gangs. I bet she's hunting for him right now. No easy task. Koa can make himself scarce when he wants to."

They stopped at the bridge over the koi pond, and Peter considered what he'd learned, watching the infinite weaving patterns of the fish. Part of him wanted to ask Tuna where he thought this Koa might be hiding. But if Detective Kealoha, with her knowledge and local resources, was looking for him, Peter's time was better spent pursuing other avenues. But which?

The raised bridge, combined with his height, gave him a view past the curtain of broadleaf foliage bordering the lower pool area. A pair of women in the gray uniforms of the housekeeping staff pushed two carts of towels and linens into a service elevator. "The maid," he said out loud.

Tuna glanced up from the koi. "Say again?"

"The maid. The concierge. Any of the staff. You told the detective that you'd checked on Kelly several times during the day—that she'd never left the room. But clearly that's not the case. We know she went down to the beach. Perhaps she even left the property. As our friend Mr. Carlisle noted, the staff sees everything. Someone here knows where Kelly went when she left her room."

"I'm sure the police are conducting interviews."

"True. But the police make people nervous. The staff might have looser tongues when gossiping with the resort doctor and his new colleague."

RULES WERE BROKEN. Of that, Peter was certain. Tuna stepped behind the reception desk and accessed the housekeeping schedule to see who had serviced the villa where he'd put Kelly. This violation bought them nothing. Before they could locate their potential witness in the service halls, a supervisor shooed them away.

They fared better with the concierge staff. After accessing another set of employee schedules, Peter and Tuna found a lobby attendant who'd called Kelly one of the resort's private cars. She'd left more than two hours after Tuna had last checked on her.

"I did what I was supposed to," the attendant told both doctors. "I ran her villa number before I called the car. The note in the file said she could pretty much have whatever she wanted." He looked up at Peter. "I'm not in trouble, am I?"

Tuna motioned for Peter to bend a bit so that he could whisper in his ear. "You should work on that hostile resting face of yours, ya? You don't even work here, and the kid is scared you're gonna fire him." He turned to the attendant and gave him a pat on the arm. "You're okay, ya? No trouble. But we're gonna need the address where she took the car so we can complete our investigation."

Tuna didn't say what the investigation was for or why a pair of doctors were investigating anything, but to add weight to his friend's statement, Peter tightened his natural frown. The kid bolted away to do their bidding as if his livelihood depended on it.

Tuna laughed. "Okay, maybe I was wrong. Keep the face. It's useful."

When the kid returned with the address, Tuna wrote it down and handed the slip of paper to Peter. "I'd better stay here. Got an appointment in twenty minutes to check on a sunburn. You go. Follow Kelly's steps and see where they lead."

"And if I run into Detective Kealoha? I doubt she'll be pleased to see me, and I don't know how an arrest for interfering in police work will look to the Royal London's board."

"I'll advise that young man to share his information with one of the police officers floating around the resort"—he checked his watch—"after my appointment. That way, you get a good head start and Lisa can't claim obstruction. Besides, I treated that girl's boo-boos until she was twenty. That gives me special dispensation. Think of me as your anti-arrest insurance policy."

It was a nice thing to say, but if Detective Kealoha decided to put him behind bars, Peter doubted there was anything Tuna could do to stop her.

CHAPTER
TWENTY-SIX

Maui PD Criminal Investigative Division

LISA DIDN'T GIVE HERSELF the same extra hour she'd given Mike. The dynamic of the case had shifted. If Peter's hunch was right, this was murder, and not a murder of some unknown victim in a massive urban crowd, like the more than fifteen hundred murders LA had suffered during Lisa's time on their force. This one was personal, a girl she'd known growing up. A girl she'd taken to Papohaku Park to get shave ice.

A girl whose family shared an unwanted bond with hers.

As if he sensed her need, Clay called as she flipped the lights on in the task force section.

"She's gone, Clay."

"Wait. What? Who's gone?"

"Kelly Alana. Yesterday, I pulled her out of the way of some falling scuba tanks. Looked like an accident, and I let it go." The sorrow that had been welling up inside Lisa came to the surface. Tears blurred her vision. Thank goodness the section was empty. She sat on the corner of a desk. "I could have put a guard on her. Could have stayed with her myself. It's not like I never babysat her before. I left her alone, Clay.

And someone bashed her skull in and dropped her in the ocean to die."

"Don't do that. You know better, right? The view after the crime is often clear, but that doesn't mean we should've seen it coming. I know you, Lisa. You made good decisions. This isn't your fault."

She sniffed and wiped her eyes with her sleeve. "Right. I know. It's just . . . this one's a lot more personal than usual. There were things I should have told her. Important things. I could have called from LA. Kelly would have answered. I could have been the big sister God meant me to be."

Lisa had to pull it together before the rest of the section came in. She grabbed her purse and walked into the restroom to assess her appearance. Puffy red cheeks. Bloodshot eyes. Great. At least there'd been no running mascara. She never wore much makeup, and she hadn't put on any before leaving the house after Mia called.

With a little touching up, Lisa's people wouldn't be able to tell the difference between a task force chief who'd been crying and one who'd been up all night getting a jump on the case. She pulled a powder compact out of her purse. "How did you know we'd hit a murder, Clay? We're talking hours here."

"I didn't. I called to give you what I'd learned." He paused, as if unsure this was the right time to give her the details.

"Go ahead. Tell me."

"You want to talk about the other thing first?"

"Later. And right now, the best way for me to get through this is to find Kelly's killer."

"Okay. I've got two items of interest for you. Number one, our system flagged the purchase of a crate of key fob cloners. Nothing illegal on the surface, but we're talking about a lot more devices than a mom-and-pop garage should need."

Lisa finished with the compact and moved on to her mascara. She'd learned how to hide bloodshot eyes a long time ago—way before she'd become a cop. "Got it. Key fob cloners. Definitely suspect. Send me the details." She paused in her mascara work. "Wait. If it flagged in the FBI system, shouldn't a notification have been sent to our department's Investigative Services Bureau?"

"Yeah, it should have. Same with my second item. I'd say there's a glitch or connectivity problem."

Lisa scowled at her reflection. Ever since her arrival, she'd been learning that the island department ran like Mayberry in 1960. Chances were, their connection to the FBI Auto Theft Task Force had never been established. She could hear the excuse from the IT department in her head. *Why bother? This is Maui.* "What's your other item?"

"Your 18th Street hint paid off. You've got a known felon on the island. Probably brought friends with him. LA transplant. You might recognize his name. Did some time for murder, but he got his start in auto theft. I'll send you the file."

"Any connection to Kelly Alana?"

"None yet. But I know you'll find it."

BY THE TIME ANOTHER SOUL entered the GTF section, Lisa had her murder board up and cooking. Frustratingly, that next soul was Jenny Fan.

Jenny walked straight up the aisle between the desks, heels clicking on the tiles, not a hair out of place. "You establish a timeline yet?"

Of course not. Lisa had a time of death—an endpoint—but no beginning. She turned, ready with a defensive remark, and saw Jenny holding out a paper cup from Aimee's.

"Figured you could use this. I heard you knew the vic. Tough break."

"Um . . . thanks." Lisa accepted the gift, too tired to come up with a better thank-you or an explanation of how she knew

Kelly. She took a long swig instead. Straight black. Harsh. She could find some creamer later. "I'm hoping to get on top of this before the clock on any perishable evidence ticks out."

"You know this isn't officially our case, right?"

"It will be." Maui didn't have the manpower for separate sections specializing in robbery, homicide, or special victims. When needed, they spun up a task force like Lisa's and assigned individuals with the right rank and training. "The fact that we're the gang task force doesn't preclude us from taking on a murder. Especially since I can link Kelly to our auto theft case."

Jenny scrunched her brow. "You mean the MetaHive posts? That's thin, Lisa. It's a small island."

"I'll thicken it up if I have to. A little conjecture goes a long way if you frame it right."

"You learn that in your big mainland city?"

Lisa nodded, her guard coming up again. "That okay with you?"

"Sure. But maybe I can help with some more solid evidence. Cross some t's so to speak." Jenny opened the satchel hanging from her shoulder and handed Lisa a file folder with a single-page legal document.

Lisa read the short paragraph. "This is a warrant to search the home of Edena Alana, Kelly's mom." She checked her watch. Not even eight yet. "You woke up a judge?"

"Didn't need to. Every morning before sunup, Judge Ikeda runs what the public defenders call the Circuit Circuit, the loop formed by Wells and Main. I met him on the courthouse steps." She gave Lisa a wry smile. "Staying in one precinct for a while has the benefit of knowing the local system."

"I'll give you that one." Lisa handed the folder back to her. "And this is good work. But Kelly's mom will let us look around without a warrant."

"Because you know her?"

"It's a little more than that, but yeah."

129

Jenny slipped the warrant back into her satchel. "I'll keep it on hand just in case. We should probably head over there now, unless you've made the notification already."

"No, I haven't." Lisa lifted her borrowed phone from her desk and headed for the door. "I wanted to let her sleep—to let her have a few more hours of normalcy before I brought her world crashing down." She didn't elaborate. But those extra hours of normalcy were what Lisa and Kelly and other families all could have used more than a decade ago when the suits from the mill came to their doorsteps.

CHAPTER
TWENTY-SEVEN

Happy Valley

EDENA ALANA SEEMED TO KNOW the truth the moment she opened the front door. She kept up enough with Lisa's mom to know Lisa had joined the force. The grave expressions on Jenny's and Lisa's faces probably told her the rest.

She didn't invite them in. Not really. It was more of a slow retreat, backing away into her living room to flee the shadows crossing her threshold. The suits from the mill all over again.

Lisa broke the news, giving enough detail to be sure Edena understood, while Jenny stood apart, looking anywhere but at Edena's eyes. Jenny had probably been through a murder notification once—maybe—given Maui's low population and crime rate. Lisa had done it a dozen times or more. She'd stopped counting after the first three. What was the point? But she'd never given a notification to someone she knew.

She let Edena fall against her—let her pound on her shoulders—and then lowered her onto a worn green couch to sob. She didn't question her at first. One of her LA mentors had taught her that moments of shock and grief often produced the most fruitful interrogations, but Lisa had never favored the tactic. She pressed Edena's hands between her own, and the two sat together for a while.

When Edena's breathing evened out, and when she showed enough mental faculty to reach for a tissue, Lisa tried an easy question. "Did she call you last night, maybe tell you where she was going?"

Edena shook her head. "We didn't speak every day. We—" Her voice caught. "We argued a lot. Most nights, she stayed at her coach's apartment over by Papohaku Park. It's a lot nicer than this place, and she loved that park." The look she gave Lisa seemed to say *But you know that as well as I do*. "And Jason had been around more, so Kelly was keeping her distance—for my sake, I think. She knew I didn't like to see my children fight."

"Jason? I thought he was living in Hana." Lisa glanced down at her shoes, suddenly feeling guilty, as if she was persecuting this family. "I mean, I know he is. I went out there and spoke to him."

"Because of that Puelani girl? There's lots of people on Maui with records, Lisa. You didn't have to pick on Jason."

"It's not like that." Lisa tried to shift her focus back to the important questions. "How often does Jason stay with you?"

"Couple of nights a week. He has a part-time job at a resort, you'd have to ask him which one. I can't keep 'em all straight anymore. He works multiple jobs just to get by after what they did to him. I keep telling him he can live here permanently, but he's too proud. Wants to be a man like his father was, you know?"

Lisa nodded. She knew. All the kids from that day carried the ghosts of their fathers in one way or another. "Was he here last night?"

"No. I haven't seen Jason since the day before yesterday. And Kelly hasn't come home since long before that."

"But Kelly does have a bedroom here, right?" Jenny asked, nosing around in the kitchen.

Lisa shot her a look.

Edena didn't seem to mind. "I always keep her room ready for her." Her phrasing seemed to dawn on her, and Edena corrected herself with a half sob. "Kept. I always *kept* her room ready. I guess that's over now. I can show you."

Jenny gave Lisa a *You were right* shrug.

No warrant necessary. One point for Lisa. At the moment, she didn't feel like keeping score.

Kelly's room looked like a platoon of mermaids riding unicorns had stormed the gates of a luxury car show—a mix of teen dreams and *Grand Theft Auto*.

"She liked her cars." Edena laid a hand on Lisa's arm. "I guess all you kids did, ya?"

"When I left, she was still in the unicorn and mermaid phase," Lisa said, standing just inside the doorway while Jenny took care of the dirty work, inspecting the closet and poking through drawers. "But she'd started to notice the differences between a Charger and a Challenger. And she and Koa were growing close. You know Koa has a history of auto theft, among other things. I hate to ask, but did Kelly ever take part in his illegal activities?"

Edena's voice caught again. Tears returned to her eyes. "Not my baby. Her brother fell into that life, but not Kelly. The freediving was going to save her." She turned and looked hard at Lisa. "Why do you ask? What did that *lolo* Koa do? Is he the one? My brother's fool child. Did he kill my Kelly? Tell me. You tell me, Lisa Kealoha. Right now."

Lisa held up her hands to calm her. "I'm not saying that. I'll talk to Koa if I can find him. And if you can point the way, I'd sure appreciate it. But I'm not making any accusations. All I want to know is if he and Kelly were working together."

"No. I told you. She didn't do that sort of thing."

"Lisa." Jenny emerged from the closet holding something the size and shape of a TV remote, but with its own screen and a heavy-duty cord hanging from one end.

Lisa closed her eyes. *I knew it.* "Anything else?"

Jenny showed her a white cardboard box with no markings. "Key fob blanks. I'm guessing they fit the port on the side of this thing."

"Okay. I think it's time to go." Lisa guided Edena out into the living room, heading for the door. "We're going to borrow that device and the box to help us find out what happened. In the meantime, you call my mom, okay? She'll come over anytime you want. Ikaia will cook you something—take care of you."

The instant she said it, the old couch, the drapes, even the smells rolled back fifteen years. They were all there together. Her brothers. Her mom. Jason. Koa. Kelly was playing with a doll on the floor, oblivious. Edena had been the strong one then. *We gotta stick together, okay? All of us. We'll get through this.*

"Lisa, why do you want that thing?"

Edena's question snapped Lisa back to the present. She'd found the door—pushed it open. The sun was blinding.

"Lisa? Why are you taking that thing your friend found? What is it?"

Lisa let Jenny squeeze past her, then stood on the stoop and faced this person she should have kept in touch with—this woman she should have loved like they'd all promised so long ago. "I'm sorry, Edena. It's a device used for stealing cars."

CHAPTER
TWENTY-EIGHT

The Elysium Grand

A LITTLE SHOPPING TRIP in the resort's overpriced shops helped Peter replace his waterlogged mobile. The proprietor helped him restore his contacts and such from the cloud, and his first call went to a rental company. Ubers and cabs didn't seem the right mode of transportation for snooping about Maui to retrace Kelly's steps. The rental place said they'd be happy to bring him a car. To remain inconspicuous, he selected a Ford Focus.

A half hour later, Peter received an automated text telling him the car was arriving. But when he walked out to the Grand's circle drive, he saw only a cherry-red Cadillac pulling in among the fountains. It stopped directly beside him, and Peter backed up, expecting either a Saudi dignitary or a cocaine dealer to step out.

Instead, a red-haired, pimply young man climbed out of the driver's side, wearing a jacket with the rental company logo. "Dr. Chesterfield?" The kid made a ta-da sign with both hands, as if he'd pulled the Cadillac out of a hat. "Here's your car."

"But I ordered an economy vehicle."

"Yes, sir. This is an upgrade."

"I chose a Ford Focus."

The kid nodded, adding emphasis to his words. "And the manager upgraded you to a Cadillac CT5-V Blackwing, part of our prestige series."

"I don't want an upgrade."

"But it's free."

"I don't care."

The kid's smile dropped. He dipped his spiky hair into the car for a moment and reemerged with a key fob and a clipboard. He flipped up the top page, reading the document underneath. "Looks like you paid with an Ultabank Diamond card, sir. That entitles you to a free upgrade. Part of their perks program or something." He dropped the page and shrugged. "Says here, there's no extra charge."

Whether Peter believed that or not was immaterial. He'd wanted something that blended in on Maui, not in the valet line at a Monaco casino. Why couldn't rental companies ever just give you the car for which you've asked? He didn't want to waste the morning arguing and demanding a different car. If he sent the Cadillac back, the kid might return with a Lamborghini. "Fine. I'll take it."

"Awesomesauce." The kid turned the clipboard around and clicked a pen open for him. "Sign here."

The Cadillac's navigation system accepted the address the attendant had acquired from Kelly's driver and identified the location as the Maui Central Baseyard. On the display it looked to be out in the wasteland of the former cane fields, almost two-thirds of the way between the resort and the island's main urban hub of Kahului and Wailuku. What could a young freediving star desire that was out there in the empty valley?

As the navigation system counted down the last miles, an old concrete drainage ditch came in from the east to parallel the road. The ditch, dried out and half filled with red dirt, terminated at an industrial complex—a few acres of concrete covered in prefab metal warehouses, chain-link fences, and converted shipping containers. Clearly once part of the cane mill's complex, the place had been taken over by garages, storage, and junkyards.

"You've arrived at your destination." The navigation computer made its declaration the moment Peter turned off the highway. Too soon. There might have been a dozen or more businesses in the complex, spread out on a jumble of roads and alleys that made little sense, even with the bird's-eye view of the Cadillac's map. He slowed to barely more than a coast.

The entry road passed between a body shop and a junkyard full of old hulks, from rusted Chevys and Mazdas to a full-size fishing trawler that listed on the gravel in eternal distress. An older Hawaiian in a stained white undershirt stared Peter down as he drove past. From the suspicion in the man's glare, Peter guessed this place—well removed from the city and the resort villages—was an appointment-only location.

He cruised the tangled streets, trying to guess which place Kelly might have visited. A boat mechanic. A stonemason. A solicitor—some ambulance chaser with a shop the size of a London street toilet. The island's garbage truck parking lot. There was a grand total of six auto body shops with a variety of declared specialties.

Near the center of the complex, he found a flimsy corrugated steel cantina-slash-bar. That was what the sign said. No name. Just CANTINA/BAR. Interesting. He hated to think this was the place Kelly had forsaken her free villa to visit, but it made more sense than any of the other businesses. He parked across the street at the front of a lot filled with shipping containers and shut the engine down to wait and watch.

THE THREE MEN had approached from behind, among the containers, as best Peter could surmise, like Lawrence at Aqaba catching the Turks by surprise. Peter had been there less than fifteen minutes, and with his attention focused on the bar, he didn't see them until he heard the thump of a hand slapping the Cadillac's roof.

After gaining his attention, the apparent leader—wearing board shorts and an LA Clippers jersey and covered in tattoos—signaled for Peter to step out.

He should have stayed in the car and driven off.

Instinct told him to flee, but Peter wanted information. He needed to know what prior events had transpired to place Kelly Alana in his path, destined to die despite all his skill and knowledge. He climbed out, locking the doors and giving them a boisterous greeting to cover the sound. "Good morning, gentlemen. Beautiful day, isn't it?"

One of the men, a little younger than the leader and about the same size, lifted his chin. "You lost or somethin', Ese?"

"You got a nice ride," the other subordinate added—a great bulging bear of a man. "But this ain't no place for a Sunday drive."

The leader let out a huff. "You been sittin' outside the cantina for a while now. Why don't you man up and go have a drink. In fact"—he glanced at his two friends, then back at Peter—"I'm thinkin' you should buy all of us a round."

In Afghanistan, as a naval surgeon assigned to a special unit of the Royal Marines, Peter had endured negotiations with the worst kind of men—warlords who had shed innocent blood and were proud of it. They all carried the same darkness behind their gaze, what a religious person like Tuna might call demonic. The leader and the smaller of his two friends had it. Not the big bear, though. Interesting.

"Thank you, but it's pretty early in the day. And early or late, I'm not a drinker."

The leader took a step forward.

Peter backed up an equal distance, bumping into the Cadillac. He tried the direct approach. "To be honest, I'm looking for information. Perhaps you can help."

"Information, eh?" The leader's slow grin told Peter that if he had any, there'd be a charge. There was probably going to be a charge either way. "What kinda information?"

"It's about a young woman."

"Oh, Ese," the smaller of the two subordinates said with a chuckle. "If you're lookin' for a girl, we can tell you which streets to cruise in Happy Valley. But this ain't the place."

"A specific girl, I mean. She was in this area yesterday. I'm trying to find out why."

The leader shifted his stance and narrowed his eyes. "This girl got a name?"

The question gave Peter pause, but only for an instant. Kelly was dead. What harm could sharing her name do? "Kelly Alana. The rising freediving star, if you follow that sort of thing."

The name had meaning to them. The leader didn't show it, but the big one did, darting a glance at his boss.

"Don't know her," the leader said. "She go missin'?"

"She's dead."

The first tidbit he'd given them had triggered interest. The second—the fact that Kelly had died—triggered action. All three advanced, hemming Peter against the Cadillac. The leader cocked his head left and right, cracking his neck. "If you're here askin' 'bout a dead girl, I'd say that makes you some kind of cop or cop wannabe. And guessin' by that ain't-from-around-here accent, I'm favoring wannabe. It's time you bought us those drinks." He made a pointed glance toward the cantina. "Inside."

CHAPTER
TWENTY-NINE

Maui Central Baseyard

PETER HAD NO INTENTION of entering the cantina with his new friends, where he'd likely be surrounded by more—an Abu Sa'id dining with the Castilians. "As I said, I'm not a drinker. Thanks for your kind invitation, but I think I'll be on my way."

"It wasn't an invitation." The smaller of the two subordinates caught Peter's wrist. "He gave you an order."

Peter wheeled his forearm and cracked the young man's knuckles against the Cadillac's doorframe, causing him to let go. He cringed and raised both hands. "Sorry. Sorry about that. Pure instinct. No offense. Don't like to be grabbed, that's all."

The other two tightened the circle. "Don't like to be touched, eh?" their leader asked. "Then I'm afraid what's about to go down ain't gonna be too pleasant." He nodded to the bear, who gave Peter a look that said *It didn't have to be this way*, and grabbed the front of his shirt.

Peter whipped both hands up, striking the median nerve in both forearms of his attacker. The bear grunted and let go, then growled. A flurry of punches from all three followed.

Peter deflected most of the strikes with his raised arms, pulling his elbows close to protect his organs. But one painful shot made it through to his liver. In a regrettable counterattack, he struck the leader's nose with the base of his palm. He heard a *crack*.

"That's it!" The leader backed up, nose bleeding, and pulled a knife from his waistband. He flicked out the blade. "You're done."

A siren stopped his advance.

The leader shook his head at Peter and fled with his subordinates an instant before a black Toyota 4Runner with flashing grill lights skidded to a stop on the storage lot's gravel.

Detective Kealoha leapt out with her gun drawn, tracking the men with her aim. "Peter, are you hurt?"

"Not really."

"Too bad. Get in that ridiculous car and follow me. If you turn off or fall so much as two car lengths behind, I'll bury you so deep in a Maui detention center that you won't see daylight for weeks. Understand?"

"You're not going to chase them?"

"Shut up and get in the car!"

The detective led him to a shopping center three miles away and parked next to the dumpsters in the asphalt alley between a hardware store and a mega mart. She stormed over to the Cadillac and slapped the roof, not unlike the thug from a few minutes before. "Out, you! Out of the car!"

Peter cracked the door. "You seem upset. Perhaps we should drive around a bit more so you can calm down." He shot a glance at the dumpsters. "This isn't an ideal place to talk. I've been in cadaver labs that smelled better."

"*Get out!*"

He obeyed, hands up, but not so high she wouldn't be able to reach them if she wanted to cuff him. The detective was far from the tallest of women, and he'd have hated to upset her more by playing keepaway with his wrists.

"Put your hands down. This isn't an arrest."

"Whatever you say. But if that's true, would you mind putting your gun away?"

The detective followed his gaze and seemed surprised to see the weapon in her hand. She slipped it into a holster at her waistband. "What were you thinking?"

"You'll need to be more specific."

The tilt of her head gave him the impression she wanted to draw the gun again. "Driving out there. Following Kelly's trail. What was that supposed to be? A stakeout?" She looked past him to the Cadillac. "In that? And you claim to be brilliant?"

"This car was not my—" Peter winced. What was the point in explaining? "Never mind. Thank you for the rescue, however unnecessary. How did you know where I was?"

"I didn't. A tip from an FBI contact merged with information we gained from an attendant at the resort. But I'm guessing you talked to that same kid, because it's the only way you found your way out here."

Right. Tuna had said he'd make sure the young man passed on the message. "Well, your arrival was poorly timed. I was just beginning to get somewhere with those gentlemen."

The detective's jaw dropped. She took a couple of steps as if she might walk away, muttering under her breath, "Unbelievable," then turned to face him again. "Did you talk to those men about Kelly?"

"I might have mentioned her name."

"Of course you did. Why can't you let this go?"

"I . . ." Peter didn't want to explain—wasn't even sure he could. "I want to help. That's all."

"You're not helping, okay? Get it through your thick skull that you're not an investigator or a consultant, or whatever you think you are. I had the jump on a known thug with possible ties to this case. Now he's seen me coming. You've probably killed the best lead this investigation was ever going to get."

Peter puffed himself up, tired of being the subject of her accusations. "I killed the lead? Who found your thug first, hmm? I did. Without your FBI contact. *You're* the one who came flying in with siren wailing and let them get away."

He'd gone too far, and he knew it. Another Barbara of Seville moment. The shade the detective's cheeks turned, a deep red, strong enough to be visible behind her Polynesian complexion, confirmed it.

She poked him in the chest. "I let them get away because my primary responsibility was to keep you safe. You have no idea who those men are. I do. Had I pursued them, one or more could have doubled back to come after you. They would have killed you without a second thought."

"I can take care of myself."

"I don't have the luxury of making that assumption. I saw you punch the one in the Clippers jersey. By putting yourself in harm's way, you left me no choice. I had to let them go and remove you from danger." She showed him the badge clipped to her belt. "Every morning, the act of putting on this shield makes me accountable for the lives and safety of those around me. Every move I make will be judged if someone gets hurt or killed. Do you understand the weight of that kind of responsibility?"

"Do I understand the weight?" Nigel's voice in his head told Peter to be quiet. He saw Carol warning him to back down. He ignored them both. "I hold lives in my hands on a weekly—sometimes daily—basis to a level you can't begin to comprehend. I held Kelly's life in my hands. I knew every step required to save her. I knew every tissue to repair, every drug to administer, every vessel to stitch. But I couldn't do it." He balled his fists. "You want to know why I need to be part of this investigation? That weight is *crushing* me. Bringing Kelly's killer to justice is the only remaining thing I can do for her. You don't want to let me in? Fine. I'll keep at this without you. And I'll beat you to every clue the way I did today. So help me, Detective, I'll remain a thorn in your side until you have no choice but to lock me up."

They stared at each other for a long time, both red-faced and breathing hard, until the detective finally relaxed her posture and nodded. "Okay."

"Okay? Meaning you'll let me join you in the investigation?"

"Nope." She pulled a set of cuffs from behind her back and spun him around. "Okay, meaning I believe you when you say you won't stop. I'm skipping to the end and locking you up."

CHAPTER
THIRTY

Maui PD Criminal Investigative Division

"HE'S BRITISH." Jenny Fan sat on the edge of a small desk in the observation chamber next to the CID's primary interrogation room, scrunching her brow at the man handcuffed to the interview table on the other side of the one-way mirror. "And he's a doctor—the one who pulled Kelly from the water."

Lisa closed her eyes and nodded. "Correct." She knew where this was going.

"And you hauled him in because you think he killed her?"

"No. I hauled him in because he won't stop trying to help."

This bought her a slow nod. "Right. Too helpful. That must be one of those LA laws."

"I didn't say he was helpful. I said wouldn't stop trying to help. Thanks to him I lost our best suspect at the Central Baseyard."

"The Baseyard? You're kidding, right? You think heading over there in an unmarked and looking all coppish was going to get you anywhere?"

"I guess we'll never know. But I'm gonna make sure he doesn't do any more harm. The captain says I can keep him in there stewing for another three hours if I want. After that, I either have to let him go or book him."

Jenny hopped off the desk and opened the door for her. "Which will it be?"

"I haven't decided yet. Meanwhile, what did you discover about Jason Alana?"

Lisa had tasked Jenny with following up on Edena Alana's statement that her son was driving in from Hana a couple of days a week to work part-time at a big resort. Jenny had given her some pushback on the menial task, but when Lisa had threatened to give her Rivera's task of locating the sneezy kid from the freediving event, she'd relented.

"Dead end. He was at the Oceana, not the Grand." Jenny led Lisa back to her desk and showed her a work schedule for the Oceana's housekeeping staff from the evening of Kelly's death. Jason Alana had worked the late shift—a solid alibi.

"Why didn't he tell me about this job when I interviewed him?"

"Did you ask?"

"No. But my mom is the Oceana's head concierge, and she knows Jason well. It's weird she hasn't mentioned him."

"The Oceana has thousands of employees, Lisa. Late shift. Different department. Maybe Jason didn't want her to know."

That made sense. "Yeah. Sure. I guess that leaves us only one more lead to run down. Good thing it's our best lead."

"Kelly's key fob cloner?"

"Yeah."

Auto thieves had used devices like the one they'd found in Kelly's closet almost universally since the dawn of keyless entry. Plug one into the diagnostic port under the steering wheel of most modern cars, and you could program your own key fob. Fourteen seconds. That's all it took to smash a window, plug in the device, and clone a key fob. From that moment forward, the thief's key was as good as the owner's.

Clay's information had traced a crate of these devices, including the serial number on Kelly's device, to a local mom-and-pop garage over in the Waiehu Beach area.

"Mind if I run point?" Jenny asked. "I did find the device, after all."

Lisa appreciated the recent change in Jenny's demeanor—her helpfulness. But she had the uneasy feeling Jenny could turn on her at any moment. She didn't want to seem like a glory hog, but she had to keep her defenses up. "Maybe next time. No offense, but the soft touch isn't your specialty, and that's what we need here. I don't want to spook the garage owner. Nobody's in trouble. We just want information. That kind of thing. Got it?"

"You're the boss." Jenny gave her a thumbs-up.

WITH STUCCO SIDING and red-tiled roofs, the garage and the shopping center next door looked clean and upscale. "This close to the water, commercial rent has to be a killer," Jenny said as she and Lisa climbed out of the 4Runner. "Our guy must have a pretty hopping repair business."

"Or he's making up the difference with a side gig."

A digital bell rang as they entered, bringing a young man in a green golf shirt out from the back. The name embroidered on his chest read BRANDON. Lisa leaned her elbows on the counter, keeping her badge out of view. "Hi, Brandon. We'd like to talk to your manager, if we could."

The kid looked taken aback. "Is there something wrong? Something I could help with?"

"Nope. We just want to chat with him. Would you ask him to come out?"

"He's kinda busy."

Before Lisa could stop her, Jenny flashed her badge, waving it at the kid. "Hey. This is a police matter. Stop stalling and go get him before we charge you with obstruction."

So much for the soft approach. Lisa glanced from the waving badge to the security camera in the corner above them. Not good. There was no telling whose eyes were on the monitors.

From the garage, she heard the crash of a falling tool tray.

"Great. You spooked him." Lisa pointed at the door behind the counter. "Go for the garage. I'll take the outside."

The L-shaped footprint of the building forced her quarry to run past the entrance on the way to the street. Lisa came out the door right on his heels. "Stop! Police!"

Marco Lastra—owner and manager of Marco's Garage—wore a red golf shirt tucked into khaki shorts with his gut hanging over the beltline. Lisa felt like she was chasing the local Little League coach instead of a cog in a ring of auto thieves and killers. Big gut or not, the guy had some speed. She doubted he had the breath to keep it in gear.

She never got the chance to find out.

Jenny came out of a walkway between the Pizza Hut and the Party Zone and bodychecked Marco into a beat-up Nissan Frontier. He bounced off the hood and hit the asphalt facedown.

Lisa dropped a knee into the small of his back and slapped on a pair of cuffs. "What's the hurry, Marco?"

"Just out . . . for a jog," he said, puffing. "This . . . is assault." He turned his face to the side and tried to shout at the onlookers gathering across the street. "Police . . . bruta . . . brutal . . ."

"Oh, pipe down," Jenny said, not waiting for him to get the rest of it out.

Lisa grunted, hauling him up with Jenny's help. "Get your feet under you, Marco."

"You go boneless," Jenny whispered in his ear, "and I swear we'll let your face hit the curb."

Lisa gave her a look that said *What happened to the soft approach?*

They walked him back to his garage, and while Jenny read him his rights, Lisa did her best to act as a shield against the onlookers snapping pictures. But at her height, there was only so much she could do. They sat him down in a folding chair next to the maintenance pit.

Lisa dusted off her hands. Since Jenny had thrown the whole *take it easy* plan out the window, she went with it. She added a touch of growl to her voice. "Fess up, Marco. Why'd you run?"

"You know why."

"Oh," Jenny said, holding up the cloning device. "You mean this?"

The mechanic gave her a *duh* look. "I knew it was only a matter of time. You pulled it out of that poor girl's vehicle, right? Traced it back to my order?"

They hadn't pulled any useful tech out of Angelica Puelani's stolen Porsche. She must have ditched it when the chase began, before Lisa got close enough to see.

Lisa gave Jenny a subtle chin lift. They'd keep going—let him think that's where they found the device. "Go on."

"I swear I never meant for anyone to get hurt. Just needed some extra cash, ya know? Business has been slow, and this place isn't cheap."

"So you turned to a life of crime?"

"Crime? No. A guy came to me, offered a big payday for a crate of duplicators. I didn't ask questions. He coulda wanted them for anything. Tinkering. YouTubing. They're not illegal. I had no idea a girl was gonna turn up dead."

Jenny leaned in and bumped his gut with the device. "What guy? Who'd you sell this to if it wasn't Angelica Puelani?"

Or Kelly Alana, Lisa thought. She watched him squirm, holding back barely a second before she stomped her foot. "Give us a name!"

"Koa, alright? I sold the whole order to Koa Alana."

CHAPTER
THIRTY-ONE

Maui PD Criminal Investigative Division

ALL ROADS LED BACK TO KOA ALANA, Kelly's cousin. His appearance during the first car theft, his association with both Kelly and Angelica, Jason's testimony about him keeping Kelly in the life, and now Marco's claim that Koa bought the key fob duplicators. To any investigator, all these pieces added up to Koa being the killer. So how did Lisa's new suspect—the one who'd almost gutted her problem Brit—fit in? And could she envision Koa as a murderer?

Hardly. Koa and Kelly might have been cousins, but they had the strongest big brother/little sister bond Lisa had ever seen. It was the kind Jason had never achieved with her. Their relationship could have changed since Lisa left the island, but not that much.

She and Jenny left Marco trembling in his garage. They had no interest in the hassle of booking and charging him. He'd have plenty of questions to answer with his staff and the other business owners, probably enough to scare him straight. And just in case it wasn't, Lisa had made it clear she would reserve the right to come back and charge him.

When they returned to the station, Tuna met them in the lobby. He rose from a bench by the doors and followed them into the GTF section without the slightest invitation. "Lisa, dear. I'm told you're holding my client without charge. I'd like to see him."

"Your client?" Lisa looked to Jenny and inclined her head toward their desks, indicating she could handle the resort doctor on her own. "You're not a lawyer, Tuna."

"How do you know? I have lots of time on my hands these days. I mighta gotten my law degree online between treating coral scrapes and sunburns."

"Did you?"

"No."

She lifted a laptop from a charging station at the corner of the section and breezed past him on the way to the interrogation room. "Go home, Tuna. I'm busy."

"Oh, come on. Let Peter in. Don't you remember his insights on the beach? That black rock thing?"

"He pointed at the water, Tuna. And got lucky. And he drew the same medical conclusion that Mia did when she examined the body." She started to argue that the black orb the dive team had pulled from the silt might not have anything to do with Kelly's death. But then she stopped, pausing at the door to the observation chamber. How *had* Peter gotten information out of a resort attendant before the uniforms could? "It was you, Tuna. You're the one who put him up to it this morning—Dr. Chesterfield's little caper, driving out to the Baseyard and picking a fight. You helped him, didn't you?"

"Peter picked a fight? Is he okay? I should probably check him over."

"Don't change the subject."

"Yeah. Okay. I mighta encouraged him a bit—helped out with the staff. The guy is grieving, ya? Investigating Kelly's murder is therapeutic."

She held him with her glare.

"And did I mention he's really smart?"

"You don't have to. He mentions it all the time." Lisa pushed open the door. "Get in here and keep quiet. You can watch while I talk to him."

THE MORE PETER THOUGHT ABOUT IT, sitting alone for over an hour in the detective's interrogation room, the more he despised Nigel. He'd been right about the workaholic thing. He'd been right about Peter's inability to control his mouth. And now Peter's mouth had gotten him arrested. The I-told-you-so would be epic when Peter returned to London.

If he returned to London. By the end of the day, he might be out of a job.

The detective entered the room with a laptop under her arm that looked to be a decade old—a testament to the fact that American police departments were as poorly funded as the Metropolitan Police Service these days. She slid the interrogator's chair to the side of the table and sat closer to him, setting the laptop between them. "Hello again, Dr. Chesterfield."

"I've told you, please call me Peter."

"Okay, I will. But you should stick with Detective Kealoha."

"That's fair."

Before she could begin, Peter stopped her, raising a finger with a cuffed hand. "I must apologize. As my administrator at the Royal London recently noted, I have trouble controlling my tongue. I shouldn't have questioned your ability to empathize with my frustrations—especially since Tuna had already informed me that you knew Kelly well. I'm"—his jaw tightened in involuntary resistance to the next word—"I'm sorry."

The detective gave him a thoughtful nod. "That's progress. Maybe. Are you sorry because you were almost killed, because

I arrested you, or because you're actually sorry for interfering in my investigation when I specifically ordered you not to?"

He gave her a fleeting smile. "A bit of all three, I suppose."

"That'll have to do." She cleared her throat and opened the laptop. "On to the business at hand. Since you did choose to interject yourself into the case, you are now—once again—a witness."

"Not a prisoner?"

"Don't push it."

He lifted his hands as much as he could in resignation and watched her tap a few keys.

She turned the laptop so they could both see. A video window filled the screen, showing what appeared to be a dash cam. "This is what I saw as I drove up. You'll see it pause and jump occasionally because our techs have zoomed in and out to highlight the important parts. Watch, and try to understand how close you came to death."

The video started where the biggest of the three attackers had grabbed Peter's shirt. From the camera's viewpoint in the 4Runner—and thus the detective's—Peter could see how it looked as if the men might kill him at any moment. She let it play through the end, in which the three of them ran as the car skidded to a stop, sprinting up the street to vanish between a pair of prefab buildings.

"Did any of that make what you did look like a smart play?"

He chose not to answer that question directly. Most actions Peter took were, by definition, smart. "Again, I'm sorry. And yes, the camera's point of view does make me look foolish."

She eyed him, as if sussing out his subtext, then scrolled back the footage. "Now, let me make you look even worse." She pushed play at the cleanest shot of the attackers—the moment when the one in the Clippers jersey drew his knife. The video zoomed in, an artificial zoom added by her technicians, and she froze it with the leader enlarged at the center of the frame. "I want you to take a good look at this man. What do you see?"

"A thug. A killer. And a man almost a decade older than I am living life as a twisted child."

"I won't argue with you there, but let's get more specific." She drew a pen from her shirt pocket and pointed to the Clippers jersey. "Notice the blue-and-white color of his jersey and the number 18 on the front. Those are solid indicators that this man is part of Barrio 18, otherwise known as the 18th Street Gang."

Peter gave her a flat look. "Sounds like a boy band."

"Barrio 18 is a rival to MS 13 and one of the most dangerous criminal organizations in the world, known for extreme violence."

That cowed him. He should have known better than to challenge her at this stage. Peter lowered his chin in deference. "I see. Go on."

Next, she pointed to a pair of skulls tattooed on the man's left bicep. "These represent murders, probably assassinations of high-value targets in an opposing gang. They're on his arm because he attributes his rank in the organization to those accomplishments. The cat curled up below the skulls means he began his criminal career as a thief." She manually zoomed the image even more, focusing on a pixilated toy in the cat's paws. "You can't make them out in this video, but what you see here are the kind of dice you'd hang from a car's mirror, indicating a specialty in auto theft. Ask me how I know those are dice."

He already knew. The detective had mentioned an FBI tip merging with the attendant's information on Kelly's movements prior to her murder. Recent events at the Grand included a brazen auto theft, conducted at Kelly's freediving competition. Ergo, the FBI tip must have been an identification of this 18th Street Gang member who specialized in auto theft and dabbled in assassinations. The detective's contact must have told her that the gang member had moved to Maui and given her the Baseyard as a starting point. Peter said none of this. Instead, he played her game. "How do you know?"

"My FBI contact. He pulled this thug's name from a flagged event in the world's largest auto theft database. Luan Trejo. He recently moved to Maui, and he's brought all kinds of trouble with him."

As expected. Peter fought to keep a smug look off his face, but he couldn't stop his mouth from moving. "So, what you're saying is, you needed the FBI's help to do what I—"

She held up a warning hand. "Don't. Don't even think it. And now that we're back on the subject, let's go over your actions. What exactly did you say to those men?"

"Nothing I haven't told you, or that you haven't already surmised. I told them I was looking for information on a woman who had been there yesterday evening. They asked for a name. I gave them Kelly's. I saw a reaction out of the big one. A bear of a man. He looked to the leader, Trejo, as if he should react as well. And then—"

Peter halted his account. "Wait a moment. Am I being charged? Are you aware you failed to read me my rights?"

"I didn't fail to do anything. So far, I've been keeping this relaxed, that's all."

He wriggled his wrists. "Relaxed?"

Her frown flattened into something not quite a smile— perhaps a modicum of respect. "I'm glad you noticed I didn't read you your rights, though. That tells me you're not a complete idiot, in that absent-minded professor way."

"It's what I do. I notice what's missing or out of place, and I set it to rights."

"Then tell me what I'm missing from the video. How can you possibly believe you were going to survive that encounter?"

She was playing him, gathering information in whatever way she could as a good interrogator. Peter didn't fault her for it, and he was happy to show off. "Play the video again—the ending, please."

She did, and he had her pause it as the men sprinted away.

"Right there. They're running the wrong way."

The detective scrunched her brow. "How so?"

"When they approached my awful car"—he gave her a look acknowledging the Caddy was a gaudy mistake—"they came from the storage containers behind me."

"Okay. They ran away in a different direction. No big deal."

"But it is a big deal. You came in with lights and siren. The police. No question. The police carry guns and pride themselves on employing said guns with accuracy. Your thugs, by your own analysis of Trejo's tattoos, have extensive experience with the police and their guns, yet they chose to run toward cover that was much farther away." Peter sat back, pleased with himself until he attempted to cross his arms. He'd forgotten they were still chained to the table. He regained some dignity with a light snort. "Why would Trejo take such a risk? Hmm?"

A muted voice behind the room's mirror shouted. "Ha! Yes!"

Peter looked sidelong at his own reflection, then returned his gaze to the detective. "Is Tuna behind the mirror?"

She nodded.

"Glad to hear he didn't abandon me. As I was saying, your highly dangerous thug intentionally avoided his best chance at cover. He didn't want you pursuing him into that storage lot. Detective, there's something in those shipping containers he doesn't want you to see."

CHAPTER
THIRTY-TWO

Maui PD Criminal Investigative Division

"Jenny, call your jogging judge." Lisa hurried to her desk with the two doctors in tow, one of them rubbing his recently freed wrists. She tapped at her keyboard without sitting down. "Get me a warrant for . . . Baseyard Storage."

"That's original," Peter said.

Lisa glanced back at him. "It gets the message across."

Jenny picked up her desk phone. "It's a storage place. Which units do you want to open?"

"All of them."

"That's a tall order."

"Cite special circumstances. The search may implicate a suspected killer recently off parole." Lisa had recognized the name and face as soon as she'd opened Clay's file. Luan Trejo, aka *El Príncipe*. Trejo had been the righthand man to the 18th Street boss in South LA, Francisco Hernandez. For years, Trejo had waited in Hernandez's shadow, but his boss refused to retire. "Trejo was 18th Street's permanent prince of South LA," she said. "Looks like he got tired of waiting for the king to shuffle off and decided to claim a city for himself."

Mike had brought Trejo's file and photo up on the section's big-screen monitor. He read off a string of crimes. "Extortion, distribution of a controlled substance, manufacture of a controlled substance, auto theft, armed robbery, murder. Nothing stuck until they got him on a manufacturing and distribution charge. He only did four years."

Jenny had her desk phone against one ear, covering the mic. She gave Lisa a nod and removed her hand. "Thank you, Judge. You won't regret this. We're moving on it within the hour." She set the receiver in its base and opened an email that popped into her inbox. "Warrant's good. I have the digital copy."

"Good," Lisa said. "I'll bet you Trejo is the one driving the surge in criminal activity on Maui, not Koa Alana. And he's the kind of guy who'd rather humiliate and demoralize an opponent than kill him when he moves into new territory."

"You think Trejo killed Kelly to send Koa a message that this is his turf now?"

"Most likely. Or something similar. Either way. He's our killer. I'm sure of it."

Jenny lifted the warrant from the printer. "Then let's go get him."

HALF THE MAUI PD FLEET poured down the narrow funnel of the Baseyard's entry road, then split to weave their way through the jumbled streets and come at the storage lot and cantina from three directions. SRT's Bearcat was the first into the lot, in accordance with protocol, followed by Lisa in her 4Runner.

"Stay in the car, Peter," she said, pushing open the door before coming to a full stop. "I'll come get you when it's clear."

She'd sent Tuna back to the resort but had agreed on a temporary basis to let the Brit shadow her. He'd signed the release paperwork on the way. Lisa couldn't deny that he'd been helpful by coming up with the container lot lead, but she hoped his foul-up that morning hadn't scattered Trejo's crew to the four corners of the island.

Lisa and Jenny wore vests and goggles, but none of the bulkier gear worn by the SRT. The two kept close to the lieutenant and the two sergeants leading the charge.

As they ran in formation into the storage lot, an older Hawaiian in a stained undershirt came out of a tin shack waving his arms and shouting. A good way to get shot. The officer behind Lisa split off and pressed a gloved hand to the man's chest to press him back out of the way.

Many of the containers lay open and empty, with dust from the cane fields coating the insides. The SRT moved along a central alley between the rows, weapons panning the aisles on both sides. Satellite imagery showed a double line of containers with an aisle between them bordering the east edge of the Baseyard. The SRT's formation split when they reached the wall of corrugated steel formed by the inner line, intending to enter the aisle from both sides.

A heavy clang rang out. Lisa pushed ahead of her group. "Hurry!" She paused at the entrance to the aisle and peered around the corner while the lieutenant caught up.

Three men heaved a broad door closed on the long side of a container halfway down the line, causing another loud clang, then ran. Lisa looked to the lieutenant and motioned him around her, chopping the air with her hand. "Three tangos. On the run. Go! Go!"

The suspects had too great of a lead. Lisa and several SRT members bolted after them, shouting, "Stop! Police!" But the criminals kept running, probably experienced enough to know that the cops wouldn't shoot as long as they fled and showed no weapons.

Jenny and the rest of the SRT entered the aisle from the other end, and with the suspects running along the outer wall of containers, both teams hugged the inner—trained to create as much of an angle as possible to prevent a crossfire.

"Stop!" Lisa shouted again. "You've got nowhere to run."

But they did. The suspects reached a small gap between two of the containers and squeezed through. Lisa and the lieutenant reached it a moment later, but the SRT leader's bulky gear wouldn't fit. She pressed herself into the gap without him. Side-stepping between the rusted walls, she heard the almost musical hum of an electric motor spinning up. What were these guys driving? Teslas? And where did they plan to go? The force she'd brought had the Baseyard's only exit covered.

When she squeezed out into daylight again, she saw no sign of them. No suspects. No electric vehicle. Not even a road. She saw only Jenny, jogging toward her from another gap where she too had squeezed through. It looked like she'd gotten to the other side first.

"Did you see anything?" Lisa asked.

Jenny slowed to a walk, shaking her head and breathing hard, and the two stared down together at a dried-out concrete drainage ditch ten feet wide and six deep, the border between the Baseyard and the cane fields. No vehicle, electric or otherwise, could have crossed it.

Jenny looked up and down the length of the ditch, as if she expected to see the men crouched and hiding there. "I don't get it. Where'd they go?"

The two walked down the line together, looking into the spaces between every set of containers. Most were too tight for any human being to fit. All were empty except for the shielded faces of SRT officers staring back at them from the other side. The only other place that might have provided cover for the suspects was a natural irrigation gully that split two of the cane fields. Rusted iron grates covered the culverts where the gully intersected the concrete ditch. But if the suspects had been nimble enough, they might have traversed the deep ditch, climbed out the other side, and run into the heavy foliage surrounding the gully.

But, again, what had been the source of the electric motor Lisa heard? "Did you hear a vehicle?" she asked Jenny. "Like an electric car, maybe?"

"No. Sorry. I didn't hear a thing."

As the two rejoined the SRT in the aisle between the containers, Lisa saw that the lieutenant and his two sergeants had taken the tall Brit into custody. She hurried over. "He's with the department."

The lieutenant acknowledged her with a nod and a frown. "So he claims. Detective, this idiot came rushing up behind me and Sergeant Ogawa waving his arms. Almost got himself shot. Says he belongs to you."

"I wouldn't go that far, but I'll take him off your hands."

She pulled him away by the arm, having to dig her fingertips in to hang on because Peter's bicep had a lot more firmness than she'd expected from a doctor. "I told you to stay in the car."

"But there was dust."

"Dust? In the 4Runner? Are you seriously that much of a—"

"Not in your car." Peter pulled his arm free and pointed toward a patch of tall green acacias and monkeypod trees—the only part of the irrigation gully visible from that side of the containers. "There. I saw dust above those trees. Faint, probably filtered by the leaves, but it was there, I assure you. Would you really expect to see dust rising from such lush green when there's none rising out of the dead fields?"

Dust. Out of place.

For generations, the island's natural meandering gullies had carried runoff from Haleakala into the cane fields. The early growers had allowed vegetation to thicken around them, including the tall trees that later became protected. After that, the succession of owners couldn't chop the trees down to modernize the irrigation, so the ribbons of green remained, dividing the fields.

Dust from those trees meant a vehicle. Her electric car sound. "That's it. Our suspects escaped in a car or mule, driving under the cover of those trees along the gullies. And more of them might have driven something heavier away before we arrived." But what about the ten-foot-wide, six-foot-deep concrete ditch behind the containers? Nothing on four wheels could have crossed it. "They saw us coming, emptied the containers, and escaped into the fields. But how?"

CHAPTER
THIRTY-THREE

Maui Central Baseyard

WHILE DETECTIVE KEALOHA and the lieutenant from SRT worked on a plan to get police vehicles out to the fields and the gully for a search, Peter walked over to a container that had gained the attention of a small crowd of uniforms. The other detective, who had introduced herself earlier as Detective Fan, told him three suspects had been spotted closing it up before they fled.

The officers swung open the door on the container's broad side, and a dozen flashlights shone into the dark.

"Empty," Detective Fan said, kicking the corrugated steel. She shook her head and walked away.

Peter wasn't ready to give up so easily. He borrowed a flashlight from one of the uniforms and made an inspection of his own. Less than sixty seconds later, he discovered some baffling marks on the rear wall. "Detective Kealoha!" He ran out into the open. "Detective! Over here!"

When she joined him, Peter shined his light on the marks—black smudges, several of them. He drew his finger across one. "This is rubber. And look at the pattern."

The detective stood back, taking in the whole wall. "Those are tire marks."

"I agree. How do tire marks get onto the vertical wall of a shipping container?" He moved his beam along the seam between the rear wall and the ceiling until he came to the corner. A chain hung down, welded to the upper edge of the wall and passing through an eyelet bolted to the ceiling. It pooled in a series of coils on the floor. The other high corner of the rear wall had a matching chain. Peter and the detective exchanged a look, then pushed on the wall together.

Nothing happened.

The detective left the container and addressed a huge officer. "Pika."

"Yeah, Sis?"

This familiarity earned him a scowl, but the detective seemed to shake it off and continued. "I need to borrow you for a sec. Grab Ogawa too. Tell him to bring his lovie."

His lovie?

Listening to this exchange, Peter pictured the big SRT sergeant who'd almost shot him entering the container carrying a child's stuffed lamb or elephant. Instead, Sergeant Ogawa came in lugging a black two-handled battering ram. The one she'd called Pika, whose nametag identified him as a relative, most likely her brother, entered with him.

"You two." The detective pointed at them both with two fingers, then pointed to the rear wall of the container. "Ram. Wall. Go. Knock it down."

On a count of three, the officers smashed the ram into the steel. With that one shot, the wall fell back, in slow motion at first and then accelerating, rattling the chains through the eyelets until it slammed into the dirt. The twelve-foot wall formed a perfect bridge across the deep concrete ditch.

"And that's how they did it," the detective said. "Whatever Trejo was hiding here was gone before we arrived. The three we saw were just cleaning up." She flicked one of the chains, now taut. "The first bang we heard was this wall being pulled into place. They had their electric vehicle waiting in the trees, ready to go."

She paced back and forth on the makeshift bridge a couple of times, then walked out of the container.

Peter followed, watching her. The detective seemed to survey the scene, deep in thought, gaze drifting until it settled on four police cruisers that the uniforms had driven into the aisle between the containers.

He could see where her mind was going, perhaps as clearly as the detective herself. So, when she broke into a run, Peter stayed right beside her.

The detective ran to the closest police cruiser and jumped in, and Peter slid into the passenger seat beside her.

She frowned at him. "Out!"

"I know you intend to give chase. Your chances of catching them are slim, and growing slimmer the longer we argue."

"Fine. Get shot if you want. You signed the release." She hit the gas, causing both of their doors to swing closed, sped into the open container, and bounced across the steel bridge.

To the best Peter could tell, there was no road ahead of them. A short path of dirt extended from the bridge to the trees on their side of the gully. Dried-up cane stalks hemmed them in from the left. To their right, the dirt path narrowed as the gully foliage, as dense as any jungle, took over. But the detective kept the gas pedal pinned to the floor.

"You'll hit those trees."

"There has to be a road."

"There doesn't *have* to be a road. We suspect it exists. That's all." Peter grabbed the dashboard. "Slow down!"

She hit the green. Loose vines slapped the windshield and parted to reveal a dirt track, ten feet wide. This might have been a greater relief if their cruiser hadn't hit the track at a forty-five-degree angle.

"Watch the gully!"

"I see it." She cranked the wheel. The cruiser slid sideways onto the track.

Once the detective had them going straight again, Peter got the sense she had full control. Perhaps she'd had it the whole time. By the precision of her movements and the complete lack of fear, she might have been perfectly at home on a rally track. "You've done this before."

"Once or twice. Back in the day, I used to do a lot of . . . nontraditional driving."

"On tracks like this one? Hidden in the trees next to an irrigation gully?"

She laughed. "No. This wasn't here—at least, not that I know of, and I know most of Maui's secrets. This track is new."

"Then how could you be sure we wouldn't slam into a tree?"

"You didn't see the tire tracks?"

He hadn't. Score one for the detective. Peter would've smiled if the jostling of the road weren't so bad. The thieves had carved a ten-foot-wide path, twisting and turning with the natural gully. Stumps and orphaned roots at the edges showed where they'd cut out plenty of trees, but they left enough of a curtain on the outer side to hide their vehicles. Smart. It felt like barreling through the world's bumpiest green tunnel. "Like General Slim charging along the Irrawaddy in Burma. And he had Jeeps."

"What?"

"The road is rutted and intolerably bumpy." Peter clenched his teeth to keep them from clacking together. "Are you sure the vehicle can take this punishment?"

"These cruisers have modified suspension. She'll be fine."

"All the same, your SUV would have been a better choice."

She hit him with a glare. "Are you gonna be like this all the time?"

"Probably." He pointed at the road ahead. "The dust is growing thicker. We're closing in."

Seconds later, they saw the suspects' vehicle—not a Tesla but a Mustang Mach-E raised up on fat tires and covered in dirt. Peter guessed it had never left these hidden tracks—a smuggler's quiet workhorse. "You've almost got them. Speed up."

"Yeah. Because my foot isn't already flat on the floor."

"Then shoot out their tires."

The look she gave him said something to the effect of *You've got to be kidding me.* "You think I can shoot and drive a track like this at the same time? You think anyone can?"

"I suppose not." He considered options, then gave her a confident nod. "Give me the gun. I'll do it."

The gully made a sharp bend to the right. Lisa drifted through the curve. "You're out of your mind."

"I was a military man for a time. Scored well in marksmanship—both in pistols and rifles."

"How long's it been?"

"Seven years."

She waited, as if she knew his answer wasn't entirely accurate.

Peter let out a huff. "Seven and a half. Eight since I fired a weapon."

"Forget it. Not gonna happen."

The gully turned back to the left, but the track didn't turn with it. The Mustang dropped out of sight in a billowing cloud of dust, and when the detective throttled in after them, Peter felt air beneath the car. The track had gone down into the gully.

The impact with the bottom of the great dip felt hard enough to break the cruiser in two—and possibly Peter's back. Neither broke that he could tell, but soft dirt at the bottom slowed them down. The cruiser dug itself too deep and lost too much momentum to make it up the other side. It rolled backward.

Showing her rally skills, the detective turned in her seat and used the rearward momentum to drive the car up and out for another try. On the second attempt she made it. But the Mustang was long gone. She drove onward, perhaps a hundred meters, and came to a broad swath of dirt and intersecting tracks where three of the gullies met. The thieves had built a series of dipping bridges supported by culverts. Try as they might, neither Peter nor the detective could tell which road the Mustang had taken.

She slapped the wheel with both hands. "We lost them."

"But we've found their system. These roads will lead us to their hideouts, right?"

"Hideouts?" She hit him with a sardonic glare. "This isn't a Hardy Boys novel. These gullies run all over the island, feeding thousands and thousands of acres of cane fields and extending into the jungle gulches on both volcanic mountain ranges. We could search them for weeks without result. And meanwhile, Trejo could be moving or dismantling his operation. I realize you're out of your depth here, but I need you to understand that this is far worse than a killer and his crew getting away."

"Worse?" She was right. Peter was out of his depth. He didn't understand. "How is it worse?"

The detective turned the cruiser around in the intersection of the three tracks and headed back toward the Baseyard. "Trejo is a gang lord, Peter—a ranking member of one of the most violent criminal organizations on the planet. By raiding his storage area with my task force and failing to catch him, I might have just started a war."

CHAPTER
THIRTY-FOUR

Maui Central Baseyard

BY THE TIME LISA RETURNED to the storage lot with her shadow, SRT had packed up to leave, and the uniforms had opened nearly twenty of the converted containers. With blue nitrile gloves in place, they rummaged through trunks, boxes, and garbage bags. Jenny, with Pika and another officer on either side of her, had the manager cornered next to his shack, practically pinned against its tin wall.

"She sure does like the heavy approach."

Peter chuckled. "Compensation for her size, I'd say. Not that I can blame her. In your business, someone of her small stature probably has no choice but to come on strong."

"True enough." Lisa had experienced plenty of that problem herself, and she had a good three inches on Jenny.

"The man she's interrogating—I saw him this morning. He stared me down as I entered this complex. He may be the one who brought my presence to Trejo's attention."

"That Cadillac brought your presence to everyone's attention."

As they approached, she saw the manager shaking his head

at Jenny. "Like I told you before, he paid cash. No name. No records. And he paid in full for six months. I only saw him once."

Jenny tapped a line in her notebook with her pen. "For the six containers at the back? No others?"

"No others, I swear. You already asked me that."

"I know. Just making sure." She made a check mark on the next line. "You got security cameras?"

"You joking?"

"Right. Never mind."

Pika took a couple of steps back from Jenny and the manager and quietly gave Lisa the rundown. Jenny had pulled plenty of information from the guy, who seemed to want no trouble with the police. The uniforms had opened up the five other containers identified by the manager as having been rented by the same man as the one with the false back. And all five were just as empty.

"How many others were cash only?" Peter asked.

Pika glanced at Lisa, and she nodded for him to answer.

"Don't know. The manager didn't say."

"I suggest you find out. Your gang lord could have easily rented more containers using different operatives."

He was right. Lisa walked past her brother and interrupted Jenny to ask the manager Peter's question. He didn't seem to like it. His pupils shifted from her to Jenny and back. "Who are you?"

Lisa inclined her head toward Jenny. "I'm her boss, and this is my investigation. Answer the question."

"I gotta check my records, ya?"

"Do it."

He came back with a green cardstock file folder covered in coffee and juice stains and who knew what else.

Before he could open it, Lisa took it from his hands. "Thanks." She flipped through the pages, some of which she had to peel apart. There were plenty of names and phone numbers—payments made, number of months rented—but nothing that indicated any of his customers were paying by any digital service. "These are all cash."

"Yeah." The manager scratched the back of his head. "That's kinda my thing. Guess I forgot to mention it."

She slapped the folder into Pika's chest. "Go tell your buddies to open these. In fact, open 'em all, even if they're not on this list. Open every container."

The manager took a step toward her, stopped by a forceful hand from one of her officers. "You can't do that."

"I've got a warrant says I can. Give me any more trouble, and I'll haul you in for obstruction." She turned to her brother, who hadn't left to carry out her orders. "Why are you still standing here?"

"Call Mom. She's been trying to reach you all day."

"Mom can wait."

He gave her an *It's your funeral* shrug and set off.

Once Pika had gone, Peter signaled her to speak with him off to the side. "That manager would have lied to you about the cash-only containers if you hadn't taken the folder from his hands." He said this as if it ought to be some big revelation for her. Cute.

Lisa nodded. "Way ahead of you."

"Then you know he also lied about knowing who cut a false back out of one of his containers."

"I do." Her doctor showed decent instincts. Lisa decided to test them some more. "My next move is to return to that exact line of questioning. Do you know why?"

Peter shook his head. "Pointless. He'll only lie again."

Decent instincts, but still an amateur. "I caught him trying to deceive me about being a cash-only operation. That means he might be dodging taxes, licensing fees—all sorts of low-level crime. Our manager is nervous. Shaken. So, now I'll get specific, and when he lies, it'll be obvious. Every false statement will take me closer to the truth."

Lisa returned to the manager, holding up her borrowed department phone with Trejo's mugshot displayed on the screen. "Help me out. Is this the guy who paid cash for the containers?"

The manager's jaw tightened. He rubbed his stubble, studying the photo too long. "Mm. Don't think so. Yeah. Nope. I'm pretty sure that ain't him."

By Peter's poorly hidden amusement, she could see he'd noticed the manager's array of positives, negatives, and in-betweens. A deception. Maybe Trejo hadn't physically handed over the cash, and maybe he had. Either way, the manager definitely knew Trejo was involved.

Lisa swiped the screen to bring up a picture of one of Trejo's associates, taken from her dash cam footage. "What about this guy?"

The manager gave her a similar hemming and hawing response. Two for two and totally predictable. But what about her wild card? She swiped to an old mugshot of Koa.

The manager's posture straightened. "That's the one."

"This one?"

"Yeah, he's the guy. No doubt."

No deception.

The manager looked like a kid playing the old Memory card game, finally seeing the one card he knew. "That guy paid me the cash for the six units at the back. I remember. Serious moke. No way was I gonna say no."

Lisa had expected a blank look or a hemming, hawing response that matched the first two. The former would have pushed Koa to the back of her suspect list. The latter would have confirmed he'd joined forces with Trejo. What was she supposed to make of this?

She left Jenny to supervise the search of the containers and returned to the 4Runner with Peter.

"Back to the station?" he asked as they buckled in.

"*I'm* going back to the station. You're going back to the Grand. And you'll stay there."

"Right. Naturally." He was quiet for a time as she pulled out of the lot, then cleared his throat. "Would you mind dropping me at the dumpsters instead, so I can pick up my luxury vehicle?"

His luxury vehicle? She checked his face and caught him grinning.

"Cute. Of course I'm taking you to your Cadillac. You sure you want it back? I could always have it towed away and impounded."

He laughed. "I never had the opportunity to explain my choice, did I? For your information, it *wasn't* my choice. I ordered an economy car. The rental company brought me that cherry-red monstrosity as an unrequested upgrade. I'll have them exchange it this evening."

"Don't bother. Welcome to Maui in June. The economy cars were all booked months ago. Mercedes, Cadillacs, and Corvettes are all they have left. Classic haole mistake."

When they reached the shopping center where they'd left his car, Peter asked her to stay a moment. He dipped his head into the Caddy's back seat and emerged with a gift bag. He brought it to her side of the 4Runner.

She rolled down the window. "What is that?"

"A gift, Detective. I purchased it this morning."

"You bought a get-out-of-jail-free card? In law enforcement, we call that a bribe."

"Not a bribe. An olive branch—something I thought you'd need since I'd run into the same problem."

Lisa pushed the bag away. "I can't accept gifts from people involved in my investigations."

"I'm not a suspect anymore, am I?"

No reason to keep pretending on that front. Lisa shook her head.

"Good." He thrust the bag through the window again. "Please, Detective. Take it. But don't open it now. I've never been good at watching people open gifts."

She let out a sigh and accepted. The bag had some weight to it—a particular feel. "Tell me you didn't."

"Like I said, open it later. And don't even think about giving it back. I'm sure that's as much of a faux pax in America as it is in the UK." He gave her one of his fleeting *My accent is attractive, and I know it* smiles and walked back to his car, giving her no more chance to argue.

CHAPTER
THIRTY-FIVE

Maui PD Criminal Investigative Division

LISA HAD PLANNED ON OPENING the gift bag as soon as she got to her desk, but when she arrived at the GTF section, she saw Mike drawing on her murder board. She dropped the bag in her chair and rushed over. "What are you doing?"

He glanced over his shoulder, black marker still in contact with the board. "I'm adding evidence to your evidence display." He put the finishing touches on what appeared to be a molecular formula—a series of hexagons and pentagons joined by lines and nodes to form something like a soccer ball. "See? Evidence."

To Lisa it looked more like the beginnings of a chemistry lecture. She held out an open palm. "Give me the marker."

"I wasn't actually done."

"Mike, we've never worked a murder case together before, so I'm going to give you a pass. But nobody touches my board. Nobody. So, the marker"—she curled her fingers in a *Give it here* motion—"please."

Mike started to comply, but pulled it away and hurriedly drew a question mark at the center of his formula. Then he capped the marker and surrendered it. "There. Now I'm done. Won't happen again. Do you like it?"

"I won't know if I like it unless you tell me what it is."

He seemed surprised she didn't recognize his drawing. "It's a buckyball."

"Say again?"

"A buckminsterfullerene, named after the guy who made geodesic domes popular. It's a ball-shaped molecule made up of sixty carbon atoms." Mike gestured at his drawing and wrinkled his brow at her. "You know. A buckyball. You've never heard of a buckyball?"

Lisa was also getting the sense that Mike just liked saying the word *buckyball*. But in the three weeks she'd known him, he'd never let her down, nor wasted her time—too much—so she took a calming breath. "Humor me. Why are buckyballs important to this case?"

"Ah." He raised both index fingers. "I'm glad you asked. Carbon takes many forms, not just graphite and diamonds. Most are super rare or lab-created only. Compressed buckyballs are one of these." Mike cupped his hands and made an exaggerated squeezing motion. "Squish a buckyball at crazy high pressure, and you can make a material that's harder than diamonds. That's what I think the scuba team pulled out of the silt where your doctor found Kelly Alana—an object made of buckyball carbon molecules."

"You think?"

"Think? Yes. Can I confirm it?" He shrugged. "No. Not with our equipment. The object is too hard to grind out or cut a test sample, even with our diamond-coated tools. But someone *did* cut it, and they cut it into the shape of a buckyball molecule. That has to be intentional."

Lisa studied the formula with new interest. "So, it's not some tourist trinket. The object is unique."

"Likely priceless—and maybe local too. A while back, some

Swiss scientists predicted ultra-hard carbon might be found on Maui. They called it Elysium." He glanced at Wailea on the section's wall map. "Take the tour over at the Grand. The guide does a whole spiel on the stuff. Harry Alcott was obsessed with it."

"Harry Alcott, huh?" Lisa pictured him where she'd last seen him, seated on the platform at the freediving competition with the island's rich new darling, Jack Carlisle. The object had been found at the Grand. Could it be some lost treasure of Alcott's, unrelated to her case? She nudged Mike out of the way and wrote *Alcott's obsession* next to his chemical formula.

"Whoa," Mike said. "Did I just make Mr. Alcott a suspect?"

"I'm only making a note. Keeping everything straight. How do we get confirmation the material is what you think it is?"

"I have to send it over to the state forensics lab on the Big Island. But if I'm right, the thing is so rare as to make the odds of it being found at the murder scene minuscule—next to impossible."

"Unless Kelly or her killer dropped it."

He nodded.

Lisa let her gaze drift over each of the items she'd written or posted on the board—Kelly holding her mermaid monofin, times and dates of the two accidents at the Grand, the remains of the stolen Benz sitting on the forensic lab's flatbed, the acid used in meth production that Mike had found under the destroyed bleachers, mugshots of Trejo and Koa, and finally, Mike's molecule with the name of the Grand's owner right next to it. What did LA gangs, meth labs, and auto thieves have to do with resort owners and superhard carbon?

"What on earth is going on?"

"Don't know, Boss. That's your department. I collect, identify, and catalog the pieces. You're the one who has to put them together."

"I don't think I have enough of those pieces. Go get me some more. Head out to the Baseyard and monitor the evidence collection with Detective Fan."

"You got it."

As Mike dutifully walked away, Lisa sent a text to Clay asking him to look into Harry Alcott and his friend Jack Carlisle—best to cover all her angles. Then she returned to her desk. With so much information broiling in her mind, she almost sat on the blue paper bag Peter had given her.

She frowned at the bag, set it on the desk, and sat down. Part of her didn't want to open it. Opening a gift from her problem Brit came with a slight sense of opening Pandora's box. Once she knew what the gift was, could she return it? Could she close the door of familiarity that it opened between them?

A long stare at the bag failed to reveal its contents. Finally, Lisa tugged at the white ribbon holding the paper handles together and reached inside. She closed her eyes the moment she felt the object and saw herself in the shopping center parking lot. *Tell me you didn't.* "You did," she said out loud.

Lisa withdrew a brand-new smartphone, still in its shiny white box. The latest model. It might have cost him a small fortune, but maybe that was nothing to a neurosurgeon.

Before caution and reason could change her mind, Lisa cut the shrink-wrap with a letter opener and sliced through a silver seal. No going back now.

The phone had plenty of charge, and the screen-by-screen directions made it easy for her to connect with her provider and restore her contacts and most important apps.

She hadn't quite finished the process when a rapid string of text messages popped up.

Mom
Call me.

Mom
Where are you?

Mia
Your girl was in the cane fields.

Mom
Big news about dinner. Why haven't you called
me?

Ikaia
Mom's trying to call you. She set you up. I'll
understand if you disappear to the mainland
again.

Set me up?

Her mom could wait. Lisa called Mia first. "What girl?
Which cane fields?"

"Well, hello to you too. Where you been?"

"Baseyard. SRT raid. Car chase on a secret dirt smuggling
road."

"So, the usual?"

Lisa laughed. "What've you got for me?"

"It's Kelly," Mia said, her tone growing somber. "The water
removed a lot of evidence, but the blood of her head wound pre-
served some soil particulates. And I found matching particulates
in the blood she left on the doctor's clothes."

"You mean Peter?"

"Oh." The smile returned to Mia's voice. "You two are on a
first-name basis now?"

"Only on my side. Don't start. Tell me about the particulates."

"Maui has seven different soil types. The samples I found on
Kelly and on the doctor's clothes have a pH that indicates mol-
lisol, which covers the central portion of the island."

Lisa glanced toward the wall map. "You mean the valley cane
fields. Like the fields around the Baseyard."

"Exactly. And a few fibers of decomposing cane stalk confirmed it. The fact that the samples were trapped in the blood
on her head tells me she acquired them at the same time as her
wound."

179

"So Kelly goes out to that cantina in the Baseyard to meet with Trejo or one of his boys. Then she—"

"Stop," Mia said. "Why is she meeting with these dangerous Barrio 18 guys?"

"The scuba tanks. We suspect Kelly knew about their auto theft operation. She and Angelica were friends, and Kelly cared about her. I saw it when I questioned her. Maybe she threatened to expose Trejo. The tanks were a warning to back off. Kelly, still the same girl she was at age ten, answers with defiance. She goes out to the Baseyard to tell Trejo off, and that earns her a trip out into the cane fields, where she takes a blow to the head or is shoved down and hits a rock. How does that sound?"

"Not bad. But if Trejo is your guy, why didn't he finish the job out in the field?"

A good question. A guy like Trejo would know several methods to dispose of a body. Grabbing a shovel and burying her deep in the cane field would have topped the list. Leaving her half alive and dumping her off the beach of the most expensive resort on the island didn't get anywhere near the list. "You're messing with my conclusions, Mia."

"Just passing the info."

"Yeah. You and Mike. Good work. I'll let this simmer and hopefully it'll make more sense later. Meanwhile, I've got to call my mom. She's been trying to reach me all day."

"What for?"

"I'm afraid to ask. If I send you a text tonight, call me. I might need to make another late-evening autopsy escape." Lisa hung up with Mia, took a breath, and dialed again.

"Mom? What does Ikaia mean when he says you set me up?"

CHAPTER
THIRTY-SIX

The Elysium Grand

PETER COULDN'T REMEMBER the last time he'd napped in the middle of the day—probably sometime early in his residency. After a necessary shower and a cold plate from room service, sleep had come easy and fast. He had no less weight on his mind than before, but by allowing him to join her, the detective had lightened the burden on his shoulders. They were sharing it now—their search for some kind of postmortem healing for Kelly.

His body woke him when it was good and ready. And once the fog of sleep cleared, Peter's mind felt sharper than it had since Kelly died. Or so he thought, until his new mobile rang. Then things went pear shaped and weird.

"I need you to come to dinner tonight. At my mom's place."

Peter rubbed his eyes, fighting to gain the clarity he'd had a moment before. The voice belonged to the detective, he was sure. But her words made no sense. "What?"

"Dinner. Tonight. My mom's place." There was a pause, and a slapping sound, like a palm hitting a face. "I'm sorry. Did you have plans?"

"No. I didn't have . . . How did you get my number? I only bought this mobile this morning."

"And you bought this one too. Thank you, by the way. But your number is the same as it was on your old phone, and I'm a detective. It really wasn't that hard." Another pause. "So, where do we stand on dinner?"

"How bad is your mother's cooking that you need to bring your own doctor?"

"I told her I was bringing a colleague home, someone visiting the island. Long story. No time for it now. Are you in or out?"

"Yes. Yes of course, Detective. The Cadillac and I would be glad to attend."

"Thank you. Be there in an hour. I'll text you the address. And call me Lisa."

"All right, then. Lisa. Excellent. Thank you."

That was progress. Another barrier overcome. Or was it? He'd begun to sense dinner would come with a show, and he was the show.

"Um . . . Lisa . . . Am I just calling you by your given name for tonight or is that a—"

She hung up.

A moment later a text alert chimed. An address appeared on his screen.

PETER ARRIVED AT THE ADDRESS precisely one hour after Lisa's text. The Cadillac's navigation system identified the Wailuku neighborhood as Happy Valley, which he couldn't help but remember had been the area where Mr. Trejo's friend had told him he might find a *demimonde* for the evening.

The house looked well-kempt—one and a half stories with yellow painted siding. Peter parked on the street, because a food truck had taken up the driveway. "This will be interesting."

A woman, not Detective Lisa but older and a little plumper

with Detective-Lisa-esque qualities, met him at the door. "Welcome. *E komo mai.* Please, come in. You must be Dr. Peter, the colleague, ya?" She made air quotes when she said *colleague*, and stepped aside to allow him in. "Not bad. Not bad. And you're British, right? I love a British accent. Say something."

Say something? Peter had never done well with new people, especially women, even discounting his arrest by Lisa and the slap on the face he'd received from that Welsh woman. "Um . . . Hello?" Peter gave her his best awkward visiting-stranger smile and searched the home behind her for Lisa. He found her hurrying down the stairs from the upper floor, as if rushing in to stop a mugging.

"Mom, leave him alone. I didn't ask him here to entertain you."

The big officer who'd wielded the battering ram at the Baseyard appeared from what Peter guessed to be the kitchen. "Too bad, ya? We could use some entertainment 'round here." He offered Peter a hand. "I'm Pika, Brah. Welcome. We met before, but my sis was too busy bein' important to introduce us."

Family dinners—where rocks and hard places converge to crush unsuspecting guests like the Swedes crushed the Saxons at Fraustadt. How was Peter supposed to respond to Pika's jab at Lisa? Should he take the brother's side? *Oh, yes. Your detective sister is indeed obsessed with her own rank and importance. Good show.* Or should he take Lisa's? *Not at all. Lisa kept her focus on the mission at hand. As one in a junior position, you should strive to emulate her.*

Peter intended to use some form of the latter, but what came out was a quiet tittering laugh and, "Not at all, not at all."

Brilliant.

Lisa ushered him into the family's small dining room, made all the more cramped by the size of her brothers. Peter almost fell over with shock when the second one entered from the outside, carrying a platter of grilled fruit. "Is that the last one," he whispered to Lisa, "or is there another climbing down a beanstalk somewhere?"

Thankfully, the larger brother either did not hear him or ignored him. He set the platter on a mismatched pair of knit potholders. "First round of appetizers. Watch the pineapple. The juice'll be lava hot." On his way back to the door, he offered a giant fist for Peter to bump. "Ikaia. Welcome."

"Peter. Glad to be here." He hoped the *Please don't eat me* came across in his subtext.

Lisa's mother took her time with the prayer at the start of the meal and used none of the liturgy he'd expect from his Anglican acquaintances. The words she spoke did not make him feel awkward. But the holding of hands did. At the start of it, Lisa carried his hand under the table and let go, but her mother held on with the immobilizing consistency of a surgical clamp.

She patted his arm when it was over. "Good man. The last one Lisa brought home couldn't handle a little prayerful hand-holding. His fingers got all sweaty."

"Mom," Lisa said. "I didn't *bring him home*. Peter drove himself, and he's a colleague. He's helping with my case."

"If that's all, then why couldn't Jaxon join us?"

Peter turned from mother to daughter. "Jaxon?"

Lisa said nothing.

Her mother answered for her. "The young man I wanted her to meet. My friend Lucy's boy. Very nice."

"Lawyer," Pika added with a nod and a raised eyebrow at his sister. "Not sure how a doctor stacks up against him, ya? A little higher. A little lower. Does this one get bonus points for being English?"

Ikaia took a bite of a braised rib and dabbed his lips with a napkin. "Mom moves fast, Peter. Tonight was supposed to be Lisa and Jaxon's first date."

"I'm so sorry." Peter set his roll down and looked to Lisa—a hard look. "I had no idea." The timing and nature of her call began to make sense. He narrowed his eyes and tried to burn a message into her reddening cheeks. *I don't appreciate being used as a decoy.*

"There was no date with Jaxon," Lisa said, avoiding his glare. "And Peter is also not a date. He's never been to the island. I thought he could use a home-cooked meal." She stabbed a shrimp with her fork. "No dates, Mom. Got it? I'm deep into investigating Kelly's death, so this is not a good time for me to be distracted by your efforts to fix me up."

Her mother shrugged and muttered, "There'll always be a case. If you want to find the man God has in store for you, you'll have to make room in your life for him. And playing long-distance phone tag with Clay doesn't count."

"The old boyfriend," Ikaia said, as if Peter had asked.

"FBI agent." Pika reached across the table and lifted a bowl of a purplish bean or root mash that Peter had not yet tried. "We can all agree that stacks below lawyer *and* doctor, ya? We're pretty sure it's over, anyway, but Lisa won't say."

Rock. Hard place. Fraustadt. How many Saxons had been slaughtered?

Peter knew for certain that Lisa didn't want him to hear any of this. He would have made more of an effort to change the subject, but he dared not cross her mother or her brothers.

Lisa took care of the subject change for him. "Mom, Peter is the one who pulled Kelly out of the water."

"Then you should bring him to church on Sunday. Our class— the Single Again Life Group—would love to hear your story."

"You mean the story of how I failed to save the girl?" It came out more caustic than Peter had intended. He tried to recover. "Actually, I'm not much good at church. I'm an atheist."

"I see." The hand with the surgical clamp grip returned to his forearm. "So, how are you dealing with Kelly's loss? It's not easy, is it?"

Could she see into his head? He found himself answering,

the words slipping right past the wall he meant to put up. "No. It isn't."

"I get it. I mean, I'm no doctor, but when I lost my Kai in the mill fire, I dropped into a deep depression. I beat myself to pieces coming up with ways I could have saved him. What if I'd encouraged him to speak up more about safety problems at work? What if I'd begged him to take a few days off? I got lost in what-ifs. But with help, I learned to let go of the illusion that I was in control." She pointed toward the sky. "I had to acknowledge that someone else is in charge, and give it all to Him."

Someone else is in charge. The phrase hit Peter's mind from two angles. He chose to focus on the one that was easier to face. He turned to Lisa. "Someone else is in charge. Your other suspect—Koa Alana. Didn't you speculate Mr. Trejo might have bullied him out of control of Maui's criminal society?"

Lisa glanced past him to her mother, almost as if asking permission to move on from a discussion of her father's death. She seemed to receive the permission she sought. "That's right. Why?"

"And finding Koa will help your case?"

"We've had a BOLO out on him since the auto theft, two days before Kelly's death. So far, we've had no luck. Peter, what are you getting at?"

"You've been searching for Koa under the idea that he's hiding from the police. I think he's hiding from the new man in charge. And no offense, but Mr. Trejo is a lot scarier than you are—much more so to Mr. Alana after Kelly's death."

Lisa eyed him. "I'm not following. How does the person he's hiding from make a difference?"

"If I were a criminal, hiding from you and the rest of the Maui police, I might be out in deeper reaches of the island's jungle. But if I were afraid a gang lord was out to kill me, I wouldn't be hiding on the island at all. I wouldn't be hiding on any of them."

CHAPTER
THIRTY-SEVEN

Maui PD Criminal Investigative Division

LISA HAD MIKE MEET HER and Peter at the CID to make use of their direct connection to the world's leading marine ship tracker.

"We don't have boats," Mike told her, wielding multiple remote controls to turn on the CID's network system and the gang task force section's 86-inch monitor.

"So you've said. Don't worry about it. My brother Pika knows a guy." Lisa bobbled her head. "He probably knows twelve, and hopefully one of them will lend us the boat tonight."

A digital globe came up on the display, and Mike zoomed in on Hawaii. "SeaSight AIS data is the best on the planet next to the US Navy's. If your boy is floating out there between the islands, we'll see him. We may not know it's Koa Alana we're looking at, but we'll see his dot for sure. This thing shows every boat on the water."

"We'll know," Peter said, surprising her with the confidence in his tone. The arrogant neurosurgeon had disappeared after the failed Baseyard search, displaced by someone who seemed off centered by a law enforcement operation and completely baffled by a family dinner. Now he was back. "Look in the waters close to Maui."

She couldn't argue. Koa would avoid the other inhabited islands. He'd know better than to try and sneak onto another primary island or Molokai, especially after what had happened to Kelly's brother Jason. But how had a doctor come to that conclusion? "How do you figure, Peter?"

"The Royal Navy is not unfamiliar with marine drug interdiction, even the medical branch—coastal radars, registration requirements, and so on. I expect an unregistered vessel staying close to its island of origin won't garner a second look. But visiting another island or even coming close to one of their shores without making radio contact might look like a smuggling operation and draw too much attention."

He'd nailed it—almost. "Agreed, with one caveat." Lisa used Mike's remote to enlarge the area around a small and barren island off Maui's southwest point. "If you're right about him going offshore, Koa might hang out in the water northwest of Kahoolawe. Calm seas, uninhabited island. No one will bother him as long as he doesn't land."

"If it's uninhabited," Peter said, "why would it matter if he lands?"

"Kahoolawe used to be a US Navy bombing range. It still has tons of unexploded ordnance. And the area that's been cleared is now a biological preserve. Without special authorization, it's off-limits." The map resolved into imagery of the island and the water. Digital motion effects applied to the surf gave it the look of real-time video from a military satellite.

Pink, green, and blue icons began to populate the screen. There weren't too many. Maui didn't see near as much commercial and private traffic as Oahu. And most of the tracks had names and flags next to them. Only one track, a pink dot less than three miles northwest of Kahoolawe and going nowhere, had a generic tag. UNREGISTERED PLEASURE CRAFT.

Lisa touched the pink dot to bring up its coordinates and history. It hadn't moved more than a hundred yards in twenty-four hours. "This is Koa. No one parks a boat off of Kahoolawe that long. There's nothing to see."

"What do we do now?" Mike asked.

"You stay here and call Jenny's judge for a warrant. He won't argue, it's pretty normal for warrants to come one right after another when the pieces of a murder case begin to fall into place. We"—Lisa ran a pointing finger back and forth between herself and Peter—"are gonna go get Koa. Right now."

PETER KEPT AN EYE on his side view mirror as Lisa drove them to the marina. The same bluish headlights had been with them since they'd left the CID, always two or three cars back. "Lisa, I . . ." The vehicle signaled and took a right on a side street—a dark-colored sedan.

She glanced over at him. "What?"

"Nothing. I think your statement earlier about a war made me paranoid. I'm seeing things."

"We call it the rookie itch. They see crimes everywhere they look for the first month out of the academy. Everything makes the hair on the back of their necks stand up. I went through it too, but you can't. I need to be able to trust your eyes tonight. Finding a set of coordinates on a map is one thing—"

"But finding a boat on the water is quite another," he said, finishing the statement for her. "Yes, I know. Especially when the pilot doesn't want to be found." Peter watched her for a moment, gauging her mood. "Lisa?"

"Yeah?"

"Your mother mentioned a fire at the mill. I don't want to pry, but Tuna said something similar and related it to you and Kelly."

"That history has no bearing on this case."

Peter didn't believe her denial for a moment. A doctor at

the Royal London would need an exceptional reason to gain permission to operate on an old friend. And the same psychological factors that might put a surgeon's performance at risk must have some impact on a detective trying to solve a friend or family member's murder. In fact, Peter imagined they'd have a greater impact. A surgeon trying to save a friend worked under the pressure of hope. In a murder case, hope had passed, leaving nothing to drive the detective but grief and anger.

A block later, Lisa drew a long breath. "Cane leaves are nature's rocket fuel. Have you ever heard that?"

When Peter shook his head, she grunted. "Well, that's what my dad used to say. Carbon, hydrogen, oxygen. It's all there. Wilted cane leaves burn hot and fast, while the stalks protect the juice. Burning them saves millions in annual labor and machinery costs."

"You're saying the industry burns their fields on purpose?"

She caught his eye and nodded. "Pre-harvest. If you want to know what Elijah's chariots of fire looked like, watch a Maui cane field burn while the wind charges down the central valley. That's how it was the day he died."

Lisa set her attention on a stoplight. After it turned green, she drove on but stayed quiet.

"You don't have to continue," Peter said.

"I know. But it's okay. I want you to hear this. I turned thirteen a few days before it happened, so this was a while ago. In those days, the crews used pickup trucks and propane torches to start the burns. No fancy machinery. No big safety plan. Three pairs of senior crewmen would go out and check the stalks at twelve points in the field to make sure the whole sector was ripe. Once they reported a good crop and all clear, the foreman would release the trucks to light it up." She clenched her teeth, as if struggling to maintain control. "At the trial, he swore he heard the call."

"Your father. Kelly's father. They were still out there when the foreman sent the trucks out with the torches, weren't they?"

"All six of the crewmen checking the stalks were still out when the burn started. Forty-mile-per-hour winds. Cane leaves going up like rocket fuel. Chariots of fire. They were taken up."

What could Peter say? "I'm sorry."

She sniffed—not the sniffle of a whimper, but a hard sniff. "When six close families are made fatherless in one day, the chance of trouble for the kids is high, especially when the community doesn't know who to blame."

"I can imagine."

"Can you? This island has strange dynamics, Peter. Superstition and anger are a bad mix. It drove us together, with Koa as the leader of the pack. I lost myself for years—my brothers too. And all that time, my mother prayed. With her help, my brothers found a place in our church youth programs. But not me. I fled to California. I had to hit rock bottom on the LA streets before I found a new Father. He'd been waiting for me the whole time."

Peter didn't understand. What father? A mentor? A teacher? Some kind cop who helped her join the LA police?

Before he could ask, Lisa's phone rang. The caller ID on the 4Runner's screen said CLAY.

"Who's Clay?"

"My . . . FBI contact." Lisa made what seemed an unnecessarily hurried scramble for a Bluetooth earpiece on the center console and missed, accepting the call via the vehicle's audio system instead. The greeting from her contact was less than professional.

"Hey."

Peter raised an eyebrow at Lisa.

She gave him a fleeting smile. "Hi, Clay. How's the FBI?"

Did the caller feel as much awkwardness as Peter?

By the tentativeness in his reply, Peter guessed that he did. "Um . . . fine. I guess. I have that information you requested. Alcott and Carlisle."

Lisa pulled into a lot with a sign that read MAALAEA HARBOR MARINA and parked. She kept the engine running. "Go ahead."

"I'm afraid it's not much. Alcott is your typical everybody-loves-him rich guy. A real John Hammond type."

"John Hammond brought back the dinosaurs that ate half the characters in every movie."

The caller laughed. "Good point. But Alcott's clean. No dinosaurs yet."

"And Carlisle?"

"Alcott's and Carlisle's lives intersected at a hospitality conference. Alcott was a keynote speaker. Carlisle Beef was listed as a vendor. I can't say for sure if they met there. Carlisle is an interesting guy. A few months ago, he survived a wreck that killed his dad and his CFO. Took it as some kind of life-is-short lesson. He sold his dad's company from his hospital room. Ranch, cows, and all. That's when he started making inquiries about Maui and contacted Alcott."

"Anything illegal?"

"Nada. Alcott gave him some help, but nothing untoward."

"Got it. Clay, I have to go. I'm following up on a lead with a consultant." Peter felt like she added too much emphasis to *with a consultant*.

The caller didn't seem to notice. "Oh. Good deal. I'll call if I learn anything else. And Lisa?"

"Yeah?"

"If it didn't come across in our last conversation, I just wanted to say . . . I miss you."

Her eyes widened. Peter read mild panic in them.

"I miss you too. Gotta go." She ended the call.

"Do you have such a close relationship with all your inter-agency contacts?"

Lisa pointed to a pickup entering the marina parking lot. "There's Pika. Time to go to work."

CHAPTER
THIRTY-EIGHT

Maalaea Harbor Marina

"GIVE ME YOUR PHONE."

Peter crossed his arms. "Who's Clay? Friend? Mentor? More than that?"

"None of your business, Dr. Consultant." Lisa held out an open palm. "Pika's waiting. Give me your phone."

"Didn't I already give you one?"

"Funny. I don't have a waterproof bag on me, and it'll get pretty wet out there. Would you rather suffer through another cloud respawn later or leave your phone safe and dry in the glove compartment with mine?"

As Lisa locked up the 4Runner, Pika slid out of his pickup. He showed off a single key, dangling by its ring from a foam keychain the shape of a surfboard. "Aloha, Sis. Shen says if you scratch his boat, he'll sue the department into oblivion."

She tried to take the key, but her brother snatched it away and held it above his head. "No way. I'm driving. Shen's rules."

"Shen doesn't get to make the rules." She punched him in the gut, causing him to lower his hand, and then pried the key away. "I'll drive."

In that moment, Peter realized his earlier fears of playing keepaway with his wrists had been for naught. Had he tried, she would have punched him too.

Pika coughed and frowned at his sister. "Fine. But I'm coming, ya? You need backup, and no offense to the doc, but he don't count."

"He *doesn't* count."

Peter shot her a glance. "Thanks. Nice to know where I stand."

"You know what I mean. And don't tell me you didn't want to correct him too."

After lifting a Maui PD duffel bag from the back of Lisa's vehicle, Pika led them to an old and dented blue runabout with a bow console.

Lisa muttered under her breath as she untied the bow mooring line. "Scratch his boat. We'll be lucky if it doesn't sink."

"We could always take your boat," Pika said, climbing into the boat after Peter.

"I don't have a boat," Lisa said.

"Exactly."

Peter hardly heard their banter. Movement at the opposite end of the marina had drawn his attention—in the shadows beneath a burnt-out dock lamp. "Did you see that?"

"See what, Brah?" Pika asked, following his gaze.

Whatever the creature was, whether an animal or a figment of his imagination, it had gone.

The big Hawaiian shook his head. "I don't seen nothin'. But we have a stray cat problem on this island. Close to half a million. And folks who leave food and bait in their boats don't help."

Lisa hopped in and slapped Peter's arm with the back of her hand. "Leave the cats alone and get focused." She cranked the engine. "Play this right, and tonight you'll be part of your first arrest as a consultant for the Maui CID."

While Lisa piloted the boat out to sea, Pika dug into the

big duffel bag. He produced a dark blue vest and handed it to Peter. He raised his voice over the boat's twin outboard engines. "That's Kevlar with hard plates in front and back. Put it on. Keep it on. Pretty good at stoppin' bullets. Pretty bad as a life vest."

"Not a problem. I'm an excellent swimmer."

"Shoots, Brah."

Peter held a hand to his ear. "What?"

"It means good deal. Great." Pika passed a vest to his sister, then put on a much larger version. After that he returned to pulling equipment out of the duffel—radios, a bullhorn, spotlights, flares—making it look like a police version of Mary Poppins's magic carpetbag. As if to mimic the famous Poppins hat stand, the last item he drew out was a long-barreled shotgun. "Mossberg 500 with copper slugs," he said. "This'll put a hole in a boat as big as your head at a hundred fifty yards."

"You plan to sink him?"

"Nah, Doc. But it's nice to have the option."

Peter wouldn't have minded having some options of his own. "Do you have a weapon in there for me? Nothing fancy, but some method of self-defense might be appropriate in case your suspect brought friends on his boat trip."

"A weapon for you, eh?" Pika cast a glance at his sister, whose eyes were on the water ahead. With the engine noise, Peter doubted she could hear them.

After a few seconds, Pika pursed his lips and nodded. "Yeah. Sure. I got somethin' right up your alley." He rummaged around in the duffel and produced a large knife with a black nylon sheath. "Here ya go. She's a little bigger than those scalpels you're used to, so don't stab yourself, ya?"

Peter shot him an annoyed frown, but he accepted the knife. Better something than nothing. He fixed the sheath to his belt and tied its tip around his thigh. "Thanks."

"Don't you worry 'bout Koa, Doc. We go way back. He won't hurt me or Lisa, or anyone with us. We're 'ohana."

'Ohana. Family, as Tuna had said. Lisa and Kelly, even this criminal they were after, they were all family of a sort—the sort with strong bonds. "You're . . . um . . . 'ohana because of the fire your mother spoke of. Is that correct? That tragedy brought you all together."

Despite the motors, Peter felt a quiet descend over the boat. Pika let the shotgun rest against his shoulder and narrowed one eye. "You been talkin' to my sis?"

"She told me what happened. Yes."

"Did she tell you two o' those men were brothers? Both Alanas. That family used to own thousands of acres of those cane fields before the mill bought everyone out—including the one where they died. The whole island decided Kelly, Jason, and Koa were cursed because their fathers sold out. Me, Lisa, and Ikaia, and the keiki from the other families all got lumped in with 'em. A bunch of cursed kids. We had nobody but each other to lean on."

"But now you're on opposite sides of the law. What made the difference?"

The big man shrugged, making the shotgun bounce. "A mother's prayers." He walked up to the wheel to stand next to his sister.

After another twenty minutes bounding over the low chop, Lisa idled the engines. Pika retrieved three night-vision scopes from his bag of goodies and passed them out.

"He should be ten degrees left of our bow," Lisa said, showing Peter a handheld GPS display. A blue dot on the screen marked the coordinates they'd taken from SeaSight. "About a quarter mile out."

"You think we'll see him this far out?" Pika asked.

Peter raised a hand. "Got him." He had the scope pinned to his eye, locked on a black form bobbing on the horizon. "He's keeping it dark. No lights. Looks like a small trawler, but I can't say for sure at this distance." From his naval days, he knew better than to look away and check the boat's compass. Instead, he oriented his body to face their target and thrust out an arm. "There's your heading, Lisa. What now?"

"Now we hope he doesn't see us coming before we get close enough to catch him."

Pika crawled out onto the bow deck and let Peter help him center Koa's boat in a scope. "Got it, Doc. You relax your eye and take a seat, now. Don't want you fallin' over when Sis gives this thing some throttle."

He needn't have worried. Lisa left one engine at idle and eased the other one up no more than a quarter. "The ocean will mask some motor noise, but not all," she said, "especially these clunkers."

With the tide against them, Peter wondered if they were moving at all. But the next time he raised his scope to give Pika a break, they'd cut the distance by half. He caught himself slouching down into his seat until the scope was level with the windscreen. Pika's promise that Koa wouldn't harm them didn't mean much if Koa couldn't tell who was in the boat. If he spotted the runabout before they announced themselves, he might think one of Trejo's people had come to kill him and take a preemptive shot. But there was no gunfire—only the sound of engines coming to life.

"He's running!" Lisa said, pushing both throttles to the maximum.

The rocking motion of the boat lurching forward almost cost Peter his visual lock on their target. "A little warning next time, please. Come right twenty degrees to intercept. Pika, can you pick him up?"

Lisa's brother had fixed the night vision scope to his shotgun. "I see him. But it ain't easy keepin' track of him in the dark with this chop. Sis, how about a light?"

"No lights," Peter said, blindly waving her off. "Not yet." He'd barked the order in his surgeon voice. A mistake. He didn't have to look at Lisa to know he'd earned himself a glare. "Sorry. I realize I'm not a law enforcement professional, but I do have some training in tactical operations on the water, both in theory and practice. Reflections off the waves could wash out the scopes. Best not to use the spotlight until we're sure we can follow without them."

Koa may have had a two-hundred-yard lead, but by choosing to hide on a livable boat, he'd sacrificed the option of speed. Shen's beat-up old runabout had no trouble eating up the distance. On the way, Lisa pressed the spotlight into Peter's free hand and guided his finger to the switch. "You made a good argument, so you make the call. Warn us before you flip the light on."

"Right. No problem." He waited until they were within three boat lengths, and then did as she asked. "Scopes down. Here comes the light."

Without the hazy glow of the night vision and the magnification of the scope, the trawler seemed to shrink. But it was a decent-size vessel, with a long salon-style pilothouse. If Koa had brought any of his crew with him, they'd have plenty of cover from which to defend themselves.

The thought brought a lesson from Peter's Navy days to his mind. What had that crusty warrant officer told him? *During a night boarding action, Sir, give the light to your bravest man. And if not the bravest, the dumbest. Because the man holding the light is the biggest target.*

Lisa brought the runabout alongside the trawler and shouted into a megaphone. "Police! Cut your engines! Give it up, Koa!"

Peter shined the light into the pilothouse. The figure at the wheel raised a hand in their direction.

"Gun!" Pika shouted, and fired the Mossberg.

CHAPTER
THIRTY-NINE

Two Miles off Kahoolawe

PIKA'S COPPER SLUG obliterated the pilothouse window, and the figure went down. The trawler veered hard to port, away from the runabout.

Lisa followed, cutting across Koa's wake to the inside of the turn. She prayed the engagement's one and only shot had been fired. Peter, to his credit, had kept his light steady on their target, a good way to get hit if Koa shot back.

She shouted into the megaphone again. "Cut your engine now, or we'll cut it for you!"

"You're assuming he's still breathing," Peter said. "Could anyone survive a blast like that?"

"I had no choice." Pika pumped the shotgun. "Family or not, he raised his weapon." He seated the Mossberg against his shoulder again and aimed low on the trawler's hull near its center. "You want me to stop him, Sis?"

"Do it."

He fired, cycled the action, and fired again. The trawler coughed and slowed. Smoke filled the pilothouse and poured from the broken window.

Koa Alana came sputtering out with a gun held high in his left hand, blood dripping from his right. He threw the gun into the water. "Don't shoot! I'm unarmed!"

"YOU DIDN'T HAVE to shoot me, Cuz."

Lisa cuffed her prisoner and sat him on the runabout's bench. "I didn't. Pika shot you. And in the future, if you don't want the police to shoot at you, don't point a gun in our direction."

She'd sent Pika over to secure the trawler. With its engine off, the smoke had stopped, giving no sign of a fire. The big diesel simply hadn't taken kindly to the pair of copper slugs Pika had lodged in its workings. Lisa had also ordered him to radio the Coast Guard and let them know they'd need to send a ship out to tow the derelict vessel in. The runabout was quick, but it didn't have the power for that kind of work.

"Whatever," Koa said. "I didn't know it was you. Coulda been real police. Coulda been someone else."

Coulda been real police. Who did he think she was? Lisa let it go. "By someone else, do you mean Luan Trejo? El Príncipe?"

He looked away, turning his attention to Peter, who'd quietly identified himself as a doctor and begun treating Koa's arm. "Tell her to quit playing around, Doc. Tell her to get this rust bucket moving, preferably to the Big Island. I need a good hospital."

"You need a good bandage." Peter wrapped gauze around Koa's bicep. "The slug grazed you. Barely broke the skin." He finished the dressing with tape and patted the wound—harder than Lisa might have expected from someone who'd taken the Hippocratic oath. "You'll be fine. Now quit whinging and answer the detective's question."

"Detective." Koa let out a huff. "You'll always be little Lisa Kealoha to me."

"Say what you want. I own you now. Resisting arrest. Conspiracy to commit auto theft. Maybe I'll add the murder of your cousin too."

"That wasn't me. Just like those stands in Wailea, ya? And those boosted cars. And Angelica. None of it was me and you know it."

Angelica. Koa hadn't said *that girl* or *Angelica Puelani.* The way he'd said her first name was too familiar. He knew her. Koa had just confirmed the connection from the MetaHive posts and connected himself to the auto theft ring. Lisa kept him talking. "No? I'm not so sure. You see, every time I turn over a stone in this case, I find some mention of Koa Alana—at Marco's Garage, at the storage site in the Baseyard. Every time, your name or your face comes up. Why is that?"

"It's what Trejo wants, ya? He set me up. He took over my crews. Pushed me out. And then he forced me to be his front man."

"How?" Peter asked.

Lisa gave him a look that said *Don't interrogate my prisoner,* but then nodded for Koa to answer the question. She got one name in answer.

"Kelly."

"Explain."

"You know Kelly. She had that wild streak—lived life like one of her diving competitions. Spent most of her time on the surface, but every so often she'd hold her breath and dive deep into the dark. Just for a visit. For the thrill."

Lisa crossed her arms, looking down her nose at him. "You're saying she tried to walk that line with Trejo?"

"I got word she'd offered to do a boost for him. Found him at his place near Twin Falls. Can you believe that girl?" He laughed, and then the smile fled, and his voice tightened. "She went lookin' for the devil and found him. Soon as I found out, I warned her off, ya? Put my foot down. No way I was gonna let Trejo get his hand around her throat the way he had it around Angelica's."

Fear. Mia's autopsy had told them Angelica had been living in fear. "What do you mean when you say Trejo had his hand around Angelica's throat?"

"Don't act like you don't know. That's why she ran the barricade—got herself killed. Can't say why Angelica joined up with Trejo, but once she became his favorite, she had no way out." Koa took his eyes away from Lisa's. "I don't know what he did to that girl. Don't want to know. But he told her if she tried to leave him, so much as got herself arrested, he'd kill her mom, ya? That's how Trejo rolls."

Peter caught Lisa's eye—a request for permission. She gave him a nod, and he shifted his gaze to Koa. "You placed your throat in Trejo's grip in place of Kelly's, is that it? You offered yourself up to keep Kelly from becoming Angelica?"

Koa snorted. "Not exactly, Doc. When I warned Kelly off, Trejo saw it as a weakness. From then on, he owned me. Kelly was his free-roaming hostage, like Angelica's mom. He said if I didn't play, he'd hurt her, frame her, kill her—I wouldn't know which till it was too late."

"So, what changed?" Lisa asked.

"She did, Cuz. When I put my foot down, Kelly told me she was plannin' to ditch the job anyway. She didn't like Trejo's big-money game. Said it was wrong. She was gonna rat him out." He raised an eyebrow at the skeptical look Lisa gave him. "What? Don't believe me 'cause she didn't say nothin' when you went to see her? Like I said before. You a big scary cop now. Kelly couldn't build up her nerve, and that was fine with me. I told her to keep her mouth shut."

Kelly couldn't build up her nerve. Lisa kept her expression still and stern, but inside she crumpled. A girl she had carried in her arms had been afraid to come to her. Lisa had found grace, and should have been reflecting that grace, but she'd become a frightening figure to Kelly. Had the hard façade she put up as a detective cost her the chance to save Kelly's life?

"Lisa." Peter leaned over the console, squinting out at the waves off the bow. "Where'd your brother put those night vision scopes? Something's out there."

The rookie itch. "Not now, Peter."

Koa had mentioned Trejo's big-money operations. Meth, maybe? Was that where Kelly had drawn the line? Lisa could relate. And if word had gotten back to Trejo that Kelly planned to give him up, Lisa would have solid motive to write on her murder board. "Let's get back to the collapsing stands."

"Don't know. But I'd say it was a warning, Cuz. The boosted cars were a bonus. Trejo works all the angles all the time. It shook Kelly up, the way he went after her fans, but she still planned on talkin'."

"Lisa, I'm not imagining this." Peter had found a scope. He held it fixed on a point on the black surface a good distance from the boat. "I think I'm looking at a . . . No. It can't be."

"I said, not now." Lisa was so close to having everything she needed to wrap this up—except for having Trejo in custody, and with a murder charge backing the manhunt, she could remedy that soon enough. "Koa, can you confirm Trejo knew Kelly planned to talk? Did you hear her tell him or one of his people she wanted to come forward about his meth operation?"

"Meth? Who said anything about meth? Oh, Cuz. This is so much bigger than drugs and boosted cars. Trejo's got—"

"Look out!"

Peter rushed at her, arms wide for a tackle. The impact of his body lifted her airborne, and the two went flying together over the stern. The boat exploded behind them.

CHAPTER
FORTY

THE HEAT AND ROAR of the blast gave way to cool water and rushing silence. Pain flooded Peter's skull, but he held his awareness enough to remember he needed to let go of Lisa. She pushed away from him and disappeared in the blur.

Fire burned above the swirling blue, like lanterns behind stained glass. He knew the right answer for the situation from his long-ago naval training—like knowing a procedure from a surgical textbook. But putting knowledge into action was something else entirely. Get clear. Surface. Breathe. Kick. Now.

His legs didn't move.

The pain.

A hand gripped his shoulder. Lisa? Peter managed to catch his rescuer's forearm and felt a soft layer of neoprene. A wet suit.

The person spun him around and he came face-to-face with a shifting ghost. He took the misshapen head to be that of a diver in a scuba mask. Though, with the regulator and hoses, it also gave him the impression of some evil half-squid creature.

The monster kept its hold on his shoulder and thrust its other arm at his sternum. Peter heard a muted *click*, felt the jarring impact of steel on steel—a knife tip breaking against the plate in his bullet-proof vest.

Air.

Breathe.

Kick.

Can't breathe. Can't kick.

The creature had tried to stab him in the chest. It wouldn't make the same mistake twice. Next time, it would go for his neck. It did, but Peter's hand was waiting and caught its wrist. He wrenched it over. Had the knife fallen free? He couldn't tell. Looking up, he saw the blue stained glass of the surface and the lanterns behind it seemed farther away than before.

Peter clawed at the sea monster's mask, regulator, anything. But it dodged him, and so he devoted both hands to its wrist and the knife that might or might not be there. A knife that either was or wasn't because he couldn't observe it.

Schrödinger's *knife*. Peter felt like laughing.

Air.

Breathe.

Kick.

Can't breathe. Can't kick.

His head and lungs screamed.

Peter knew of one knife he could observe, at least by feel. A practical blade would outmatch the creature's theoretical blade. He risked letting go of the wrist with one hand and drew the knife Pika had given him from its sheath.

The creature saw. Stupid mask. Unfair advantage. The creature grabbed Peter's wrist, and the two slowly spiraled.

The lanterns above were so far away. They rushed apart as the stained glass shattered, broken by another dark creature diving straight for Peter. He couldn't fend off another one. He only had two arms and the one nontheoretical knife.

Air.
Breathe.
Kick.
Peter couldn't kick. There was no air.
This was the end.
His mouth opened on its own. The sea poured in.

CHAPTER
FORTY-ONE

Maui Memorial Medical Center

LISA HATED HOSPITAL GOWNS. Feeling the rough, overused linen against her skin took her back to her worst days, back to big mistakes and bruised cheeks. A hospital gown meant too much exposure. It meant uncomfortable questions from a nurse and an inevitable visit from the cops, none of whom seemed to care if she lived or died—none except Clay.

The weight of the knock at her door told her it was Pika.

"Give me a sec." She hadn't worn the gown a second longer than necessary. She finished buttoning the jeans he'd delivered earlier and opened the door. "Hey."

"Hey, yourself, Sis. You okay?"

"I'm fine. The tests were just a precaution."

"You know that's not what I meant."

"Yeah. I know." Lisa backed up and sat on the bed, lowering her gaze. "Peter tried to warn me. I should have listened. If I'd had two more seconds, I could have . . ."

"You could have what, Sis?"

"I could have saved him."

Pika sat beside her, his weight depressing the mattress so

much she fell against him. Lisa didn't mind. She let him put his arm around her. He squeezed her shoulder. "You don't know that. For all you know, walking to the front of the boat to get a look mighta put you in a worse spot—given you less time. And don't give up. The docs are still working."

"Tuna said the chances were slim."

"Yeah." Pika gave her a smile that didn't fool her, and sure didn't seem to fool him. "A slim chance is better than no chance every day o' the week."

A white coat appeared in the door's narrow window, and an empty gray feeling hit Lisa's chest before the lever even moved.

The look on the surgeon's face left no doubt. Tuna, entering behind him, looked equally defeated. "I'm sorry," the surgeon said. "We did all we could. He's gone."

Lisa buried her head in her brother's shoulder, where she could feel the shuddering in his chest. She didn't sob. Her tears were quiet, held inside like Pika's. They'd known Koa most of their lives. For years, he'd been the boy father who stepped into their dad's shoes and the shoes of five other dads—a void he wasn't capable of filling and was never meant to. She straightened, wiping her eyes. "I could have done more. I should have."

Pika gave her a frown. "We just talked about this, ya?"

"Not tonight. I mean before. I didn't speak to him for years, didn't ask about him. And when I finally did hunt him down, it was for an interrogation. The same with Kelly. We were 'ohana because we had no one else. But when I found a new family in Christ, I didn't do anything to invite them along."

Tuna thanked the surgeon and released him, then walked closer to the bed where she sat with Pika. "I treated Koa's boo-boos the same as I treated yours. But his wounds grew progressively more serious each time until the day I retired. Cuts from a broken window became stab wounds. The same wrist that broke in a fall, broke years later when he beat some poor boy down. I'm not blaming him, but Koa was rushing toward this moment no matter how hard I or anyone else tried to turn his path."

"I could have tried."

"We both could," Pika said.

The doctor didn't argue. "I know this is a difficult time and a crushing loss. But I do have some good news. Our friend Peter is awake and alert and self-diagnosing up a storm. I hear he's already ordered a couple of tests." Tuna centered his gaze on Lisa. "You'd better go and get control before he takes full command of the residents."

"But I don't like Jell-O, green or otherwise."

The nurse raised a flat hand as she departed, leaving the jiggling green mass on Peter's tray where she'd set it moments before. Apparently being a surgeon-slash-patient was an invitation for a terrible bedside manner.

Peter realized that some of the fault might lie with him. The pain of breathing had made him disagreeable. But still. Jell-O?

As soon as the door clicked closed, it opened again.

Peter held out the Jell-O cup. "Oh good, you've reconsidered. Now if you wouldn't mind—"

Not a nurse. He set the cup down. "Hello, Detective."

She'd come alone. No bandages that he could see. Tuna had given him a glowing report, but he'd needed to see for himself. Peter breathed a sigh of relief. He hadn't realized how much he'd needed to see her. What did that mean?

Lisa gave him a smile. "Detective? Are we back to formalities, or have you lost a full day of memory?"

"Sorry. Lisa." He slid the Jell-O toward her. "Want some?"

"No thank you."

"It'll only go to waste."

"I'm okay with that." She set his new mobile down next to the Jell-O. "I brought you this."

"Thanks. Mobile giving is becoming a sort of tradition with us, eh?" He tried to laugh and winced. "Ouch. I'll be hurting for a while, I suppose."

"You should know. You're the doctor. Peter, what *do* you remember?"

He remembered a great deal, but he knew some of it was a terrible fiction from the nightmares that came after the water flooded his lungs—black memories of writhing monsters. At least, he hoped it was fiction. "I remember the explosion. Stinging thumps against my back. The fire. A diver dragged me down. I remember a knife." Peter crinkled his brow. "Perhaps two knives. That part's a bit fuzzy. I sank a long way. And then I saw a second man—a big one—and I knew I was done for."

Done for. Lights out.

The end?

All Peter's medical knowledge, even his Royal Navy training, couldn't have saved him. In that moment, all control over his fate had been stripped away, the way his control over Kelly's fate had been stripped away.

Lisa picked up the Jell-O and dropped it in the hazardous waste bin beside his bed, plastic spoon and all. "The big guy you saw was Pika. He tore your attacker's mask off and pulled you up—said you were so deep that the two of you might have broken all of Kelly's freediving records."

"And the attacker?"

"Pika didn't waste time going after him. He knew you were in trouble. You weren't breathing when he got you to the surface, even after we got the water out."

Not breathing. Tuna hadn't mentioned that part. Peter narrowed his eyes. "Which one of you did mouth to mouth?"

She walked to the end of the bed. He had to wonder if she'd used the maneuver to hide a smile.

"What about you?" he asked. "Where did you go after we fell in?"

"You mean after you tackled me off the boat?"

Peter started to protest, but Lisa held up a hand. "Thank you, by the way. You saved my life. And then Pika saved it again by taking a shot at the man who tried to drag me down."

"There were two divers."

She nodded. "Pika was the X-factor. If he'd have been on the runabout with us, either the explosion or the divers would have killed us all. But he was still on the trawler, going through Koa's stuff for evidence."

Lisa rubbed the back of her neck, exposing a bruise. So, she hadn't come out of it unscathed. "After we went in, I pushed away and surfaced clear of the fire, close to the trawler. A diver caught my ankle and tried to drag me down, but Pika was right there with the Mossberg. One shot, and the guy let go."

"Did your brother kill him?"

"Don't know. In the dark, with the fire, shooting through the surface. He couldn't see if he'd hit the guy, and we couldn't tell if there was blood in the water. All I know is that no body surfaced. Then Pika grabbed a mask he'd seen while going through the pilothouse cabinets and dove in to find you. He says he saw you almost instantly. And not long after we pulled you out, the Coast Guard arrived. Both of those factors beat some dim odds, Peter." She paused for a few heartbeats, then shrugged one shoulder. "You should think about that."

He knew what she meant. But he didn't want to think about it—not right now, in the bright light of a hospital room with clean sheets and green Jell-O to reject if he chose. "Pika showed great presence of mind to remember the mask and great calm to use it with such effectiveness. The shotgun is one thing, but to realize in that moment that a scuba mask meant the difference between life and death? He's an exceptional officer."

"I know."

"Have you told him?"

Peter gathered from the way her hands slid into the pockets

of her jeans that she hadn't. He didn't press. They were both avoiding the important lessons. What a pair they made. "And Koa?"

She shook her head.

"I'm sorry. Not to be crass about it, but I'm sure you know you've lost more than an old acquaintance. He was your big witness against Trejo. We're back to square one, as it were."

Her eyes came up to meet his, no longer the eyes of Pika's sister or Koa's old friend. Peter saw only the detective.

"We lost a witness," she said. "But we haven't lost the case. I now have two murders, the assault and attempted murder of a civilian, the assault and attempted murder of two police officers, and enough circumstantial evidence to pin it all on one known 18th Street felon." Lisa returned to his side and rested a hand on his bedrail. "You're about to see what a former LA cop can do when she lights a fire under a sleepy island PD with one of the highest officer/citizen ratios in the nation."

CHAPTER
FORTY-TWO

Maui PD Criminal Investigative Division

LISA'S MURDER BOARD FILLED UP FAST once she returned to the CID the next morning. Her timeline had few numbers, but it had plenty of events.

According to Koa, after Trejo muscled him out of his territory, Kelly had gone to the gang lord to ask for an auto theft job. Koa had stepped in to protect her, unwittingly making Kelly a greater target and a *free-roaming hostage*, as he had put it. But Kelly had seen something she didn't like in Trejo's operation. Lisa made a tick through her line and labeled it with the words *Kelly visits Trejo, big money*, and a question mark. She heard Koa's voice in her head.

Meth? Who said anything about meth? . . . This is so much bigger than drugs and boosted cars.

Whatever Kelly had seen, she'd threatened to reveal, earning herself a couple of warnings and a death sentence. Lisa darkened the marks where she'd already written the dates and times for the bleacher sabotage and the pool incident. She wrote *Trejo* above but added question marks. She needed solid proof. And she'd get it soon enough when she hauled Trejo in.

"Where are we on the place near Twin Falls that Koa mentioned?"

Rivera looked up from his desk. "Mike's cyber team identified it early this morning based on the report you filed from the hospital. After they heard what happened, they pulled an all-nighter." He returned his eyes to his computer screen. "Says here, Trejo rented it under an alias. Paid with a stolen card. The captain put two units on the house. If he shows his face, they'll bring him in. We have him on identity theft."

"We need to get him on murder." Lisa had started a war. Trejo had escalated a hundredfold. She wouldn't settle for anything less than burying him under the jail.

She looked past Rivera to survey the office. The section, sized for her six-member task force, now held more than twenty department personnel, some standing three or four to a desk, all in deep discussions or on a phone, including Captain Griffith.

"Good," she heard him say. "Now that the National Guard request is in your system, I need you to expedite up the chain. We need those bodies for an island-wide search. These people may have miles of hidden roads in the cane fields to hide their movements. I've already spoken to the commissioner. He wants the request on his desk by nine for his signature, and in front of the governor before noon."

In the short time she'd been with the department, Lisa had learned to recognize the captain's *not playing around* voice. The sharpness of that tone didn't fade in the slightest when he hung up and stormed over to her. If anything, it intensified. "Kealoha, we haven't had a chance to talk since the attack."

"I apologize, sir. I wanted to get right to work on this. I did upload an after-action report from the hospital."

"Noted. And maybe that's enough in a big department like Los Angeles, but here on Maui, we prefer a more personal touch."

"Yes, sir." Where was he going with this?

"You should thank your friend Detective Fan. She was in my office at dawn to give me a full briefing, running cover for you."

Your friend Detective Fan? Forcing those two phrases together raised the hairs on the back of Lisa's neck. "With respect, sir, Detective Fan wasn't there."

"Yet your brother, who is not a member of this task force and with whom Detective Fan conducted a thorough interview, was. That's part of the problem, Kealoha." He waved Jenny over, and Lisa noticed a lightness in her step as she complied.

Jenny handed the captain a single sheet of paper. "These are the bullet points you asked for—from my briefing, sir."

"Yes. Good. Thank you." The captain scowled down at it through his rectangular readers. "This Dr. Peter Chesterfield. Isn't that the man you arrested?"

"He proved useful. I asked him to consult on the case."

"I didn't authorize any payment for consultants, Kealoha."

"He's a volunteer."

This earned her a pointed look over the top of the readers.

Lisa got the message. "Okay. No more consultant. I'll let him know."

"And your brother. It says here he shot the witness before the assassins destroyed the commandeered civilian vessel and killed him."

Jenny's bullet point had combined three facts in the worst way and with the worst semantics possible, making Lisa's actions sound indefensible. "Sir, Koa was a suspect before he was a witness, and he pointed a gun at—"

The captain raised a hand to stop her. He looked up from the page again. "And you apprehended . . ."

"No one."

"No one. No arrest. Nothing to go on but conjecture and a description of two divers in the dark. A pair of bogeymen." He lowered Jenny's paper and Lisa felt the knife being yanked out of her back. "We are an island police force, Kealoha, not the

Pirates of the Caribbean. I've given the full weight of my support to your follow-ups this morning because of the severity of the attack. Neither I nor the commissioner are in the business of letting assaults on our people or witness assassinations go unanswered. But last night, you crossed so far over the line you'd have to fly to the mainland to find it again."

He let out a long breath. "Detective Kealoha, at this juncture, I think it best to allow Detective Fan to step into the leadership role for this task force. From now on, you answer to her."

CHAPTER
FORTY-THREE

Maui PD Criminal Investigative Division

LISA'S MOUTH FELL OPEN as she watched the captain walk out of the section.

Jenny patted her arm. "I didn't ask him to do that. I swear."

"You didn't have to, and you knew it." Lisa backed up two paces, not so much to escape Jenny's touch, but to get Jenny's neck out of the reach of her own hands. "I can't believe you."

"Me? You're the one who went rogue."

"I followed up a lead."

"With only friends and family in tow. And it ended in disaster. If you had looped me in, maybe it would have ended differently."

Had this maneuver come from Jenny's bitterness over being left out? Lisa doubted it. Jenny had wanted the task force leader position since before Lisa arrived on the island. Lisa darkened her glare. "We didn't have room to invite you along. It was a small boat."

"Which blew up, thanks to you."

"Actually . . ." Mike approached with a stack of printouts. "The credit for blowing up the runabout goes to a real live torpedo."

He lifted the top form and then hesitated, as if unsure to whom he should offer it.

Jenny grabbed the paper and flipped it around. "What's this?"

"The report from Oahu's Coast Guard Investigative Service team. The CGIS. Sea-gis." He frowned, pupils drifting upward. "Sea-jis? Sea-jees?"

"Mike," Jenny and Lisa both said at once.

"Right. Sorry. The Coast Guard takes exploding boats pretty seriously, so they've had a team sifting the debris all night."

Jenny scanned the printout. "This says our gang friends used a 3D-printed weapon."

"Yep. The body and propellor fragments were layered PLA, a common 3D-printing material. And they think the motor came from an RC boat. The CGIS team found 3D files that matched the propellor dimensions on a family fun project site. The project had instructions for everything except the explosives, including an impact fuse to release an air charge." Mike beckoned to imaginary children. "Hey, kids, let's build a working torpedo!"

"A guy like Trejo could make the explosives for it in his sleep," Jenny said.

Mike nodded, handing her the next sheet from his stack. "The commander of the unit also sent this letter."

Lisa grew impatient while Jenny read it. "Well?"

"It says he's impressed with your *consultant*." She gave Lisa a flat look. "It appears your British doctor took it upon himself to call their unit and make a few suggestions."

Lisa sighed. "He's always making suggestions."

"Which CGIS followed up on." Mike stepped around to Jenny's side of the letter and tapped the second paragraph. "See? The doc says a couple of divers couldn't get that far out on their own. A boat had to follow you."

"No kidding," Lisa said. "The question is, how did they learn we were heading out in the first place?"

"Don't know. But the doc did some math and came up with

a search area, then asked CGIS to go back and check the data recordings from the Navy's coastal defense radars."

Jenny lowered the paper. "That data is classified. The Navy never shares it with law enforcement."

"But CGIS has access. Says it right there." Mike pointed to another paragraph, then quickly pulled his hand back when Jenny flicked his finger. "The commander says it'll take time to redact the nonessential information, but with the doc's narrowed search area, he expects to have a radar trail on our perps' boat later today."

"Fine." Jenny handed the letter back to him. "What else you got?"

"These." Mike waggled the rest of his stack. "They're the reports from the containers at the Baseyard."

Lisa had been waiting for that data. She took the summary off the top before Jenny could get it. And scanned the page. "Let's see what they found."

Not much. The summary said that the uniforms had recovered two fiberglass fragments matching the stolen Porsche that had crashed in the salt marsh. Two of the tread marks on the false container wall had matched the tire models listed for the stolen Mercedes. And they'd found one crate of electronics with no manuals or serial numbers. Nothing was traceable to a purchase or a person.

"No drugs?" she asked.

"None. They did find traces of hydriodic acid in the blankets covering the crate, but no other drug-related chemicals."

Illicit drug operations always left evidence behind—residues, powders, discarded containers, or equipment. They left more than a trace of a solvent in some blankets. Always. Koa's last words kept coming back to haunt her. *This is so much bigger than drugs and boosted cars.*

Jenny took the summary out of Lisa's hands and read it. "What were the electronics for?"

"The evidence team is digging into their circuit boards as we speak, but the analysis will take time. I can tell you there were six black boxes with flat composite plates that looked like radar panels. But we'll need time to confirm."

"When you have it, send the information directly to me. I'm going to get this investigation under control." Jenny popped the cap off a black marker and turned to face the murder board— Lisa's murder board. "I need to refresh my memory on these details. Lisa, if you want to be helpful, I could use a coffee."

She had to be joking. Lisa headed for her desk. "Coffee's in the corner where it's always been. Get it yourself."

CHAPTER
FORTY-FOUR

Happy Valley

AFTER THE HOSPITAL RELEASED HIM, Peter took an Uber to Lisa's place to pick up the Cadillac. She hadn't answered any of his texts. He hoped she was okay.

Before he took the car, he knocked on the door. Lisa was at the station. He knew that. But her mother might know how she was doing.

Ikaia, the big cook, opened the door instead. "Yo. Dr. Chesterfield. Howzit?"

"All right, I suppose."

"Really? Pika says you almost died."

"Did he tell you he saved my life?"

Ikaia smiled, coming out and letting the screen door close behind him. "He mighta mentioned it. To hear him tell the tale, he snatched you from the tentacles of a kraken, ya?"

His phrasing struck Peter. "A what?"

"Kraken. You know, one o' those—"

"No. I mean, I know what a kraken is. It's just . . . Never mind."

Ikaia watched him, cocking his head. "Getting dragged down

like that, into the chokin' dark, makes a man think, eh?" He waited, but when Peter gave no answer, he went on. "We talk about the water heaps around here. The bounty. The danger. Some say drownin' is the most terrifyin' way to die. Some say it's the most peaceful."

"I'm sure it depends on your perspective."

A short laugh rose from Ikaia's great chest. "For sure. For sure. But the one thing they all say is drownin' and survivin' brings you so close to death's gate you can peer through the bars. When you had the chance, Doc, did you open your eyes and see?"

Open his eyes? Peter wished he could have closed them, but whatever he'd experienced—whether a nightmare or something else—hadn't left him that option. In any case, he had no desire to describe the tentacled creature he saw dragging him into the dark after the water had flooded his lungs.

Peter glanced at the Cadillac. "I'm sorry. I should be going. I just came to pick up my car and thought I'd ask how Lisa was faring."

"You haven't heard?"

"She hasn't answered my texts. And I don't want to call and interrupt her work."

"I see." Ikaia looked down. "She . . . uh . . . she's havin' a hard time. Got a text from her a half hour ago. Said the captain came down on her hard."

"How so?"

"He fired Lisa from her big-time gang-hunter job and gave it to her best frenemy—Jenny Fan."

DETECTIVE FAN. Peter had seen the way she and Lisa were together. He'd seen the glances Detective Fan gave her when Lisa wasn't looking. If Lisa had been removed as head of the gang task force, he could imagine it had as much to do with

Jenny's actions as her own. More than either of them, however, Lisa's loss of position came down to Peter's foolhardy interference in her case.

He pounded the seat beside him as he turned onto the long stretch of highway leading to Wailea and the Grand. With his meddling and pushiness, he'd cost Lisa the position she loved—that she'd worked for. No wonder she wouldn't return his texts.

To think he'd had the gall to call the Coast Guard from his hospital room, inserting himself once again without invitation or permission. "I am such a muppet."

When Peter raised his eyes to the rearview mirror to get a look at his muppety face, he noticed a black Dodge Charger two cars back. He'd seen the same Charger pull in behind him from the first cross street he passed after leaving Lisa's place. Pain radiated from his sternum—a dead match to the pain he now experienced every time he laughed. But nothing about this was funny.

Peter's right hand quivered at the wheel—not a pronounced shaking, but present.

A psychogenic tremor? Anxiety? Cold fear?

During an ambush in Afghanistan, while digging lead out of a Marine who'd not yet reached twenty, Peter had hardly noticed the rounds whizzing past him. Afterward, when the adrenaline wore off, he hadn't experienced the post-action shakes other Navy doctors had described. The next time he ventured outside the wire with his unit, it was the same.

Peter did not do fear—not on the battlefield and not in the operating theater.

He tightened his grip to force back the tremors and checked the mirror again.

The Charger was gone.

Instead of a comfort, he found the vehicle's absence a cause for greater concern. On the way to the marina the night before, the bluish headlights had turned away. And the movement on the dock had ceased. In both cases, a shadow had faded, giving him a false sense of relief. And then the monster reappeared beneath him in the deep.

Breathe.

Air.

Kick.

He couldn't breathe. He couldn't kick.

The light at the upcoming intersection turned yellow, and Peter tried to shift his foot to the brake. His foot didn't move. He tried his left. Same. Just like in the water. All through his fight with the diver, he hadn't been able to kick. He hadn't been able to move his legs at all.

At the hospital, Peter had demanded tests with good reason. Fragments from the explosion had impacted his back. The vest had stopped them from penetrating, but that didn't mean he hadn't experienced a spinal concussion. He'd requested X-rays and an MRI, but the doctors had found nothing, forcing him to decide his partial paralysis in the water had been temporary.

But here it was again.

Glancing down at his obstinate limbs, Peter saw writhing black tentacles locking them in place. The floorboard had vanished, leaving nothing but emptiness below. He had no control. Control was an illusion.

Horns blared. Tires squealed.

His legs came free. Peter stomped on the brake, skidding to a stop on the far side of the intersection. The driver of an Audi that had been turning left gunned past him, shaking her fist.

He eased the Caddy onto the shoulder. As a neurosurgeon, Peter knew the risks of anoxic/hypoxic brain injuries, the most likely physical trauma to result from a near-drowning. He knew the symptoms too. Motor impairments were common, but not hallucinations. He collapsed back against his seat. "What on earth was that?"

CHAPTER
FORTY-FIVE

The Elysium Grand

PETER HAD NO INTENTION of trying to park the Caddy in one of the Grand's narrow garage spaces, not with his motor skills in question. He passed it off to a valet, leaving the key fob and ten pounds on the dash.

At some point, he'd have to remember to get some US cash.

"Dr. Chesterfield, right?"

The Dallas accent. Peter winced, then glanced up as the valet drove away with the Caddy.

Jack Carlisle sauntered out from the Grand's open lobby. He thrust his chin at the attendant out front. "Hey, son. Order up a car to take me back to my villa. And this time make sure the driver hasn't been smoking before he comes. I don't need to smell that reek."

Peter pretended he hadn't heard Carlisle call his name and tried to walk by. He kept his right hand, still plagued by a slight tremor, behind his back.

Carlisle stepped into his path. "You all right, Doctor? I heard you had quite a scare—spent the night in the ER."

Peter didn't know this pompous buffoon and didn't want to.

And he certainly didn't want to discuss the attack with him. "I'm fine." He tried to step around.

Carlisle sidestepped to block him. "Really? I could swear I heard Dr. Iona telling the concierge that you had a boating accident. Pretty serious. I wasn't eavesdropping, per se, but you know me. I like to get all the scuttlebutt." He made a *tsk* sound. "A ship going down at night and far from shore? Fire and black water? That kind of scare has a big effect on a man. Makes him rethink his life choices."

"Again, I'm fine. Now if you'll excuse me, I—"

"The ocean is all the more dangerous for landlubbers like you and me, Doctor. Folks like us oughta stay on the beach where it's safe. Stay in our own lanes, if you know what I mean."

For an instant, Peter saw the same look behind Carlisle's gaze as he'd seen in that of the Afghanistan warlords and Trejo. Only an instant, but enough to send a chill straight through him. Then it was gone.

The resort car pulled up, and Carlisle patted Peter's arm, brimming with friendliness and concern. "You feel better now, Doc, you hear?" He headed for the door the bellhop had opened for him. "Get some rest. Stay off your feet a while. That's a nonnegotiable prescription."

Stay off your feet. Nonnegotiable. Was he offering advice or a warning?

THE FACT THAT CARLISLE had issued Peter an order to relax and stay off his feet prevented him from doing anything of the kind. The tremors in his right hand ceased on their own, but apart from that, he couldn't settle himself down.

Peter showered, had a bite, and paced so much he thought he might wear a path through the room's woven bamboo flooring. In the grand scheme of murders, gang lords, and hidden smuggler's tracks, Jack Carlisle was the one thing most out of place.

What did a cattleman and Luan Trejo have in common—apart from a killer's gaze?

Cattleman. Car thief. Smuggler's routes. What did they have in common? Wasn't it obvious? How could he have missed it?

Peter sat on his suite's couch with a home nebulizer treatment prescribed by the hospital's cardiothoracic team and occupied himself by checking his theory on the internet.

The information was easy enough to find. Maui's media outlets had all covered Ono Beef's big purchase of cane field acreage. As if they'd all plagiarized the same Ono Beef press release, every article described the purchase as a swath of land stretching from Route 311 to the slopes of Haleakala. "And that includes the Maui Central Baseyard," Peter said to himself between deep breaths on the nebulizer.

The network of hidden tracks he and Lisa had discovered among the irrigation gullies of the old cane fields were all on Ono Beef property.

If Lisa already despised him for getting her removed from her leadership position, what would one more text matter?

Peter typed it in.

> jack carlisle owns cane fields near baseyard.
> other connections to trejo?

For the first time since the hospital, he received a response.

> captain says you're out. i need you to stop
> texting me. sorry.

So that was that. No more Dr. Detective.

Peter puffed on the nebulizer a few minutes, casting occasional glances at the darkened screen of his iPad. He couldn't help himself. He pulled it into his lap again and opened the browser.

The website for Carlisle's new island cattle operation looked legitimate, and so did Ono Beef's social media pages, but that didn't mean much. Peter got the feeling Carlisle could put up a realistic digital front if he wanted. He certainly had the means.

Over the last several months, Ono had maintained a steady schedule of posts on all the major social media platforms. Most were images of large white facilities—giant square barns with long-horned steers, palm trees, and blue water photoshopped in. Only one facility currently existed. Ono Beef had built its first barn on terraced land near the forested slope of the island's big volcano. According to the announcements, the herd would grow from those pastures to fill the rest of the acreage over the next decade.

The herd.

Peter switched from Ono Beef's propaganda to the local media coverage. A series of articles showed the first facility under construction, the transformation of terraced cane fields into pastures, and the final product of white picket fences and big green fields. But one key feature was missing from all the photos. Where was all the beef?

CHAPTER
FORTY-SIX

Maui PD Criminal Investigative Division

HAD LISA BEEN TOO HARSH with Peter in her text? She hadn't meant it to be a slap in the face. But when his note about Jack Carlisle had come in, she'd felt like she needed to hide her phone. The captain wanted Peter out—as in *zero communications* out. With Jenny's eye on her and Peter's name popping up on her phone, it might look like she was keeping him in the loop. And wouldn't her new boss have a field day with that?

Still, he'd been right about a lot of things.

Lisa sat at her desk, typed out a quick text to Clay, asking him to take another look at Carlisle and any connections to Luan Trejo, then tucked the phone away and watched the new boss bark orders at *her* task force.

"Where are we on the National Guard support?" Jenny had parked herself in front of Lisa's murder board like an empress on her throne, pointing her whiteboard marker scepter at Rivera. Was that how Lisa had looked?

Rivera answered. "Nowhere, yet. The request reached the governor's desk a half hour ago, but he hasn't made a decision."

"I don't blame him, not in this climate. No more inquiries. Either we hear something from his office, or we don't. I'd hate for the governor's staff to think we're overstepping our bounds." Jenny turned back to the board, putting her hands on her hips. "Keep me informed."

A chair bumped Lisa's, making her jump.

"Whoa," Mike said. "Wound pretty tight, aren't we?" He ducked below her monitor, out of Jenny's view. "I get it."

"Do you? You weren't much help earlier. Where were you when the captain dropped the hammer?"

Mike inclined his head toward his desk. "Over there. Keeping my job. But I'm not entirely gutless, thank you. I intercepted something." He laid a folded paper on her desk and slid it the six inches it needed to travel to be directly in front of her. "Didn't think you'd want the captain to see this at that particular moment, or Jenny for that matter."

Lisa unfolded the paper to see an email with a lot of numbers and exclamation points and the words I LOVED THAT BOAT.

"It's a bill," Mike said, "from some guy named Terrance Shen for a 1972 Formula F190 Twin Engine Classic. He seems pretty mad. Also, I snagged a piece of info from Rivera, told him to keep it to himself for now. He found the sneezy kid."

"The one I saw in the stands?"

"Yep. Rivera tracked him down, conducted an interview."

"And?"

Mike bobbled his head. "Annnd he didn't get much. The kid remembered seeing a guy under the stands before his allergies flared up. The suspect wore a hoodie."

"In eighty-degree weather—the international sign for 'I'm up to no good' or 'want to look like I'm up to no good' as a fashion statement."

Mike touched his nose. "Yep. No facial description, but the kid did catch a glimpse of what he was wearing under the hoodie. A white shirt."

Lisa immediately thought of the undershirt she'd seen one of Trejo's men wearing. "A tank top?"

"More like a golf shirt. The kid described a brown collar on the white shirt and a couple of tan buttons. You want Rivera and me to keep this to ourselves?" Mike peeked over the screen and gave the detective-in-training a conspiratorial nod. "He'll do it. Rivera doesn't like Jenny. She steals the chocolate-covered macadamia nuts he puts in the fridge—the dark chocolate kind the ABC stores never have."

Lisa shook her head. "Tell him he did good work—hard work. As the task force leader, Jenny needs to see the report, and Rivera needs to get his due credit. Besides, I'm more interested in solving this thing than sticking it to Jenny."

Mike raised an eyebrow.

Lisa frowned. "Not *much* more interested, but enough I'm not planning to bury evidence."

One of the officers who'd been added to the task force that morning raised a desk phone receiver, hand covering the mic. "Detective Fan, I've got the Coast Guard on the line."

Jenny crossed the room with rapid strides and took the phone. "Detective Jenny Fan . . . Yes . . . That's right . . . No, I'm afraid he's no longer associated with this case . . . Mm-hmm . . . Excellent. Thank you." Still holding the cordless receiver, she rolled Mike and his chair out of the way and waved at Lisa's monitor, keeping her voice low. "Your email. Open it up. Your doctor friend had them send you the radar results."

Lisa brought up her inbox and saw a new message from the Oahu office of the Coast Guard Investigative Service.

Jenny took control of her mouse and clicked it open. "CGIS isolated a track from last night's scans. Probably your attackers. They traced it to the place where it came ashore after the explosion."

"That's the kind of lead that fades fast," Lisa said. "We should get out there."

"We?" Jenny put a hand on her hip. "I don't think so. You're sidelined. And don't tell anyone else. I want to keep this need-to-know until I've checked it out."

Sidelining Lisa hadn't been part of the captain's hammer. She fought back her indignation. "Jenny, I'm asking you, don't do this. And you can't go alone. Trejo may have people guarding the boat."

"Then I'll take Rivera. He knows how to keep a secret. And why shouldn't I sideline you? You did the same to me."

"True. I cut you out of the good leads, and look how it turned out. I lost my position."

Jenny squinted at her, as if trying to read her intentions.

Lisa held her pleading expression. "I'm telling you, I just want to help. Don't shut me out."

"Fine. It's you and me. Let's go find these creeps."

CHAPTER
FORTY-SEVEN

The Elysium Grand

PETER SPIED TUNA the moment he stepped off the elevator, seated on a lobby lounger sixty meters beyond the pool and its Greek heroes. The resort doctor held a surfing magazine at eye level, pretending to read. Transparent.

"Waiting for me?" Peter asked, lowering Tuna's magazine with a finger a few moments later.

"You don't know that. It's a big resort, ya? I got a lot of friends here, a lot of potential patients."

"But you're waiting for me."

"Yeah. Okay. I was waiting for you."

Peter sat on the lounger beside him. "I'm fine."

"You're gonna keep saying that. You and I both know it. And we both know it's not true. You almost died, Peter. It'll be a long time before you're anything close to fine."

"How many people are going to harp on this today?" Peter laid his head back on the cushion, staring up at the blue sky. "You, Ikaia Kealoha—"

"Maybe Ikaia got a message he was supposed to talk to you about this."

"From you?"

Tuna laughed. "No, silly. From on high, like me."

Messages from the sky deity. These Christians and their superstitions. Peter lolled his head over to give Tuna a look of derision. "God told you and Ikaia to grill me about my near-drowning."

"Is that so hard to believe?"

"It is. Especially since—as I was going to say—I also received a bit of a grilling from Jack Carlisle, who doesn't strike me as the kind of man with whom God has congenial conversations."

"Jack Carlisle? The cattle guy?"

"The same."

"How did he even know what you'd been through?"

Dumb question, or at least ironic, since Tuna was Jack's source. "He said he overheard you describing the whole thing to the concierge."

Tuna turned and laid a knee up on the lounger. He rested a hand on his leg to give Peter a somber look. "Never happened."

"Are you sure? The man is a gossip addict, listening to everyone's conversations."

"That's the thing. The conversation itself never happened. I haven't spoken to anyone at the resort about the attack. Not one word."

The two doctors stared at one another for several heartbeats, then both stood.

Tuna slapped his surfing magazine down on the end table. "I think it's time I showed you my villa."

"AND YOU NORMALLY USE this telescope for . . ."

"Whale watching." Tuna hauled a long telescope and its tripod to the southern corner of his lanai, angling it up the curving beach.

His villa had a certain '80s luau charm, Peter thought, but it also had a certain scent. For too many seasons, the place had soaked in the humid, salty air. "That's a powerful sea odor."

"She's a classic, ya? Pure Hawaiian. None of that McMansion marble and stucco like the others. All that stuff is too mainland for my taste."

Water stains on the grass-cloth wallpaper. Coffee stains on the bamboo matting that carpeted most of the floors. The place was due for a renovation. Peter considered taking a seat on a love seat near the lanai's sliding glass doors but saw more stains—some of which he couldn't identify—and decided to remain standing. "So, the telescope. Whale watching."

"And sailboats. I have a camera attachment that lets me get great shots of the boats and whales." Tuna nodded at the wall behind Peter.

Sure enough, a framed photo of a sailboat hitting a dark blue wave in a mist of spray hung there above the love seat. "Fine. Whale watching and sailboats. I'll buy it."

"But today"—Tuna adjusted the scope with one eye buried in the vertical eyepiece—"we're spying on the neighbors. Thanks to the westward curve of the beach in the villa section, this puppy can see"—he made another adjustment—"right through Carlisle's lanai doors and into his pretentious all-stainless-steel kitchen."

Jack Carlisle. As far as Peter was concerned, he'd earned himself some spying. If Tuna had never told the concierge or anyone else at the resort about the attack, then Carlisle had lied. Not only had he lied, but he'd hinted at details he shouldn't have known.

Going down like that. Fire and black water.

Where had Carlisle gotten his information?

Peter waited his turn at the telescope while Tuna described what he saw.

"Carlisle's on the phone. Looks mad. Clenched fist. Now he's pounding on the counter. Oh, yeah. I think he's trying to keep his voice down, but it's taking every bit of his willpower."

"What's he saying?"

"How'm I supposed to know? I'm a doctor, not a lip reader."

"I wish we had some kind of listening device. The unit I worked with in Afghanistan had laser microphones. Incredibly useful toys."

With his eye still in the scope, Tuna flopped a hand in the direction of the lanai's outdoor storage closet. "In there. Top shelf."

"Really?"

"No." The resort doctor slapped Peter in the side. "Don't be ridiculous. Here, have a look."

Peter gave it a go. He hadn't used a telescope since his boarding school days, but he remembered how the eyepiece took some getting used to. Tuna's telescope was no different. For several seconds, he saw nothing but his own eyelashes. Then the kitchen came into view—an empty kitchen. "He's gone."

"You sure?" Tuna pulled him away and looked for himself. "Yes, you are. Carlisle must have walked out of the shot, ya? Don't worry. He'll be back."

A throaty engine cranked up from somewhere in the vicinity of their target.

Tuna straightened. "Or not. That's Carlisle's Bentley. He makes a point of revving it for the neighbors once a day. We should get my car."

"You mean tail him?" Peter held up both hands. "Hang on a tick. Are we taking this too far?"

"Brah, a second ago, you were staring into the guy's house through a telescope. But now you think following his Bentley is crossing some sort of line?"

How could he argue? Peter stepped out of Tuna's way and made an *after you* gesture. "Lead on."

CHAPTER
FORTY-EIGHT

The Elysium Grand Villas, Wailea

"THERE ARE ONLY TWO ROADS out of Wailea," Tuna said, backing his 2000 Toyota Tacoma compact out of the villa's garage. "One is the world's slowest beach roads past all the resorts, and the other is the Pi'ilani Highway. Unless Carlisle has a lunch at one of the other resorts, we'll catch him on the highway. The odds are in our favor."

The odds. Was that why the bluish headlights had stopped following Peter and Lisa once they turned toward the marina? That dead-end road had only two or three destinations. Not long after, a boat of killers had found them on the open water. Was it why the Charger had turned away when Peter took the Pi'ilani Highway toward the Grand? Where else would he have gone but back to his resort? Like magic, Carlisle had been waiting in the lobby when he arrived.

At the thought of the attack and the mysterious Charger, Peter's right hand began to quiver again. *Not now. Please, not now.* He lowered it behind his thigh to keep it out of Tuna's view.

"There he is." Tuna snapped his fingers and eased off the

accelerator. "Ha! I told you we'd find him, ya? Black Bentley, four cars up."

"Should we get closer?"

"Nah. Broad daylight. Big car. We won't lose him. Settle in. With our island speed limits, this might take a while." Tuna laughed. "Let's hope he's not going to Hana, ya?" He glanced across the pickup's small cab at Peter. "So, uh . . . There anything you wanna talk about?"

Did he know? Peter tucked his quaking fingers under his leg, willing them to be still. "Lisa. I'm worried about her. She's been removed from her position as the head of the task force, and it's my fault."

Tuna returned his eyes to the road, looking disappointed. But to Peter's relief, he played along. "Lisa's okay, Brah. She's a big girl. Makes her own choices. If she didn't want you on that boat, she'd have left you standing on the dock. Believe me."

Peter hadn't thought of it in those terms—that Lisa had wanted him on the boat. The whole time, he'd been imprisoned within the view that his actions propelled the world around him and everyone in it. He'd inserted himself in the investigation. He'd pestered her until she let him tag along. But was that really true? Lisa was the one who'd invited him to meet her at her house for dinner. And he hadn't needed to ask permission to join her on the water. She'd practically pushed him into the boat.

Play this right, and tonight you'll be part of your first arrest as a consultant for the Maui CID.

Control hadn't been stripped from Peter when he dove into the water. He'd let go of it the moment he answered her text. When was the last time he'd voluntarily put someone else in the driver's seat of his life? Outside of his military days, he couldn't remember. "Well, whether it was her choice or mine, I'm sorry for her. I feel like a first-class muppet."

"A what?"

"A muppet, a floppy, brainless doll that cannot move unless someone else animates it, utterly unaware of its own cluelessness." Peter's hand had settled. He leaned back in his seat, watching the Bentley. "And here I am again, still interfering."

Tuna caught his eye. "You wanna turn back?"

"Not at all. Before, I was a clueless fool. Now I am a fully aware fool and happy to own it."

The Bentley followed a big loop of highways around the island's central valley, east on 36 and south on 37. As it reached the lush slopes of the Haleakala volcano, though, it turned west, downslope, on a gravel road. "Where's he going?" Tuna asked.

"I think I know." Peter pulled up Ono Beef's Instagram feed on his mobile and showed Tuna a picture of their inaugural cattle facility. Lowering the device and looking out through his window, he saw the same green terraced pastures.

"Huh," Tuna said. "He's going to work. Who knew?" He slowed the truck. "I can't follow him anymore. We'd be the only two vehicles. Carlisle would spot my little Wahpa for sure."

"Wahpa?"

"My pickup. It's short for Wahine Paniolo. Means 'cowgirl.'"

Peter eyed the faded Toyota emblem at the center of the steering wheel. "You know your cowgirl came from a factory near Tokyo, right?"

"Don't dig too deep, ya?" Tuna nodded toward an asphalt road leading east from the main highway not far ahead. "We'll take that one. I've got an idea."

He drove them upslope to a hillside golf course—one with a fairly upscale clientele, judging by the other vehicles on the road.

"I don't think they'll let you park Wahpa on the green," Peter said, "if that's your plan."

"Don't have to. There's a golf academy at the top of this rise. I caddied there to pay the bills during med school. The parking lot has a fantastic westward view."

Fantastic didn't begin to cover it. Tuna backed Wahpa into a narrow space with a commanding view of the western slope of the volcano and the valley below, including a developed section of Carlisle's cane fields. Peter watched the black Bentley pull up to Ono Beef's square white barn and park next to a lone tractor trailer.

Nothing about the facility or the surrounding pastures looked ominous. Quite the contrary. A pristine white barn. Terraced pastures with white picket fences. Ono Beef had created a look that fit right in with their golf course neighbor on the other side of the highway.

"If I saw that place on any other day," Tuna said, unzipping a long black bag in the pickup's bed, "I'd think it was a polo club. But let's get a better look." He pulled the sides of the bag apart, and with Peter's help, pulled out the telescope and tripod.

They had almost finished setting it up in the back of the truck when a Black man about Tuna's age came out of the golf school. Peter thought they were finished, but the man smiled and waved. "Hey, Tuna."

Tuna kept on working, screwing the eyepiece into place. "Hey, Fred."

"Been a while since you brought the scope out. Whatcha looking for today? Birds?"

"Cows."

Fred stared at them, but only for a moment. Then he made a goodbye salute with three fingers and walked on. "Well, okay then. You have a good one."

"You too, Fred."

In answer to the questioning look Peter gave him, Tuna shrugged. "Told you, ya? I used to work here. Fred knows I like to get pictures of wildlife."

"You said whales. Cows are not whales. Nor do they qualify as wildlife."

"Whatever. We're all set." He moved away, giving Peter a

240

crack at the scope. "Carlisle's with the semi driver next to the trailer. I think they're about to open it up."

Peter bent his eye to the scope and watched. Tuna had it perfectly centered. He could see Carlisle and his mystery driver at the back of the truck. Two men in brown coveralls came out of the barn carrying sections of rails. They pulled a long steel ramp out from a slot beneath the trailer, anchored it in place at an open gate in one of the white fences, and then set the rails in place along the ramp's sides.

A sinking feeling hit Peter. Everything about the scene was all wrong—because it was all exactly what he should have expected to see based on Ono Beef's public profile. Their first facility. A budding herd that might take a decade to build. Sixty seconds later, the men in coveralls opened the trailer doors and utterly destroyed his picture of Carlisle as an evil mastermind.

"I can't believe it," Peter said.

"Can't believe what? What do you see?"

Peter took his eye from the scope, because what the men drove out of that truck were easily visible from their parking lot perch. "Cows," he said as the cattle thundered down the ramp and into the pasture. "I see nothing but cows. Jack Carlisle and Ono Beef are exactly what they claim to be."

CHAPTER
FORTY-NINE

Haleakala Golf Academy

"I'M SORRY, BRAH," Tuna said, zipping up his telescope bag.

Peter hopped over the side of the Tacoma's bed and opened the passenger door. "Sorry that our beef hustler is a pestiferous busybody but not a murderer?" He rested his forearms against the doorframe and looked at his friend over the cab. "Me too. And now I owe that disagreeable blowhard an apology."

"I'm as guilty as you, ya? Tell you what. We'll take him out to dinner later, offer an olive branch."

"Deal." Peter squeezed himself into Wahpa's tiny cab. "But whatever you do, don't order a steak. We'll never hear the end of it."

How had Peter's sense about the man been so far off the mark? Lisa had warned him about the rookie itch—the paranoia that plagues new cops, causing them to see crime and threats everywhere. But how had Carlisle learned of the boat attack?

"Steak." Tuna let out a grunting chuckle as he pulled out of the parking lot. "Yeah, right. Not to play mean girl, but we should order the steak tonight. Both of us. The Grand gets its beef from Hanai Ranch, who'll be Carlisle's biggest competitor on Maui. They've got maybe six hundred head on the old cane fields east of Paia—whole setup can't be more than three thousand acres. Ono Beef is gonna put 'em out of business."

"Three thousand acres? Didn't Carlisle say he'd bought thirty?"

"That's what I mean, Brah. Ono's gonna be too big when it's all grown up. I'll bet Carlisle buys Hanai out for pennies on the dollar in under five years."

Thirty thousand acres. Peter had never considered the actual size of an acre. He pulled up a map and a converter on his mobile's web browser and did some mental math. The pastures they'd been watching—the first small, developed section of Carlisle's land—more than doubled the size of Hanai's operation. Peter frowned. "Huh."

"You got a look about you." Tuna eyed him. "A kind of connecting-the-dots look. What's that all about?"

"It's . . . nothing." A Fuel Stop, a combination petrol station and convenience store, stood at the corner where the golf course road met the highway. Peter tapped the dashboard. "Would you mind pulling into that station? I'd like to pick up a few snacks."

Tuna slowed but scrunched his brow. "Brah, we have all the grindz you need at the resort. You'll never pay more for a candy bar, but I didn't take you for the penny-pinching type."

"It's not the price. It's the selection. I have a weakness for cheap, high-preservative, prepackaged foods." He winced inside. Was Tuna buying any of this? He hoped so.

Peter had involved the old doctor in too much foolishness thus far. It was time to cut him loose, for his own sake. He cracked the passenger door before Tuna could park, forcing him to stop in front of the convenience store entrance. "There's no need to wait for me. I'm quite the finicky shopper—read every label and all that. I'll catch an Uber."

"You sure?"

"Quite sure. You head back. My escapades have kept you

derelict from your sunburn-treating duties long enough." He got out and shut the door before Tuna could protest. "See you soon."

PETER MILLED AROUND THE STORE until he was sure Tuna had driven off, long enough to worry that the young man behind the counter might harbor contempt for him if he left without making a purchase. To assuage this guilt, he purchased a three-dollar hula girl lighter from a display next to the cash register.

Outside, barely twenty meters of highway and red dirt separated the petrol station from the white fence of Ono Beef's nearest pasture. An empty pasture. From what Peter could see, only the lowest of the terraced fields—the one adjacent to the facility—held cattle. It made sense. There'd been only one truck.

"Window dressing," Peter said under his breath. He waited for a car to pass on the highway, then hurried across and vaulted the picket fence.

One semitruck might hold what—thirty cows? Where were the rest? Tuna had mentioned the smaller Hanai Ranch had six hundred head. If that was true, a set of pastures like these could hold twelve hundred or more. And Ono intended to grow its herd to fill another twenty-four thousand acres. Carlisle should have imported a much larger seed herd.

There were other explanations for such a thin bovine veneer on the landscape. Perhaps Carlisle was testing his operation before calling in the bigger haul. Or perhaps this truck was only the first of several shipments. But the numerical difference was enough to make Peter want a second look.

He ran through the grass in a low crouch. Among many other lessons, Afghanistan had taught him the value of cover. The pasture offered no cover, and its high position upslope from the facility did not help. Peter altered course and headed for a thick line of foliage—most likely a meandering irrigation ditch like the one where he and Lisa had chased the Mustang.

The thought gave him pause. How much like that other irrigation ditch might this one be? Would it have a smuggler's track hidden inside? After all, Carlisle owned them both.

Peter reached the foliage and kept going, pushing through a wall of green. Vines tangled his legs. Branches tore at his face and arms. But after a short battle with the bushes, he emerged victorious, standing on a dirt track ten feet wide. He knelt to run a finger through the shallow groove of a tire track and snorted. "Hmph. Cattleman, indeed. What are you up to?"

A smuggler's network through the unused cane fields was one thing. But with the level of development Ono Beef had committed to for these first pastures, Peter found it hard to believe Trejo's gang could have cut this track unnoticed. Unless Trejo had been here first, using the dormant fields. That would mean Ono Beef's purchase had infringed upon the gang lord's operation. Had he and Carlisle formed an uneasy alliance?

Lisa would want to know of this. Look deeper. Peter pulled out his mobile and dialed her number.

Captain says you're out. I need you to stop texting me. Sorry. Her last text came to his mind. Peter pressed the red button to terminate the call. He couldn't risk making things worse for her without solid evidence. He tucked the mobile away and set off downslope at a jog.

Ono's terracing of the mountainside fields had left the irrigation ditch untouched, leaving Peter with perhaps three more kilometers of steady decline to cover. The tunnel of trees held in a choking mass of stagnant air to which his own footfalls added dust. And the meandering ditch stole his sense of direction. But Peter slogged on in an act of faith. Not faith in Tuna's favorite deity, but in his own conclusion that the track would lead him to within a stone's throw of Carlisle's square white barn, if not right to its back door.

His faith proved founded. The track leveled out, and forty meters or so beyond that, it disappeared, consumed by the foliage. Exhausted, sticky with sweat and grime, Peter fought to control his breathing and crept closer to the wall of green. Above the steady pound of blood in his ears, he heard voices—one in particular.

"I'm not made of money, kid." Jack Carlisle's accent no longer sounded as thick. "I have a schedule to keep—investors who need results in a specific time frame. If we don't meet their expectations, this whole thing falls apart. Do you get that?"

Peter parted the vines and found his cattleman resort mate standing a mere fifteen meters away, berating a young man of Hawaiian descent.

The young man kept his head low, without answer, and Carlisle continued. "I brought you on because you swore you could keep those machines running. I trusted you, despite your record. Was I wrong?"

At this, Carlisle's employee looked up. "You brought me on because of my record, not my résumé."

Those defiant eyes looked familiar. Had Peter seen this young man somewhere before? At the resort, perhaps?

"You need me."

"Do I? You think yours was the only name on my list?" Carlisle brushed past the young man and headed for the Bentley. "Get us back on schedule, or you're out. And you know exactly what leaving my employment means."

The Bentley's tires spun on the gravel, leaving the employee coughing in a billowing gray shroud. The young man stared after him for a time, then retreated to the barn.

I brought you on because you swore you could keep those machines running.

What machines? Peter had to get a look inside.

The smuggler's track had curved, bringing Peter to the rear of the facility, just as he'd expected. He waited, but after Carlisle and the kid left, no one else appeared who might spot him covering the short distance across the gravel lot. He needed a peek, that was all. And perhaps a picture.

He wished Carlisle's people had thought to add a few windows. But, of course, a man hiding his true objective wouldn't want such things.

After a deep breath, Peter parted the vines and ran for it. He reached the building with his mobile ready and its camera app open. He almost couldn't believe his luck when the lever turned. Unlocked. Careless, unless Ono Beef had other security arrangements.

Something was missing from the air seeping out as Peter cracked the door. What was it?

The smell. Too clean.

No manure. Nothing remotely animal about it. Peter tried to peek in and see if his path was clear, but he froze before his eye reached the crack. He felt a hand on his shoulder and turned to find a knife at his throat. "Hello," Peter said, lifting his chin to keep it clear of the blade. "Can't say I'm surprised to see you."

"Well, look who it is." The smaller of Trejo's two companions from the confrontation at the Baseyard moved the knife to the side of Peter's neck and propelled him toward the foliage. He wore the same brown coveralls as the men who'd herded the cattle out of the truck. "Where's your Cadillac, Ese? I thought you might be lost when we found you outside the Cantina. This time, I know you are."

CHAPTER
FIFTY

Haycraft Park

LISA AND JENNY CROUCHED beside one of the CID's unmarked sedans at the edge of the Haycraft Park wooded natural preserve. "We're less than a mile from the marina where we put out last night," Lisa said. "It's like they knew our plans before we did."

"Are you saying the department has a leak?"

Lisa let out a frustrated breath. She'd been toying with the idea all day. "The Baseyard containers were cleaned out by the time we got there. I mean, *cleaned out*. Trejo had plenty of warning. And Mike and I pulled Koa's coordinates off SeaSight, using the Investigative Services network. A lot of people have access to that feed, which could be how Trejo's men knew where to find Koa."

Jenny shrugged a shoulder. "His people could've been watching us. They might have followed you from the marina. And if they were listening with the kind of surveillance gear you can get online, they wouldn't need an inside man." She rested an arm on the sedan and looked over at Lisa. "About that night. What made you pull up SeaSight to find Koa Alana? Did you have a stroke of genius or something?"

"Peter did. He had this epiphany at dinner when my mom—" Lisa stopped, but too late.

"Forget I asked. I don't ever want to hear about your doctor friend again. Got it?"

"Yeah. Got it." Lisa checked her Glock's magazine, and then kept the gun out and ready, muzzle down. "All I'm saying is, without help, I don't know how these guys knew what we were up to. In LA, Barrio 18 infiltrated one department. Trejo is part of that organization, working from the same playbook."

"Well, I'm not playing anymore." Jenny gave Lisa the signal to follow her. "This ends today."

The Coast Guard had traced the radar hit to a thirty-foot-wide point on the narrow stretch of beach between the preserve and the ocean. A couple of able-bodied crooks could have easily dragged or carried a small craft across the sand and into the woods.

Jenny led them on a straight GPS path toward the coordinates, ignoring the thickening bushes, some taller than either of them.

"We could go around," Lisa whispered. "Find a better path. Better visibility."

But Jenny swatted the air, signaling her to keep quiet. She tramped through the undergrowth, right past the boat.

Its hull caught Lisa's peripheral vision through the tightly knit branches, and she made a low whistle. When Jenny swung around to snap at her, Lisa pointed to her eyes and then into the brush toward a small clearing.

They separated themselves by ten feet, and Jenny gave Lisa a silent countdown.

Three. Two. One.

They pushed in, Glocks leveled.

The clearing was empty—no people, at least—nothing but a single outboard fishing boat with a gray-and-blue camouflage paint job sitting on a concrete pad.

"Where did this come from?" Lisa asked, tapping the concrete with her foot.

"Looks like Trejo's putting down roots." Jenny lowered her Glock and walked around the boat. "He's building infrastructure. Gutsy pick for a location. The Coast Guard station is just down the road, at the marina you launched from. Either Trejo or his people followed you right under their noses."

"They didn't have to follow us. If there's a leak at the department, they had the coordinates almost as soon as we did. The problem for Trejo's people was, our borrowed boat was faster than this piece of junk. Since we got there first, we became targets along with Koa." Lisa bent over the gunnel, inspecting a large black spot on the boat's floor. She frowned and flipped on her phone's flashlight to push away the shadows.

Not black. Red. Deep red.

"Jenny. I've got blood here. Lots of blood."

TEN MINUTES LATER, Jenny had a department laptop open on the roof of their unmarked unit, running off a hotspot inside the vehicle. "Your brother said he shot one of the divers, right?"

Lisa grimaced inside at the mention of Pika and the thought of how Jenny had twisted his honest report to use against her. But they had bigger issues to deal with. She set her anger aside. "After the explosion, the diver came up underneath me and tried to grab me. Pika saw him and fired. But waves could have thrown off his aim, and even a shotgun slug starts going wonky once it breaks the surface. The guy was five feet or more under. We couldn't be sure Pika hit him."

"You can be sure now." Jenny scrolled through line after line of data on the laptop screen. "Question is, did Officer Kealoha kill him or just wound him? I don't see anything about a DOA from a gunshot in the hospital reports. They might have dumped the body. We should get every person we can spare out here to scour these woods."

"And tip our hand?"

Jenny stopped scrolling and gave her a look.

Lisa softened her expression to keep her calm. "Trejo is running a sophisticated operation, which means he may have eyes on this park right now. Hopefully, our one unmarked sedan didn't raise any flags. But if you bring the whole department out here . . ."

Jenny stayed quiet for a moment, then nodded. "Fine. No troops. Do you have an alternative?"

"We call Mike. I trust him. Get him out here in another unmarked unit to process the scene. Meanwhile, we check the activity of a certain class of local perp. Medical types."

"Meaning former doctors with records who might have pulled the slug out of your diver?"

"Not doctors. In—" Lisa almost said, *In LA*, but Jenny had bristled earlier when she referenced her big-city experience. "In . . . other cases, gangs like 18th Street have shown a preference for paramedics. They don't trust doctors, even the disgraced type."

"Paramedics it is. Let's see."

Jenny called up a database of local offenders and ran a filter for previous employment. Three names popped up. One was back inside, doing time for robbing a pharmacy in Lahaina.

When she moved on to the next file, Lisa pounded the roof next to the computer. "That's the guy. That's our dirty paramedic."

"How do you know?"

"Check out the mugshots on his known associates—third pic from the left." After a *May I?* gesture, Lisa took control of the laptop and clicked on the photo, enlarging it in the browser. She circled the pointer over an eighteen tattooed on the side of the man's face. "See it now?"

Jenny let out a humorless laugh. "Yeah. I see it. Subtle."

CHAPTER
FIFTY-ONE

Unknown Location

"WHY HAVEN'T YOU killed me yet?"

The fertilizer bag over Peter's head muted his question, but his captors should have had no trouble hearing him, especially since the vehicle into which they'd shoved him had a remarkably quiet engine. If he had to guess, he'd say he was in the back seat of a Mustang Mach-E.

Neither of them answered.

"I know you want to. I saw it in your eyes—in the twitching of your blade."

"Shut up, Ese. You got a death wish or somethin'?"

He didn't. He truly didn't. And if they had a reason to keep him alive, Peter wanted to know. He was almost grateful they'd zip-tied his hands behind him. That way they couldn't see the tremors.

Air.

Breathe.

Kick.

He couldn't kick.

Even with the bag blinding him, Peter could see the smoky

black tendrils coiling around his legs, constricting. If his captors reached their destination and realized he was paralyzed from the waist down, what would they do? Toy with him? Torture him? Decide he'd lost his usefulness and end his life? What did the end of his life mean anymore?

Peter breathed deep, ignoring the stench of the bag and fighting through the pain in his lungs. He had to get control, and knowledge had always been his source.

Why were they keeping him alive? They had tried to kill him on the water—not just Koa. After the explosion, the divers had come for both him and Lisa. What had changed?

Two possibilities.

One—nothing had changed, and Trejo's men were simply taking him to a convenient place to ditch his body.

Two—they needed him. For what? Information? Peter had no information. If not information, then they needed him for his skills.

"You need a doctor. The diver who was shot. He's still alive and you need me to save him."

"I said, shut up, Ese."

The vehicle stopped. The men spoke to each other in some dialect of Spanish—a language Peter had never bothered to learn. A rough hand hooked him under the arm and dragged him out, stumbling. He fell to his knees in the dirt.

The bag came off. Trees surrounded him—tall, thick with overgrowth and vines. From the rising terrain on three sides, Peter determined they'd brought him up into one of the rain forest valleys on the side of Haleakala. Perhaps they had, indeed, brought him to the middle of nowhere to kill him.

Air.

Breathe.

Kick.

He couldn't kick.

Bolting was no option. The black tendrils locking his legs in place wouldn't allow him to stand, let alone run. He swallowed and lifted his chin. If fear was his new reality, he wouldn't show it, not when he only had minutes left. "Slapdash work, killing me here. You could at least do it properly by taking me the rest of the way up and dumping me in the volcano's mouth."

Trejo's man hit him across the face, splitting his lip. "I'm getting tired of your mouth, Ese. From now on, don't speak unless we ask you a question." He nodded to his compatriot and spoke Spanish again. This time, Peter picked up two names— Jorge, which he took to be the name of the compatriot, and El Príncipe.

Trejo.

The second man hauled Peter to his feet, and Peter found his legs willing to support him. They moved under his command. Control.

Now, how else could he exert control over this situation?

A stepped path of dirt and stone led from the Mustang upslope through the trees to a two-story shack with green siding, painted to match the forest. A multilayered canopy of netting woven with vines covered the roof and overhung a small parking area to the side with a pair of quads and a dirt bike. Solid camouflage work from a military perspective. No aircraft or helicopters would spot this place from above. To find Trejo here, Lisa would need a massive ground force of searchers. Even then, it would take days.

When they shoved him through the door, Peter saw his analysis had been spot-on. Trejo's large associate from the confrontation at the Baseyard lay groaning on a couch in a large open room, still wearing his wetsuit from the waist down. His friends had cut the top away. An IV bag hung from a nail in the wall above him. His left shoulder looked like hamburger, held together with two lines of sutures. Someone had done quite the hack job digging out the slug.

Another man sat in the adjacent kitchen, white T-shirt soaked with blood, medical tools and used gauze scattered across the table in front of him.

"This your work?" Peter intended to add a crack about the young man's future as a butcher, but he never got the words out.

Jorge buried a fist in his sternum, doubling him over. "What'd we tell you about your mouth?"

"Let him speak." Trejo appeared, walking down a set of creaking wooden stairs. He had a white bandage across his nose. "If he's gonna fix Diego, he'll need to chat with young Mark." The gang lord hit the man in the kitchen with a glare. "The doc needs to know where our paramedic went wrong."

Mark stared down at his tools. "I told you. I'm not a surgeon."

"You took the job. Where I come from, that's a promise you can get it done, and get it done right."

Freed from his zip-ties by Jorge, Peter went to the kitchen table and lifted a vial, inspecting the label. "Morphine. How much did you give him?"

"Last hit was ten milligrams. An hour ago. I've been dosing him every four hours since they brought me in."

"Anything else?"

"Vancomycin, to stave off infection."

"Vancomycin is too strong for this situation. You could put him into shock."

The paramedic scowled up at him. "It's all I had. My clients pay for the good stuff."

"Your clients." Peter snorted. "Sterilize your tools and let's deal with this the right way, shall we? When you're ready, meet me in the"—he shifted his gaze to the open living area—"the operating theater."

Peter washed his hands at the sink and stole a pair of black nitrile gloves from the paramedic's bag. While waiting for Mark to join him, he knelt with his patient. Diego, if he'd heard the name correctly, stared up at him with terrified eyes.

"I'm . . . gonna die. Yeah?"

"Most likely."

"Hey!" Trejo leveled an oversized handgun at him—a gaudy nickel-plated .357 Magnum. "Don't give me an excuse to kill you too soon."

Peter raised his hands. "You want me to coddle him? After all, this man tried to kill me and my friend. He only has this wound because he tried to drown her."

"You still gotta save him, yeah? You took an oath or somethin'."

"I have to try. And I will. But I'm no miracle worker. What you did to Kelly proved that."

"I had nothin' to do with what happened to Kelly." Trejo shook the end of the Magnum at him. "Get on with it."

Get on with it. The major in Afghanistan had said those words in a situation much the same. Back then, Peter had been kneeling beside the cot of a wounded man he knew to be a Taliban fighter, though no one in the mudbrick house would say it out loud.

The young Marine out of whom Peter had pulled nine slugs while still under fire had survived. A US UH-60 Blackhawk had evacuated him to Bagram, and the reports from the doctors there were good. But that evening, Peter and the major had been called out to a village near their forward operating base. They'd been told Peter needed to treat a young girl who'd been hit by a stray round during the day's events. When he and the major arrived, there'd been a second patient with a burly friend watching over him.

The girl's parents, clearly terrified, insisted the two extras were family. Their daughter was in dire shape, with a bullet lodged in her chest near the heart. The fighter had taken one in the gut. He didn't look much better, but Peter knew he was more likely to survive a field operation. The rules of triage told him to treat the fighter first, and so did everyone else in the room—especially the burly friend. But for all Peter knew, these men had been the ones who put those bullets into his Marine hours before.

"Major," he'd said, leaving the rest of the protest unspoken.

"Just get on with it, Chesterfield."

Get on with it. Those words had implied that the fighter was to be saved, and the girl left to die. But Peter had refused to let it happen. That day, he'd saved the Marine, the fighter, and the little girl. He'd worked a miracle. Complete control. After returning to England, he'd kept the campaign coin on him at all times—a reminder that by fighting to maintain excellence in knowledge and skill, he could wield power over life itself.

Kelly Alana and Luan Trejo, or whoever had killed her, had shattered that illusion.

"Right," he said, pushing the major out of his mind. "Let's have a look."

CHAPTER
FIFTY-TWO

"You left a fragment in his left subclavian artery." Peter held out an open palm, expecting the paramedic to know by his statement that he wanted a clamp. "And it's a good thing you did. That sliver of copper is the only thing keeping our patient from bleeding out."

In the absence of a suction device and Carol to wield it, Peter had stuffed poor Diego's upper left chest with gauze. But the artery kept oozing blood around the offending sliver of copper. If Peter removed it without clamping the tube on the upstream side of the laceration, he'd be faced with a flood on the same scale as Barbara's. The paramedic placed the clamp in his hand, and he set it in place, immediately holding out his hand for another. "One more. And I'll need you to irrigate while I suture the cut. Fetch me the nonabsorbable sutures—polypropylene. These are going to be a permanent fixture in his chest."

How Diego remained awake, Peter could not fathom, yet the big man's eyes never left his as he worked—pupils focused, comprehending. The Taliban fighter had not been so strong. He'd passed out from pain and blood loss before Peter had arrived, and he'd remained out during the surgery.

Peter tried to reassure him. "I'm going to cut off the blood flow from your heart toward your shoulder. This will intensify your pain, perhaps make your heart feel as if it's stopping. I assure you I won't let that happen."

Diego nodded, and when Trejo followed Mark into the kitchen, he motioned with his good arm for Peter to lean closer. "He's . . . going to kill you," he whispered. "As soon as you finish . . . you're a dead man."

With the strain in Diego's voice, Peter had trouble determining whether he'd offered a warning or a threat. But his next words answered the question. Diego gritted his teeth and swallowed. "I'm . . . I'm sorry."

Mark returned with the irrigation syringe and a sealed pack of fresh sutures, with Trejo close behind him. Peter gave Diego the subtlest nod he could manage. "Stay quiet and stay as still as you can. This is delicate work."

Too delicate. Peter's right hand began to quake.

Not now. Please, not now.

He moved his body to block Trejo's view. But he couldn't account for the paramedic. Holding the irrigation syringe in place, Mark gave him a sidelong look. "You okay, Doc?"

"I'm fine. Stick to the job I gave you and keep quiet. Let a man work."

He couldn't work. Not like this.

Black tendrils.

Air.

Breathe.

I need to breathe. I need help. With no other recourse, and without a conscious decision to scrap years of steadfast pragmatism, Peter found himself making a silent plea to Tuna's deity— the one who'd composed the sunset. *Please, if you're there, let me save this man.*

The tremors ceased. Peter sutured the first pattern, then the next, while repeating the same constant request. Like breathing in and out.

The rest of the procedure went well, although Diego would live with quite a scar. Thanks to the disgraced paramedic's searching and hacking, Peter had to make an ugly crisscross pattern of four suture lines when closing up. He glanced at Trejo before beginning the final line. "So, what's next, El Príncipe? Now that I've saved your man, will you take me out back and shoot me?"

Trejo raised the Magnum. "You think I'm worried about a little blood on my couch? Diego stained it pretty good already. Maybe I'll just shoot you right here. You broke my nose, Ese. I can't let that stand."

Air.

Breathe.

Help me.

"Before you do, you should know your man Diego needs a hospital. He needs a proper course of antibiotics, constant monitoring of his heart. Not that you care."

Peter and his mouth. Would he never learn to control it?

That last barb earned him a growl and a gun barrel pressed against his temple. "You think I don't care 'bout my men—that I don't love my brothers? What do you know? You got no idea what we been through."

Peter's hand froze in the midst of his sewing. He pleaded silently for Tuna's and Lisa's God to keep the tremors at bay. "My apologies. You're right. But all I can see is what's in front of me. It's all I've ever been able to see. What I see now is a man who needs more help than I can give." Inspiration hit him—an idea born of desperation, but worth a try. "If you truly care about your men as much as you say, perhaps you should get them out of here." Peter resumed his sutures, remaining as casual as he could under the circumstances. "I'll stay with Diego and get him the help he needs."

"Why would I clear out?" Trejo kept his gun in place, pressing harder. "You know somethin' I don't, Doc?"

"My mobile—my smartphone, as you Americans call them. The police can trace it. They may arrive at any moment."

Trejo shot a scowl at his short companion. "You didn't take his phone, Miguel?"

Miguel shrugged. "Why would I? Our guy says he's on the outs with Kealoha. He got her fired or somethin'. Ain't nobody lookin' for him."

Our guy. Interesting. Peter scrambled to save his lie, words flowing as fast as his mind could assemble the pieces. "He's wrong. We know about your mole. The torpedo attack made it obvious. And we knew about your wounded man. Why wouldn't we? Our officer is the one who shot him. The rest was a ruse. By bringing me here, your friend Miguel led the whole department right to you." He finished the sutures and stood, hoping both they and his lie would hold.

The sutures held. The lie didn't. Trejo seemed to buy it, but not his short companion Miguel—the one who'd caught Peter outside the Ono Beef facility. "I'm tellin' you, he's lyin'. The Maui cops ain't that smart."

"Maybe not," Peter said. "But I am."

"Get his phone," Trejo said. "And get Jorge back in here. We might have a fight comin'."

Miguel reached into Peter's left pocket and drew out the phone, which he dropped on the floor and crushed under his heel. Then he set off to find the other man who'd brought Peter in.

Trejo walked to the front window, grinning at Peter. "I don't believe you. Carlisle says you got that detective fired from her high-horse job. She don't care about you no more. And you ain't been gone long enough for anyone else to worry." He lifted a wool blanket beneath the window, showing Peter a pile of weapons and ammunition, including an old military breech-loading grenade launcher. "But hey, let them come. My boys and me? We're ready for a fight."

CHAPTER
FIFTY-THREE

TREJO PUSHED BACK a linen curtain to peer out the window. "Don't see no one, Doc. I'm afraid that means you're outta time."

"At least let me clean up." Peter gestured to Diego's bloody chest. "I'd hate to leave my last procedure on this Earth unfinished. It's unprofessional."

"Whatever. Make it quick."

Air.

Breathe.

Please help me.

The black tendrils faded, and Peter's legs carried him into the kitchen, where Mark, paramedic to the gang stars of Maui, sat at the table, putting his bag of tricks back together.

Peter tossed his nitrile gloves in the rubbish bin and waved the young man out of the way. "Move. I'm not done."

I'm not done. Not without a fight. Not with new questions to answer.

Positioning himself with his back to the paramedic and Trejo, Peter rummaged through the bag. He'd wanted alcohol, but he found something better. *Ether*. Who besides veterinarians used ether? But Peter supposed Mark's clients accepted whatever anesthesia he could get his hands on. He palmed the vial and grabbed a stack of gauze and a bottle of alcohol.

Trejo eyed him as he returned to Diego. "I said, make it quick."

"I'll only be a moment. I'd hate to make killing me a bother for you." Again, he worked with silent pleas, in and out like breathing.

Despite his protests of not believing Peter's lie, Trejo kept returning to the window. He handed weapons to each of his comrades—the paramedic as well—and claimed a grenade launcher for himself. While his captors were distracted, Peter unscrewed the cap from the ether vial and tucked a strip of gauze inside before screwing it back on a single turn to hold the gauze in place. The fabric immediately soaked up the sweet-smelling fluid, forming a fuse, and the loose cap would allow oxygen inside. Or so he hoped.

The small amount of fumes he'd released set his head to spinning. He hadn't played with ether since his medical school days, and he'd forgotten how powerful the stuff was—powerful in more ways than one.

He finished cleaning up Diego's chest, and felt the strength of the man's grip at his wrist.

"Don't, Doc," Diego said in a hoarse whisper. "Don't be done. Tell 'em you need to keep workin'."

Peter gave him a smile, in part out of genuine care for this criminal who had tried to murder Lisa. He forced himself to believe Diego had failed in his attempt to drown her because his heart wasn't in it—that the hole Pika had left in his shoulder might have proved unnecessary. But more than out of care, Peter offered Diego that reassuring smile because the hand attached to the wrist he'd grabbed was holding his makeshift bomb.

The bomb needed one more ingredient. Ignition. Peter's guilt-purchase at the petrol station would provide that. In school, when making a similar bomb, he and his friends had devised a more complex and yet elegant ignition source using pure potassium and a water balloon, giving the explosion a lovely pink hue. But in a pinch, a hula girl lighter would do the job nicely.

"You were one of my bravest patients," Peter said to Diego, pushing himself to his feet as soon as the man let him go. He dipped his hand into his pocket, gripping the lighter. "I hope you find your way out of this life. It doesn't suit—"

The sound of a helicopter interrupted what had turned out to be some of the best potential last words Peter could imagine. And it didn't move on. The pounding of the rotors grew louder and louder. Had he been wrong? Could a searching aircraft see through Trejo's camouflage?

No. A search craft wouldn't drop so low in a place like this, where it couldn't land.

Trejo pulled back his curtain and shouted at his men. "He was tellin' the truth. They're here!" He pointed at Miguel, the short one, and then at Peter. "Kill him."

"Gladly." Miguel aimed the automatic rifle slung about his shoulder. "*Te veo*, Ese."

With a roar, Diego came off the couch. He knocked Peter to the side and threw his massive form at the shooter, taking a sickening ripple of rounds to the chest Peter had just stitched up.

"No!"

Peter didn't waste the big man's sacrifice. When he hit the floor, he rolled to remain a moving target and came up with the lighter held against his gauze wick. The flame took. He chucked the explosive into the center of the room and covered his head.

The vial exploded. Shards of glass flew in all directions, cutting Peter on the arms and back.

Air.

Breathe.

Please.

Peter leapt up and charged the disoriented Miguel, calling on his rugby days, and rushed the killer backward into the window. They smashed through, curtain and all, tumbled down the slope, and slammed into a boulder.

Peter heard Lisa's voice. "Hold fire! The tall one's a friendly. Peter, stay down! Stay down!"

Miguel did not get the message. He jumped to his feet, bleeding from the head and neck, and tried to level his rifle.

A host of weapons erupted from the crowd in front of the shack, and Miguel crumpled, body jerking with the impacts.

Answering gunfire came from the broken window, and more came from a window on the upper level. An armored officer went down.

Peter kept his head and body low, behind the boulder. "They have grenades!"

"Any more hostages?" The other detective's voice. Jenny Fan. "Any friendlies?"

The image of Trejo handing the disgraced paramedic a weapon returned to him. "No!"

That was all the permission the small army needed. The volley unleashed by Peter's statements dwarfed the response to Miguel's threat. The rain forest thundered. Lead pelted the shack and shattered its remaining windows. Canister grenades sailed inside, trailing gas. Two men came out, one through the first-level window and the other through the door. But neither showed signs of giving up. They fired their weapons and died for the offense.

Peter did not see Trejo, and decided the ether bomb must have killed him or knocked him unconscious. Otherwise, he would have used the grenade launcher by then.

The sound of a dirt bike cranking up proved his assumption wrong.

"We have a runner!" Lisa shouted. "Hold fire! Hold fire!" She raced toward the quads.

Peter caught a glimpse of Trejo. He still had the launcher. Did Lisa understand what she was getting into by pursuing him?

He crushed back the instinct to stay down and ran after her. "Lisa, wait!"

CHAPTER
FIFTY-FOUR

Waikamoi Valley
Koolau Forest Reserve

LISA THROTTLED UP THE QUAD, ignoring the jarring impacts of rocks and roots on the trail. No way was she gonna let Trejo escape. By taking off after him without Jenny's leave, she had probably ended her career, but she no longer cared. She had to take this joker down.

The sight of Peter flying through that window, grappling with one of Trejo's men, had turned her world on its side. How had he gotten here? They had found the shack with good old-fashioned investigative work by stalking former paramedic Mark Ryland through interviews and traffic cameras. A familiar Mustang Mach-E had picked the former paramedic up in Wailuku. The same Mustang had been seen by a local leaving the paved road near Twin Falls. From there, Lisa and Jenny had tracked it up the Jeep trail in the Waikamoi Stream valley. When the two saw the shack, Jenny had called for reinforcements, including SRT and a Coast Guard chopper to watch for runners.

The chopper now pounded the air above, keeping pace with Trejo. There wasn't anything else they could do. The Coast

Guard didn't have the authority to shoot him, and in this terrain, they had no way to land and block his path.

Seeing Peter had stunned Lisa enough that she hadn't thought to ask him for intel. Jenny's quick and pointed questions had been lethal in their consequences as Peter's *No!* brought a storm of gunfire down on the house. But Lisa hadn't wanted Trejo dead. Far from it. She'd wanted answers.

The trail widened as it turned downhill, paralleling the Waikamoi, a stream that carried runoff down the northwest slope of the volcano. With less foliage to block her view, Lisa got a better look at Trejo. Blood soaked his shirt, and he had a rifle slung over his shoulder—a shotgun, maybe.

The helicopter rose higher, and once its incessant thumping no longer dominated the valley, Lisa became aware of another motor behind her. A second ATV. Had one of the SRT guys joined her in the chase? She glanced back.

Peter.

Seriously?

He was shouting something she couldn't understand.

She had no intention of slowing down for him. If Peter wanted to chat, he could catch up.

Trejo cut through the stream to a trail on the other side. Lisa tried to follow, but the shorter ATV struggled in the streambed. Before she reached the far bank, her tires spun. She tried switching into reverse, and the engine failed.

Trejo turned his dirt bike broadside on the trail. He aimed the shotgun.

Finally, she heard Peter's call. "Grenade, Lisa! Get out of there!"

Not a shotgun. Peter had warned them back at the shack. *They have grenades.* In her mind, Lisa had pictured homemade bombs constructed of scored grease cans and black powder like she'd seen in LA. But this was a military launcher. Where had he gotten that?

She rolled out of her seat to get behind the ATV and drew

her Glock, but she heard the telltale thump before she could rise and fire. She dove, throwing her body flat in the streambed. An explosion rocked the quad and shook the ground. The Glock flew out of her hand.

Lisa's ears rang. Gray closed in at the edge of her vision. She looked behind her to see the quad burning, no longer giving her cover. Trejo had the launcher open, loading another round. Lisa needed her gun.

She willed her arm to reach for it, but Peter was standing there with the Glock already extended, his finger on the trigger. He fired. Once. Twice. A third time. Straining against the pain in her shoulders, she looked back again and saw Trejo fall to the dirt. A grenade, never loaded, rolled from his lifeless fingers.

CHAPTER
FIFTY-FIVE

Maui PD Criminal Investigative Division

"TELL ME WHY I shouldn't fire you, Kealoha." Captain Griffith stood between Lisa and Jenny in the observation chamber, all three watching Peter. He sat, once again handcuffed to the interrogation table, staring down at the bandages on both forearms.

"Your actions encouraged a civilian—a foreigner—to involve himself in the most dangerous police investigation Maui has seen since the days of the Yakuza/Triads wars. As a result of his sense of entitlement and your lackluster regard for department policy, he was almost killed in a waterborne confrontation." The captain drew in a loud breath through his nose, a bull preparing to charge. "And now, by his own admissions, your Dr. Chesterfield has performed an illegal surgical operation at the behest of a gang, improvised and detonated a bomb, and gunned a man down"—he turned to glare at Lisa—"with your service weapon. Did I miss anything?"

Lisa let her eyes focus on the reflection of Jenny on the dark side of the one-way mirror. She had not left Lisa's side since the return from the valley, as if supporting her by her presence. But

269

Lisa could sense a cold glee radiating from behind her somber expression. Jenny could not have asked for a better result than this.

The case had been concluded in spectacular fashion, with the sole survivor from the gang house being the paramedic, Mark Ryland. The killers were dead, eliminating any potential for foul-ups during prosecution. Jenny would claim victory, and the whole department could celebrate with her, all except Lisa.

"No, sir. You didn't miss anything."

"Then I'll ask again." The captain crossed his arms. "Why shouldn't I fire you? In fact, why shouldn't I make sure you never work in any police department anywhere ever again?"

"Sir," Jenny said. "If I may. Det—"

Lisa held out a hand to stop her. "Peter saved my life."

"Is that your only reason?"

"No, sir. I wasn't finished." She tore her gaze from the one-way mirror and matched the captain's glare. At this point, what did she have to lose? "Peter beat us to the Baseyard, becoming the first to confront Trejo. It was Peter who figured out how to find Koa Alana. It was Peter who knocked me off the boat before it exploded. It was Peter who gave the Coast Guard what they needed to track our attacker's vessel." Lisa shifted her glare to Jenny. "And when we finally tracked Trejo down, Jenny, where was Peter?"

Jenny didn't answer.

Lisa gave her a frown. "Already there, stitching up a wounded man because of the oath he's taken. He found the killers before us, even after I had completely cut him out." She returned her gaze to Peter, shaking her head. They should be pinning a medal to his chest, not treating him like a criminal. "You want to fire me because I allowed him in? Fine. But the fact is, I made the right call. And by cutting him out, you made the wrong one. If you hadn't cut him out, Captain, this whole thing might not have ended in a blood bath."

Out of the lower corner of her eye, she saw the captain's fists tighten. "Are you finished?" he asked.

"I don't know, boss. Am I?"

"Go home, Kealoha. And leave your gun and badge with the desk sergeant on your way out. You're suspended."

CHAPTER
FIFTY-SIX

The Grand

PETER SAT ON HIS LANAI, a steak salad in front of him—the same dish he'd ordered on the night he'd failed to save Kelly.

Lisa had never come to see him in the interrogation room. He wasn't quite certain why that particular fact hurt so much, but it did. It hurt a lot.

He'd never been an emotional man. Disagreeable at times—quite often if you asked Nigel—but never emotional. Yet every fiber of his being wanted to shed great alligator tears into that salad, enough to soak and salt it beyond edibility. But Peter didn't cry. In all the years since he'd left home for boarding school, he'd never cried—wasn't sure he was even capable anymore.

Tuna had picked him up from the station in the Cadillac. "I wanted to give it a shot, Brah," he'd said. "See how it felt. I think I'll stick with my little Wahpa."

As always, Tuna's small talk had been a not-so-subtle attempt to get him chatting—a sort of prelude to a friendly interrogation. Peter had kept silent, and Tuna had filled the void with unsuccessful prompts and prods. He knew about Diego. He knew about Trejo. All of it information he could not have learned without talking to someone who'd read his report/confession. Most likely Lisa.

Peter watched the waves far out on the horizon, numbly chewing his steak. Why hadn't she come to talk to him herself?

The captain had come instead—a stern man, broad shouldered and broad chinned. He'd released Peter without charge with the caveat that Peter should return to the Grand and not leave again except to get on an airplane. He advised Peter that an investigation was pending and that a report of his actions would be sent to the London precinct with jurisdiction over his home address, including the fact that he'd conducted an illegal vigilante investigation.

And the fact that he'd killed a man.

There was a knock at the door.

Peter set down his fork and sighed. Why wouldn't Tuna leave him alone? What part of *I don't want to talk about it* could that man not understand?

Since he had no intention of taking visitors, Peter had not properly dressed after his shower. He'd chosen a light set of striped pajamas Carol had bought him and the plush bathrobe provided by the hotel. No man should be seen in that state. He waited, hoping Tuna would take the hint.

Not a chance. The knock came again, a little louder.

"Go away!"

"Peter, open up. I'm sorry."

Not Tuna. Lisa.

He hurried to the door, struggling to tie the robe closed. And because part of him worried that hearing her voice had only been wishful thinking, he checked the peephole.

There she was in a white cotton blouse and jeans, hair down— a style he'd never seen her wear before. Apart from the cuts and bruises, she looked like any other young woman out for a casual evening. No gun that he could see, and no badge.

She made a frustrated, sorrowful face and turned to go.

Peter jerked open the door. "Apologies. I wasn't dressed." He stepped aside, making room. "Please. Come in. You . . . um . . . You're not wearing your badge. Should I take that to mean you're not visiting in any official capacity—for instance, to arrest me . . . again?"

He meant it as a joke.

She didn't laugh.

"I have no official capacity," Lisa said, walking past him. "I'm on suspension, pending an investigation into both our actions. I—" She looked out at the lanai. "Oh. Were you in the middle of dinner?"

"Same dish you saw last time you visited, though not yet as cold."

It was a stupid thing to say, and Lisa seemed to take it as a criticism, as if she was keeping him from the meal. "This is a bad time," she said. "I should have called first. I can go."

"No. No, that's not what I meant." Peter rushed the tray into the suite's kitchenette. "I could get you something as well. They have anything you could want here."

Lisa shook her head.

"Not hungry? Me either. Not truly, anyway. I was just filling time." He rolled the lanai table out of the way and offered her a chair out there in the breeze, then took the one beside it. "The last time, you came out here to check my story. You thought I might be a killer." He glanced over at her, watching her expression. "This time we both know for certain that I am."

She touched his arm. "Peter, don't—"

"I must, Lisa. Today, in one of the ugliest surgeries of my career, I saved a man's life, only to have him trade it for mine. And what did I do with that gift? Minutes later, I put three rounds into a man's skull."

"You had to. Trejo would have killed me. He probably would have killed us both."

Peter nodded, sitting back. Rain clouds had gathered to obscure the moon, leaving the water black. Black water. Black tendrils. Peter flexed the fingers of his right hand, half expecting them to shake. "Today, when they took me . . . and through the whole surgery, I . . ."

"You what, Peter?"

He wasn't ready to talk about it, not even with her. "Have you ever taken a human life?"

She swallowed, then nodded.

"I see. I'm sorry. I hadn't killed anyone, not until today, not even in Afghanistan."

"You weren't expected to. You were there as a doctor, right?"

"True. But the old ideal of medical personnel as noncombatants vanished when our adversaries stopped playing by the same rules. And the difference between now and then becomes quite real the moment you drive outside the wire. When I traveled with our specialized team, I carried a weapon, and I was willing to use it."

"But you never did."

He shook his head. "When the bullets started to fly, my job was to keep my team alive, not to return fire. There were severe days, but never so bad I had to step outside my role. The same rounds that occupied my magazine on our first patrol remained there until the conclusion of my tour. My team took some pride in that—the idea that they'd carried me through without letting me compromise a commitment to do no harm. And now look what I've done."

"You stopped a killer, Peter—Kelly's killer. Trejo will never hurt anyone again."

At this, Peter scrunched his brow. Suspension or not, he hadn't expected Lisa to call it quits on the case so soon, not with such a big thread still hanging loose. "Are you certain of that?"

"Of what? That Trejo won't kill again?" Lisa let out a dry chuckle. "Yeah. Pretty certain. He's not coming back."

"No. I mean, are you certain Trejo murdered Kelly?"

"Him or one of the gang members who died today. Why? Did you have another suspect in mind?"

Peter turned his chair so he could face her more directly. "I should think the man upon whose property I was snooping when they captured me might at least be a person of interest."

The blank look Lisa gave him told him she had no idea what he was talking about.

"Carlisle," he said. "Jack Carlisle. I was at the door of his new facility when Trejo's men grabbed me. It seems a far stretch to call that a coincidence." He squinted at her. "Didn't you read my statement?"

"Of course I did. The transcript said nothing about Carlisle, only that Trejo's men had caught you following them and grabbed you." She looked down at the lanai's slate floor for a time, then back up at Peter. "That's a big discrepancy. We have some leeway in paraphrasing witness transcripts, but not that much. Who took your statement?"

The two had been separated immediately after the shooting, since they'd both been participants. Peter didn't know where they'd taken Lisa, but he'd been put into the back of an ambulance with the doors closed. Aside from the refreshingly non-criminal paramedic who'd ministered to the lacerations on his arms and face, there'd only been one other person in the bay—a Maui PD detective.

"It was your colleague," Peter said. "Detective Jenny Fan."

CHAPTER
FIFTY-SEVEN

The Grand

"JENNY'S THE LEAK." Lisa couldn't believe the words coming out of her own mouth. Was this jealousy? Anger? No. Okay, maybe a little, but she had some firm ground underneath her suspicions.

Jenny had downplayed Lisa's hunch about a leak at Haycraft Park. And she had worked against Lisa at every step of the case. Lisa had assumed the sabotage was aimed at undermining her position as the head of the task force. But what if it was something more sinister?

Omitting a detail in a witness transcript could still be explained away. Jenny could claim she misunderstood or was protecting Carlisle from wild accusations—that she simply didn't trust Peter. Lisa needed more. "What exactly did you tell Detective Fan?"

"What *didn't* I tell her?" Peter stood and walked back into the suite, heading for the refrigerator. "Want something? I have bottled water. POG—passion fruit orange guava juice. During my stay here, I've grown particularly fond of the POG."

"Peter." Lisa followed him inside. "What did you say to Detective Fan?"

"Sorry. I was stalling, trying to remember. Keep in mind that I had just killed a man, which occupied most of my thoughts." He opened the fridge. "I do remember telling her I was trying to get a peek inside Carlisle's facility when Trejo's men picked me up and that the men wore the same brown coveralls as those who'd driven Carlisle's tiny herd into the pasture." He paused to pop the tab on a can of POG, then snapped his fingers. "Oh. And I told her I suspected your department had a leak."

"You told her that?"

"I didn't know it might be her. Trejo's man had practically admitted it. 'Our guy,' he said, then told Trejo this mystery contact had told them I had been ousted from the investigation."

None of that had been in the transcript Lisa read. Matching coveralls linking the gang to Ono Beef—brown, the same color seen on the clothes underneath the saboteur's hoodie when the bleachers collapsed. A witness overhearing talk that implied a CID mole. No investigator would leave details like that out of a transcript, especially the last one. Unless she *was* the mole.

She. Problem.

"Trejo's man said 'guy,' right? He used that specific word?" Peter nodded.

Lisa waved the discrepancy off. "Maybe she's working through an intermediary. But Jenny is the leak. I'm sure of it."

"I'm sorry." Peter poured her a glass of POG that she hadn't asked for. "Betrayal ranks among the worst of ills. Like Ephialtes at Thermopylae. The Greeks were slaughtered." He took a sip of his own drink, then added, "I myself feel quite Greek at the moment."

Lisa accepted the juice and sank down onto Peter's couch. She'd been avoiding POG since returning to Maui, the way a recovering alcoholic avoids whiskey. POG went down smooth, but it had the sugar content of a glassful of jelly beans. "Jenny

Fan has been working against us this whole time. That's why the Baseyard was empty when we got there. And that's how Trejo's people found us when we hunted Koa down."

"Be careful with your conclusions. Some of that can be explained by surveillance. I did see a car following us that night."

"All the way to the marina?"

"No. It peeled off before the last street."

"They were checking her information or maybe racing us to the coordinates. Jenny and I found their boat less than a mile from there."

Peter sat on the edge of a chair and took a long swallow of his juice. "You and her. If Jenny was working against you, why would she help you find the boat, and subsequently the shack?"

"She had no choice. Thanks to you, the Coast Guard sent the coordinates directly to me. Jenny had to push in because she knew I might investigate that lead without her. I should have known she was stalling when I had to walk her through finding Mark Ryland in the criminal database."

A lot of Jenny's behavior over the last few days began to make sense. She had taken over the crime scene at the Grand in an effort to suppress evidence. She had used Lisa's lack of local precinct knowledge to get a lift in the fire department's helicopter without her. By cutting Lisa and everyone else out of the aerial search, she'd given Trejo a head start in hiding the stolen vehicles. And then she'd magically shown up with the remains of the Benz, a feather in her cap that proved almost useless to the investigation.

Anytime Jenny had been around, Lisa had been working with one arm tied behind her back.

Peter still wasn't convinced. "What about the showdown at Trejo's shack? If she warned him before your department invaded the Baseyard, why not then?"

"Good question. Jenny did step away from me to make a call while I interviewed the witness near Twin Falls. And Ryland's statement mentioned the gang had some kind of warning—that they armed up before our arrival."

"Yes. That." Peter coughed, looking away. "That was me."

"You warned them we were coming?"

"I didn't know you actually *were* coming. It was a ruse to get them to leave."

She frowned at him. "So, no phone calls from a mole?"

"None. Trejo was downstairs with me the whole time, and his people argued against, not for, my prediction of a police assault."

Lisa stared at the gold threads in the beige fabric wallpaper. "She had ample opportunity to give Trejo a heads-up that I was coming and bringing the whole department and part of the Coast Guard with me. So why would she suddenly hang him out to dry?"

"Perhaps for the same reason she omitted key details from my statement. Detective Fan isn't working for Trejo."

Lisa met his eye, and they both spoke at the same time.

"She's working for Carlisle."

"Carlisle is the intermediary," Lisa said. "He was the one working Trejo's strings."

CHAPTER
FIFTY-EIGHT

Captain Griffith's Residence
Kahului

THE CAPTAIN'S HOME hadn't been the first stop in Lisa and Peter's effort to revive the Kelly Alana case. Lisa hoped it wouldn't be their last. She had to take the risk—do this right. "Let me do the talking, okay?"

Peter gave her a thumbs-up.

Mike leaned out from behind him and gave her two. "You got it, boss."

She closed her eyes and shook her head. "Don't say that in front of the captain. I'm not your boss right now—not as long as I'm on suspension."

"You will be." Mike had that smile that always seemed to be there, no matter what. "We're gonna set this right. You'll see."

Captain Griffith answered the door in board shorts and a Rainbow Warriors jersey. "Kealoha. You have something to say that couldn't wait until after your review?"

"You have a leak in your division."

"That's quite a claim. You have proof?"

"Dr. Chesterfield."

The captain tried to close the door.

Lisa stopped it with a flat hand. "Wait. What he has is circumstantial, but I believe him, and it's enough to warrant a hard look."

"Then take it to internal affairs."

"Sir, this is a small division, and you know it. If word of an inquiry gets out, we might spook the mole."

"Translation—your name is mud with IA right now, and you want me to give you permission to do an end run around them. Correct?"

Lisa had to give the man credit. He'd seen right through her line and picked out the far more accurate subtext. "Correct."

He pressed his lips together for a long time, then swung the door wide. "Come in. Let's hear what you've got." When only Lisa crossed the threshold, the captain rolled his eyes and thrust his chin at the other two. "All of you. Get in here before someone sees you hanging out on my stoop. Like she said, it's a small division."

The captain sat them down at his dining room table and asked his daughter to bring them coffee. Lisa took that to be a good sign that he was willing to listen. Drinking caffeine after sundown was a commitment. She laid out her case and let Peter chime in with an occasional detail.

Captain Griffith scowled at his steepled fingers. "This is more than a leak. You're accusing Jack Carlisle, who has ingratiated himself no small amount with the mayor and the chamber of commerce, of being an evil mastermind and a murderer who had both Trejo and Detective Fan on his payroll."

"Has," Peter said. "He still *has* your Detective Fan on his payroll. And her actions in his service have caused multiple deaths and severe injury to your officers, including one that I saw go down at Trejo's shack."

Lisa touched his knee under the table to quiet him. "I have . . . a friend in the FBI looking into Carlisle. A good friend. If he's as dirty as we think, he'll have slipped up in the past. We may have more on him soon."

The captain glanced at Peter. "Officer Kapas, whom you saw take a hit today, is fine. His vest absorbed the round, and he has nothing worse than a bruised rib. And you," he said to Lisa, "haven't given me enough to justify involving the FBI. If your contact trips the wrong digital wire while snooping around Carlisle's life, we might all be in trouble."

Mike had raised his hand early in the captain's statement, and he kept it up, squirming like a first grader with the answer to a math problem.

"Yes, Mike?"

He looked to Lisa, as if he also needed her permission to speak. She tilted her head toward the captain. "Go ahead. Tell him what you found out."

"Sir, I can tip the scales in Detective Kealoha's favor. It all goes back to buckyballs. I first noticed it when—"

Lisa thumped the table beside him.

Mike's pupils darted to hers, and he nodded. "How about I skip the buckyballs and get to the important part. We found an object in the silt at the drowning site, and I sent it to the state lab on Oahu for testing. But I never got a result."

"No result?" the captain said. "That's your proof of Detective Fan's malfeasance?"

"In a way, yes. I hadn't heard from them in a couple of days. Nothing too unusual for a busy state lab. But when Detective Kealoha came to me this evening, I grew suspicious. I called a colleague there, and he told me they had canceled the tests at Detective Kealoha's request."

"A request I never made," Lisa added. "Someone called the lab from the CID and impersonated me to keep them from testing the object. Those phone lines are recorded. We'd need a warrant to get the audio file, but if we do, Jenny's voice will be on it. I'm certain."

The captain stared down into his coffee, brow furrowed. "If we ask for a warrant, we'll need justification. And I know for a fact Detective Fan has made a life's goal of making friends with judges. I don't think we could keep that quiet. The evidence will still be there if it comes to that, but before I try to get it, I'll need more to back it up in court."

Mike continued to squirm, and the captain let out an exasperated sigh over his cup. "You have something else, Mike?"

"Yes, sir. It's my colleague at the state lab. The object, a black stone faceted like a tiny soccer ball, intrigued him too much. He ran the battery of tests anyway. He was planning on sending me the results tomorrow."

When Mike didn't continue, the captain set his cup down. "And?"

"And we need more testing for verification, but it looks like the object is a formerly theoretical form of carbon called Elysium, mined illegally here on the island." Mike spread his hands, eyes lighting up. "Imagine, right under our feet, giant blocks of ultra-hard diamond, so dense light can't pass through them, with ferromagnetic and superconducting properties heretofore unseen in nature."

"Which no one can touch," the captain said. "Because mining on Maui is illegal."

Lisa shrugged a shoulder. "We think Carlisle is doing it on the sly, using Ono Beef as a cover."

"But what does mining Elysium have to do with Trejo and the auto thefts?"

"Most likely, Trejo had already set up his network of smuggler's tracks before Carlisle bought the dead cane fields, driving the uptick in auto thefts you brought me here to stop. I'd guess he would have moved into drugs next, but then Carlisle showed up."

Peter wrapped his fingers around his coffee cup. "And what's one criminal to do when he finds another camped out on his territory?"

The captain snorted. "Only two options. Start a war or join forces."

"Agreed." Peter sat back with his cup. "And we think what happened is a little of both. The two brokered a deal. Trejo used his smuggler's tracks to support Carlisle's illicit mining operations and provide security. Carlisle used his influence to keep Trejo off the police radar."

"But after Kelly died," Lisa said, jumping in, "things got too hot for Carlisle's comfort. He had to get rid of Trejo, but he couldn't just get him arrested. Trejo knew too much. Carlisle used Jenny to touch off a war to get Trejo and his men killed, and we played right into his hands."

The captain left the table and crossed the hallway between the dining room and a small open office. "It all fits, but like you said, most of it is circumstantial."

Lisa stood and laid her hands on the table. "Will you take action?"

"No." The captain opened a safe behind his desk and brought out a gun and badge, both resting on a clipboard. "You will. I thought about what you said at the station—not your most diplomatic moment, but you made good points. That's why I brought these home with me. And now you've backed those points up." He set his burdens down in front of Lisa and offered her a pen. "Welcome back, Detective. Sign for your badge and gun. Then go get me enough hard evidence to put Carlisle and Fan away for good."

CHAPTER
FIFTY-NINE

LISA AND PETER DROPPED MIKE OFF at his place in Wai-luku, only a few blocks from Lisa's. "Get in touch with your buddy on Oahu," she told him as he climbed out of the Jeep's back seat. "Tell him the division wants those lab reports after all. We want them first thing in the morning. Make sure Jenny doesn't get wind of it."

She waited until he was inside the house before driving off. Maybe it was an overabundance of caution. Maybe not. An opponent like Carlisle, willing to work with a notorious gang, put a dirty cop on his payroll, and play the two sides against each other in a deadly confrontation, would do anything to stay ahead in the game.

Peter seemed to sense her mind. "He's been watching us, hasn't he? Carlisle, that is."

"Probably. But he might have been using Trejo's men."

"Trejo's gone. Does that mean we're in the clear now?"

Lisa put the Jeep into drive and pulled away. "I don't know."

As she turned north onto Route 30, away from Happy Valley, Peter glanced over his shoulder. "I thought your house was the other direction. Shouldn't we get Pika?"

"The captain was clear. No one outside that room is to know

286

about this investigation. That includes Pika. For now, it's just you and me."

"And where are we, this dynamic duo, headed?"

"Ono Beef."

"Oh." His expression darkened. "I should think we'd need a warrant for that."

Instead of answering, Lisa squared her shoulders and took on an official tone. "Dr. Chesterfield, is it your assertion that earlier today, while at the Haleakala Golf Academy, you witnessed members of Barrio 18 working on the Ono Beef property?"

"Well, I was looking through a—"

"Aa-aa!" She stopped him with a sharp look. "Yes or no, please."

"Yes."

"I see. And is it also your belief as a consultant for the Maui Police Department Criminal Investigative Division that these are the same gang members who later abducted you?"

"Yes." He said it slowly, narrowing his eyes at her. "Yes, it is."

"And finally, Dr. Chesterfield, is it your belief that Jack Carlisle, owner of the Ono Beef property in question, knows you survived your encounter with Barrio 18 and spoke to the police, and as such, may rush to hide any connections to said gang?"

This time, Jack gave her a confident smile. "Yes, Detective Kealoha. That is, indeed, my belief."

"Good." She settled her eyes on the road ahead. "You've given me a legal justification known as exigent circumstances. Combine that with our belief that a dirty cop is involved, and we have no other option than to sneak in and collect our evidence unseen and without warning."

"The unseen part won't be easy. The only access road winds downslope through the pastures. If Carlisle or one of his people are at the facility, they'll see us coming quite literally a mile away."

"We won't use the access road." Lisa patted the Jeep's dashboard. "I've been dying to take this baby off-road since I bought her. It's time to see what she can do."

CHAPTER
SIXTY

Smuggler's Route
Ono Beef Property

"HOLD THE LIGHT STEADY, Peter, unless you want us to end up in the ditch."

"I am holding it steady. Perhaps you haven't noticed, but this isn't the smoothest road on the island."

What was going on with him? At the pace Lisa was driving, his excuse didn't hold up—not in the slightest.

Lisa had entered Trejo's smuggler's network from Route 30, at a gulch two hundred yards south of the gas station where Peter said he had ditched Tuna. Predictably, a section of white picket fence blocking the start of the hidden track rose free of its post holes with only a small effort. They kept the Jeep at a crawl, using nothing but a five-inch MagLite from the glove compartment to light the dirt track. Headlights were too strong. They might shine through the walls of the foliage tunnel and give them away.

Ever since Lisa had given Peter the flashlight, he'd been fidgety and awkward. When he spoke, his tone remained as confident and as annoyingly *I am verifiably brilliant* as ever, but he kept adjusting his position—elbows on the dash, forearms, elbows again.

He switched the flashlight from one hand to the other for the umpteenth time, dropping the beam from the track. When he shined it forward again, Lisa found her left front tire inches from a deep dip where an intersecting track joined theirs. She jerked the wheel right to keep them from barrel-rolling into the gully. "Okay, what is up with you?"

Peter wouldn't look at her. He thrust his chin at the track ahead. "Eyes on the road, please. And I don't know what you're talking about."

"Yes, you do. You've gone all . . . shifty."

"Pardon?"

"You heard me. And don't pretend you don't know what I'm talking about. You might have some off-the-charts IQ, but I've spent years at the interrogation table, learning to read people. You're hiding something, Peter. What is it?"

"Between the dark and my clumsiness, you're imagining things."

"You're not supposed to be clumsy. You're a neurosurgeon." Lisa meant it as sarcasm—humor to lighten the argument. But from the wall of ice that instantly grew between them, you'd have thought she'd punched him in the nose.

"Perhaps we shouldn't talk," he said. "This is, after all, a mission of stealth."

More stealth was not a bad idea. Lisa stopped the Jeep. "We're close enough that anyone at the facility might hear the engine. Let's walk from here."

Peter laid the MagLite on the dash, forcing her to grab it before it rolled off. He got out without a word and trudged down the slope.

She caught up to him, and they walked onward with no sound but their footfalls and the buzzing of the mosquitoes swarming in the beam of the MagLite that Lisa now held. Finally, Peter grunted, as if giving in to some unspoken point she'd made. "Do you experience fear?"

Didn't everyone experience fear? "I'm not sure what you mean."

"Just what I asked. You're in law enforcement, a dangerous profession. In life-threatening encounters, do you or do you not experience fear?"

"I guess." Lisa adjusted the MagLite lens to narrow the beam. She kept it pointed down at her feet. At this range, even that small light might give them away if she lost her focus. And the strange turn of Peter's mood was becoming a distraction. "Any cop who claims he doesn't experience fear is lying, especially in those moments when you don't know where the bullets will be flying from."

"Good. Good." He seemed to brighten. "What are your fear symptoms?"

"Symptoms?"

"Humor me. I'm a doctor attempting to craft a diagnosis."

"I . . . uh . . ."

"Tremors, perhaps?"

Really distracting. Who was Peter trying to diagnose? "No tremors. My heart pumps. Hard. At the academy they taught us breathing techniques to counter that kind of thing."

"Breathing?"

"Yeah."

To her surprise he took a heavy breath in and out, and then another.

Lisa touched his wrist. "Not like that. It's complicated. I'll show you . . . later." Tremors. Against the tips of her fingers touching his wrist, Lisa felt quaking. "Peter, what's going on? Level with me, or we're turning back."

He stayed quiet, and Lisa stopped to show him she was serious. She almost shined the light on him. *Focus.* She turned it off instead. "Talk, Peter. This kind of distraction can get a cop killed."

"I expect that's true. Or such a distraction could get the doctor who is sneaking around with the cop killed. And at the moment, Lisa, even though I don't feel afraid in the traditional sense, I find that I very much don't want to die."

CHAPTER
SIXTY-ONE

PETER AND LISA STARTED WALKING once more, taking the growing swarm of mosquitoes in the torch beam with them. Peter could see he'd made Lisa uncomfortable—one of several reasons he hadn't wanted to talk about his sudden bout of anxiety in the first place.

"It's not as if I've never experienced fear before," he said, splitting from her to dodge a rut in the dirt track. "As one with medical training, I never suffered from the delusion of invincibility, a malady that plagues many young soldiers."

Lisa kept the light between them as they merged again. "Then why the change?"

"I'm not certain. While the invincibility delusion never infected me, I contracted a type of fatalism from my adopted team. 'You have to die of something,' they would often say, equating a bullet to the head or an IED with cancer or heart disease. Thus, they recognized the black ending of death as inevitable, whether it came sooner or later."

"I've heard the phrase. A lot of cops use it."

"I expect so. I've carried that fatalism with me ever since. But . . ." Peter kicked at a rock in their path. "What if death is not the end of the road, but a fork? And what if one must choose which path to take without seeing beyond that fork? Lisa, I've defined myself by knowledge. I know the results of every decision before I make it. But if death is a threshold beyond which I cannot see, I find myself paralyzed."

He didn't say how paralyzed, or how truly physical that paralysis had become. He also didn't tell her that this sudden fear of death was not restricted to his own. He couldn't save Kelly. He'd saved Diego, only to have the man throw himself in front of a gun to save him back. He had no control. Peter had tried relinquishing control through prayer during that surgery, and the results were self-evident. But was that effect real, or the benefit of a psychological panacea?

Lisa slowed, and in the darkness behind the torch beam, he could feel her looking at him. "Did all this start after you nearly drowned?"

"Close enough. During the incident, I experienced something darker and more terrifying than pure nothingness. I considered it a hallucination brought on by lack of oxygen. But . . . I've had similar visions since, as if, in a way, I'm still drowning. Your mother said—"

"I know what my mom said. But this isn't really the time, Peter."

"Then when will be the time? Should I learn to pray now? Pray later? If I decide I believe all of this, I certainly shouldn't wait until after the bullets finally catch us and we each go our separate ways at the fork."

He heard her sigh in the dark. "Like Kelly and Koa."

Peter was not entirely sure what she meant by that, but Lisa went quiet for several paces. "Lisa? Are you praying right now?"

"Yes, Peter. I'm praying for patience. With you. My experience of coming to God had a different genesis. I came out of longing, rather than questions about the unknowable. I longed for a better life, a better purpose. And I had help."

"The father you mentioned before."

Lisa let out a quiet laugh. "Uh. Yes and no. By Father, I meant God. He pulled me up out of my despair. He restored my sense of worth. But I also had human help. A young police officer took the time to help me understand God's love in a way I never had before. He helped me trust and relinquish control over my own happiness."

"Control. Yes. That's where our experiences meet—mine, yours, your mother's. Control of happiness. Control of circumstances. Control of life. How can anyone give these up?"

"By recognizing we never had them in the first place."

The track outside the torch beam seemed to grow brighter, almost like the clouds covering the moon above their tunnel had parted. But the moon was not up. Peter glanced ahead and saw twinkling pinpoints. It took his mind a moment to register what they were, and then he caught Lisa's elbow.

"Douse the torch," he said. "We're almost there. And I think Carlisle's people are on the move."

CHAPTER
SIXTY-TWO

Ono Beef Facility

ONE LOOK THROUGH THE VINES hiding the tunnel told Lisa her exigent circumstances argument would hold up. Carlisle's people had raised a broad overhead door at the rear of the structure. She didn't have the angle to see inside, but the equipment they were towing into the light spilling across the threshold gave her all the information she needed.

"Those are drills," Peter whispered, peering through the vines beside her.

Lisa raised her phone and snapped a photo. She nudged him. "Get some pictures. I'll switch to video."

"I can't."

His phone. Of course. Trejo's people had destroyed it, and the remains were still locked up in the evidence storage room at the station. *Peter's phone.* Lisa made a mental note. "Keep watch, then. Let me know if you spot someone looking this way."

The workers, wearing everything from dress shirts and slacks to shorts and slippahs, used a small crane to lift the last of four tracked drills onto a pair of flatbed trucks. To these they added piping, computer racks, and hard-shell cases. More than one argument broke out, and Lisa got an excellent close-up video of Carlisle telling them to quiet down and get on with it. The whole operation seemed rushed and chaotic. "Carlisle's got all hands on deck," she said, zooming out again. "This is last minute. Reactive."

"Agreed. Combine that with the conspicuous absence of brown coveralls, and we can confirm your friend Jenny is the leak."

Lisa lifted her gaze from the video to shoot him a questioning look. "How so?"

"Not one person out there is wearing the brown coveralls I described in my report—the coveralls Detective Fan left out of the final transcript. Only she knew about them. Ergo, only she could have warned Carlisle to get rid of them."

Clay had once told Lisa that the absence of a piece of evidence is often more telling than the evidence itself. Peter had summed up the principle nicely. But an absence of evidence rarely held up in court. "I'll need more than that to nail Jenny," she said, still videoing. The workers had started pulling big black tarps over the equipment. "I need phone calls or emails. Or I need Carlisle to flip on her."

"Do you think he will?"

"Not over an illegal mining charge." She panned the phone to catch a shot of what looked like a ground-penetrating-radar rig before Carlisle's people covered it with a tarp. "We have to get him on something bigger, like Kelly's murder."

"So, you're not ready to arrest him and go public?"

"No."

"Then we should probably move. Because Carlisle's heading this way."

Lisa looked up from her phone to see headlights coming toward them. Carlisle's Bentley, moving at a slow roll. The driver of the first truck released the brakes with a loud hiss and pulled in behind him. Neither gave any sign of turning toward the asphalt road out of the facility. Could they drive those flatbeds on the dirt smuggler's track? Maybe that's how they'd gotten the equipment to the facility in the first place.

Lisa yanked Peter back into the darkness of the tunnel. "My Jeep. It's blocking the track. We need to get there before they do."

Uphill. Stumbling over roots and stumps. Whenever the track made enough of a turn to hide the MagLite, Lisa flashed it on and off, trying to memorize the path ahead. She saw the Jeep sooner than expected, but in the same moment Peter went down with a pained grunt.

The wash of the Bentley's lights would reach them at any second. Lisa helped him to his feet and put his arm across her shoulders.

At his first step, he nearly dropped again. "Ow. Didn't need that knee, I suppose."

"We're almost there. Can you make it?"

"That's what the other one's for."

When they reached the hood of the Jeep, he pushed her away toward the driver's side. "Get her cranked up. I'm all right."

The noise from the big flatbeds in the column masked the sound of her engine coming to life, but Lisa had no room to turn around. "I have to do this in reverse."

"So?"

"I can't control the back-up lights."

"Either they'll see, or they won't. Just get moving!"

She put it into gear and found the reverse lights were a blessing—bright enough to light the track a few yards behind them but dim enough to stay hidden from Carlisle and his people. "Here we go."

Twisting in her seat, hand constantly in motion at the wheel, Lisa pushed the limits of her driving skills. She drove in reverse faster than she ever had on a paved surface, let alone a winding dirt track in the dark. And it paid off. The column fell behind. But her arms and eyes were tiring. She couldn't keep it up much longer. "Where is it?" she asked herself out loud. "Where'd it go?"

Peter turned to look. "Where'd what go?"

"That!" Her lights found the dip where an intersecting track crossed the gully to meet theirs—the place where she'd almost rolled the Jeep on the way in. Lisa gave the steering wheel a hard turn and dropped into neutral. The Jeep rolled backward into the dip. She cut the engine before it settled to a stop.

The two sat in the dark, listening to the approaching column.

"Is this depression deep enough to hide us?" Peter asked.

"We'll find out."

The Bentley came first. Carlisle had stayed close to his trucks, acting as a lead car for the larger vehicles. Smart. He had better visibility on the narrow track. He'd done this before.

Lisa and Peter sank down in their seats until they could no longer see the roof of the passing car and only the very tops of the following trucks. None of them stopped, and once the red glow of the last truck's lights had disappeared around the next bend, she started the Jeep again.

"What now?" Peter asked.

"Now we find out where they're going."

CHAPTER
SIXTY-THREE

Central Maui

PETER'S KNEE THROBBED. He tried probing it with his fingers, looking for a chip or crack in the kneecap, but the swelling and pain blocked his analysis. He'd need an X-ray. His back. His knee. His lungs. How many body parts could a man have safely X-rayed in a single week?

"You okay?" Lisa asked, glancing at him.

He'd shown enough weakness for one night. "I'm fine. It's a bump, nothing more." He pointed at the trucks, now running with their lights off. "Focus on our friends. Don't lose them."

"I don't plan to."

The Ono Beef column had left the smuggler's track at the place where Lisa and Peter had entered and taken Route 37 north. But they hadn't stayed on the paved roads for long. Shortly after the highway bent westward, the column had veered southwest onto a gravel road that took them into the heart of the island's great valley plain. The dust they kicked up obscured Peter's view so much that he often wondered whether he or Lisa could still see them, or if they were following a mirage.

"Where are they headed?" Peter asked.

"You don't recognize this area?"

"Not in the dark, with all this dust."

"The dust is your clue. These are the old cane fields. We're on Ono Beef property again." Lisa took out her phone and dialed. "Pika? Yeah . . . Yeah, I know . . . I'm fine. Really. Just listen. I need you to call Detective Fan. Tell her your sister's doctor friend called and said he's been snooping around Jack Carlisle's facility again."

"Have you gone mad?" Peter grabbed at the phone, but Lisa dodged him and gave him a look that said *Keep quiet*.

"Yeah," she said. "The Ono Beef facility on the southwest side of Haleakala. Tell her the doctor claimed he saw mining equipment and thinks Carlisle is moving it to the storage containers at the Baseyard."

She paused, listening, then frowned and shook her head. "It doesn't matter how he figured it out. He's smart. Jenny knows that. She'll buy it. Tell her the doctor was on foot, but that your sister has already left to intercept Carlisle's trucks at the Baseyard. Say I took my personal weapon with me. Pretend to be worried—you think I might get violent."

Peter heard Pika's voice on the other end, and Lisa held up a hand like a puppet, mimicking someone who won't stop talking. "Rat me out to Mom all you want, but not tonight. The captain wants us to keep this quiet . . . Yes, *the* captain." She rolled her eyes at Peter. "Do as I say, Pika. Call Detective Fan right now, and make sure you record everything."

Lisa hung up and opened her camera app, then handed the phone to Peter. "Video me. But not yet. Let's wait a while to let things simmer."

"What are you up to?"

"You'll see." She drove on, following the ghost column through the dust at their slow pace for several minutes. "Okay. We're good. Let me know when you hit record."

He gave her an okay sign and Lisa began.

"This is Detective Lisa Kealoha. The digital time signature on this video will show I'm recording at the same time Officer Pika Kealoha is feeding Detective Jenny Fan leading intelligence. If Detective Fan is our leak, the Ono Beef convoy ahead of us will stop." She motioned for Peter to shift his focus to the trucks.

He followed her direction but shook his head, squinting at the black screen. "It's too dark and dusty out here. The camera can't pick them up."

"Give it time. Don't pan away."

He held the camera steady, waiting. Nothing happened. "Lisa, perhaps we should—"

Red brake lights appeared at the edge of the screen. Peter adjusted his aim to bring them to the center, and they grew larger. The trucks had stopped.

Lisa smacked his arm with the back of her hand. "Got her. And now Carlisle is out of options."

It took Peter less than a minute to reconstruct her thinking. Carlisle intended to hide the mining equipment at the Baseyard, because the police had already searched it and found nothing. Not a bad idea. But by telling Carlisle—through his mole—that Peter had foreseen this plan, Lisa had forced him to abandon it. He watched the trucks, still idling. "Where will they go now?"

Lisa nodded at the road ahead. "Keep shooting."

On the screen, Peter saw the trucks shifting into reverse. "They're coming back. We should move."

"No need. They won't get too close."

As she spoke, the reverse lights went out. The closest truck turned, seeming to vanish into the cane field. Peter laughed. "He's gone into the trees lining an irrigation gully—part of Trejo's smuggler's network."

"It's the only option Carlisle has left. He'll have to leave them there on the dirt track, hidden only by the trees, and hope nobody looks." Once the second truck had pulled into the trees,

Lisa hit the stop button and took the phone from Peter's hands. She put the Jeep into gear and made a K-turn. "But we'll be looking. First thing tomorrow."

"Where to now?" Peter asked. "Back to the resort?"

"Nope. It's time I dealt with my office bully."

CHAPTER
SIXTY-FOUR

PETER DIDN'T QUESTION Lisa much as she drove. The pain in his leg made conversation difficult. The swelling had not stopped. He imagined his knee had grown to the size of a grapefruit—oddly not one of the many juices offered to him at the Grand.

His tumble while running in the dark could have gone a lot worse. A bump on the knee from a root could have easily been a knock to the head or a stray branch through the spleen. The world didn't need the help of rogue divers, gang lords, or grenades to kill him.

Done for.

Lights out.

The end?

Peter clenched and unclenched his right fist to stave off the quivering. He needed to figure out for sure what lay beyond the fork at the end of life's road.

More life waited for him there, if he was to believe Tuna and Lisa. And if Lisa, especially, believed that death was a crossroads instead of a bleak nothingness, perhaps Peter should give the view more weight than he had in the past.

He darted a glance at the woman driving the Jeep. So intelligent —more than him in many respects. Peter had always been good with numbers and facts, procedures and processes, even hand-eye-coordination skills. But Lisa seemed to understand people and their motivations in a way that he didn't, or couldn't. He hadn't seen her simultaneous trap for both Carlisle and Detective Fan until after the trucks had stopped.

"There she is," Lisa said, pointing out his side of the Jeep toward the orange streetlights and concrete expanse of the Baseyard. "See the Chevy Bolt parked behind the Cantina? Jenny thinks she's so sly. Her car won't be visible from the main Baseyard road or the container lot, but we can see it from here."

Once they entered the Baseyard, Lisa drove past the Cantina, all the way to the back of the storage lot where they'd found the container with the false back. When she got out to stretch her legs, she told Peter to stay in the Jeep and remain inconspicuous. As far as Jenny knew, he wasn't supposed to be there. Peter was happy to oblige, not certain he could stand if he tried.

He did his best to hold his poker face and not show his pain. "When do you expect her?"

"Watch this." Lisa turned to face the far end of the double container line. "Cue the traitor in three, two, one . . ."

With a blue/red flash and an obnoxious *whoop* of a dashboard siren, Jenny came idling down the gravel aisle. By appearances, she was in no hurry, savoring her rival's moment of total self-destruction.

She climbed out of the Bolt and rested a hip against the door. "Hey, Lisa. Whatcha doin' out here?"

"Waiting for you."

The answer seemed to throw Jenny, but only for a heartbeat. "Are you sure you weren't waiting for an imaginary suspect?" She gave a dramatic gasp and covered her mouth with her hand. "Oh wait. You can't have suspects. You're on suspension. Oo. That's not good." With a smirk, she knocked on the top of the Bolt.

The Bolt's passenger door opened, and a large form rose beside it.

Lisa straightened. "Captain Griffith."

"Hello, Miss Kealoha."

Peter didn't like the way he'd said *Miss*. Was this part of Lisa's plan?

Jenny gave the captain a somber look. "Sir, I hate to say this, but I think former Detective Kealoha has taken things too far. This violation of her suspension rises to the level of criminal conduct. For the public good and her own safety, we should place her under arrest."

The captain gave Lisa a dark look, then drew a set of cuffs from a round holster on his belt. He and Jenny approached together.

"Sir?" Lisa said.

The captain shifted his gaze to Jenny. "Secure the suspect so I can apply the restraints."

A smile spread across Jenny's lips as she reached for Lisa's wrists. "Gladly."

Peter gripped the Jeep's dashboard, right hand going to the door handle. He would hobble over there and tackle the captain if he had to. But before he could make such a doomed move, Lisa made hers. She dodged Jenny's grasp, caught one of her wrists, and stepped behind her. Jenny struggled, but Lisa held her by both arms and dropped her to her knees with a kick to the back of the legs. "The captain was talking to me."

Two Maui PD squad cars came in from either end of the container line, sirens on and lights flashing. One turned broadside to block Jenny's Bolt. The other stopped within a few feet of their group. Pika stood up from behind the wheel. "Aloha, Sis, Cap'n. Howzit?"

The captain slapped the cuffs on Jenny, and together, he and Pika lifted her up. "Jennifer Fan," Captain Griffith said. "You are under arrest for corruption, hindering an investigation, and accessory to murder."

"What? But . . . How—"

"Oo," Lisa said, cutting her off. "That's not good."

Peter laughed despite the pain in his knee.

After the captain put Jenny in Pika's squad car, he met Lisa and Peter at the Jeep. "Your brother and I will book Fan. And I'll have Mike and Rivera get the warrant for the Oahu lab's phone lines in the morning. But the truth is, our case is still paper thin. A good defense lawyer will shred us in court. We need either Fan or Carlisle to confess. Do you have a plan?"

"I might, sir. Right now, Dr. Chesterfield needs medical attention. He's been trying to hide it, but his knee is in considerable pain. Then I'll need to locate Carlisle. I let him go so we could grab Jenny." She darted a glance at Peter. "And now I'm afraid he'll try to tie up a vital loose end."

CHAPTER
SIXTY-FIVE

Maui Memorial Medical Center

SINCE THE BEGINNING—since he first rode into the ER on Kelly's cart, fighting to save her life—a part of Peter's mind had noted the deference with which the Maui doctors treated Tuna. In his experience, ER docs and surgeons weren't rude to general practitioners, per se, but they didn't treat them as equals. And they certainly didn't allow GPs to practice medicine in their exam rooms.

Yet here he was.

Tuna finished wrapping Peter's knee. He had lanced it to drain fluid and applied a subcutaneous patch to secure a crack in the kneecap, talking Peter through every step of the procedure. "Stay off that as much as possible," he said, removing his blue gloves and walking to the head of Peter's bed. "I'll make sure Margaret gets you a cane, and I'll assign one of my keiki at the Grand to wheel you around."

Margaret. He and the head nurse for the shift were on a first-name basis—the old-friends kind. "You were the trauma surgeon here, weren't you?"

Tuna gave him a wistful smile. "Chief attending, ya? A long

time ago, but near enough that folks around here remember me that way."

"What made you give up the life?"

"Heart attack, Brah." Tuna patted his chest. "Even God-fearing men can let stress and too many sugary grindz get the best of 'em. But praise Him. We have a great cardiothoracic team. Especially Dr. Wen. She saved my life." He shrugged. "Maybe just so I could stick around and save yours."

Peter thrust both hands at his wrapped knee. "That was hardly a lifesaving procedure."

"I wasn't talking about the knee, Brah." Tuna helped Peter take a couple of pills, then pressed the button to lower his bed into the sleeping position. "It's late. That was a sedative, which should help you get some rest. I'm sure you need it. Me too, ya? Tomorrow, over some pulled pork sandwiches at Aunty Noelani's, we'll talk more about the way you ditched me to go on your adventure." He switched off the room's light, giving Peter a wink as he did. "Next time you hop a fence and sneak through a cow pasture, I want in."

Peter lolled his head over to look at the blue digital numbers of the room's clock. 1:14 a.m. The ER had gone quiet—something that never happened at the Royal London. Despite the pain, despite everything, he feared exhaustion might actually take him. He couldn't let that happen.

His life depended on staying awake. He should have told Tuna his plan—to become the bait in a fishing expedition.

Fishing. Bait. Tuna.

Hadn't he been thinking about something important just now? Whatever it was, he'd lost it in a wisp of amusement.

After a time, the blue glow of the numbers disappeared. Had he closed his eyes? No. A shadow had moved in to block them. Black shadow. Smoky tendrils reaching for him. "Is someone there?"

"Go to sleep, Dr. Chesterfield." The voice was so familiar, so steeped in death. "You need sleep, and I'm going to give you a shot to make sure you stay asleep for a long, long time."

Peter felt the hand on his arm. He felt the tendrils, this time around his neck, pulling him down, down. "I'm not ready."

"Oh. I think you are."

The lights came on. With effort and searing pain in his knee from the motion, Peter jerked his arm away from the needle.

The privacy curtain flew back. Lisa dove at the attacker and wrapped him in a bear hug from behind as Mike and Rivera burst into the room.

The lights snapped on, blinding Peter at first, but when his vision resolved, he saw Carlisle fighting his captors, struggling to stab Lisa's arm with the deadly needle.

Rivera cracked him across the wrist with a club. The syringe fell to the floor, and Mike held him fast while Lisa yanked his arms behind his back.

She slapped on a set of cuffs. "What's wrong, Carlisle? No one left to do the dirty work for you?"

CHAPTER
SIXTY-SIX

Maui PD Criminal Investigative Division

THE SECONDARY INTERROGATION ROOM at the Criminal Investigative Division didn't get a lot of use. It had no observation room like its larger cousin, so it had no mirror, just four gray walls and a table and chairs. That wasn't entirely true. The room also boasted two standing cabinets, since it doubled as the division's spill-over supply closet. In her short time in the CID, Lisa had been in there only once before—to get paper for the printer.

She brushed the dust off the seat of an aluminum chair and sat down across from Jenny and her public defender. "How was your night?"

The public defender, on the heavy side and all of twenty-five, glanced at his client. "Don't answer that."

Both Lisa and Jenny shot him a frown.

Jenny lifted her chin. "I'll tell you whatever you need to know to nail Carlisle, as long as you get me a good deal. What are the terms?"

Lisa opened a leather folder and notepad, tilted so that Jenny couldn't see the contents, and clicked a ballpoint pen a few times, making her wait. Her mother would have frowned on her behavior. But really, was there anything in the Bible precluding her from enjoying this moment a little bit? "I don't know about deals," she said slowly. "The assistant DA doesn't like you much. She says you hang around the courthouse too much, politicking. She felt like you were after her job." Lisa scowled at her over the top of the notepad. "I can relate."

"I'm sorry, okay?"

Jenny's lawyer opened his mouth, probably to warn her not to apologize, but she brushed him off as best she could with both hands cuffed to the table. "Call it ambition. Call it jealousy. Call it whatever you want, but don't mix up our little rivalry with the charges against me. That's not professional."

"Not professional?" Lisa had to clench her teeth to keep from coming out of her seat. "You passed on information that got my suspect, an old friend, killed and almost got me and Peter killed as well. Then, to wipe away any sense that you didn't know the depths to which Carlisle might stoop, you did it again."

"I didn't know your doctor friend was in that house."

"Prove it. Right now, I have you on corruption, accepting a bribe, and accessory before and after the fact on Koa Alana's murder. And once I go through your phone and email accounts, I'll have you on a conspiracy charge for Kelly's murder too."

"My client denies all charges of conspiracy to commit murder," the lawyer said, looking pleased with himself for getting a word in.

Lisa didn't even look at him. "Tell me one thing up front, Jenny. Why Kelly Alana? What did she do to deserve getting beaten over the head and left in the ocean to drown?"

"I don't know anything about Kelly."

"Wrong answer." Lisa snapped the leather folder closed.

"Wait. It's true, I don't know about Kelly, but I can tell you other stuff. Like the cache of weapons at Trejo's hideout—that military surplus grenade launcher. Carlisle supplied all of it. He asked me for the name of a gun runner and then had me keep an eye out to make sure the transaction stayed off our radar."

"You're off to a good start. What else?"

"Tell me the deal first."

"That's not how this works, and you know it." Lisa removed a stack of lined confession forms from her leather folder and slid them across the table. She unlocked Jenny's cuffs. "Write down everything you can, and the DA and I will decide what it's worth." She clicked the pen and set it on top of the pages. "And Jenny, don't forget to sign and date every page. By the book. That's how we do it here in the Maui PD."

JACK CARLISLE HAD THE DUBIOUS HONOR of getting the primary interrogation room, which came with a packed-house audience in the observation chamber. As she entered, Lisa wondered if her suspect could sense the host of gazes through the one-way mirror. She certainly could.

Carlisle had declined a public defender. He didn't need one. He had a full team seated on either side of him. Two men and one woman, all in three-thousand-dollar suits.

Lisa didn't say a word when she sat at the table. She closed the leather pad and folded her hands on top of it, then stared at Carlisle as if his lawyers weren't there.

Carlisle answered her stare with a grin.

One of the lawyers, the older of the men, laid a stack of papers in front of Lisa. "Good morning, Detective. This is a list of our client's complaints against your department, including false arrest, false imprisonment, and brutality."

"You've got to be kidding. We caught him attempting to inject Dr. Chesterfield with concentrated vitamin K, more than enough to cause a pulmonary embolism and—"

The female lawyer on the other side of Carlisle interrupted her with a second set of papers. "And these are the complaints against you personally as a joint defendant with Dr. Peter Chesterfield. For the record, our client found that syringe in the hospital while visiting his sick friend. He had no knowledge of its contents and had no intention of injecting them into anyone." She took on a sad expression. "But since our client's friendship with Dr. Chesterfield has soured beyond repair, he is now suing you both for harassment, damaging trespass, and defamation. You might want to hire a legal team of your own. Dr. Chesterfield can certainly afford it."

Lisa almost believed the hurt in the lawyer's voice, expressed on Carlisle's behalf. She tucked both stacks of paper under her pad and once again folded her hands and settled her gaze on Carlisle. *Don't forget to breathe,* she could hear Clay saying.

In fact, Clay had said those very words to her on the phone less than an hour before. Dawn had broken on the FBI offices in Philadelphia long before it had on Maui, and Lisa had called Clay while he was still driving to work. Clay had been busy following up on her previous text about Carlisle, and that morning, with slam-dunk murder charges pending, he'd been able to go even deeper.

"Mr. Carlisle," Lisa said, maintaining her stare. "Your complaints will hold little water once the court realizes you've made them under a stolen identity."

All three lawyers turned to look at him. "What is she talking about?" the oldest asked. "What stolen identity?"

"Oh. He didn't tell you? Your client's real name is Daniel Moore, former CFO of Carlisle Beef."

This earned Lisa her first response from Carlisle since she'd entered the room. "Daniel Moore was our CFO and my best friend. He died in a car accident—the same wreck that killed my father."

"Did he? Or did you seize an opportunity to take over the life of one of the richest ranchers in your state?" Lisa glanced left and right at the lawyers. "Let me paint you a picture, counselors. Late at night. Rural Texas. The road is empty except for a rancher and his son heading home. Coming the other way, after leaving the ranch, is a reckless driver going way over the limit."

The female lawyer started to protest, but her boss shut her down. "Go on, Detective. We're listening."

Lisa gave him a nod. "The speed demon survived, but he knew he'd go down for vehicular manslaughter—his life over. He had to act quickly before emergency responders, called by the automated system in Carlisle's Mercedes, arrived on the scene. Daniel Moore traded wallets and phones with his best friend, Jack. The two were close enough in age and appearance that no one would give the ID a second look. Then he dragged Jack to his car and put him behind the wheel. With all the gas on the road, a little spark did the rest. Moore let himself get burned to finish the effect and lay down in the ditch to wait for the responders to find him."

Clay and his team had pieced the rest together for her. They believed Moore had swapped lives with Carlisle, an easy con when dealing with a best friend whose only living relative had been killed in the same crash. As the company CFO, Moore had all the right knowledge and passwords. He'd shut down the ranch and sold off the property from a hospital in Dallas, citing his grief and a need for change.

"Too many people in Longview might have recognized you if you went back," Lisa said. "You came up with a new plan— a new dream to chase—a pet idea about Elysium in Hawaii, planted in your head by Harry Alcott when he spoke at a conference you attended. Too bad you didn't meet then, or he would have recognized you as a fraud when you contacted him later, posing as your dead friend."

The head of the legal team cleared his throat. "Detective, at this time, I'd like to request a few minutes to confer with our client."

"That's your right." Lisa got up to leave. "But I'll be back shortly." She dropped the absurd complaints against her, Peter, and the department on the table with a loud slap. "And don't waste my time with any more games. Fraud is the least of your concerns. Your client is facing multiple murder charges."

She made it to the door before Carlisle spoke. "It wasn't a dream."

"Excuse me?"

"The Elysium," he said, shaking off the lawyers' attempts to quiet him. "We found it, as you well know. You have a piece in your possession, the smaller of two we pulled out of the ground. One of our own team members shaped them for me with a laser cutter."

"Mr. Carlisle," Lisa said. "Mr. Moore, I should say. You just placed yourself at the scene of Kelly Alana's murder."

"No. I gave that rock to Trejo when I promised him a piece of the Elysium windfall, and the idiot lost it within days. I can prove I didn't kill Kelly. Trejo didn't either. We met at my villa that night. With Angelica Puelani's crash, his side hobby had brought too much attention from the police. I wanted to rein him in."

"Why should I believe you?"

"I have security footage." Carlisle shrugged. "I'll cop to the illegal mining charges, and to letting Trejo use my land for his auto theft enterprise. The rest, we can fight out in court. But I'm telling you right now, neither I nor Luan Trejo killed that girl, and I have no idea who did."

CHAPTER
SIXTY-SEVEN

The Elysium Grand

"SO, YOU *WON'T* BE SENDING CARLISLE to jail for trying to kill me? Attempted murder gets a pass. Is that some odd nuance of the American justice system?"

Peter sat in a wheelchair at a sleek ebony conference table in one of the Grand's decked-out boardrooms. He'd rented the place for the day, complete with an interactive whiteboard on which he and Lisa had re-created her murder board.

She was filling in the timeline, adding the meeting between Moore/Carlisle and Trejo on the night of Kelly's death. "The conspiracy to commit murder charge carries a bigger sentence, especially when Jenny's testimony proves Carlisle bought the explosives Trejo's men used in their homemade torpedo." Lisa finished her work on the timeline and looked back at him. "Oh, don't look so hurt."

"It is hurtful. He tried to kill me"—Peter rolled his eyes—"again. And he's getting off scot-free."

"Peter, he's going to jail for a long time."

"For someone else's murder. Not mine."

Lisa threw up her hands. "You weren't murdered. Can we

focus please? We're back to the original question. Who killed Kelly Alana?"

"Are you certain our fraudulent Carlisle isn't lying about the meeting? You checked the footage?"

"Every second of it." Lisa dragged her finger across the screen below a window that showed the Fake Carlisle's security video, running it forward at high speed. "Mike says the time stamp is authentic and the changes in light back it up. These two fought over Trejo's auto theft ring deep into the heart of our murder window for Kelly. This video is our best piece of evidence that the two were working together, and it gives them both an alibi for her murder. They didn't do it."

"Trejo could have ordered one of his men to kill her. He had motive."

"They both had motive. Kelly threatened to expose Carlisle's operation, which was Trejo's big-money game that Koa tried to tell me about. We can presume Carlisle knew of Kelly's threat." Lisa crossed her arms, shaking her head at the board. "But I believe him when he says he doesn't know who killed her or how Trejo's chunk of Elysium wound up in the ocean with her."

"Kelly stole it."

"What?"

Peter laughed to himself. "Kelly's killer didn't drop the Elysium stone. It fell from her pocket. She'd stolen the rock from Trejo's house as proof of what they were doing."

"But why?"

"Your brother answered that question for me when we were in the boat. He said the Alana family once owned the land Carlisle had bought."

"They did, for many generations, before they and other cane farming families sold their acreage to the mill company. The Alana lands made up the largest section." Lisa met his eye. "Honu."

Peter nodded. "Honu. The Alanas' 'aumakua. Carlisle and

Trejo were illegally mining on land sacred to her family. Apparently, that was where Kelly drew her line in the sand."

He wheeled his chair away from the table and over to a set of file boxes Lisa had brought with her. "All right. If Carlisle and Trejo are out, and the Elysium no longer points to our killer, let's go back to the beginning. We'll pore over the body of evidence until we find what we've missed." He lifted a notebook with warped pages from one of the boxes and wiggled it at her. "What is this?"

"The evidence notebook I was carrying on the day of Kelly's competition. I filled it up until it went into the pool with me at my interview with Kelly, and then I switched to a new one."

"Sounds like a good place for me to start—a new set of eyes and all that." Peter found a smile spreading across his lips as he opened to a crinkled page dated to the day of the freediving competition. Book study came with a sense of excitement when it involved a good puzzle, like diagnosing a particularly baffling set of symptoms or finding the safest route to a hard-to-reach tumor. He glanced up at Lisa, who had joined him at the file boxes. "We should order something to eat. This might take a while."

THREE HOURS and a great many shrimp toasts and other hors d'oeuvres later, Peter had created a system of images and notes that covered the boardroom table. Tearing the first few pages out of Lisa's notebook had seemed to annoy her for reasons he couldn't quite understand. But once that was done, she grew accustomed to it and acquiesced to the rest of his organizational demands.

"I've laid our evidence out in similar fashion to my favorite offshoot of brain mapping," he said, waving his hands over the papers. "While the physical brain doesn't always cooperate, our visualization system takes the coordinates of nodes with the most related functions and interactivity and repositions them close to each other. When the source of a patient's neurological issue is hard to identify, examining portions by degree of relatedness helps us discover what's out of place."

"And what are you seeing that's out of place with my evidence?"

Her tone suggested that Peter had put it *all* out of place—irreparably so—but after hours of study and searching, he had an answer. "I'm glad you asked."

He used a device that had come with the interactive board to snap pictures of two different pages from her notebook. These, he sent to the board. "The incidents here at the Grand—the falling scuba tanks and the collapsing bleachers. They seem like childish pranks compared to the violence of the other events in the case, hardly worthy of men like Trejo and our Fake Carlisle."

"You're saying they're not related to Kelly's murder?"

"Not at all. To call the common victim and location coincidence defies common sense. No. They're not *un*related to the case, but perhaps they're not *as* related as we thought. And here's the thing." He snapped a picture of Kelly's autopsy file and sent it to the board as well. "When you set it apart from gangs and car thefts, guns and explosions, Kelly's death is similarly nonviolent. No bullets, no bombs, no knives. Just a blow to the head from an unusual angle and a poor attempt to dispose of a not-yet-expired victim."

Lisa walked to the board. "If Fake Carlisle or Trejo or one of their lieutenants had been part of Kelly's death, the murderer would have killed her more quickly and disposed of the body more cleanly. Our killer is outside the inner circle of the Carlisle-Trejo conspiracy."

"Perhaps," Peter said. "Out or in, if I were to try my hand at some amateur profiling, I'd say our man—or woman—was physically strong but something of a mental wimp. This person doesn't think his or her actions through to their full conclusion."

He rolled up beside Lisa, rereading the pages on the digital board to reinforce his analysis. "Yes. Yes, that's it. I should have seen it earlier. Kelly's murderer is reactionary, easily manipulated by events or strong personalities." He glanced up at her. "Looking back on your investigation, can you think of anyone who fits this description?"

"Possibly. But he's so far removed from the case, I had completely written him off." She hurried back to the table. "Where is it? I can't make heads or tails of your system."

"What are you looking for?"

"This." She took a photo with the smart board's device and sent it to the screen, where it forced the two pages Peter had placed there to shrink and move down. "Mike's people took this picture of a crate of electronics when they searched the containers at the Baseyard. We know these devices to be part of Fake Carlisle's mining operation, used for subterranean radar and analysis." She laughed a sad *I finally get it* laugh. "I saw matching devices during the auto theft investigation before Kelly died. They were in pieces, hard to recognize, but I'd swear now they were the same."

Lisa returned and knelt next to Peter's wheelchair, laying a hand on his arm. "I know who the killer is. We just have to figure out how to prove it."

CHAPTER
SIXTY-EIGHT

Maui Memorial Park

PETER STOOD APART FROM THE CROWD praying under the stone-and-timber awning at the center of the cemetery park. The rising sun washed the white prints on their dark aloha shirts and dresses in shades of orange and pink. A Sunday sunrise funeral, laying to rest both Koa and Kelly Alana.

Rest.

What rest would they have? Which fork had they taken?

Peter was thankful for the cane Tuna had gifted him. Leaning on its bronze dolphin head put constant weight on his right hand to hide the tremors, which had grown to a near constant. For that reason, he doubted he'd give the accoutrement up once his knee healed. Peter did not take part in the prayer—wouldn't know how—but kept his eyes moving, watching for their suspect.

Lisa had bid him discover the identity of the killer on his own. And he had. But she refused to let him forget that she'd gotten there first. As he'd acknowledged before, she was smarter than him in many ways. For Peter, the answer had come down to the array of evidence he'd laid out in his spiraling brain map.

All became clear once he reached a simple conclusion that had changed the meaning of a single printout—if Jenny Fan was a traitor, then she had lied about almost everything.

The mill company, now gone, had paid for the gravesites after Koa's and Kelly's fathers died in the fire. One complete row in the park belonged to the six victims and their wives and children. The spaces for the Alana children were not far apart. So many from their extended family had come, easily identified by the sea turtles on their shirts and dresses.

Honu.

Kelly's family.

Lisa had assured Peter their suspect would come—would not be able to stay away. Such behavior matched Peter's analysis of the suspect's personality. But the pastor had already begun his sermon, and so far, the killer had not shown his face.

"Where are you?"

Let Lisa and Pika mourn. Peter set off to walk the grounds. He wouldn't miss this chance to find the man who'd robbed him of his illusions.

Movement. A shadow behind a bonsai tree at the corner of the park. Peter picked up his pace.

When he reached the tree, the shadow had gone. But the cemetery park had few hiding places. A stepped, maze-like garden served as a path between the park's upper and lower lawns. Peter hurried in, wincing with every step, and saw his quarry among the hedges after the first turn. "Jason Alana!"

The young man tensed and shifted his weight as if preparing to bolt.

"Don't. I'm not a cop, just a man looking for answers. Turn and face me, Jason."

Peter left no room for disobedience in his tone, and it worked. The young man turned. Peter nodded. "Good. Look at my leg. This cane. I won't be chasing you if and when you choose to run. But if you do, you'll never get what you came for."

"Which is?" Jason refused to meet his gaze.

"Absolution. Release. The secret of what happened that night is eating you alive from the inside. They're about to put Kelly in the ground, Jason. This is your last chance to let it out, to be free."

"I'll never be free. She made me a monster."

Shifting the blame. *She did this.* Peter recoiled from the offense to Kelly. But then, had he been any different in the operating theater? Barbara had made a mistake, yes. But her mistake had not forced the harsh words out of Peter. That cruelty had come from within.

"If you run, Jason, they'll find you. We know everything."

"You can't know everything."

"No? We interviewed Carlisle last night. He identified you as the man he hired to keep his radars and on-site analysis lab running. Your criminal record and IT skills made you the perfect man to find his Elysium. Too bad you couldn't."

Jason lifted his gaze to meet Peter's. "I *did* find Elysium. I found a big chunk of it for Carlisle, the one he cut in two. One for him and one for his pet gang lord Trejo."

"But after that first, thrilling find, you couldn't deliver more."

"No, that's all Haleakala would give me."

"And while you kept searching, Kelly learned of your operation."

Jason's eyes narrowed. His right hand inched toward his back. "Kelly had no idea I was involved. She went to Trejo's place. He bragged about the Elysium, showed off his piece." He let out a huff. "Party tricks. Did you know that if you put an Elysium stone on a block of ice, it melts straight through, like it still holds the volcano's fire inside? But Kelly wasn't entertained. She could only think of what might become of our family's old lands once Carlisle found the mother lode."

When Jason's hand reappeared, it was holding a Beretta 9mm. He kept talking, as if unaware he'd drawn the gun. "She wanted to stop us. She was gonna ruin everything."

In their Saturday-night interview with Carlisle, Lisa and Peter learned that he'd promised Jason a share of his profits. To a kid with a felony record, barely scraping by, it must have seemed like a fresh chance at all his dreams.

"You tried to warn her off, didn't you?" Peter said. "With the bleachers? The falling tanks?"

He and Lisa had found Jason on the Grand's security footage, wearing a white shirt with a brown collar and tan shorts—the uniform of the maintenance staff. He'd gotten a job there under an alias, giving him access to the bleachers at the freediving event and the pump room behind the doomed scuba shelf. But thanks to Jenny, Lisa had missed that evidence the first time around. When he'd learned Lisa was interested in Jason, Carlisle had directed Jenny to manufacture an alibi. Any heat on the kid keeping his high-tech equipment running might burn the operation.

When Jason failed to answer, Peter pressed him. "We know you used acid from your mineral analysis equipment to weaken the bleacher bolts. But what about the scuba rack? How'd you do it?"

"The fender washers," Jason said, his tone bland and distant. "I took them off and overtightened the nuts until the fake rock holding the rack in place cracked. After that, any new weight, like Kelly's wet buoyancy vest, would bring it down. It was supposed to scare her. I wasn't trying to kill her."

"No." Peter took a hobbled step toward him, holding his gaze but watching the gun in his peripheral vision. "You didn't want to kill her. I understand that. You only wanted to warn her off, make her think Trejo was sending her a message."

"And it worked. Kelly thought Trejo was behind it. She called me, told me everything as if I didn't already know, and asked me to meet her."

"In the cane fields."

"Yeah. The cane fields." The phrase triggered a change in his expression. Jason's eyes grew darker, more focused. His gun started to rise. "That's where it happened."

"Jason, don't!" Lisa appeared from the hedges behind Peter—Pika too. "Move that gun one more inch and I *will* shoot you."

The gun stopped, angled down at forty-five degrees, roughly pointed at Peter's good knee. Peter would have preferred Lisa had ordered him to *Drop it!* as police always did in the movies.

"Lisa?" Jason glanced her way with the look of a man addressing a ghost. "Why did you have to come back? You made Kelly want to be brave like you. Not freediving or car-boosting brave, but the real kind. The kind of brave that makes you stand up for something."

"Is that what she told you?" Lisa asked. "That night in the cane field."

"She showed me the Elysium, as if I hadn't been the one to pull it out of the ground for Carlisle. She wanted us to go and talk to you together." His gun arm relaxed, giving Peter a measure of relief. "I told her everything, what Elysium could mean for us. For me. I couldn't be a famous athlete like her or a cop like you and Pika." He snorted. "On Maui, a felon can't even get a food truck license. I told her I had to make my own path. She had to let me. It was only fair."

Peter could guess what happened after that. "The argument grew heated. She pushed you verbally. You pushed back physically."

Jason answered him through clenched teeth, grip tightening on the gun again. "I didn't mean to push so hard, you know? She was putting the Elysium in her pocket, so her hand got trapped as she fell. I tried to catch her, but I only made it worse, like pushing her again. Her head hit a rock. She stopped moving. There was nothing I could do."

"You could have taken her to the hospital," Peter said.

"No." Jason closed his eyes tight, shaking his head. "No. It was too late. The doctors couldn't have saved her."

"*I* could have saved her."

Peter felt Lisa's eyes on him, warning him he'd crossed a line. His mouth—even now, after everything, he couldn't control it.

When Jason opened his eyes again, they locked onto Peter's, filled with tears. "Is that really true? You could have saved her?"

Whatever Lisa might want him to say to talk this kid down, Peter wasn't going to lie, not about this. He gave Jason a subtle nod. "Me. The doctors at Maui Memorial. There was time."

A sob burst from Jason's chest. "I'm sorry. I'm so sorry." His gun hand twitched.

Lisa advanced, keeping her weapon leveled. "Take it easy, Jason. We found the Elysium with her body—must've fallen out of her pocket. It corroborates your story. I promise you, there's light on the other side of this. I can show you, the way I should have showed Kelly and Koa. All you have to do is put that gun down, nice and slow."

His body shook with another sob, arms going limp. He turned his gaze to Lisa and tilted his head as if to offer one more *I'm sorry*. His gun came up.

Lisa pulled her trigger.

CHAPTER
SIXTY-NINE

Okeanos Restaurant
The Grand

PETER ROSE FROM HIS TABLE in the corner of Okeanos as Lisa arrived. "Thank you for coming. It's good to see you."

"And you." She let him adjust her chair for her as she sat. "I was glad you called."

He hadn't seen her since the funeral, six days earlier. Peter had needed some time—to regroup, to put some affairs in order. And he'd sensed she'd needed time as well. "How've you been?"

"As well as can be expected. I went to visit Jason. They'll be releasing him soon." She let out a quiet laugh. "Released from a week in the hospital only to spend the next twenty years behind bars."

In the hedge garden at the cemetery, Jason had tried to point the barrel of his gun at his own chin. The round Lisa put into his shoulder stopped him and loosened his grip. In the next instant, Peter hit the weapon with his cane, knocking it to the ground. After that, Jason had given no resistance.

"And his mother?" Peter asked.

"She won't see me. And I get it. Mom says she'll come around when it's time. All we can do is keep trying."

A waiter interrupted them, arriving to pour their waters. He offered a wine menu that they both declined, then recited his litany of specials. Peter hardly heard a word. He ordered the fish. The type and preparation didn't matter, as long as nobody brought him a steak.

"So," Lisa said once the young man had gone. "You're still here. I thought maybe you'd gone home to London without saying goodbye." She toyed with her water glass. "You know the investigation into Trejo's shooting is over, right? You're free to go. No charges."

"I know. Captain Griffith told me when he delivered the check for my consultation services. Quite generous."

She coughed on a sip of water. "Generous?"

"By that, I mean it's paying for our dinner this evening."

When Lisa gave him a pointed look over her glass, Peter shrugged. "Fine. If I'm honest, between the Grand's prices and your department's budget, that check will barely cover the first course. But it's the gesture that counts."

Peter thought he'd successfully dodged the real question, but Lisa circled back to it.

"Not that I'm chasing you off the island, but if the department isn't holding you here for the investigation and your conference ended days ago, why haven't you gone home? You must have patients waiting."

"None I can't pawn off on other surgeons."

The waiter returned with a loaf of rye, which Peter left on its wooden plank. He looked down at his empty plate. "To start with, I stayed to make some funeral arrangements."

"Funeral arrangements?"

"Trejo and his man Diego. No one claimed their bodies, so I took care of both. Your pastor helped me arrange the ceremony. We had it this morning. Just the two of us."

Lisa watched him, perhaps seeing right through him to the reasons behind those actions, more shameful than noble. "I would have come."

"I know."

"And now? Is that what this dinner is? A goodbye?"

"Not at all." Peter gave her a quick smile. "In fact, I think I'll stay for a time. You have Tuna to thank for that. He talked to Alcott, who apparently has more money than the Queen, and convinced him that the largest resort on Maui should boast two staff doctors instead of one. He's even building us a new surgery." He bobbled his head. "A clinic, in American medical parlance. No major procedures, but a nice space for us to work on coral scrapes and sunburns without stepping on each other's toes. Which is good, because we may be at each other's throats before too long."

Her brow furrowed. "Why? Are you two fighting?"

"Tuna swayed me on this scheme by noting that as a resort doctor, I would make my home in a villa. He failed to mention that it was his villa. My suite is paid up until tomorrow. After that, Tuna and I will be housemates."

Lisa found this more amusing than Peter had intended. But her laughter won him over, and by the time the food came, they were joking together about his future life with Tuna as bosom buddies.

She prayed and gave thanks for the meal and for Jason's survival. She spoke as if God were seated there at the table with them, as if she knew it for certain. Was such sight beyond the dark threshold possible? Is that what believers like her and Tuna meant by faith?

At the end of Lisa's prayer, she thanked God for Peter and asked for His hand to guide Peter's future there, however long he might stay. This seemed to spark a new question once she opened her eyes. "What about neurosurgery? Will you practice here, at Maui Memorial?"

He'd been dreading the topic. Peter's right hand rested on his knee, out of sight below the tabletop, where it had been all evening, plagued by the occasional tremor. They came at every instance of stress, and—as it turned out—a dinner with Lisa was no exception. If he couldn't get through a meal with a woman for whom he harbored feelings without losing control of his fine motor skills, how could he ever practice neurosurgery again? "No," Peter said and used his left hand to take a sip of water. "I'm taking a hiatus. By . . . indirect means, my boss recently pointed out that I've become a workaholic. A break will do me good."

As he spoke, Lisa's purse buzzed. She drew out her mobile. Peter wasn't trying to pry, but he couldn't help but notice a text from Clay, her FBI contact. Wasn't he on the US mainland? It must have been quite late there.

Lisa frowned at the message and returned the device to her purse without sending a reply. "Where were we?"

"My hiatus."

"That's right. Well, I'm glad you're staying."

The words and the smile that came with them warmed him. "You . . . You are?"

"Absolutely. To be frank, Peter, I need you."

So direct. Peter cared for her, and he'd suspected Lisa felt the same. He hadn't expected her to be so open about it so soon, though. "Um." He swallowed. "Great."

"Good. Good," she said, returning to her purse. "Not to pressure you, but I'd like to get started as soon as possible, if your new schedule as a resort doctor allows."

Get started? My schedule? Peter had not dated for some time—or much at all—but didn't romance require a touch of spontaneity? He laid his left hand on his right to try to calm the tremors. Maybe he should take time to work things out on his own instead of leaping right into a relationship.

Before he could broach the subject, she surfaced from the dive into her purse, moved the bread plank aside, and laid a file between them. "There's been a string of burglaries from resort boutiques—art, jewelry. Really high-end stuff. And now there's a body."

Lisa opened the file, revealing an image of the victim that Peter doubted the other diners would appreciate. "Weird, right? Not your typical armed robbery. And it gets weirder." She moved the photo. The page underneath was covered in symbols. "That text was from Clay, who's looking into these. He didn't find anything solid, but it's still early."

She folded her hands, resting them on top of the file. "Peter, you did great work on Kelly's case, with all kinds of odds stacked against you. If you can bring that same passion and unique perspective to this one, combined with Clay's resources, I think we can nail this joker."

"The three of us?"

Lisa nodded.

So, Peter was her resource, not a potential boyfriend or whatever Americans called their dating partners these days. He should be offended or disappointed, yet he couldn't muster either feeling, not while studying the puzzle she'd laid between them.

So many pieces out of place. So much to set right.

The quaking in his hand stopped. "Yes. Yes, I'm sure we can. Let's see the rest of that file."

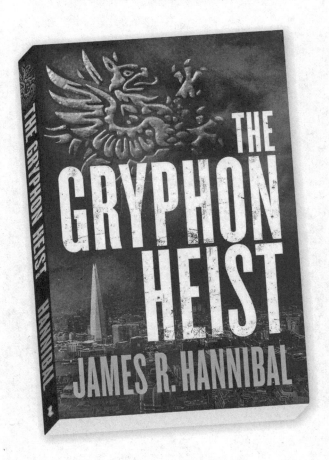

CHAPTER
ONE

PRESENT DAY
UNDISCLOSED LOCATION

TALIA INGER CLUTCHED HER SIDE, letting her shoulder fall against the alley wall. The pain had been growing for the last half hour, threatening to overtake her as it had in Windsor.

Eddie Gupta, her team specialized skills officer, sat cross-legged on the asphalt beside her, hidden from the street by a dumpster defaced with Cyrillic graffiti. He looked up with concern, fingers hovering over a tablet computer. "Are you all right?"

"I'm fine." Talia shoved the pain to the back of her mind. She wouldn't fail—not again. "Bring up Whisper One. Show me the square."

An app expanded to show infrared video of a small city square. A few gray, lukewarm figures drifted across the cold black of the cobblestones. A white heat source flared near the center, blocking out a good bit of the image for a moment before the filters kicked in. The flash subsided to reveal a single individual seated on the edge of a fountain. The hot spot remained where his hand should be for several seconds, then dropped to the ground and was snuffed out, crushed under his heel.

"There's Borov." A hint of British Indian colored Eddie's accent. "He's giving us the all-clear signal. Do you remember his code name?"

Talia shot him a look, and he answered with a sly smile. She remembered everything. Always. Eddie knew that. Her eyes returned to the drone feed. "Escort, Siphon is ready. Move in."

"On it, Control," a young woman replied through Talia's earpiece. "Moving now."

The infrared camera on Eddie's Whisper nano-drone picked up another gray figure entering the square from the west, moving toward the fountain at a brisk pace. Even from behind the alley dumpster, two streets away, Talia could hear the echoing *clop* of the linguist's designer heels on the stones. "Take it easy, Kayla," she said, using the girl's name instead of her call sign to be sure she caught her attention. Kayla hated the handle *Escort*, anyway. "Slow is fast, remember?"

The linguist slowed her pace to an exaggerated stroll. Talia closed her eyes and shook her head. She should have kept her mouth shut. The abrupt change looked out of place in the quiet square—enough to draw the attention of any local opposition. She held her breath. The pain in her side flared. But no enemy forces stormed in to grab Kayla.

Alexi Borov's deep grumble came to her through the comm link—a low, intense string of Belarusian. When he moved to stand, Kayla touched his arm and sat beside him, offering what Talia hoped were whispered assurances of his safety. After a few tense seconds, he nodded. More grumbles. Kayla switched to English. "Two, six, nine, seven."

A third player read back the sequence. "Two, six, nine, seven. Black Bag copies. Stand by."

In the silence that followed, Eddie glanced up at Talia. She gave him a smile, made thin by her pain. "We'll make it. It's been a year. We can last another twenty minutes."

One year.

One year of academics, field craft, and mock missions, knowing everything—fake embassy balls, live-fire exercises, chance meetings with undercover agents in Chestertown—everything was a test. Talia's only break had been the TGT—the Trainee Grand Tour—which had taken her across four continents in two months, sampling every menial, low-risk job the Agency could offer. And even that had ended in a twenty-page evaluation from six different supervisors. One year of weeding out the chaff.

Only five candidates remained. Tonight was their final exam.

Success hinged on two interconnected objectives: extract a Belarusian scientist from an urban environment and use his access code to steal a device from a corporate lab. They had Siphon in hand. Once Black Bag recovered the device and Talia got them all to the extraction point, the rest was pomp and paperwork. She would pass through the black curtain into the CIA's Directorate of Operations, better known as the Clandestine Service.

Scott, the candidate who had read back the numeric sequence, broke the silence on the comms. "Green light, Control. Code one was solid. Black Bag is inside the compound."

"Copy." Talia widened her eyes at Eddie in a *here we go* look. "Escort, Siphon's info is genuine. Get him to the bridge."

Eddie tapped the screen again. The first window shrank to half its size and a second window labeled WHISPER TWO opened beside it, giving them a bird's-eye view of a walled compound. Four L-shaped office buildings surrounded a flat bunker. Two gray figures, her teammates Hannah and Scott acting together as Black Bag, slipped through a gate in the south wall and crouch-ran to the shadows of the nearest structure. Another pair casually strolled in their direction, leaving the central bunker. None of the candidates knew what waited inside that bunker, the infamous Sanctum. No graduate had ever revealed the answer. They were spies, after all, and what good were spies who couldn't keep secrets?

"Black Bag, two guards are headed your way. Use the eastern approach."

"Copy. Black Bag is moving east. We'll be at the door in minutes, Control. We need the second code."

Talia gave Kayla a chance to reply, but the linguist was busy. She and Borov had stopped at the exit from the square, arguing in whispered Belarusian.

"Escort?"

"Siphon says the western street will be watched." Kayla turned north, letting the mock scientist take the lead. "He knows a better route, to the south."

Eddie opened his mouth to protest, but Talia held up a hand to quiet him. She called up a map of the city in her head and looked for a route to the bridge. It would work. "That's fine, Escort. Tell him we need the second code, though."

"He says we'll get it when we're out of danger."

"Great." Scott's usual pessimism came in loud and clear. "So we play hide-and-seek with armed guards until Siphon gets a warm, fuzzy feeling inside? Escort, shove your gun in his ear and see if that changes his mind."

"Negative, Black Bag," Talia said. "That's not how we do business."

"Right. I forgot who was running this op. Miss Everything by the Book."

Strange motion on the video feed cut the argument short. Talia watched as the roof of the Sanctum expanded to fill the frame. "Eddie, check Whisper Two. You've got a runaway zoom."

The SSO tapped the screen, frowned, and tapped harder as granules of cinder on the roof rushed toward the lens. The feed went black.

Scott's voice grew tense on the audio link. "We heard a *crunch* from the Sanctum. The guards are moving that way."

Eddie locked eyes with Talia. "That was not a zoom issue."

"I know. Redirect Whisper One. We need to get eyes on our team."

Kayla and Borov moved out of frame as the drone left them behind. Through the SATCOM, Talia distinctly heard the scientist say "*Prabaččie*." With his sorrowful tone and inflection, it sounded so similar to a phrase she knew in Russian. "*Prostitye*."

Forgive me.

She heard a metallic *sptt*. Kayla let out a muffled cry. At the same time Whisper One dropped out of the sky and crashed into the Sanctum roof beside the first.

"Escort, check in!"

Nothing but static.

"Kayla? Kayla, respond!" Talia clenched her fist, pounding the brick wall behind her, and then doubled over to stop the needles shooting through her midsection.

The pain had been with her for years, most of her life. But it had not become crippling until the previous spring, at Windsor, in the middle of the national rowing championships. It had cost Talia the gold medal. The team doctors at Georgetown had found nothing. The specialists had checked her kidneys, her liver, her bloodwork. Nothing. Now with her career—her future—on the line, it was back.

"You are *not* fine." Eddie stood, taking her elbow to support her.

She pushed him back. "Doesn't matter. Black Bag, Siphon sold us out. You're walking into an ambush."

Scott didn't answer. They had no visuals and no comms. They would have to breach the Sanctum both deaf and blind.

CHAPTER TWO

EDDIE SLAPPED THE TABLET down into his lap. "I have heard rumors about this. Whole classes wash out on Sanctum night. This is the Kobayashi Maru."

Talia gave him a blank stare.

He spread his hands. "The Kobayashi Maru. *Star Trek*? How is it possible you don't know this?"

She jerked him out of the alley.

With their SIG Sauer P226s drawn, Talia and Eddie hurried across the square. She kept her weapon down, reminding herself to aim chest level if she encountered a threat. The Farm's Simunition paint rounds looked and fired like real bullets, carrying enough velocity to make a head shot deadly.

"I can hack the instructor cameras," Eddie said, puffing hard and pushing his glasses into place as the two threw their backs against the compound wall.

She made no answer, leaning forward just enough to look up and down the perimeter.

"Hacking the system is exactly what they want us to do—thinking outside the box and all that." Eddie nudged her with an elbow. "We are spies now. Sometimes spies break the rules. Besides, it worked for James T. Kirk."

Spies played dirty. Talia understood. At the Farm, there had been plenty of morality discussions. The book was for the über-nerds at the FBI. But how quickly would good guys cease to be good when they crossed every line? "We're not hacking the instructor cams. That's cheating. And since you went there, Kirk slept with every green alien girl who crossed his path. Maybe you should find a new role model."

Eddie stomped his foot. "You *do* know *Star Trek*."

Siphon's code still worked on the southern door to the compound. Talia and Eddie ran to the shelter of a colonnade of trees bordering the same building where they had last seen their teammates. "Black Bag, say your status."

Nothing.

"Hannah? Scott?"

White static filled the comms. In the darkness beyond the trees, there were muted flashes, accompanied by four rapid spits. The two crept to the edge and found Hannah and Scott lying motionless on the cobblestones. Red blotches marked their tactical vests. There was no sign of the shooter.

Eddie poked Scott with the toe of his boot. "So much for Black Bag."

This earned him a glower from below. Scott bared his teeth, but he remained silent. The rules were clear.

Meanwhile, Talia grabbed the collar of Hannah's vest and dragged her back into the enclave of trees. She thrust a chin at Scott. "Grab him, Eddie. We have to get them out of sight."

"Why bother? We're blown."

"We're not blown. We're betrayed. Where are the guards? The sirens?" Talia reached the bushes and lowered Hannah to the grass. "Borov must have doubled back. He got the Agency's money. Now he wants his corporate payday, but he'll have to silence us first. That has to be the scenario we're facing."

When Eddie failed to move Scott, Talia did the job herself, grunting against the phantom pain in her side. "I saw a jeep

. . . outside . . . the compound. We retrieve the device, drag the bodies out . . . and drive to the bridge." She didn't have enough strength left to lower Scott gently to the grass. She dropped him.

Scott let out an involuntary *"Oomph!"*

"Shhh!" Talia gave him a stern frown, then pointed at Eddie. "I am *not losing this*. Got it? Get the charges. Hannah has them."

Eddie folded his arms. "We don't have the second code. How are we supposed to enter the Sanctum?"

"Hannah. Has. *The charges*."

"Oh, right." As Eddie squatted next to his teammate, Hannah opened one eye and stared at him hard. He pulled his hands back. "Um. Where *exactly* did she put them?"

"Now, Eddie."

"Okay. Not a problem." The SSO winced as he patted the pockets on Hannah's thighs and midsection. "Sorry. So sorry."

"Eddie," Talia hissed at him, "what are the two keys to infiltration?"

"Uh . . . Shut up and hurry up."

She gave him a *you're not doing either* glare.

"Found them." He held up two black discs, the size of hockey pucks, and followed her up the lane leading to the Sanctum.

The bunker looked unguarded, but that was too much to hope for. Talia and Eddie were halfway to the Sanctum's steel door when two silhouettes wandered into the orange circle of light spilling from the lamp above.

Talia pressed Eddie back against the wall, her side throbbing.

The guards looked their way and started down the lane.

An alcove a few feet away offered the only shelter. She pulled Eddie into it. He sniffled, and she dug her fingernails into his arm in the universal signal for *Don't you dare sneeze.*

The guards walked past.

When Talia and Eddie reached the circle of light, she held an explosive disc close to the door and let its magnetic backing do the rest. The disc jumped from her hand and clamped itself to the metal with a soft *clink*. She glanced at Eddie. "Backpack."

"What about it?"

"Give it to me."

"Uh . . . This is my *personal* gear, Talia. This bag is a Givenchy."

"You bought a designer bag? This is why you haven't had a date since our junior year." Talia glanced up and down the intersecting street. They couldn't stay in the light, exposed, for much longer. "I'll need your tactical vest too. And your sweatshirt. Hurry up."

A knife through the strap, wedged into the doorframe, held the pack in place over the charge, and Talia stuffed it near to bursting with the vest and sweatshirt. She dialed the charge to its lowest setting and started the timer, and the two retreated to a safe distance.

There was a light *pop* and a muted flash. White smoke rose from behind the Givenchy bag.

Eddie let out a quiet whimper. "Twelve hundred dollars."

"For a backpack?"

"It's *real* leather."

Somewhere, watching through the instructor feed, a judge must have decided the mock explosive had done its job. The steel door swung inward with a long, awkward *creak*. The two crossed the circle of light and pushed inside.

"Whoa," Eddie said, smoking backpack hanging from his right hand.

The Sanctum.

Weapon ready, Talia peered over a polished green rail. Five levels of arched mahogany galleries and light green pillars descended below them, all the way to a bottom floor made of the same stone. The balcony walkways each formed a different shape—hexagon, pentagon, square, and triangle.

Eddie slipped his tactical vest over his head. "If we were in

341

a video game, this would be the palace of the final boss. Is that . . . jade?"

"Someone at the CIA has a flare for the dramatic." Talia shook her head. "And no regard for the taxpayers." On the floor at the bottom of the chamber, she saw an old, worn briefcase with the letters CEMP painted sloppily on the side. "The target is down there. Out in the open."

"Then let's grab it." Eddie made for the nearest stairwell.

Talia caught his arm. "Wait. This is too easy."

"Tell that to Scott, Hannah, and Kayla."

"Think about it. The case *must* be guarded. Maybe they're hiding beneath the balcony."

Eddie produced the second charge. "So drop this baby down the disturbing green well. Boom. Problem solved."

"We can't. Those guards are just doing their job. No collateral damage, Eddie." Talia's pain flared again. She winced, but she gritted her teeth and waved off the offered explosive, starting toward the stairs.

She expected a surprise around every corner, but found none. The jade floor at the bottom level remained quiet and empty. The briefcase called to her from the center.

"Perhaps that's it." Eddie panned his SIG from left to right. "Inside the case we'll find a message. 'Congratulations. You win.'"

His suggestion didn't sound right. Talia still had to get her team, bodies and all, to the bridge. But in the moment, she saw no obstacles. She walked out across the floor, reaching for the briefcase.

Thunk.

Talia heard the spit of the suppressor and wheeled in time to see Eddie drop to the floor, a red blotch on his chest.

No. No, no, no. She dodged the bullet she knew was coming and made a grab for the case, but her hand fell short.

Thunk.

The impact of a Simunition round slamming into the small of her back only added to the pain. Talia spun. The room around her spun as well.

Amid the slow pitch and tilt of the jade floor and the mahogany arches, the fake Borov grinned, covering her with a silenced Stechkin pistol. "It appears I've caught intruders within the Sanctum."

He wasn't talking to Talia.

Mary Jordan, chief of the CIA's Russian Eastern European Division and the woman who had recruited Talia two years before, walked deliberately to the center of the room and picked up the case. She wore a submachine gun slung at her side, a twin to those carried by the guards. "You're tenacious, Talia. But you still failed." She cocked her head, squinting a little. "And by the way, when the opposing force shoots you, you're supposed to fall. Rules are rules."

She raised the gun and opened fire.

ACKNOWLEDGMENTS

I'M GRATEFUL TO GOD for the opportunity to write books in His service—to bring fiction to men and boys, who've become an underserved group in the Christian fiction industry.

As always, there are a number of others to thank, starting with my wife Cindy, who acts as my frontline editor and occasionally keeps me from making an utter fool of myself with an off-the-wall chapter. And to our friend JL for acting as a consultant in shoes and hairstyles. I'm grateful to everyone on the Revell team for bringing this book to publication, and to my wonderful agent Harvey Klinger for bringing us together. I'm also thankful for DiAnn Mills, Steven James, James Stoddard, David Morrell, and others in the Thriller Writers community who've helped shape my writing style.

Finally, I'm thankful for you, the readers, whose support makes my job possible. Your encouragements on social media and in reviews mean a great deal, not just to me, but to all the authors battling the worry that every book we write is going to be an utter disaster. Thank you for everything, and God bless you.

JAMES R. HANNIBAL is no stranger to secrets and adventure. This former stealth pilot from Houston, Texas, has been shot at, locked up with surface-to-air missiles, and chased down a winding German road by an armed terrorist. He is a three-time Silver Falchion Award winner for his children's mysteries, a former Thriller Award nominee, and a Selah and Carol Award winner for his CIA series that starts with *The Gryphon Heist*. James is a rare multisense synesthete, meaning all of his senses intersect. He sees and feels sounds and smells, and hears flashes of light. If he tells you the chocolate cake you offered smells blue and sticky, take it as a compliment.

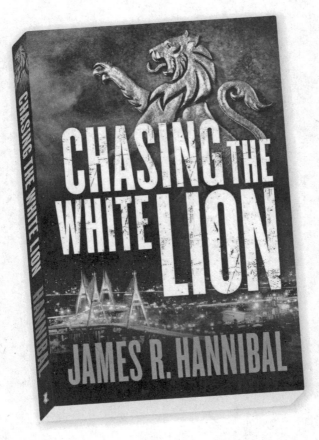

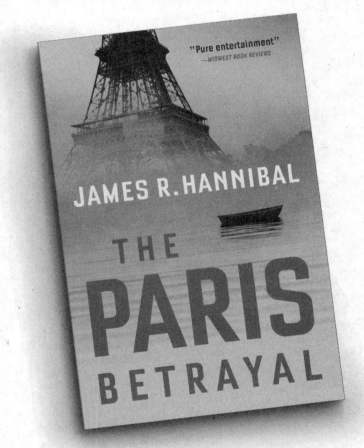

CONNECT WITH
JAMES R. HANNIBAL

f	JamesRHannibal	**◎**	JamesRHannibal
𝕏	JamesRHannibal	**g**	James R. Hannibal